The Bouchard ☑ **W9-BRW-714** *d Frenchman who left his children a legacy written on the wind. With hope, courage, and determination, the Bouchard family could inherit the earth. He laid claim to the Alabama land and to his heritage by building a strong foundation—Windhaven Plantation—and it is from this fortuitous beginning that our story continues. . . .*

* * *

In this passionate novel of men and women driven by powerful forces beyond their own comprehension, we once again follow the lives and loves of the Bouchard clan. This time Laurette and her husband, Charles, take center stage as they seek new worlds to conquer. Eddie Gentry, a Windhaven Range cowhand, falls in love with their pretty governess, Polly, but tragedy strikes. At the Creek Village, Ben Wilson, the Quaker doctor and his young Indian wife, Elone, decide to move to Wichita, but danger lurks. And this time, Lucien Bouchard will go to Sangrado's rescue, if he's in time. . . .

* * *

For those readers who have loyally followed the Bouchards, a preview of the next Windhaven novel, WINDHAVEN'S CRISIS, is included at the end.

THE WINDHAVEN SAGA

Produced by Lyle Kenyon Engel, creator of the WAGONS WEST Series, THE AUSTRALIANS, and THE KENT FAMILY CHRONICLES

DEFENDERS OF WINDHAVEN

Marie de Jourlet

PINNACLE BOOKS   LOS ANGELES

DEFENDERS OF WINDHAVEN

Copyright © 1980 by Book Creations, Inc.

An original Pinnacle Books edition, published for the first time anywhere.

Produced by Lyle Kenyon Engel

First printing, December 1980

ISBN: 0-523-40723-8

Cover illustration by Bruce Minney

Printed in the United States of America

PINNACLE BOOKS, INC.
2029 Century Park East
Los Angeles, California 90067

Dedicated to the memory of Dugan,
loyal companion and friend.

ACKNOWLEDGMENTS

The author wishes to acknowledge her indebtedness to Marla and Lyle Engel, to Leslie and Philip Rich, and to Marjorie Weber, all of Book Creations, Inc., for their continuing support and aid in the writing of this series.

Thanks are also due Mrs. Mary Barton of Carrizo Springs, Texas, who, because of her many years as a rancher's wife, has contributed invaluable and authentic data on the locale and history of Windhaven Range; to M. Walters, D.V.M., Chicago, Illinois, for his expert professional documentation on the behavior of dogs and wolves; to Dave Richmond, former manager of the gun department of Abercrombie & Fitch, for his historical expertise on the weapons of the period this book covers; and to Professor Joseph Milton Nance of Texas A & M University, one of the nation's most eminent historians.

The author also wishes to thank Kathy Estes of the Galveston Historical Foundation, Galveston, Texas; Cynthia Huggins of the Newberry Library, Chicago, Illinois; and Robert Stevens of the Rosenberg Library, Galveston, for their assiduous research in verifying many obscure facts of the period in which this novel is set.

Finally, the author expresses her deepest gratitude to Fay Bergstrom, transcriber-typist, whose expertise in transferring taped dictation to error-free and beautifully typed pages is happily augmented by her close attention to details of the story. She sees the material as a reader would, and thus has saved the author from many an embarrassing error.

Defenders of Windhaven

Luke Bouchard

Gloria Bouchard 1872~

Edwina Bouchard 1868~

Hugo Bouchard 1861~

Gary Davis 1871~

Lawrence Davis 1849~

Kenneth Douglas 1865~

Joy Hunter 1869~

Arthur Douglas 1863~

Howard Douglas 1863~

Andrew Hunter 1854~

Fleur Douglas 1872~

Charles Douglas 1835~

Melinda Hunter 1852~

Jimmy Belcher 1853~

Connie Belcher 1855~

Laurette Bouchard 1837~

Sybella Wilson 1868~

Millie (deceased)

Maybelle Williamson 1820~

Mark Bouchard 1819~1864

James Hunter 1822~

Arabella Bouchard 1824~

Henry Belcher 1821~

The Bouchard Family

RON TOELKE 1978 Op.IX

COPYRIGHT © 1978 Book Creations Inc.

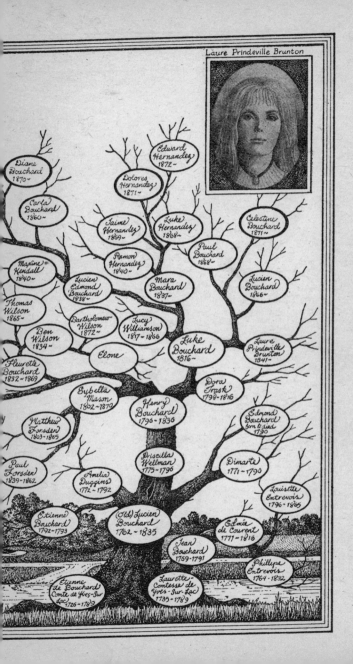

Laure Prindeville Brunton

Diane Bouchard 1870~

Carla Bouchard 1860~

Edward Hernandez 1872~

Dolores Hernandez 1871~

Celestine Bouchard 1871~

Maxine Kendall 1840~

Jaime Hernandez 1869~

Luke Hernandez 1868~

Paul Bouchard 1868~

Lucien Bouchard 1866~

Thomas Wilson 1865~

Lucien Edmond Bouchard 1838~

Ramon Hernandez 1840~

Mara Bouchard 1837~

Ben Wilson 1834~

Bartholomew Wilson 1872~

Lucy Williamson 1817~1866

Luke Bouchard 1816~

Laure Prindeville Brunton 1841~

Fleurette Bouchard 1832~1869

Elone

Sybella Mason 1802~1879

Henry Bouchard 1796~1836

Dora Trask 1799~1816

Matthew Forsden 1803~1865

Edmond Bouchard born & died 1790

Paul Forsden 1839~1862

Amelia Duggins 1772~1792

Priscilla Wellman 1775~1796

Dimarte 1771~1790

Louisette Entrevois 1796~1865

Etienne Bouchard 1792~1793

(Old) Lucien Bouchard 1762~1835

Edmée de Couvent 1771~1816

Etienne de Bouchard Comte de Yves-Sur-Lac 1726~1789

Jean Bouchard 1759~1791

Laurette Comtesse de Yves-Sur-Lac 1735~1789

Phillepe Entrevois 1764~1832

PROLOGUE

The red wolf yearling was alone, an outcast from his pack. His mother was dead. She had been leader of the pack of twenty wolves for more than a year, deciding where they should hunt and where they should den. Two days previously, she had brought them to a thick forest near the little Mexican village of Guerrero, where she and two males made a fine kill of three young javelinas, the wild pig of the region. She made sure that her yearling cub, the only one of her litter to survive, had his ample share of food. But when she went to the little creek just outside the forest to wash down her gorge of meat, she was bitten by a coral snake and died a few minutes later.

The yearling stood watching his mother's death throes, as did the two males who had accompanied her. When she was still, the two turned on each other to fight for leadership of the pack, and the larger, a seven-year-old male, was the victor. His tail erect, his hairs bristling, he watched defiantly, snarling, as his conquered rival backed away and then trotted off. When the yearling timidly tried to approach him, he bared his strong teeth and made an attacking lunge. Turning tail, the yearling moved off toward the north. He stopped at a little bank to look back at the body of his dead mother, and then, with a soft whine, set out alone.

She had taught him everything he knew. After weaning him, she had provided food, regurgitating the partially digested meat into his mouth. Two other females had helped train him; with his needle-sharp milk teeth, he had bitten them on the ruff of the neck in mock battle as they lay placidly watching his antics. Just two months before her death, his mother had taken him on his first hunt.

Now he was frightened, not certain where to go. He

1

tried once again to return to the pack, but the new leader snarled again and came running at him. Terrified, the young red wolf scampered off and this time he did not look behind. The air was cool, for it was the beginning of January.

By instinct, the red wolf understood that he could never go back to the pack and that he must survive on his own. He had already learned how to catch mice and rats and even hares. He did not think he was old enough to kill a javelina by himself, but he felt strong and he knew that his teeth were sharp. His mother had taught him how to run swiftly and dodge laterally and how to find shelter when there was a storm. That was enough to keep him alive.

He headed north, instinctively drawn toward the place where he had been born the previous winter, near San Buenaventura. His father had died there, shortly after mating with his mother, who had then led the pack south. Thus the yearling was retracing a path he had traveled; nevertheless, he felt lost and alone.. The sun set, and the wolf felt all the strangeness of the barren terrain. It stretched flat well beyond his vision, and it was broken by little hills, tiny clumps of mesquite, and here and there a scrub tree. Half a mile farther on, the yearling stopped, looked back, and emitted a low whine, wanting to return to his dead mother. But there was silence and nothingness all about him, and all his instincts told him that to return would be useless and doubtlessly fatal. Perhaps he would find another pack that would accept him. Perhaps even now they were watching from their hiding place to observe how he acted. So the yearling laid his head down on the ground and twisted his body, rolling his scent, leaving his odor to be marked by the unseen watchers of his kind. He went on a few yards more and repeated this, then trotted onward.

He had eaten enough javelina meat today so that he felt no hunger. It was being abandoned by his fellows that disturbed him most. He came to a little creek and drank his fill, once again wistfully turning back to look in the direction whence he had come. From afar there was the sound of a night bird calling to its mate. His ears pricked up and his tail stiffened and lifted a little, and then he went on. A few hours later, he found a small cave in the side of a little hill and went to sleep with his head on his paws. Perhaps

2

he dreamed, for he whimpered softly now and again when the sound of a night bird drifted through the silent air. When dawn came, he emerged from his den and continued journeying northward. Shortly before noon, he came across a chipmunk scurrying from one scrub tree to another and, with a swift sideways lunge, caught it between his strong jaws and bolted it down.

Pleased with himself, he quickened his pace to a trot again, stopping only to roll his scent several times and then to defecate; his droppings would tell other wolves of his species that he was in the area. Because he was healthy and vigorous, weighing nearly seventy pounds, he would not be set upon and killed as crippled or stunted yearlings often were.

By evening, he passed the outskirts of a little peon village, and a wild dog came out and barked at him. The yearling snarled a defiant challenge, but the dog went back into the circle of little adobe huts. Satisfied that he had put the enemy to rout, the yearling went on till he found another small cave for his nocturnal den. From time to time, throughout this second lonely day, he stopped and urinated, wanting to mark his boundaries in the hope that other, friendlier wolves would be alerted to his presence.

By the next morning, he had begun to feel adventurous and proud of his own survival. He thought of his mother only briefly now, and he was impatient to find a new pack with whom he could hunt, to whom he could prove his powers. A young hare bolted across his path an hour after he had left his den, and he killed it swiftly and gorged himself till he could eat no more. Then he drank, rolled his scent several times, and defecated again. By late afternoon, he came upon a slightly higher stretch of ground, verdant with wild grass and clumps of mesquite. As he paused near one of these clumps, he saw a dark form move near him and turned to engage it. It was a young skunk, and it was rabid. The yearling killed it by sinking his fangs into its throat, but not until it had nipped him on the shoulder. He bounded off from the carcass, not wanting to eat it, glancing back at his shoulder and snarling at the remembrance of its stinging bite. Then he drank thirstily from a stagnant pool of rainwater in a narrow gully. The wound in his shoulder had begun to throb, and he rolled himself in the wet mud to assuage the pain of it.

When he wakened at dawn the next morning, he hesitated, uncertain which direction to take. The pupils of his eyes had dilated, and there was a heat in his body that he had not felt the day before. Several times he turned in his tracks to stare back to the south; then, with a plaintive little growl, he ambled northward. By evening, he had come to a fork of the Rio Grande, so shallow that only a few inches of water covered the sandy riverbed. Dipping his muzzle to drink, he saw his own reflection lighted by the rays of a full moon. He snarled at it, dipped his muzzle, and bit at the wet sand, then scrambled across to the other side and shook himself.

An excited restlessness had come over him. The slightest sound, even the whir of a bird's wings, made him spring to one side and glance around, his pupils enormously dilated. From time to time, he emitted a strident little yelp. Because the sun was intense, it pained his eyes, so he took refuge most of the day in a sparse clump of mesquite bushes. He had seen no other red wolves all this way, and now he did not want to meet them. He was suddenly unsure of himself and shy. He did not know how strong he was, or whether that strength would be enough in an encounter with a strange pack.

With each new day, the sunlight became more excruciatingly painful to the wolf's eyes, so he stayed hidden by day and roamed at night, racing back and forth aimlessly across the sandy plain. His shoulder throbbed, and there were long spasms of swirling pain that made him whine and squeak, dashing off in one direction and then another, turning to snap at his own hindquarters. He was ravenously hungry and thirsty, but he could scarcely swallow water when he came upon it, for his larynx was almost totally paralyzed. There was tension in the muscles of his feet that kept his footpads spread when he was walking on dry ground. At times it puzzled him, and he stopped to snap at his feet and to whimper, before goading instinct drove him relentlessly on.

On the tenth day after his encounter with the rabid skunk, the yearling was slavering, his eyes were blood-flecked, and he snapped frequently at stray pieces of driftwood or even rocks——not out of hunger but in a mad frenzy to vent the ferocious, burning agony that engulfed his strong young body.

4

At last, his aimless trotting fixed on the north, and he crossed the Nueces River and came toward a ranchhouse surrounded by a tall stockade. It was late afternoon, and as the agony seethed within him, he sank his fangs into the wood of one of the pickets. Then he saw, even through the glaze of his hideously dilated eyes, an eroded hollow between two of the upright posts and, with an eerie, unnatural stridency to his whine, began to scrabble through it to reach what was beyond.

On the night of October 8, 1871, Charles Douglas, an ambitious young merchant, lost his department store in the great fire that swept through two thousand acres of downtown Chicago. Undaunted by his loss, Charles was determined to rebuild his store, believing firmly that Chicago would rise again and prosper as never before.

Since construction of the new store would take six months or more, Charles decided that he would give his family a change of scene after the ordeal of the fire, in which they had very nearly lost their lives. Accordingly he took his wife, Laurette, and their three children, Kenneth, Arthur, and Howard, and traveled south, so that they could visit various members of Laurette's family, the Bouchards of Alabama and Texas.

After two days at Windhaven Plantation in Alabama, with Laurette's uncle, Luke Bouchard, and his wife, Laure, the Douglases went on to New Orleans, where they were entertained for a week by the Bouchards' family banker, Jason Barntry. From there they traveled by ship to Corpus Christi, Texas, with a two-day stopover at Galveston, where Laurette was reunited with her aunt, Arabella Bouchard Hunter. Finally, traveling by horse and wagon from Corpus Christi, with four armed cowboys as escorts, the Douglases reached Windhaven Range, near Carrizo Springs. Here, Laurette was tearfully welcomed by her mother, Maybelle Belcher. They had not seen each other since May, 1865, when the family had gathered in New Orleans after the destruction of Windhaven Plantation by Union soldiers.

Laurette was ecstatic to see the Texas Bouchards once again: her cousins, Lucien Edmond and Mara, and their families. What pleased her most of all, though, was finding her mother serenely happy in her marriage to the widower

Henry Belcher, and clearly loved by Henry's children—Timmy, eighteen, and Connie, sixteen. Laurette well remembered her mother's desolate anguish during all those years after 1838, when her husband, the rebellious Mark Bouchard, then eighteen, had deserted Maybelle and her baby, Laurette, to become a partner of the infamous Creole slave-trader and gambler, Pierre Lourat. Even when Laurette and her mother had met in New Orleans just seven years earlier, Laurette had been disconsolate to see how little hope her mother had expressed for the new life she was to lead in Texas. And now, what a joy to find Maybelle radiant and looking far younger than her fifty-two years because of the devotion of Henry Belcher and his children.

Laurette's husband, Charles, also enjoyed the reunion, confident in the knowledge that he had already laid plans to recoup the loss of his Chicago department store. Some months before the great fire, he had struck up an acquaintance with a wealthy young Easterner who was looking for a sound investment and who had tentatively offered to buy some of Charles Douglas's stock. He had met the man again a few days after the fire, and the two had come to an optimistic agreement. The Easterner would help finance the rebuilding of the Chicago store in return for thirty-five percent of the capital stock and would become a partner in the venture. And now that Charles was here in the sprawling, young, thriving state of Texas, the idea of starting a second Douglas Department Store in one of the larger cities greatly appealed to him. For the past few days, he had been conferring with Lucien Edmond Bouchard on that very topic.

On an afternoon in January 1872, Lucien Edmond's wife, Maxine, and her sister-in-law, Mara Hernandez, were in the kitchen preparing a sumptuous evening meal for the family and their guests. Their conversation was joyful and animated, for Mara had just told Maxine that she was expecting another child in the summer. Her husband, Ramón, who was Lucien Edmond's foreman, had just taken their two little sons, Jamie and Luke, two and four respectively, out to see the horses in the corral, while their six-month-old sister, Dolores, slept. Polly Behting, the flaxen-haired German woman who had accompanied Laurette and Charles Douglas to Windhaven Range as the nurse

6

of their three little boys, was chatting with Eddie Gentry, a lanky young Texan who was one of Lucien Edmond's best cowhands. Eddie had offered to whittle some wooden horses for the Douglas twins, Arthur and Kenneth, and their little brother, Howard. Although Polly was engaged to a hardworking butcher's apprentice back in Chicago, she knew that it would be at least another year before he could have his own shop and be in a position to marry her. Consequently, when Charles and Laurette had begged her to come along with them to Texas, she had told her fiancé of her determination to go with them and obtained the permission of her widower father, who thought very highly of the Douglases.

Maxine Bouchard's older children, Hugo and Carla, who were ten and twelve, had volunteered to take the Douglas boys out into the yard for a walk before supper; Hugo and Carla's younger sister, three-year-old Edwina, played happily on the kitchen floor near her mother and Mara. Maxine's youngest child, Diane, now fourteen months old, was upstairs taking a nap, as were Ben Wilson's two children, Thomas and Sybella, seven and three. The Wilson children had lived for nearly a year on a Creek reservation, where their father, Dr. Ben Wilson, was doctor to the tribe. The preceding September, Ben and his second wife, Elone, had brought the children to Windhaven Range for a visit. Then he had been induced by Maxine Bouchard and Maybelle Belcher to leave the children there so that they might enjoy the Yuletide holidays. Ben and Elone, meanwhile, had returned to the Indian reservation.

Jubal followed Hugo and Carla and the Douglas children as they went outside, barking nonstop at their antics. He was nine years old now; he had lost several teeth and his hind legs were stiff, but he still reveled in being the watchdog of Windhaven Range. Seven years ago, Djamba had bought him from his owner in New Orleans, to save the poor dog from being pitted against a bear in a bloody contest of the sort popular in that city. He had brought Jubal along to Texas, where the dog had more than earned his laurels a few months later by barking to warn the Bouchards of the attack of the bandit Diego Macaras. Hugo and Carla stroked his head, and his mournful amber eyes glistened with affection as he pressed his long, lean muzzle against their legs and wagged his tail. At their urging, the

7

twins and Howard moved over to pet Jubal too, though Howard seemed reluctant to give Jubal more than a hasty pat, impressed as he was by the dog's size.

Gratified by this show of affection, Jubal was eager to show his vigilance as well as his tricks. He suddenly caught sight of a field mouse scampering near the stockade and took after it with a joyful bark. But before he could reach it, it outdistanced him and disappeared under one of the pickets. With an angry little bark, he turned back toward the children. And at that moment the yearling wolf emerged from between two of the pickets and came running at the five children. From its slavering muzzle there emerged a screeching whine of unspeakable torment, and it bared its fangs as it made for them.

Carla and Hugo froze, stark terror congealing their faces as they planted themselves in front of the twins and Howard, their only instinct being to protect the little ones. Jubal spied the rabid wolf. With an angry growl, summoning all his strength, he raced toward the terrible intruder and, just before the yearling could reach Carla and Hugo, sank his teeth into its neck. Savagely, the yearling turned on Jubal, biting repeatedly in its intolerable agony, but Jubal, though bleeding from half a dozen cruel bites, tenaciously kept his hold on the yearling's throat. They rolled over and over, thrashing, snarling, and whining, until at last Carla uttered a wild scream for help: "Daddy! Daddy, come quick, it's a big dog, he's killing poor Jubal!"

Once the young wolf managed to shake off Jubal's desperate hold, and it stumbled to its feet, its enormously dilated, glazed eyes fixing on the cowering children. But despite the pain of his wounds and his loss of blood, Jubal lunged again, sank his teeth into the wolf's jugular, and bore the yearling down onto the ground. In his death throes, the young wolf kicked and screeched, thrashing and twisting with the demoniac strength of the ravaging disease that consumed it, just as Charles Douglas and Lucien Edmond, the latter with drawn pistol, came running out of the ranchhouse.

The wolf stiffened and, with a last gurgling whine, lay still. Panting, bleeding, Jubal staggered to his feet, his amber eyes fixed on the children. He lurched and staggered, then rolled onto his side, looking up pleadingly. His throat was cut, one eye was blinded, and from his flank and

8

shoulder blood dripped from the marks left by the fangs of the rabid yearling.

"My God, Jubal's saved them! See, Charles, the slaver on the wolf's muzzle and those dilated eyes—it's got hydrophobia—when I think that the children might have been bitten by it! Jubal, poor, loyal, brave Jubal, God bless you for what you've done!" Lucien Edmond's voice broke with a sob. He knelt down and very gently touched the head of the old gray hound, and then, whispering softly, "Forgive me, dear, loyal friend," put a merciful bullet into Jubal's valiant heart.

The twins and Howard had begun to cry hysterically, and Hugo and Carla, though themselves shaken, tried to comfort them. Charles, very pale and trembling, herded them back into the house.

Lucien Edmond stood, smoking pistol lowered to the ground, staring at Jubal's body. He said aloud, "You had the spirit of Djamba himself, who saved you from the bear seven years ago to bring you here to watch over us. And now that Djamba and Grandmother Sybella, who meant so much to each other and whose lives were interwined, have gone ahead of you, I know you will join them and your spirit will help guard them as they look down at us on Windhaven Range."

CHAPTER ONE

Two days after Jubal's heroic defense of the children, Charles Douglas sat in the living room with Lucien Edmond, sipping coffee and enjoying an early Beethoven sonata played on the spinet by chestnut-haired Maxine Bouchard. Maybelle Belcher had prepared a lavish dinner, aided by Mara Hernandez and Laurette Douglas. The meal had been enjoyed by the entire family, including Lucas and Felicidad, who by now were considered an integral part of the clan, and a toast had been offered at Felicidad's announcement that her son, James, would have a little brother or sister in seven months' time.

Still basking in the feeling of well-being which the festive dinner had produced in him, Charles Douglas took another sip of his coffee and smacked his lips. "It's plain to see how Laurette comes by her skill at cooking, Lucien Edmond. It's direct from her mother, because tonight's was as fine a dinner as I've ever enjoyed."

Lucien Edmond chuckled and nodded. "I don't think Laurette will be offended if she hears you tell her mother that, Charles. Since she came with us to Texas, she's certainly blossomed out into a happy new life."

"Yes, and you don't know how pleased I am about that for her sake as well as Laurette's," the affable Chicago department store owner agreed. "I want to thank you again for your hospitality, Lucien Edmond, and most of all for the kindness Carla and Hugo have shown my three little boys. It certainly has helped to offset the impact of that dreadful thing yesterday afternoon." He shook his head and uttered a fervent sigh. "I don't even want to think about what might have happened if poor old Jubal hadn't been there. There's no cure that I know of for hydrophobia—Laurette and I saw a mad dog in Chicago last

11

summer that bit three people before a policeman killed it, and the three died horribly. Thank God, I say, for Jubal!"

"Amen to that, Charles. Best not to dwell upon it. Well now, what do you think of Texas?"

"It's a fabulous state, just about limitless in its potential now that the war's over."

"Yes," Lucien Edmond smiled in agreement, "it's big, all right. And you may recall that, years ago, it was much bigger. It used to include parts of what are now Kansas and the New Mexico, Colorado, Wyoming, and Indian Territories. At least that's what Texans laid claim to back in forty-five, when Texas joined the Union. Those claims were given up in 1850, but Texas is still our largest state. And I agree with you that it offers boundless opportunities—once we establish law and order."

"I'm convinced of that. In fact, Lucien Edmond, I've been thinking about starting another department store. Maybe in San Antonio. I might take Laurette and the boys there for a visit and see if I can find a site for my second store. My new partner, Lawrence Harding, is back in Chicago helping rebuild the one that the big fire destroyed. I'll confess that one of my main reasons for coming out here, apart from giving Laurette a long overdue opportunity to visit with her mother, was to get to work on this new venture."

Lucien Edmond finished his coffee and nodded. "The only argument I'll give you is that I don't think San Antonio would be the ideal place for a department store, Charles. You'd have to ship your goods to the port of Corpus Christi, and from there it's more than two hundred miles overland northwest to San Antonio. The goods would have to come in wagons, of course, since there's no railroad yet. And believe me, that terrain is very difficult. Father and I remember it well from the time when we came out here from New Orleans after the war was over."

"You know, Lucien Edmond," Charles said, "I always wondered why you chose this part of Texas so close to the Mexican border rather than up in the Panhandle."

Lucien Edmond's face was grave. "There was one very good reason. A great many Confederates had already fled to Texas before the Civil War was over. Most of them were

12

slaveowners, and the thought of accepting their slaves as equals was repugnant to them. So they settled mostly in north Texas. Father and I were always opposed to slavery, and we knew that if we went toward the Panhandle to found our range, we'd have hostile neighbors who would try to revive the old hatred and bigotry that helped cause the war. That's why we came here, Charles."

"I understand. And I'll bow to your superior knowledge about this part of the country as regards shipping goods for my store, Lucien Edmond. But if you don't think it should be in San Antonio, what city would you suggest?"

"I'd say Houston. You see, you can ship your goods from New Orleans to Galveston, and then you'd have an overland journey of about seventy miles over much less hazardous terrain. Besides, Houston is beginning to flourish, whereas San Antonio is an older city, more settled in its ways, and in my opinion, much too sedate for your imaginative ideas."

Charles grinned boyishly. "Thanks for the compliment, Lucien Edmond. I guess I have been talking a blue streak about starting another store ever since I first got here. But then, you see, I can't help getting restless doing nothing. While I'm waiting for that Chicago store of mine to be ready for business, I'm here with time on my hands and nothing to do. And naturally I want to make a good future for Laurette and the boys."

"You'll do that, never fear," Lucien Edmond grinned back. "Nobody would ever believe you were born in Tuscaloosa. You think and talk like a big-city tycoon."

"I hope I'm not as bad as that, Lucien Edmond," Charles laughingly protested. "The fact is, even when I was a store clerk in Tuscaloosa, I always wanted to serve people and help them get what they needed at fair prices. I guess wherever I'd be, I'd have the same feeling."

"And it's a good feeling, don't be ashamed of it. Now if you want to go to Houston, I'd be glad to send Eddie Gentry and Lucas with you. You'd need an escort, because there are still a few outlaws roaming this part of the country. It won't be long before we have Texas Rangers again, but till then it's always a good precaution to be armed and ready when you travel."

"Well then, I'd like to get started as soon as I can. Let

13

Laurette and the boys stay here and rest up for a spell—if that's not stretching your hospitality too far, Lucien Edmond?"

"Of course it isn't!"

"Thanks again for everything." Charles rose from the couch and extended his hand to Lucien Edmond, who shook it. "I think I can manage riding a horse; Laurette and I both went horseback riding in Chicago. It'll be good exercise, too, to trim this down." He patted his waist with a sheepish grin.

"Fine. I'll talk to Eddie and Lucas, and you can leave tomorrow, if you've a mind to."

"It was kind of you, Mr. Gentry, to make those little wooden horses for the *Kinder*," Polly Behting said as she walked toward the corral with the lanky, towheaded cowboy. Two hours before dinner he had finished whittling the toys for Kenneth and Arthur and Howard and brought them to the Douglas nurse, then invited her to see the corralled horses and the bunkhouse.

"My pleasure, ma'am. It won't be long before those kids are old enough to have their own ponies back in Chicago, I'd say."

"*Ja*, that's so," Polly agreed. "I do so hope they'll forget what they saw yesterday afternoon. It was so dreadful—I should have gone with them and not let them be by themselves in the yard there—"

"Now you just put that notion right out of your mind, Miss Polly," Eddie declared. "Anyhow, even if you'd been there, you couldn't have done a thing about that mad wolf unless you'd had a gun. Now you stop blaming yourself."

"But—it's nice of you to say that, Mr. Gentry."

"Eddie," he smilingly corrected. "I'm just a simple cowhand here, and calling me Mr. Gentry might give me a swelled head."

Polly sent him a covert look from her soft blue eyes and then blushed. "I do not think, Mr. Gentry—Eddie, I mean—you are the sort of person who would ever have that. Were you born here in Texas?"

"Sure was, Miss Polly. In Laredo, if you want to know. My daddy, he was a Texas Ranger."

"Oh? And what is that, if you please?" She stared inquiringly up at him, then blushed again at her forwardness. She told herself that it was wrong to look at any other man when she was engaged to Dieter Hellwig. All the same, Mr. Gentry was very nice, and he had really beautiful manners, considering he was only a cowboy, as he said of himself.

"Well, you see, Miss Polly, you might call them sort of policemen. They rode horseback and they were organized about thirty-five years ago, during the revolution we had here in Texas. When Texas became a republic, they guarded the frontier against Indians and Mexicans. They served in the Mexican and Civil Wars. Lately, though, they've sort of been disbanded, but I'm hoping they'll reorganize because we need protection here for the big cattle ranches and the settlers who are flocking to this big country."

"Your father must have been a very brave man, Ed—Eddie, to fight the Indians."

Eddie nodded. "He was all of that, Miss Polly. Took a Comanche arrow in the side eighteen years ago, when I was just a little kid, but he rallied his men and fought the raiders off before he died."

"I—I'm sorry." She touched his hand, then drew hers back, blushing more furiously than ever. "And—and your mother?"

"She was a Georgia girl visiting her cousin in New Orleans when she met my daddy. But she loved Texas as much as he did. When he died, she started fretting and ailing, went to join him about six months later."

"But then you were an orphan! What did you do, Eddie?" Polly turned to stare at the cowboy, her eyes wide with compassion.

Eddie shrugged. "Went to live with my uncle, who had a small spread near Laredo. He was good to me, sort of a second father, you might say, even though he got drunk a lot. Taught me just about everything I know, from making flapjacks to breaking horses and working with cattle. Then about ten years ago, he took sick with yellow jack and died. After that, I worked in a San Antonio stable for about five years for a cranky old widower. Then I got hired as a hand by a Mexican who'd bought some ranch land near Corpus Christi. Seems he bought it from a fellow who called himself a Spanish baron, only the fellow turned out to be a swindler and my boss found all he'd got was desert land

15

you couldn't even ranch on, much less farm." He shrugged again. So he fired me and I went to Corpus Christi to hire myself out as a post rider for any settlers who were coming through this way."

Eddie paused, shook his head, and went on. "You know, it turned out to be the luckiest day of my life when Missus Sybella's son-in-law, Dr. Ben Wilson, came out here to visit with her after her daughter Fleurette died of diphtheria back in Pittsburgh. Mr. Lucien Edmond was kind enough to take Dr. Wilson's say-so that I was a good cowhand and signed me up. I've been here ever since. Best boss I ever had, I can tell you."

"I'm glad for you, Eddie," Polly softly said. "But it must be awfully lonely for you, without any family or anyone to look after you."

"Shucks, Miss Polly." Eddie nervously twisted his sombrero between his strong hands. "I guess I haven't had much time to feel sorry for myself that way. For certain I keep busy here on Windhaven Range, and there's plenty to be done, what with Mr. Lucien Edmond cross-breeding cattle for the market and planning where he's going to drive his cattle this spring. We've been to Abilene the last few years, but that's just about played out, and I think we're going to have to look somewhere else this season. Getting ready for a drive means plenty of work, and then when you're on it, you're always worrying about bushwhackers or unfriendly Indians. And you make friends with the fellows you ride with—everybody depends on each other and that's good, so there's no time to feel lonely—you know what I mean, Miss Polly."

"Yes, I—I think I do, Eddie. I'm glad you told me about yourself. You're a very nice man. And the *Kinder* like you very much."

"Thanks for that, Miss Polly. You know, if you think Mr. and Mrs. Douglas wouldn't mind, the twins could have the fun of riding on a nice old, gentle mare. I'd see they got along fine, I promise that."

"Why, that's very nice of you to suggest, Eddie. I'll ask Mr. Douglas about it tomorrow."

Eddie hesitated a moment, twisting his sombrero again, then blurted, "And if you ever want to go riding yourself, Miss Polly, just say the word. I'll pick a nice gentle horse for you. There's mighty pretty country just east of here

16

that I could show you. That is, of course, if they'll let you off for an hour or so. I wouldn't want to interfere with your work."

Polly blushed again. "Oh, I'm sure there would be some time for me to ride—except I wouldn't be very good at it."

"I'd show you in no time, Miss Polly," Eddie eagerly volunteered.

"Thank you so much, Eddie, for everything. But now—well, I think I'd best be getting back to the house."

CHAPTER TWO

Polly Behting's horseback riding lessons with Eddie Gentry were destined to be postponed, since Lucien Edmond went out to the bunkhouse the next morning to ask the young cowboy if he would be willing to ride along with Charles Douglas on the journey to Houston. Lucas eagerly agreed to accompany the two men, and the Kiowa scout, Simata, also volunteered. The four would ride overland to Corpus Christi, where they would board the *William Wallace* for Galveston and then take the land route to Houston. It was still a journey fraught with danger.

Ramón Hernandez, because of his skill in choosing horses for the annual remuda, selected the four geldings, as well as two sturdy pack horses for the supplies the four men would need. Charles spent an hour riding the gelding Ramón had picked for him and was as excited as a schoolboy about the adventure.

Several hours before the men were to leave, a group of six vaqueros rode in with some supplies and mail they had picked up in San Antonio. There was a letter addressed to Charles, who eagerly read it and then exclaimed, "Now I really have to get started on my new project, Lucien Edmond! This is a letter from old Frederick Tyson, president of the bank I do business with in Chicago. He tells me that my new partner has just made a substantial deposit in a fund earmarked for the rebuilding of my department store, and he also mentions the fact that a new mail order firm is starting up in Chicago. Now that's a novelty indeed! I'm so used to selling over the counter, I hadn't for a moment imagined there was any other way of doing it. Yes, I'll really have to get to work now."

Later, Charles went with Lucien Edmond to the shed where the guns and ammunition were stored.

19

"Take along a Starr .44," Lucien Edmond urged, "and a Spencer carbine. Simata, Eddie, and Lucas will be armed with the same weapons. The carbine is good even at long range and has it all over the single-shot rifle, believe me. It's proved its worth more times than I care to remember when we were under attack from bandits or bushwhackers."

"I know how that pistol works, Lucien Edmond, but you'd better show me how to load and fire the carbine," Charles replied doubtfully.

"Nothing to it, Charles," Lucien Edmond smiled as he took a carbine from the rack and filled the tubular magazine in the butt with rimfire cartridges. "You see, it's lever-operated, with a side-hammer. It'll pump seven shots quickly and with accuracy—that's all you can ask of any gun. Here, I'll unload it. Now you load it and see how it works. Go outside and pick a target."

"It feels easy to handle, I'll say that for it," Charles remarked as he walked along with Lucien Edmond to the back of the stockade.

"And that's exactly the way it works. See that little stunted tree on the other side? Now you lie down and pretend you're napping, and all of a sudden some bandits close in on you. Reach around, grab the carbine, aim it, and squeeze the trigger. See if you can hit the base of that V where the trunk forks off into two gnarled branches," Lucien Edmond suggested.

Charles lay down on his back, then rolled over and seized the carbine. Squinting along the sight, he squeezed the trigger slowly, then levered and fired several more times. Simata, Eddie, and Lucas watched with interest, and Eddie applauded. "That's pretty good shooting for a city boy, Mr. Lucien Edmond! He's got at least three of the shots right at the base of that V!"

"Very good, Charles. I think you'll be able to handle yourself, and the three men riding with you are just about the best I've got. You'll get back home safely to Laurette and the boys, never fear."

"Yes, and maybe with the site of my new department store as well!" Charles declared.

After a brief lunch, Charles said farewell to Laurette and embraced his three boys, promising to bring them presents on his return. The four riders then mounted and departed, with Simata in the lead as guide and Lucas at the rear holding the reins of the two pack horses. The sky was a brilliant blue and the sun blazed down, though the air was still cool. Simata rode ahead alongside the shallow bed of the Nueces River as Charles slowed his gelding and turned to wave back at Laurette and their three boys. With a last wave of his hand, he turned to stare at the landscape ahead, admiring the rich valley that Luke and Lucien Edmond had chosen, several years before, as the site of Windhaven Range.

Charles and his companions rode out along a trail that was crucial to the Bouchards' family history. This was the path Luke had taken six years before as he returned from Windhaven Range to New Orleans to claim Laure Prindeville Brunton as his second wife. Before her marriage to Luke's good friend John Brunton, Laure had playfully seduced Luke, and Luke was convinced that the Bruntons' first child—named Lucien after old Lucien Bouchard—was actually his own. John Brunton died shortly afterwards, and Laure capitulated to Luke and went back with him to the red-brick chateau in Alabama, rebuilt after the Civil War. There she was now mistress of the thriving household and the mother of two more children: Paul, three, and the baby, Celestine, now eight months old.

The trail ahead was marked by a profusion of yellowish reeds, as high as a man, which framed the sluggishly moving river. Beyond lay rolling prairie, picturesquely ornamented with pecan, elm, and oak trees, as well as huge clumps of mesquite, their large, brownish pods strewn upon the ground. The river wound like a serpent, and the soil near it was dark and rich at this season.

There were hills and some small canyons visible now, and Charles drank in the silent beauty of the rugged, primitive landscape. He could comprehend the elemental force of this fertile earth which had drawn Luke and Lucien Edmond Bouchard to it as steel is drawn to a magnet, because in their very blood was a love and respect for good land that could be tilled and harvested. And because his wife, Laurette, had told him so many stories of Luke and Lucien Edmond, he felt an ardent kinship with the Bouchards.

"We will make camp at sundown, Mr. Douglas. Best not to do too much your first day out." Simata reined in his gelding and rode back to the Chicagoan. Few of his colleagues would have recognized Charles Douglas this afternoon, wearing a sombrero and riding boots, chaps, a sturdy jacket and riding breeches.

"But I'm fine, Simata," Charles laughingly protested. "You mustn't think that just because I come from a big city, I'm soft and fat. Not a bit of it! I told you, I rode horseback in Lincoln Park quite a few times back in Chicago, and I got plenty of exercise walking up and down the aisles of my store from eight to ten hours a day!"

"What he's trying to say, Mr. Douglas," Eddie Gentry broke in, "is that you're really still a tenderfoot out in these parts, and it's a good idea not to overdo it for the first couple of days. You'll be saddle-sore by morning, you mark what I'm telling you. Besides, there's no real rush. We've got provisions for more than two weeks and we'll just take it nice and easy."

"I'm in your capable hands, gentlemen," Charles chuckled. "It's really beautiful country, and I don't mind seeing it from the back of a horse, I assure you." Then, soberly, "Do you think we might run into any trouble, Eddie?"

"Hard to tell, Mr. Douglas."

"Look, Eddie, just call me Charlie. There's no need to stand on ceremony. Time enough for that when I unlock the door of my new Texas department store!"

"I'd like that mighty fine, Charlie. You do ride pretty well for a tenderfoot, I'll give you that," Eddie couldn't help joshing. "But to answer your question, we're following the safest and best trail we know. All the same, keep your eyes open. You never know when some outlaw might take it into his head to come our way, riding toward Mexico ahead of a posse. Or we might meet some raiding Indians. Fortunately, Simata speaks a couple of Indian languages just in case we have to parley with the redskins."

"I'll heed your warning, Eddie. Thanks. I've got my pistol in a holster where I can get at it in a hurry, and my carbine in a sling. I won't be a hindrance to the rest of you. I'll pull my weight, you've got my word on it," Charles solemnly declared.

"We never had any doubt about that for a minute, Charlie. Now let's ride on a ways, while it's still light."

When he had ridden east to claim Laure as his bride,

Luke Bouchard had made this same journey in eight days. He had been escorted by ten Kiowa braves and their old chief, Setangya, who had given him a wampum belt of shells as a token of friendship. Luke had also carried with him a turquoise given him in friendship by the Comanche chief, Sangrodo, whom Luke had aided when the ambitious officer at Fort Inge, Captain George Munson, had ruthlessly raided Sangrodo's stronghold.

The turquoise later saved Luke's life. When a drunken settler at Corpus Christi cursed Luke as an Indian-lover and fired a pistol at him, the great stone deflected the bullet, and Luke was unharmed. Upon his return to Windhaven Plantation, Luke climbed the tall red bluff where his grandfather, old Lucien, and the latter's Indian bride, Dimarte, lay buried. There, beside old Lucien's grave, Luke buried both the belt and the stone, saying that truly these tokens of friendship most rightfully belonged to him who had first come to live among the Creeks, to put into practice his humanitarian beliefs of equality and justice regardless of race, color, or creed.

The turquoise was later involved in the Bouchards' ongoing struggle with the Cournier clan, whose enmity toward the Bouchards stretched back more than eighty years. Before old Lucien Bouchard had left Normandy, on the eve of the French Revolution, he had been in love with flirtatious young Edmée de Courent, only to find that she had decided to marry his older brother, Jean, because Jean, as first-born, would inherit their father's title of count. Edmée and Jean de Bouchard had gone to Haiti, and there the faithless young woman had had an affair with a neighboring sugar plantation owner, Auguste Cournier. When Jean had discovered the intrigue, he had challenged Cournier to a duel and hopelessly crippled him for life. As a result of this, Auguste's two grandsons, Armand and Henri Cournier, years later swore a vow to discredit and destroy the Bouchards.

Armand was the first to seek revenge. He challenged Luke to a duel in New Orleans after he had unsuccessfully tried to take over the Brunton and Associate Bank, which Luke Bouchard was managing at the time for Laure Brunton. But he violated the code of dueling by firing at Luke's back, and Luke's friend, Arthur Traylor, serving as Luke's second, had to kill Cournier. Luke then had to fire at Cournier's second to prevent the murder of his staunch friend.

Armand's death did not put an end to the Cournier menace. When Luke and Laure had gone back to Windhaven Plantation, Arthur Traylor wrote to Luke to warn him of the existence of Armand's older brother, Henri. Meanwhile, an old conjure woman, Ellen, who had been mercilessly flogged by the Ku Klux Klan and given sanctuary at Windhaven Plantation, told Luke of her dream that a dark cloud would come over his two little boys, Lucien and Paul, and she instructed him to mark them with a sign so that, if lost, they could be found again. Struck by this presentiment of evil, Luke dug up the great turquoise of Sangrodo and had a Montgomery jeweler chip tiny pieces from it and make lockets which the little boys wore.

The warped vengeance of Henri Cournier soon struck. He hired ruffians who ravished Laure and kidnapped little Lucien. Then he gave the child to his valet and an unfortunate young woman who had fallen into his power because of her brother's gambling debts. They transported the boy west, for it was Cournier's plan to hand Lucien over to a wealthy man in California. Along the way, however, the couple's wagon was attacked by a warring band of Penateka Comanches. The Comanches killed the valet and the young woman, and discovered the locket around Lucien's neck. Recognizing the stone as part of Sangrodo's legendary talisman, they took the child to Sangrodo who, in turn, brought him to Windhaven Range. There the boy was reunited with his father, who came out to the ranch after confronting Henri Cournier in New Orleans and dueling him to the death. Father and son returned joyfully to Windhaven Plantation, and there Luke built a chapel to thank God for all His blessings to the Bouchards.

Charles Douglas had been told of all this by Lucien Edmond during the former's stay at Windhaven Range. As he rode now, in the waning hours of the day, Charles thought to himself that his own life had been sheltered, never really touched by any of the violence or hatred that had threatened to consume the Bouchards, and his admiration for this remarkable family grew even stronger. Not only had they met the challenge of a rugged country where there were few friends and neighbors and where they had had to depend upon their own resourcefulness, but also they had to endure attacks by bandits, thieves, and—worst of all—guileful and sinister enemies who kept their motives and their plans cunningly concealed.

All these thoughts exhilarated Charles and made him scarcely conscious of the physical strain of riding long hours. His reverie was at length interrupted when Simata called a halt and pointed to a cluster of towering oak trees, where they would make camp. Charles realized suddenly how tired he was, and when he dismounted he winced, discovering aching muscles he didn't know he had. But he merely grinned when Eddie Gentry slyly offered, "Wait till morning, Charlie, then you'll get your second wind."

Using his tinderbox, Simata soon started a cheery fire. After Maybelle Belcher's lavish dinner of the night before, the supper of bacon, beans with molasses, chunks of Maybelle's homemade bread baked early that morning, and strong black coffee might have seemed plebian, but Charles ate with a ravenous appetite and proclaimed the food the best he had ever tasted. When he had a rueful afterthought and began to amend his praise, Eddie smilingly interposed, "We know you're not knocking your mother-in-law's vittles, Charlie. All of us know how downright good the simplest meals taste when you're outdoors, like on the cattle drive to Abilene—isn't that right, Lucas?"

"I'm certain it is, Eddie," Lucas responded. "I can remember countless times, after a hard day's driving cattle and eating dust all day long, when just plain coffee and hard biscuits soaked in bacon grease tasted like a feast, and that's no lie."

After supper, Charles listened, entranced, to Simata's stories of his Kiowa kin and Eddie's yarns about horses and rustlers and land swindlers. Charles heard for the first time the story of how wily speculator Norman Cantrell, posing first as a Spanish baron and then as a count, had arranged for the murder of an old German couple who had bought the land next to Windhaven Range. Cantrell then sold the land to a Scotsman, Andrew Moultrie, who brought his beautiful young Spanish wife, Anna, from Taos. Moultrie also brought sheep, which ate the grass on Windhaven Range. When Lucien Edmond Bouchard's men rode out to protest, Moultrie's *pistoleros* fired at them. Anna Moultrie soon discovered her husband's ruthlessness,

25

and she threatened to leave him. Moultrie then whipped her, and when Lucien Edmond tried to intervene, Moultrie drew a six-shooter and fired at him, forcing Lucien Edmond to kill him.

More than ever, Charles Douglas was impressed with the courage that the Bouchards invariably showed in their times of greatest adversity. When Eddie Gentry had finished his story about Andrew Moultrie, and the tragic episode of how Robert Caldemare had bought Moultrie's land, set up fencing, and planned to kill Lucien Edmond and steal his cattle, Charles said aloud, "Here I was thinking that coming down to Texas to start up another department store was something unusual. After what you've told me, Eddie, I think, I'll keep my mouth shut from now on about my plans."

"Don't you fret, Charlie," Eddie amiably encouraged. "We haven't reached Corpus Christi yet. For all I know, we might have more excitement than we can handle— though I sure hope not."

"Well, we'll be ready for whatever happens, with those carbines along," Lucas broke in with a solemn nod, and Simata grunted assent.

As they bedded down for the night, wrapping themselves in blankets, Charles uttered a happy sigh and fell asleep at once. His last conscious thought was that this camaraderie between himself and his three companions was an unforgettably heartwarming experience and that he was grateful for it. So soundly did he sleep, indeed, that Lucas had to shake him gently several times to call him for breakfast. He sat up with a start, then groaned and reached back to rub his shoulders. "Stiffened up some, I reckon?" Lucas remarked. "That's mighty natural. Once you're back in the saddle, you'll be as good as new. I brought you the first cup of coffee so's to clear the cobwebs away right off."

"Thanks, Lucas." Charles took a tentative sip and grimaced. "It's scalding and it's strong!"

"Way a man wants it on a cold morning when he's a spell of riding ahead of him, Charlie," Lucas grinned. He had already taken a great liking to the gregarious Chicagoan because of the way the latter had adapted himself without complaint to the rigors of the trail.

Charles soon found that Lucas had been right: his aches and pains seemed to vanish once they were riding again along the trail that would lead them to Corpus Christi and the *William Wallace*. Nonetheless, Lucas saw to it that there were several stops during the long day to let the horses quench their thirst in the shallow bed of the Nueces River, and Charles shot him a grateful look each time. By the time they made camp on the second night, he was delighted to find that he was scarcely fatigued, and once again ate ravenously and fell asleep immediately. Thus far, the four riders had seen no one, and all that they had heard during this second night of the journey was the howling of a distant coyote.

In the morning, over breakfast, Simata regaled his companions with stories from Comanche folklore, in which the wolf was often equated with the benevolent creator, whereas the coyote, the wolf's younger brother, was regarded as a mischievous spoiler. Simata added, "We of the Kiowa think the coyote may once have been a demigod who offended the more powerful ones, and so they sent him to earth and made him a cunning but foolish beast. So when we hear him howl at night, we laugh and say, 'It is Coyote lamenting that he is no longer one of the gods.'"

By the end of the third day, the four riders had covered nearly sixty miles, about a third of the distance to Corpus Christi. Charles was elated and urged them to keep on at this pace, but Simata shook his head and answered, "Perhaps we will finish in ten days instead of two weeks, but it is always wise, especially when one so new as you rides with us, not to waste one's strength."

On the fourth day, shortly after noon, as they rode near a large clump of mesquite, Simata suddenly wheeled his horse to one side, drew his Starr .44, and fired. Charles's gelding whinnied and reared for a moment, and the young Chicagoan, taken by surprise, had all he could do to keep hold of the reins and maintain his balance in the saddle.

"A big rattlesnake," Simata triumphantly announced as he gestured with the barrel of the pistol at the thrashing body of a six-foot diamond rattlesnake in its death throes. "I heard the buzzing of its rattles just as I came to this mesquite, and it was about to strike at my horse when I shot it."

Charles shuddered and instinctively put his hand to the holster of his pistol. It was the first such incident to remind him of Eddie Gentry's warning that there could be trouble

27

ahead, even in this deserted country where they had still come upon no other human beings.

By the end of the eighth day, they were within fifty miles of Corpus Christi. By now, Charles's impatience had been tempered by the pleasures of outdoor living and the companionship of three men whom he now counted as his closest friends. Also, he had never felt healthier, more full of energy. His mind was completely ready for his future undertakings without feeling the slightest anxiety or stress. It would be fun, he thought, to have Laurette camp out with him for a few nights after he got back from Houston. What a wonderful second honeymoon it would make! He fell asleep with a smile, conjecturing the saucy comments his red-haired wife would doubtless make when he proposed this to her.

CHAPTER THREE

The six bandits had ridden hard all day long and their horses were foundering with exhaustion, their sides heaving, white foam puffing at the corners of their muzzles. Ten days earlier, they had held up a bank in Austin, killed the cashier and an innocent bystander who had been in their line of fire, crossed the Colorado River, and headed south toward Lockhart, where one of them had a cousin who ran a stable and could furnish fresh horses to outdistance the citizens' posse that had quickly formed and was riding after them. Then they crossed the San Antonio River near Kenedy and, three nights ago, made camp on the edge of a small forest near a stagnant creek.

Two miles eastward, a small hunting party of Kiowa Apaches had also made camp after an unsuccessful day's hunt in which they bagged only a small prairie antelope and two jackrabbits. There were twenty of them, led by tall, dark-skinned Hitosay who, though it was against the custom of his tribe, had yielded to the pleading of his beautiful new squaw, Elanit, who wanted to go with the men on the hunt. She was nineteen and had already shown great prowess with bow and arrow and the lance. She was as tall as a man and slim, and she pleased him greatly. Since they had no water, he sent her to find some. Elanit mounted a mustang, took two dried buffalo bladders, and rode westward in search of water.

It was nearly midnight when she spied the little creek, dismounted, untied one of the bladders, and hurried to the water, wearing high moccasins and a dress of deerskin. Her glossy black hair was parted in the middle and plaited in two braids, with a bright headband round the top of her head, and its markings designated her proud status as the squaw of the Kiowa Apache leader.

29

Two of the outlaws were standing guard while their companions slept. One was Jeb Durott, a black-bearded, swarthy Kansan who had ridden with the infamous William Clarke Quantrill. He had escaped a Union troop ambush intended to hang him and two other Quantrill lieutenants and made his way to Texas where he had formed his murderous band. When he saw the young woman squat down and begin to fill the buffalo bladder, he drew in his breath and turned to his companion.

"Hsst, Benjy," he whispered to the tall, rabbit-faced blond youth who was standing guard with him, "just take a gander at what's out there by the creek. Mighty nice. You 'n me 'n the boys could stand a little pokemeat right about now, I'm thinkin'."

Benjamin Carson was only twenty, but he had already killed a dozen men. He grinned wolfishly as he cupped his lean hands to his pale blue eyes and squinted at Elanit. "Real nice, Jeb," he pronounced. "But why the hell do we have to share her with the others? Just you 'n me, I'm saying."

"First let's get her. But be careful, don't let her make a sound. Figgers if she's comin' here to fetch water, there must be a passel of redskins not too far from here," Durott cautioned. He and the blond youth began to sneak toward the unsuspecting squaw, whose back was toward them.

Elanit rose, lifting the heavy buffalo bladder whose edges were pinned together with smooth wooden pins to make it look like a large, short-neck gourd. At that moment, Jeb Durott clapped his right hand over her mouth and seized one of her plaits with his other hand, while Benjamin Carson, with a lecherous cackle, his face flushed with excitement, clasped her round the waist with both arms and dragged her back toward their camp. He flung her down on the ground on her back as Durott maintained a vise-like pressure with his palm against her mouth. Drawing his hunting knife with his left hand, he menaced her and muttered, "Just let out one peep, you redskin bitch, and it'll be your last, savvy?"

Elanit's dark eyes were huge with terror: she understood no English, but she comprehended what was about to happen to her. With all her desperate courage, she kicked and thrashed furiously and tried to sink her teeth into Jeb Durott's palm. Infuriated, the black-bearded outlaw, dropping the knife, clenched his left fist and stunned her with a savage blow to the temple. Then, swiftly, the two men tore off her deerskin dress and Durott savagely violated her. Squatting down, unfastening his breeches, licking his lips in anticipation, the blond youth hissed, "C'mon, Jeb, for crissake, I'm dying to git at her—don't take so damn long—you'll wake the others up!"

One of the four sleeping men had already been wakened by the sound of Elanit's struggles. He got to his feet and came lumbering toward the two ravishers. He was Jerry Keeson, a thirty-five-year-old deserter from the Union army who since the war had been a pimp in Chicago and a shakedown artist in St. Louis. He was wanted for murder in two states, and he had killed at least two of his victims with his bare hands. Fleeing the law, he had made his way to Texas, where he met Jeb Durott in a little Panhandle town and joined the bank robber's band.

"Hey, fellas, whatcha got there?" he muttered thickly as he watched Benjamin Carson replace the black-bearded leader on Elanit's inert, naked body. "Tryin' to keep it all fer yerselves, are you now? Oh, no, you don't, boys—I'm gittin her next, else I'll wake up Denny, Marty, and Tom and tell 'em how you're tryin' to cheat us out of our share. Remember, Jeb, when we joined up, you promised a fair 'n equal shake all round, you did!"

"All right, all right," Durott snarled back. "Keep your voice down. You'll be next with the redskin bitch. All right, Benjy, ain't you had enough yet? Git off 'n let Jerry have a poke. I'm gonna git her horse. We can sure use a fresh one." Staggering to his feet and putting his clothes back in order, the black-bearded ruffian moved toward Elanit's mustang, which had been placidly grazing near the creek. But when it saw him approach, it whinnied and raced off to the east. Durott swore under his breath: "Damn it to hell—now it'll get back to the rest of those goddamn Injuns and they'll know something's up." He turned and hurried back to the two men just as Keeson flung himself down on the sprawled body of the young Kiowa Apache squaw. "Make it fast, fer Jeez' sake, Jerry! Her mustang's run back to wherever the rest of her dirty, murderin' band is camping. They'll be by to find out what's takin' her so long to git her water, so we best skedaddle."

31

"Yeah, yeah," Keeson softly panted as, his stubby fingers gripping Elanit's shoulders, he thrust savagely back and forth. "Too damn bad I hafta hurry—hell, this tricksy redskinned piece could make a fortune for me back in Chicago. There—I'm done."

He raised himself from the unconscious girl, his darkly contorted face twisted in an appreciative leer, while Durott calmly knelt down, gripped Elanit's plaits in his left hand, and drew on them to stretch her neck, which he expertly cut with a sideways slash of the hunting knife in his right hand.

"Best thing to do. Might gain some time that way. All right, Jerry, go wake up Denny, Marty, and Tom and let's git ridin' hard! We'll head for the border."

A few minutes later, all six men mounted their horses and furiously rode off southward, in the direction of the little settlement of Beeville.

When Elanit's mustang made its way back to the Kiowa Apache camp, Hitosay, who had been awaiting the return of his favorite squaw, sprang to his feet and strode toward it. He patted the horse's forehead, and it nickered softly and nuzzled his shoulder. He scowled angrily, then barked an order to two braves who, lances in hand, had been standing guard nearby. "She has not returned, but her mustang returns alone," he told them. "Go to the west where she sought water and find her—be quick!"

Mounting their mustangs, the two braves rode off toward the stagnant creek. Discovering Elanit's body, one of the braves told his companion, "I see the tracks of many horses. Follow them. I go back to tell Hitosay what terrible thing has been done to Elanit."

Hearing the dreadful news, the Kiowa Apache chief uttered a howl of agonized rage. He summoned the other warriors of the band, and, leading Elanit's horse behind him, he rode with them to the camp of the bank robbers. Then, vowing vengeance by the most grisly torture on those who had dared defile and murder his beautiful squaw, he and his men followed the track of Jeb Durott and his accomplices.

First Simata and then Lucas had stood guard during the eighth night of the journey from Windhaven Range to Cor-

32

pus Christi. The four men had camped on a slightly higher rise of ground thick with cottonwood scrubs, and as the first light of dawn broke upon a thickly clouded sky, Lucas began to make preparations for a fire for breakfast. Laying down his carbine, he squatted and took out his tinderbox, then began the fire with leaves and dried branches. There was no need to wake the others yet. They had made very good time, and perhaps in two days more they would come within sight of the range of low bluffs at the outskirts of the port of Corpus Christi. He looked round him, out of habit, and then his face became taut with a sudden anxiety as he saw, in the distance, a group of horsemen riding from the north. They were as yet indistinct in the hazy light of a wintry dawn, but they were the first people he had seen since the party had left Windhaven Range. Swiftly, he stamped out the fire and called out, "Wake up, wake up, there's men coming this way!"

Eddie Gentry and Simata sprang to their feet, and Charles Douglas, who had been deep in sleep, sat up blinking his eyes, his face blank with a drowsy wonder.

"See, off there? They're riding hard, a couple of miles off, but heading this way for certain!" Lucas warned.

"Sure, I can see them now, Lucas!" Eddie exclaimed as he squinted northward. "Five or six of them, I can't make out for sure—we'd best forget about breakfast, saddle up, and ride east. I can smell trouble already. I had a feeling it was too peaceful to last till we got to Corpus Christi. Forget your sleeping bags and blankets. Let's just get out of here quick as we can!"

In a few moments, the four men had mounted their horses, Simata taking the reins of the two pack horses, and the men spurred their geldings to a swift canter as they headed in the direction of Corpus Christi.

The outlaws were still riding hard. Jeb Durott, swearing at his foundering horse, turned back to bawl at his companions, "We're in luck, boys! See those four riders breaking camp and heading east? They've got two pack horses, by God! We'll just kill them, take their horses and what guns they've got, and make it over to Mexico before those damned redskins catch up with us!"

"I'm all for that, Jeb," Marty Callahan, a scar-faced Texas rustler and bank robber, shouted back. "These

33

horses we got aren't going to last much longer, though. We've got to head them off and start shooting once we're in range!"

"Damn sure," the black-bearded leader shouted back. "There's six of us and only four of them, and they're held down by those two pack horses—it'll be easy pickings, boys." So saying, he drew his old Whitworth rifle out of its saddle sling and, gripping his slavering horse between his knees to maintain his balance in the saddle, squinted along the sight and fired. Lucas's horse screamed in agony and toppled, but Lucas agilely leaped off before he could be injured in the fall. Swiftly, his carbine already gripped in his left hand, he whirled, flung himself down on the ground, aimed at the approaching riders, and levered the trigger seven times. Denny Brewster, a sallow-faced, nearly bald man in his early forties who was wanted for murder in Kansas, stiffened in his saddle and pitched lifelessly to the ground. A moment later, his exhausted horse sank to its knees and rolled over, its sides heaving. Tom Delby, who had urged his horse in a wide circle to Jeb Durott's left so as to head off the four riders, dropped his Starr .44, clutched at his throat, and toppled to one side, his foundering horse dragging his lifeless body by one foot caught in the stirrup, till at last it too, dying of exhaustion, rolled over and pinned his corpse beneath it.

Benjamin Carson, Jerry Keeson, and Marty Callahan, each armed with pistols and Sharps rifles, leaped from their saddles as their weary horses slackened, neighing plaintively, their eyes rolling to the whites and their muzzles smeared with foam. Running toward a clump of mesquite, the men opened fire on their four victims, and a bullet from Keeson's Sharps grazed Lucas's scalp. Having swiftly reloaded his Spencer, Lucas directed his fire toward the mesquite shelter, and a howl of agony rang out as Benjamin Carson staggered to his feet, his mouth gaping, and fell backwards, dead.

Jeb Durott had leaped from his dying horse and taken cover with Marty Callahan and Jerry Keeson, swearing violently. "Son of a bitch, where do they get that fire power? Three of my boys dead already, and not a one of them made to pay for it yet! Keep shooting, they'll have to run out of ammunition soon! Aim for their horses if you can't do any better, Jerry, Marty!" Having reloaded his Whitworth, he took careful aim and fired. Charles Douglas, who at Eddie Gentry's hasty order had dismounted and taken refuge behind a jagged boulder along with the young cowboy and Simata, had peered out from one side of the boulder to aim his carbine at the clump of mesquite, and the black-bearded leader's next bullet took him in the left arm, just above the elbow. With a cry of pain, Charles triggered his carbine and Durott, a startled look on his ugly face, sank to his knees, dropped the Whitworth, and fell forward, his boots kicking at the dusty red soil in death.

Jerry Keeson and Marty Callahan reloaded their rifles, sweating and pale at this unexpected turn of events. "The bastards," Keeson panted to his sole companion, "we're for sure in a bad fix now! They've got carbines and they know how to use them. Damn it to hell, who'd have figured that?"

"Just shut up and keep shoooting," Callahan hoarsely muttered as he reloaded his rifle, then crawled toward the edge of the mesquite clump and, both pistols in his hands, fired them at the boulder. Lucas, crouching low to the ground, had run toward the boulder behind which his three companions hid, and one of the bullets whined past him just as he took cover. He reloaded his Spencer and triggered off two shots toward the two remaining outlaws, but without effect.

"There's just two of them left now," Eddie muttered to the Kiowa scout. "You three others keep firing, and I'll crawl out a little and see if I can get them to come out from behind that mesquite."

"Be careful," Charles gasped between his gritted teeth, for his wound was beginning to throb painfully. "Lucas, you're bleeding badly."

"It just grazed me, Charlie, no time to worry. I can still see good enough to shoot," Lucas grimly assured him.

Cautiously, Eddie began to crawl out from behind the boulder while Simata, Charles, and Lucas fired a volley from their carbines. One of Simata's bullets took Marty Callahan in the fleshy part of his right shoulder, and he yowled with pain as he dropped his pistols. With an oath, Jerry Keeson, moving to the other side of the clump of mesquite, saw Eddie crawling away from the boulder and, leveling his Sharps, pulled the trigger. The Texas cowboy

35

winced and groaned as the bullet went cleanly through his right shoulder. Disregarding the pain, he leveled his Spencer and triggered off the remaining bullets. Keeson screamed as two of those bullets found their marks in his belly. Sinking to his knees, dropping his Sharps, he clutched at his middle, bowed his head to the ground, and coughed out his life in a welter of blood.

Shuddering with terror and the pain of his own wound, Marty Callahan vindictively aimed his two pistols at the pack horses and fired, killing them both. As he grabbed for his Sharps and began to reload it, Eddie got to his feet, holding his carbine at the hip, and loped, crouching low, toward the clump of mesquite, firing as he came. The outlaw spun around, two bullets in his side, then fell over onto his back and lay sprawled, his lifeless eyes staring up at the sky.

"Whew, that was too close for comfort," Lucas panted as he opened his canteen and poured the water over his bleeding scalp, then tore off a piece of his shirt and pressed it to the slight wound. "But we've only got three horses left now, and a good fifty miles of riding ahead of us."

"That's much better than lying here like those six," Eddie humorlessly joked. "Simata, help me bind up this nick in the shoulder. Bullet went clean through, thank the Lord! You, Charlie, you're hurt!"

"It's not too bad, just in the fleshy part of the arm—and I think the bullet went through, just like yours. I can stand it," the young Chicagoan panted.

"I'll make you a tourniquet too, Charlie," the Kiowa scout said as he finished binding Eddie's wound. Lucas, who had at last stopped the bleeding of his own scalp wound, grinned at Charles. "Well, Charlie, you did mighty fine the first time you were under fire—it was that, wasn't it?"

"It certainly was," Charles wanly exhaled. "I can't say I'd like to have any more experience at it, though."

Lucas chuckled and clapped him on the back. "You did just fine, just fine. And don't you dare look ashamed for being peaked now, Charlie. It's only natural for a man to feel a little queasy after he's been through a shooting fracas. He wouldn't be human if he didn't. But it's when the action was hot that you showed the guts you really have—and that's all that counts."

36

Charles closed his eyes and nodded. "Thanks, Lucas. Thank God all of you didn't let me panic."

"Why, man, there wasn't time for any of us to panic, that's what!" Lucas burst into hearty laughter.

"Ho, there, off to the north—Indians!" Simata suddenly exclaimed, pointing.

"Oh, my God," Charles groaned, "don't tell me we've got another fight on our hands without any time to rest after this one!"

"I do not think so. I think they ride after these men who attacked us. Wait, I can see their markings—they are Kiowa Apaches," Simata announced. "I can speak enough of their tongue to tell them that we are friends."

Hitosay and his braves had relentlessly pursued the six outlaws, and now they neared the scene of the attack. Simata mounted his gelding and rode out to meet the tall, dark-skinned chief, holding up his hand in the sign of friendship. Hitosay gestured to his warriors to lower their weapons as he called out in his guttural tongue, "I seek those who dishonored and killed my squaw Elanit!"

"Chief of the Kiowa Apaches, I have Kiowa blood in my veins," Simata replied. "These three men and I have ridden from a ranch which is protected by the mighty Comanche chief Sangrodo, and we make for the port of Corpus Christi."

"The name of Sangrodo is known to all," Hitosay solemnly declared. "There are dead men here."

"Those were the men you seek, great chief of the Kiowa Apaches," Simata responded. "They wished to take our horses and guns from us, and we defended ourselves."

"I see that you speak truth, O Kiowa. There are the dead horses of the wicked men who took Elanit's life and shamed her before its taking. Since this is so, I am in your debt and that of your friends. But I will take their scalps and bury them beside my murdered squaw, that her spirit may know she has been avenged."

"It is right that you do this, O chief of the Kiowa Apaches," Simata agreed.

Hitosay nodded. "Then go in peace. Your friends have been wounded, I see. Is there help we can give you?"

"If the great chief could spare a horse, since three of our horses were killed by the outlaws, we should be grateful to him," Simata replied.

"It shall be done. Because you have done me a service, I will give you my own horse. I will ride Elanit's." Hitosay dismounted and led his mustang by the reins to Simata, handing them to the Kiowa scout. Then he gripped Simata's left shoulder with his right hand and said, "You are truly Kiowa and brave. May the Great Spirit watch over you and your friends. And now, I do what must be done and then I return to mourn Elanit."

CHAPTER FOUR

Hitosay, the Kiowa Apache chief, made one more gift to the four men who had avenged the dishonor and murder of his young squaw. After scalping the six outlaws and tying their bloody scalps to the tail of Elanit's mustang, in a solemn ritual that held Charles Douglas spellbound, he turned to one of his braves and made a gesture, then pointed toward the young Chicagoan and his companions. The brave dismounted, took a pouch from the belt of his deerskin leggings, and handed it to Simata, with a brief explanation in his own tongue which none of the three others could understand. After the brave had remounted again, the Indians wheeled their ponies toward the north and galloped off. Hitosay looked back and raised his right arm, waving it in a circle, and then galloped swiftly to lead his band back whence they had come.

Simata, his face very grave, turned to the wondering trio. "He has seen our wounds, and his lieutenant has given us these herbs and the bark. I am to make a poultice with them, and they will heal the wounds you have suffered. And he has made the sign that he will never forget your friendship and that he is bound in honor to remember always how you, white-eyes though you are, avenged his honor and dealt out justice to those murderers."

"It was good of him to give us that horse, Simata," understand. After the brave had remounted, the Indians who had almost vanished from sight by now as they spurred their mustangs on to the north.

"From such as the Kiowa Apaches, or even my own people, the Comanches, it was almost the greatest gift of all," Simata explained. "The Plains Indians value their horses nearly as much as they do their wives. In battle and in hunting, their horses are the extension of their own

39

courage and endurance. Some of the tribes of my own people, as my father once told me, used to put to death the favorite horse of a chief who had died, so that the spirit of that animal might accompany him into the world beyond. Now, before we resume our journey, I will make these poultices for the three of you. It will help heal the wounds quickly. Still, I think we should not hurry, and if it takes three days to reach Corpus Christi, we shall still have made good time."

Charles nodded, lost in reflection, his handsome young face somber. "I don't think I'll ever forget what happened or what I saw," he said aloud as if it had to be said. "I didn't ever think anything like this would ever happen to me. I'm not sure I'll tell Laurette—it'd frighten her silly—"

"You will tell her one day," Simata gravely nodded. "And because she is a woman and her life is bound with yours for the evil as for the good, she will understand and respect you for what you say now. Never reproach yourself for what you feel. It is good that a man is humble and knows that he is not so brave as he thinks, and again, not so cowardly as he fears. All of us, this day, have had a new look into ourselves and found something good that we may remember in the years ahead."

"Yes—yes, you're right. That's exactly how I feel." Charles put out his hand to Eddie Gentry, then Lucas and then Simata, and the four of them wordlessly shook hands.

After Simata had cared for the wounds of his three companions, they rested for a few hours at his suggestion, and then mounted their geldings and the Indian mustang, the remainder of their supplies tied to their saddles, and rode on toward Corpus Christi.

When they rode down the dusty main street of the little town three days later with the glare of the midday sun beating down upon them, Eddie let out a joyous whoop. "We're in luck! The New Orleans packet is still there at the main dock. Charlie, you go on ahead and make arrangements for us and our horses to get aboard."

"I'll do that," Charles grinned. "That's the most welcome sight I've seen since we left Windhaven Range—it feels like a century ago."

"Doesn't it!" Lucas agreed. "You're planning to stay

over a couple of days in Galveston before we set out for Houston, aren't you, Charlie?"

"Yes, that's right, Lucas. Lucien Edmond told me to be sure to look up his Aunt Arabella and her husband, James Hunter. Besides, judging from what I've seen of Galveston as a bustling port town, I'd say there's a chance that I might even have a store there one day—who knows?" Charles spurred his gelding and galloped on ahead of his companions toward the dock.

Eddie shrugged as he turned to Lucas. "I'll bet you a month's pay, Lucas, Charlie won't ever want to have a store here in Corpus Christi. Oh, sure, there are more shacks and a couple more of those stores with false fronts, since the last time I was here. And more gulls dipping over the docks. But it's not a growing town. Look at how old and rotting the posts of the loading docks are! And for sure he wouldn't want to have his merchandise shipped here and then take it in wagons all the way to San Antone."

"I agree," Lucas said, as he sat in his saddle and stared over the harbor. "I recollect when Pappy and me first came out here—seems like a mighty long time ago, just about seven years. I don't see much change either."

Charles Douglas eagerly made his way up toward a group of stevedores who were listening, with abashed respect, to the angry tirade of a bearded man with fierce blue eyes and enormously bushy eyebrows, bedecked in the natty blue jacket and trousers and cap of a packet captain. The latter concluded, smacking his right fist into his left palm for added emphasis, "Now just mind you, look sharp, for you're a bunch of lazy landlubbers, and the good Lord'll bear me out on that. If you don't put this cargo away so we can sail with the afternoon tide, I'll have you all replaced, if I have to hire cowhands and shopkeepers for the job! Now get back to work!"

"It's the same Captain McMurtrie who brought me here," Charles laughingly spoke up.

The bearded Scotsman whirled, glaring ferociously at Charles, then squinted and stroked his beard. "Seems like I know you, mister, though I swear I can't place you just this minute."

"Well, you brought my wife and my three little sons here from New Orleans, Captain McMurtrie, back in November."

"So I did, so I did! Let me see now—don't tell me— why, that's right, you're Mr. Charles Douglas, and you came all the way from Chicago where they had that big fire," the captain triumphantly pronounced.

"Full marks for memory, Captain McMurtrie. Now, can you take my three friends and me and our horses aboard? I suppose you'll stop over a few days in Galveston? You see, I want to look over Houston and build a new store—I was telling you how mine was burned in the fire."

"I remember. And I said to myself, the good Lord in His infinite wisdom kept old Jamie McMurtrie on the sea and on the Gulf so he wouldn't have to die of fire. I'd as soon choose water any time—unless, of course, it be good Scotch whiskey!"

"Perhaps you'd be good enough to share a tot of that with me as a paying passenger, Captain McMurtrie," Charles chuckled.

"That I will, Mr. Douglas, with the greatest of pleasure! Yes, this time we'll stay two days in Galveston, then go back to the Queen City and come back to Galveston—let me think now, well, about a week after we dock in New Orleans to pick up passengers and supplies. And probably a new crew—you heard me giving the very dickens to those lazy sots."

"That's how I recognized you," Charles chuckled again.

Captain Jamie McMurtrie's face grew somber for a moment, and he uttered a heavy sigh. "This will be my last year on the *William Wallace*. The company's thinking of retiring her. Well, can't say as I blame them. She's weather-worn, and she's been in service nigh unto thirty-five years. And they'd as soon put me off on the beach and give me my walking papers. I'm going to try to fight that, if I can. Why, Mr. Douglas, I'm just seventy-two and in my prime, and you heard how I handled that bunch of musclebound stevedores. They know I'm still spry enough to take a rope's end to their ornery hides if I have to."

"I'm sorry to hear that they're trying to make you retire, Captain McMurtrie. It won't be the same without you, if that happens."

"Well, sir, let me tell you I'm just one step ahead of them. If they do give me my walking papers, I'll take me out to San Francisco. I've an old friend there who's starting a ferry, and he's written me often the last year or so, urging me to come out and start a new life. And I may just do that. But that's enough about me, Mr. Douglas. Have your friends bring the horses aboard and we'll let the men put them up in fine fashion. And now I know where you've come from, too—Windhaven Range. Yessir, I sure remember Mr. Luke Bouchard, how I brought him here and how I took him back. I was sure glad to hear—when you were aboard last time—that he and his family are doing well."

"They are indeed," Charles replied.

"God bless them all and give them long life. Mr. Bouchard's one of the finest men I ever met, Mr. Douglas. Matter of fact, you might say that I'm going to take a leaf out of his book, in a way. I mean, here's a man who had everything, came out here to Texas and founded a ranch and beat off bandits and Injuns and such, then he goes back to start over again where he began as a boy. Well, sir, if he can do that, I can take myself off to San Francisco and handle the wheel of a ship just as good as ever I did."

"I know you can. I'll tell my friends to come aboard. And here's the money for our passage to Galveston."

It took three days for the chugging old packet to negotiate the nearly two hundred miles from Corpus Christi to the flourishing Port of Galveston, but Charles Douglas did not regret the peaceful hiatus. He spent many hours on the captain's bridge with Captain McMurtrie, who possessed an amazing memory for people, places, and dates as well as an inexhaustible fund of anecdotes.

"One thing you want to remember, Mr. Douglas," Captain McMurtrie assured Charles just before the landing in Galveston, "is that shipping cargo on the Gulf can be a chancy thing, especially in an old scow like the *William Wallace*. I've run into hurricanes and rough waters many a time since I first had my captain's papers, and I've lost some cargo from time to time. But I'm sure there'll be sturdier packets built in the next few years, now that more and more settlers are coming to Texas. And, if you don't mind my saying so, I wouldn't overlook Galveston as a place for one of your new stores, along with Houston. It makes sense to have the goods taken right off the dock and straight to your store here, doesn't it?"

"Yes, I'll admit that's very logical, Captain McMurtrie. But what *do* you think about Houston? Do you think it's

43

worthwhile to transport goods the seventy miles from Galveston to a store there?"

"Well, right off, Mr. Douglas, you ought to be aware that it's really more like fifty miles than seventy from Galveston, if you take the old Indian trail. Couple of months back, I heard that some of the merchants out Houston way were trying to get a brand-new road built along that trail. It seems to me when that goes through, shipping your goods will be a mite easier. And it won't be long, either, before they start building railroads all through Texas, you mark my words."

"Yes, I agree with you, Captain McMurtrie," Charles said. "And that's what I'm really thinking about; the possibilities for the future are boundless. Of course, a man has to be realistic: railroads won't be big in this state for a while yet, and carrying goods by wagon isn't easy. But I think it may be worth the effort, because if a man gets a foothold by pioneering early in the game, he'll be in a great position to profit once progress and growth catch up with him."

"Well, Mr. Douglas, that's the spirit that built this country. It's been a real pleasure getting to know you on this trip." The old Scotsman sighed and stroked his beard again. "When you've finished your business in Houston, you'll probably still find me here ready to take you back to Corpus Christi. But I can't promise that you'll see me again by the time the year's over—not unless your business takes you out to San Francisco."

"Well, who's to say that there won't be a Douglas Department Store out there one day, too, long before your time's up, Captain!" Charles smiled as the two men warmly shook hands.

It was early afternoon by the time the four riders from Windhaven Range disembarked, secured their baggage, and rode away from the dock toward Darden Street. After a few minutes' ride, they halted their mounts before the Hunters' rambling, two-story frame house, and tied their horses to a hitching post outside the wide gate. There was a brass knocker on the front door of the house, in the shape of a soldier carrying a musket at his hip, and Charles studied it a moment with considerable interest before rapping it loudly to announce his presence.

He had heard the sound of women's voices just before

knocking, and now there was a startled gasp and then a high-pitched "Just a minute, please!" from within. A moment later, the door was opened by Arabella Hunter herself, whose eyes widened at the sight of four unshaven riders in sombreros, jackets, and breeches. "What can I do for you gentlemen?" she asked in a nervously flurried voice. "Are you looking for someone?"

"Mrs. Hunter, don't you recognize me?" Charles Douglas smiled, doffing his sombrero.

There were only a few streaks of gray in Arabella Hunter's glossy black hair, and her face was as lovely as it had always been, but with a greater serenity and maturity. Now her eyes widened and she exclaimed, blushing, "Oh, my gracious—why, of course, it's you, Charles! I do declare, I didn't recognize you at first, with your beard. And you're so brown from the sun! Oh, do come in, please! My daughter Melinda is here, you see, and she brought over my grandson, Gary."

"I do hope we haven't bothered you, Mrs. Hunter. These are my friends, Eddie Gentry, Lucas, who as you know is Djamba's son, and Simata, the very best scout in all of Texas. We're on our way to Houston, really, but I did want to see you and James again."

"Why, I'm delighted," Arabella exclaimed. "Do come in, please, all of you. My gracious, you look tired—and no wonder, after such a long journey. Just make yourselves comfortable on the settee, and I'll bring some lemonade."

"Thank you. Really, I hope we're not disturbing you, Mrs. Hunter," Charles apologized as he gestured for his friends to enter.

"Melinda, darling, here's Mr. Douglas back to visit us, and the three men who rode with him." Arabella turned toward her black-haired daughter who was holding a four-month-old baby in her arms. At nineteen, Melinda Davis was an almost exact duplicate of her mother, save that her face was fuller. She had her mother's eyes and shapely mouth, with the flare of spirit evident in the firmness of her jaw and high-set cheekbones.

"It's nice to meet you again, Mr. Douglas," Melinda curtsied. "And you gentlemen, too."

"This is Eddie Gentry, and Lucas and Simata," Charles said to Melinda, then turned to Arabella. "We really shouldn't have barged in this way, Mrs. Hunter, but—"

"Why, that's just nonsense, Mr. Douglas!" Arabella eagerly broke in. "I'm glad you came and I want you and your friends to stay with us. James would never forgive me if I let my niece's husband and good friends put up at a hotel—not that we don't have a good one here in Galveston, of course. But, my goodness, this big house has rooms enough for all of you, and I just insist that you remain till you're ready to continue your journey. Oh my, you've been hurt, some of you, I can see from the bandages—"

"Nothing to fret about, ma'am," Eddie put in. "We had a spell of trouble with some outlaws, but everything worked out just fine."

"Well, I know that James—that's my husband—will be just as excited as anything to hear all about your adventures. My goodness, I'm excited. I don't often get a chance to show off my grandson to company, and I guess I'm not making good sense."

"You're making very good sense, Mrs. Hunter," Charles replied. "He's a fine little boy."

"He is, Mr. Douglas, he's just a precious lamb," Melinda spoke up. "Why, he goes right to sleep as soon as I feed him. He's going to grow up to be an important man just like his daddy." Melinda hugged the baby to her and bent down to kiss his forehead.

Eddie Gentry watched and suddenly felt his eyes water with unaccustomed tears. Surreptitiously, he rubbed them with the back of his jacket sleeve. All of a sudden he had thought of Polly Behting, and how nice she had been to him and how eager she'd been to take riding lessons from him. Now, suddenly, because he saw this pretty girl and her baby, he was jumping to conclusions just like a tenderfoot who goes into the corral and thinks he can break the orneriest mustang on the ranch. He glanced down solemnly at his boots, averting his gaze from young Melinda and her child. He told himself that maybe it was because of his narrow escape from the outlaws, back on the range, that he'd had a chance to look back and see how lonesome he had been most of his life, and how much he had missed along the way by not having a family.

"I'm sure he'll be just that, Missus Melinda, ma'am," Lucas spoke up, having noticed Eddie's sudden, inexplicable confusion and wanting to draw attention away from the cowboy. "From what I've heard tell about your mother here and your daddy, that baby comes from fine stock, and with what you and your man have to offer, he's bound to have a head start in life."

"Why, thank you, Mr. Lucas." Melinda blushed and gave her mother a happy glance. "Mama, if you'll take Gary, I'll bring in the lemonade."

"With pleasure, dear. I'd like to hold my grandson all I can. You and Lawrence don't visit us nearly as much as James and I would like." Arabella held out her arms for the infant, and as she took him, her eyes glowed and there was a radiant smile on her lips.

Though Arabella had been a flirtatious girl, she had weathered the storms of her own flightiness and she now was settled happily into a secure marriage. As a consequence of her affair with Durwood McCambridge, her husband, James, had taken a hairbrush to her and then made passionate love to her. Thus, at the advanced age of forty-five, she had given birth to her third child, little Joy, now two years old. And Arabella also had achieved another goal: a happy marriage for her grown daughter, and a fine grandchild.

The only indulgence Arabella had permitted herself, as a late mother, was to ask James whether they might have a nurse for Joy, and he had at once agreed. She enjoyed the luxury of having someone else relieve her of the often onerous chores of rearing an infant. Moreover, the nurse, Mrs. Ella Samuels, had proved to be an excellent cook, and Arabella had cozened her into preparing occasional dinners for James.

After the four men had enjoyed the lemonade and Arabella's sponge cake, she graciously suggested, "Do you know, I think you gentlemen might like to rest before dinner. I'll show you upstairs."

"That's mighty hospitable of you, Mrs. Hunter," Eddie rose to his feet. "I'll just take you up on that offer. I sure could use some shuteye."

"I'm sure you all can. Come along, I'll show you the way," Arabella offered. As she led the way to the staircase to the second floor, she turned back to announce, "I'm so sorry you couldn't meet my son, Andrew. You know, at eighteen, he's almost as tall as his father. He's reading law with Judge Clinton, here in town. I know he'll make a good lawyer. You'll meet him at dinner." Then, to her daughter, "Can you and Gary stay for dinner too, Melinda darling?"

"Oh, no, Mama, Lawrence says he wants to take me to the theater tonight. Mrs. Jenkins will look after Gary. She's so good with him, just the way Mrs. Samuels is with Joy."

Arabella blushed again and quickly changed the subject. "That's a shame, Melinda! But maybe you and Lawrence and Gary can come over again and meet Mr. Douglas and his friends before they go to Houston—or maybe when they come back?"

"I'm sure we can, Mama. Well, I'd best be getting back home now. It was nice meeting you, Mr. Douglas, Mr. Gentry, Mr. Lucas and—and Simata?"

"That is how my name is pronounced, yes, Mrs. Davis," the Kiowa scout grinned and nodded. "I'm glad to have met you and your fine little son. May he ride straight in the saddle and his shadow be on this great earth for many long years."

"Why, what a sweet thing to say! Well, goodbye again, and it was so nice meeting all of you!" Melinda hurriedly kissed her mother on the cheek and then left the house as Arabella led the way up the stairs.

After seeing her guests to their rooms and arranging for baths to be drawn for them, Arabella prevailed upon Joy's complaisant nurse to prepare a delectable dinner for her four guests. She then retired to her dressing room, and when she came down to dinner an hour later, she was dressed in a fashionable white silk gown, with an elegant lace-trimmed bodice which, though modest, still displayed the remarkably smooth, creamy skin of her throat and upper bosom. She had styled her hair with little curls at the top of the forehead and a thick chignon falling below her nape, since that was the way James always liked to see her. As her tall, gray-haired husband rose from the settee where he had been talking with Charles and the others, the admiring glow in his eyes told her that she was still desired and loved, and she flushed in the secret knowledge of this.

There was wine before the syllabub, nuts, and cheese, port with the coffee, and an excellent French brandy of which Arabella and Andrew partook, the latter at his father's genial suggestion. During the meal, Charles, with ample embellishments from Lucas and Eddie, related their harrowing experience with the outlaws, but they had been careful to leave out the ritual of scalp-taking, lest it disturb Arabella. Then Arabella excused herself and went back to the kitchen to help wash the dishes with the widow, while the men and young Andrew remained at the table to converse.

"Gosh," Andrew exclaimed in a surprisingly deep voice, "it's sure lucky that you had plenty of guns and ammunition and someone like Lucas to warn you! I wish I'd been there to see how you made out—six against the four of you, that was really something!"

"You're much better off studying in Judge Clinton's office, Andrew," his father reproved him, but with a twinkle in his eyes. "The law is a solid foundation on which to build a good society, and don't forget it. Yes, of course, things are still unsettled after the war, and sometimes the only way to survive is by the gun. But the trouble with law by the gun is that all too often the stronger and more brutal prevail over the weak. Besides, if you're so eager to handle a gun, Andrew, you and I can go hunting in the spring for doves and jackrabbits, and maybe even for deer. It's been a while since we've enjoyed venison at this table."

After dinner, Andrew went off with Eddie, Lucas, and Simata, prevailing upon them to tell more stories about life on a Texas cattle ranch, while James and Charles refilled their goblets with brandy and retired to the sitting room.

"Well now, Charles." James settled back in his thickly stuffed armchair, took a sip of his brandy, and gestured with his goblet. "Have you recovered from the shock of that dreadful fire in Chicago? You know, I think Chicago, like the legendary phoenix that rises out of the ashes, will be bigger and better than ever."

"Yes, it will, James. I've got myself a partner back there who's taking care of rebuilding the store, and I admit that one of the main reasons I came out this way was to find a place for another store. Maybe several. I want a chain some day. And I think that Texas is the right place."

"I couldn't agree with you more, Charles. Here, let's both enjoy a cigar. These are from Havana and they came in from New Orleans just the other day." He reached to the sideboard for a teakwood box and offered it.

Charles made his selection, accepted the metal clipper that James handed him to clip the drawing end of the cigar, then lit it and took a few experimental puffs. "Wonderful aroma, good and rich. I'm glad Laurette isn't here. She detests tobacco in any form, so I have to sneak an after-dinner cigar when I'm traveling, or when I stay downtown for dinner so that I can return to the office in the evening."

"Arabella doesn't mind tobacco. She's learned to put up with my ways over the years—that's one comfortable dividend of a long and happy marriage. Mind you, I'm speaking like a veteran, because you're still a young man and practically newlywed, compared to Bella and myself." He lit his cigar, then took another sip of brandy. "So you're thinking about Houston? I'll agree that it's likely to show more progress in the next few years than San Antonio. But what's wrong with Galveston? It's two or three days by wagon to Houston, and while there's a small railroad already operating to that city, I doubt that it's adequate for what you have in mind."

"You're the second person to suggest Galveston," Charles chuckled. "I heard the same from old Captain McMurtrie on the *William Wallace*. You know, I may wind up opening two stores." Charles smiled at his own brashness.

"I like a man who thinks big, and also, you're a straightforward and likable fellow, and those are admirable attributes, believe me, for undertaking any new venture."

"You flatter me, James."

"No, I don't at all. And you know, I never believed in that old yarn about not being able to teach an old dog new tricks. Now that Bella's a grandmother and still as beautiful as the day I first met her, I don't see any reason why I shouldn't try my hand at a different line of trade. Cotton's all I've known all these years. Well, the country's expanding, and people will have money to spend, that's for certain. I've done very well out here in Galveston. I'm practically a partner now with Cousin Jeremy. And we've lived well, but we've also learned how to save, even with three children. I might just have a little extra capital to invest in, say, another Douglas department store."

"You really mean that?" Charles leaned forward, his eyes wide with excitement.

"Yes, I do, very much so."

"I'd be honored to have you as a partner." Suddenly

50

Charles's face grew grave. "You know, in all my planning, I forgot one thing. If I spread out and have a lot of stores, it means plenty of travel. I don't know how Laurette and the kids are going to like that. Of course, she could spend some time with me and it would be like a vacation. But then there's the schooling to think about. You don't want to take children out of school and change them around every six months or so or even every year."

"You can work that out, I'm confident. Once you get your stores started, you can appoint good managers you can rely on to carry out your plans. Then you'll only need to make just an occasional trip—maybe once or twice a year," James suggested.

"Yes, that's true enough. Well, what do you think about railroads expanding in this part of the country?"

"They're coming, Charles. The cities are growing and they'll want more trade. The only sensible way to get it is by having connecting railway lines. Oh yes, all of that's certain to come in the next five or ten years. I'd stake a good deal of my capital on that."

"That's what I'm thinking, too. That's why, right off, it doesn't worry me too much about having to take goods by wagon on to a place like Houston. If I have my store in place by the time the railroads are ready to haul my goods, I'll be way ahead of the competition."

"You think just about like a Texan, Charles," James smiled as he reached for the decanter. "Have some more brandy. And think over what I said. Whether you want a store here or in Houston, I'd be willing to invest some capital, either way. Who knows—maybe I could even be a working partner—that is, if you'd have me."

"I'd be proud, James." Charles rose to his feet and held out his hand.

CHAPTER FIVE

Two days after their arrival in Galveston, Charles Douglas and his three companions set out for Houston. Remembering what Captain McMurtrie had told him about the shorter Indian trail between these two cities, the young Chicagoan urged Simata to take it in preference to the longer route for the purpose of determining just how arduous it would be for heavily loaded wagons. Also, in a grocery store where he and his friends were buying supplies, Charles happened to chat with an amiable cowhand who often worked as a courier for his Houston employer. The courier declared that of course the longer road was wider and with fewer hazards along the way, but it skirted many small settlements, while the Indian trail, though sometimes treacherous and difficult to follow, was more direct.

As the four men rode along the old Indian trail, Charles made a rough sketch of the route, clearly marking the paramount hazards. His alert mind was so stimulated by the prospect of this new enterprise that he had almost forgotten the dangers of the outlaw attack. Thanks to Simata's poultices, his wound had healed well, and he had never felt healthier or more eager for the future.

By evening of the second day, they came within sight of the thriving city on the plains northwest of Galveston Bay. Harrisburg, which had become part of Houston, had been first settled in the year 1823, and Houston itself founded thirteen years later. Between 1837 and 1839, Houston had stood valiantly as the capital of the new republic of Texas. Charles turned in his saddle to look back the way they had come, and mused aloud, "You know, some day they could build a canal between here and the Gulf and turn this into just as big a port as Galveston itself. And I wouldn't be surprised if all of us lived to see it."

53

"I bet you're right," Eddie Gentry agreed. "Until then, the trail we've come over isn't too bad, though some of the spots back there would make me jittery if I had to drive a wagon loaded with barrels and crates and be sure I'd get to Houston safely."

"I know, Eddie. I've made a sort of map showing the way we came, but I've got a few ideas about how my drivers could avoid the rough stretches without wasting too much time. But just listen to me! I'm talking as if the store were already built and I were coming here for the grand opening!"

"Are you going to try to buy a piece of land right off, Charlie?" Eddie asked.

"Well, James Hunter gave me the names of the two leading banks in Houston and suggested that I go in and talk to the presidents. They'll know what land's available, what the going price is, and what's happening to the town right now. We'll find ourselves a place to stay overnight, and then in the morning I'll try to do my business quickly. I don't want to hold you fellows up too long. It certainly was wonderful of you to come along with me. Not just because you helped save my life, either—I feel that you're good friends and will be for the rest of my life."

"We feel the same way about you, Charlie," Lucas gently said.

Charles found it a good omen that the hotel where they sought a room was so crowded with cowmen, stock dealers, and settlers that he and his three companions were obliged to share a single room. "Lucien Edmond was certainly right about Houston's forging ahead," he commented. "And so far, I like what I see in this town. Well, let's have a meal and a good night's sleep, so we can be up bright and early. I'd like to walk around the main street before I go to visit the banks."

James Hunter had told Charles that the two leading Houston banks were the Houston National and the Houston Mercantile. After a leisurely breakfast, armed with his Chicago letter of credit, Charles and his friends walked down the main street, stopping at times to answer friendly salutations from passersby. Charles profited from these casual meetings by asking questions about Houston, and by the time he had arrived at the imposing facade of the Houston Mercantile Bank, he was more than ever certain that he had made a wise decision in planning that the cornerstone of his second department store be laid here.

While Simata, Lucas, and Eddie seated themselves on a mahogany bench near the entrance of the bank, Charles went up to the counter and asked to see the president. He was ushered into the office of a portly, nearly bald man in his fifties, with thick, graying sideburns and a fastidiously trimmed Van Dyke beard. "This is our president, Mr. Calvin Jemmers, sir," the teller obsequiously explained. Then, turning to the banker, he added, "This gentleman asked right out for you, Mr. Jemmers, that's why I brought him to you."

"You did exactly right, Henson." Calvin Jemmers rose, dropping the stub of a well-chewed cigar into a gleaming brass spittoon beside him, and beamed at his visitor. "Haven't seen you in these parts before, sir. How may I be of service?" Then, with a glare at the teller, he curtly ordered, "That'll be all, Henson. I see Mrs. Crowder just came into the bank. Take care of her and see that she's satisfied."

"Yes, sir, right away, Mr. Jemmers." The teller bobbed his head and hurried back to his cage as Charles came forward.

"My name is Charles Douglas. I'm visiting relatives in this part of the country, and I'm thinking of building a department store here in Houston, Mr. Jemmers." Taking out the letter of credit, Charles unfolded it and handed it across to the banker, while accepting the latter's invitation to seat himself, an invitation offered with a sweeping gesture of Calvin Jemmers's pudgy hand.

"Well, Mr. Douglas, I like a man who comes right to the point. Hmm, I can see from this you're a citizen of some distinction back in Chicago. A dreadful thing, that fire you had last October."

"Indeed it was. My store was burned down, but it's being rebuilt right now. And, since I came out here partly for my wife's sake, to give her a vacation away from that disaster, and partly because I've come to admire the real potential of this state, I'm eager to go ahead with an idea I've had for some little time. . . ." Charles then carefully explained his ambitious plans for the store in Houston.

"A very sensible plan, Mr. Douglas," Jemmers said when Charles was finished. "Of course, we do have a general store now, but I don't see any reason why your store couldn't prosper here in Houston. Here, have a cigar. I have them sent to me straight from New Orleans, and they're the best Havanas money can buy."

"Thanks, I'll confess I'm partial to good Havanas." Charles grinned as he took a short, thick, dark-leaved cigar from the ornate box that Jemmers held out with a gesture so grandiose one might think he was offering his visitor the Kohinoor diamond. The banker took a cigar for himself, produced a silver clipper, and hospitably cut both his visitor's cigar and his own, then lit them. After handing one of the cigars to Charles, he settled back in his upholstered chair, cleared his throat, and drew the conversation directly back to business. "Well, as it happens, Mr. Douglas, you couldn't have come to a better place than the Houston Mercantile, if I do say so myself. I've got a finger in just about every pie in this town. The first thing you'll need, obviously, is land, isn't that right?"

"Of course." Charles smiled assent. Then, by way of flattering his interlocutor, whose pomposity had already convinced him that such tactics would be helpful in smoothing out a future business relationship, he commented, "This is really a first-rate cigar, Mr. Jemmers. I'm indebted to you for it."

"Pshaw, Mr. Douglas, sir, my pleasure!" Once again, Calvin Jemmers waved his right hand with such a majestic sweep that one would have believed he had been on the stage earlier in life. "Nothing's too good for a smart fellow who's going to help the good people of Houston to a better life, Mr. Douglas!" he expostulated. "Yes, sir, I'm the very man in this town you ought to have come to, and I must say that it speaks well for your business instincts. Now then, as it happens, I think I can find you a good piece of land. It's good property, a block or two north of the main street. Now, sir, how much capital were you thinking of investing in this enterprise of yours?"

"Well, as I told you, my Chicago store is being rebuilt by a partner whom I met just before the fire. I can have my Chicago banker send you a financial statement on what my store was doing with his house. I'd say that I could afford to invest about twenty-five thousand dollars as a starter. Also, I might tell you that one of my kinfolk by marriage, Mr. James Hunter of Galveston—who, by the way, spoke highly of your bank—indicated that he's willing to put up some capital, too."

"Capital, capital!" Jemmers chortled, beaming at his own puerile joke, and Charles managed an applauding grin, which he tried not to let fade too quickly. "Well, Mr. Douglas, if you like, we've a telegraph office down the street and you could wire your banker. That way, I'd have your banker's statement in short order and could get to work on arranging to have you pick up that outstanding location for your new store."

"That's a good idea, Mr. Jemmers. I'll do just that," Charles promised. "I'll be going back' to Windhaven Range, near Carrizo Springs—that's where my wife and children are staying for the time being—and you can reach me there. Mr. Lucien Edmond Bouchard, who runs the ranch, gets his mail and wires out of San Antonio in care of the Citizens' Bank."

"I know it well, and Pericles Lysander is an old friend of mine. That's a good recommendation too, Mr. Douglas. Yes, sir, I think you've begun your first day in Houston on the right side of the ledger. I'll be getting in touch with you, you can count on it. Here, take along some more cigars. Are those your friends sitting out there by the door?"

"Yes, Mr. Jemmers. They came with me from the ranch."

"Not a bad idea for someone like yourself unfamiliar with this part of the country to have good men who know how to handle shooting irons along with you, sir. I trust you didn't run into any trouble?"

"Just a bit, but it didn't amount to much," Charles deprecatingly replied. "Thank you, I'll take some cigars for my friends too, if you've no objection."

"Help yourself, by all means. A pleasure to have met you, Mr. Douglas, and I promise you, you'll be hearing from me just as soon as I have word from Chicago. I'll see you to the door. My great pleasure, sir."

Eddie, Lucas, and Simata rose as they saw Charles coming toward them accompanied by the fat banker. As he introduced them, the young Chicagoan thought he saw just the flicker of a contemptuous curl of the lips on Jemmers's small but fleshy mouth. It was dispelled, however, by the bank president's effusive greeting and his good wishes for a safe journey home.

57

As they walked back to their hotel, Eddie piped up, "I'll bet that man was a politician once. He sure looks like a mealymouth to me, Charlie."

"Well, Eddie, appearances can be deceiving," Charles retorted. "After all, when I started out with you fellows on this trip, you thought I was the rankest kind of tenderfoot. I hope by now you've changed your opinion a little."

"That's putting it mildly, Charlie," the lanky young cowboy grinned. "Come on, let's go see the sights of this town—or do you want to get back right away to Windhaven Range?"

"To be truthful, I'd just as soon start right away on the trail back—just as soon as I pick up some presents for my family. I can't do anything more here until Mr. Jemmers gets word from my bank in Chicago and is satisfied that I have the wherewithal to start a store here. Then I'll be back here quickly enough, believe me. Only the next time, I'm not going to have Lucien Edmond take you away from your work on the ranch, because I've learned enough about Windhaven Range to know that you'll be getting ready for the spring cattle drive as soon as you get back."

"Well, maybe if you stay out here long enough, you'd even like to go along with us on one of those drives, Charlie," Lucas joked. "I think you'd make a right good hand."

"Thanks, but I don't think my wife would like my being away three or four months playing nursemaid to a cattle herd. All right, then, I'll just stop in this store here, and then we'll go pay for the hotel, get our horses, and ride back to Galveston."

Calvin Jemmers watched the young Chicago businessman leave the bank with his three friends, chuckled softly to himself, and tapped the profuse ash of his cigar into the spittoon. He tapped rapidly, his fingers moving vigorously, as if he were a concert pianist displaying to an admiring audience his virtuoso technique in a staccato passage. For the Houston banker, it was a characteristic mannerism that denoted his avid anticipation of a profit to be turned to his own special interest.

He had been born fifty-three years ago to a Schenectady sign painter and a pretty, plump, blond barmaid who had worked for her father in the town's leading tavern and who had inherited the tavern after her father's death. This capi-

tal had given Calvin Jemmer's father the necessary afflu-
ence to enroll his only son in a fashionable boys' academy
and after that in a private college. A lonely child plagued
by an unnatural corpulence during puberty and adoles-
cence, young Jemmers had early in life come to the conclusion that the only way to forge ahead and to be accepted
by his more fortunately endowed peers was through the
accumulation of money and, best of all, through work in
an institution devoted to its accumulation.

By the time Jemmers was thirty, he was the principal
cashier in the only bank in his home town. He had had
little success with the opposite sex, mainly because of his
excessive unctuousness and the tendency to obesity against
which he had fought unsuccessfully most of his life. When
he was spurned by the attractive nineteen-year-old daughter of the bank's major investor, he proceeded to drink
himself into a stupor. Then he absconded with $45,000 of
the bank's money and drove a horse and buggy to New
York City. There he changed his name for the first time—
he had actually been born Samuel Joliffe—and after enjoying the fleshpots of New York for about two years, moved
to St. Louis.

There, at the age of thirty-three, in the same year that
Harriet Beecher Stowe's *Uncle Tom's Cabin* became a
published firebrand to ignite the flames of Northern hatred
for Southern slavery, he talked himself into an important
post in the Great Missouri Bank and Trust. Here for a few
years he worked diligently, for he was competent in bank-
ing affairs and had begun to specialize in land mortgages.
By the time he was thirty-seven, he had become president
of the bank and induced Amelia Maxwell, the twenty-
eight-year-old daughter of a prosperous greengrocer, to
marry him.

Amelia Maxwell had been the oldest of five daughters,
and her chance of marriage had nearly gone when the glib
banker began to pay court to her. She had plain features
and pale blond hair coiffed in a prim bun at the back of
her head, and though her figure was that of a Rubens Ven-
us, she was retiring, insecure, and usually inarticulate. Indeed, she had long since resigned herself to being her father's housekeeper, having seen her four younger sisters
happily wed and each with at least one child from their
felicitous unions. Calvin Jemmers, who by then was going

59

by the name of Horatio Ellison, knew exactly what he was doing. Amelia brought with her a dowry of $15,000 and a small house near the fashionable Clayton section of St. Louis. Moreover, her father was past his sixtieth year and had been ailing for more than eighteen months; he would surely not live much longer, and Amelia was certain to benefit by his will.

Amelia's father indeed passed to his eternal reward five months after attending his daughter's wedding, and just as Calvin Jemmers had anticipated, the will left his bride another $30,000 in hard cash and title to the grocery store. Jemmers deposited the cash in his own account and then promptly sold the store with its inventory for $25,000, taking a severe loss because of his plans to quit St. Louis as soon as the deal was closed. Finally, taking advantage of an oversight by one of the bank's mortgagees, he forced the property up for public auction and bought it himself, only to turn around and sell it for twice what it was worth. At this point, on the pretext of taking Amelia on a second honeymoon, he transferred all his holdings into a single, huge bank draft and boarded a steamboat with her, bound for New Orleans.

Because of his own flamboyance, Jemmers enjoyed the easygoing life of the Queen City. Along the way he had learned enough French to be able to converse fluently with the Creoles, and his manners—especially toward attractive women—were as ostentatious as those of any dandy. As for Amelia, discovering her husband's secret infidelities did not prove overly distressing: having little innate sensuality of her own, she secretly found it a relief not to be obliged to satisfy her husband's conjugal demands except on infrequent occasions. To Jemmers's credit, it might be said that he saw to it that his wife had the finest gowns, attended the best restaurants, the theater, and the opera, and had her own carriage. And since Amelia had never dreamed that any man would show her such material attention, she was in her undemanding way reasonably satisfied. Meanwhile, Jemmers was fortifying his growing fortune by speculating in land, buying and selling at considerable profit, based on tips he managed to glean from influential Creole acquaintances whom he wined and dined for that very purpose.

Since Jemmers had been born in Union territory, he realized—when he felt the first grim forebodings of the Civil War—that it was high time to seek a new theater of operations. The South would lose the war, he was convinced; the Port of New Orleans would surely be under Union naval siege almost from the very outset. And he had no illusions about what men like Butler would do once they marched into the city and took over all the banks. By this time, he was a major stockholder in one of the most successful banks of the Queen City, and just a week before war was officially declared, he converted his stock into gold, packed it in two wagons made for him by old Emile Dagronard, the same wagonmaker whom Luke Bouchard himself had commissioned for the journey to find Windhaven Range, and set out for Texas aboard the *William Wallace*.

At Galveston, he hired a dozen *pistoleros* to escort his wife and himself and the two wagons to Houston, more fearful of an attack by Indians than of the possible greed of the *pistoleros*. As a boy, he had been terrified by his father's stories of the warring Iroquois and the Seneca and the Huron tribes who massacred innocent settlers. But he was clever enough to convince the gunslingers of his escort that he had fragile and expensive household goods in the wagons; had they guessed what was really hidden under an ornate settee (as well as inside of it) and inside tarpaulins purportedly wrapped around fine oil paintings and cases of French wine, he might not have lived to be president of Houston Mercantile.

Once arrived in Houston, he changed his name for the last time to Calvin Jemmers, and approached the elderly president of a small bank on the verge of collapse, offering to take over the failing institution and make a success of it.

Jemmers knew that there would be a great demand for land after the Civil War, and that many Confederates (quite a few of whom had had the foresight to secrete their fortunes just as he had done) would head for the vast expanses of Texas. He deposited only a small portion of his gold in his new little bank, which he promptly renamed the Houston Mercantile; the rest he hid for the time being under a tool shed adjacent to his residence.

Because of his own proclivity for ingenious larceny and his success at it over the years, Jemmers had developed a sixth sense for finding those who would become helpful accomplices in his schemes to acquire more and more of the

61

precious yellow metal buried under the tool shed. One of these was Arnold Shottlander, a lean, melancholy man of forty-three, who had come to Houston from Chicago five years before the Civil War and set himself up as a dealer in real estate. In Chicago, he had pulled off several ingenious deals by buying condemned land in the Bridgeport slum area and erecting false-front frame houses that he turned into brothels. In return for incredibly low rental rates, the madams who ran these houses were compelled to turn over to Shottlander forty percent of their earnings. This arrangment came to an abrupt end, and Shottlander left Chicago just ahead of the police, because he had been forced to kill a man who had been victimized by one of his real estate swindles and had sought revenge. But he was able to carry with him most of his money, in Union greenbacks sewn into the lining of his carpet bag.

As his next base of operations, Shottlander chose Houston, because he was sure that in Texas few people bothered about one's past and because he believed that the town was due for a land boom. He very quickly bought up several pieces of property and turned a handsome profit in the next few years, and now he was the leading realtor of the town. He was also an intimate friend of Calvin Jemmers. And it was to his office on Elston Street that Jemmers now went once he had seen Charles Douglas and his three friends leave the bank.

CHAPTER SIX

So heartened was Charles Douglas by his meeting with Calvin Jemmers at the Houston Mercantile Bank that, as he told his three companions, he saw no reason for delaying his return to Windhaven Range or, for that matter, for making even a token visit to the other bank James Hunter had suggested. So, shortly after lunch, the four retrieved their horses from the stable, mounted up, and rode back to Galveston. When they got there, it was nearly evening of the second day, and a stevedore at the dock informed them that the *William Wallace* had left for New Orleans on the previous afternoon and would be delayed in its return to Galveston because some routine minor repairs were necessary.

At this news, Charles uttered a groan of disappointment, for the alternative of riding to Corpus Christi and then on to Windhaven Range was much too arduous to be considered. But the stevedore quickly added, "You're in luck, mister. There's a new packet due in here tomorrow morning, the *Belle of the Gulf*. Just finished building her last fall—I know, 'cause me 'n some of my pals did some carpenterin' on her for a spell. She's a lot faster 'n trimmer than Cap'n McMurtrie's ol' paddlewheeler, 'n that's a fact, mister."

"All right, then." Charles's spirits were quickly restored by this information. "I'd be much obliged if you'd tell the captain, in case you see him before we do, that we'd like to book passage for the four of us to Corpus Christi, along with our horses."

"Be glad to, mister. One thing I'll tell you in advance, you'll pay more passage money on the *Belle*. The company's out to make a better profit than it did on the old *William Wallace*. I'd guess it'll cost each of you fellows another five or six bucks, 'n a dollar more than you used to pay for taking your horses along."

"I guess I can stand that. I'm obliged to you, Mr.—?"

"Purlie Jenkins is my handle, mister." The stevedore, a young black in his late twenties, as powerfully built as Lucas, grinned and extended his hand. Charles shook it. "And mine's Charles Douglas. These are my friends Eddie Gentry, Lucas, and Simata."

"Glad to know you fellows. Sure, I'll tell Cap'n Evans. The *Belle*'s due in here about eleven tomorrow. We haven't got much cargo for Corpus Christi this time, so like as not Cap'n Evans will sail with the late afternoon tide tomorrow."

"I'm obliged to you, sir. Well, see you tomorrow then." Charles turned to his friends. "Might just as well check in at a hotel for the night and find a stable for our horses. I'm not aiming to take advantage of Mr. Hunter's hospitality, though I do plan to call on him this evening and tell him what happened in Houston."

James Hunter nodded his approval when Charles had finished relating the meeting between himself and Calvin Jemmers. "From all I've heard, Charles, it's a solid bank with plenty of capital. And if things don't work out, there's always the other one. Matter of fact, since you're a smart businessman, you might want to go see the other bank— even if you get this deal from Houston Mercantile—and just hint at what their competitor is offering by way of terms. You might be surprised. Houston's growing, and when you've got two strong banks flourishing, each of them is after the lion's share of investments and speculatory land profits. Well now, I imagine you'll be starting back to Windhaven Range tomorrow?"

"Yes," Charles nodded. "I'm sure Laurette and the boys will be anxious, since I must confess I've been so preoccupied with my own affairs that I didn't think of sending a wire. I'm eager to tell her the good news. Then we have to figure how long she'll stay on there with the boys. I certainly don't want to wear out my welcome. And at this point, I don't even know if our house was spared in the fire. Things were happening so fast, we never did go back to the house when the fire was out—we met on the far North Side of the city in a boarding house that still had rooms, and then we made our plans to come out here.

That reminds me—I'll have to send a wire to my partner and ask him to take a look at the house and see if we can return to it. If not, I'll ask him to rent something for us temporarily to tide us over until we can build a new house or buy one."

James smiled and rose from the settee, stretching his long legs. "You're going to thrive no matter where you find yourself, Charles. You've an ingrained self-discipline and determination that help you overcome difficulties and problems. A man is blessed by having such dedication, because it steers him safely through the reefs and shoals of life, helping him to keep his difficulties in proper perspective. Yes, I predict you're going to do very well. And you may one day look back and say that fire was a blessing in disguise."

"I certainly hope you're right, James. Well, I'm going back to the hotel now. Mrs. Hunter, I'm deeply grateful for the gracious hospitality you've shown me, and do please pass on my very best wishes to your daughter and the new grandson."

"I'll be happy to, Charles," Arabella beamed, exchanging a glance with her husband. "Remember, you and your wife and the boys will always be welcome here. Now that you're going to build that store in Houston, it's very likely we'll be seeing a good deal of you. We'll almost be neighbors. And don't you forget what my husband told you, that right here in Galveston wouldn't be a bad place for another Douglas store."

"That may just happen," Charles said as he took his leave.

Captain Josiah Evans was the direct opposite of genial old Jamie McMurtrie. Laconic, stout, with a dark-brown bushy beard and a sourish disposition, he seemed older than his mid-forties. During the voyage to Corpus Christi, he gave no indication of being interested in the slightest in his passengers' personal well-being, and apart from an occasional gruff "Good afternoon, sir," kept aloof from them.

The ride back to Windhaven Range took nine days and was totally without incident. Along the way, Charles's mind was occupied with plans for the Houston department store. James Hunter's unexpected offer of capital investment had expanded his already large-scale schemes, and the possibility of opening two stores and thus gaining a strong merchandising foothold in the developing Southwest was a tempting one. There was no doubt that having two large stores within fifty miles of each other was an exciting concept. Indeed, a store at Galveston could maintain a larger inventory, part of which could be periodically diverted to Houston. Yes, he had a great deal to talk over with Laurette when he got back, and it was with eager anticipation that, on the first Thursday in February, he rode with his three companions through the stockade gate of Windhaven Range.

"Oh, Eddie, did you hurt yourself when you rode to Corpus Christi?" Polly Behting anxiously asked. It was two days after Charles had returned to Windhaven Range, and on this unseasonably warm midafternoon, the young cowhand was strolling along the bank of the little creek. He had plucked some of the tall reeds that grew near the bank, intending to make some more toys for the Douglas children, and he had tried not to show his secret joy when he had seen the blue-eyed, flaxen-haired young nurse slip out of the house, come running through the open gate, and then, very primly, as if she wanted to make it seem like an accident, stroll toward him.

"Why, no, Miss Polly, not really. Why do you say such a thing?" By now, his shoulder wound had healed, but there was still a slight stiffness in the muscles, and when he had bent to pluck some of the tallest reeds, he had moved his right arm slowly and then straightened after a pause. Solicitously, she had noticed this.

"I thought you made a face just then, as if maybe something hurt your arm."

"Oh, that!" He gave a nonchalant shrug and a soft, reassuring chuckle. "Got thrown off my horse, that's all. It shied at a snake, and I shot it, but not before my horse threw me. It doesn't happen very often. I felt like a fool, I can tell you that, Miss Polly. But let's not talk about me. Is everything all right here at the ranch house?"

"Oh, yes, yes," she breathed. "The little boys are just fine. They've forgotten all about that terrible—you know."

"Yes." He nodded, turning to smile at her. "I was just thinking, maybe I could make a reed flute, or, if not that, fix up some make-believe birds. These reeds are nice and long and they bend pretty well. Some of them are thick enough, and if I press a darning needle down through the middle, I'll bet I can make a flute. I'm going to try, anyway."

"You're so good, Eddie. You're always thinking of others."

"Well," he flushed at her unexpectedly fervent praise, "I guess maybe it's because I really never had much of a family. I told you I was the only kid my folks had, and around us we had lots of big families. I made friends, sure, but it wasn't the same thing as having brothers and sisters—you know."

"*Ja*. I know what it's like. I too am an only child. Oh, yes, I did have a little brother, but he died from the fever when he was only four—I hardly even knew him."

"Gosh, that's tough." He turned to the reeds again and chose a few, not wanting to seem too brash in his eagerness to talk with her. "Got any idea when you'll be going back to Chicago?"

"No, Mrs. Douglas hasn't said anything about that yet. But now that Mr. Douglas is back from his business, I suppose maybe she'll be telling me one of these days soon. Did you go to Houston?"

"Sure. First we stopped at Galveston, and we met Mr. Hunter and his wife—they're nice people. Their daughter's baby is so cute, and Mrs. Hunter seemed ever so happy."

"I like children. I hope—I mean, that is, one day—" Flustered, Polly suddenly turned aside, closing her eyes and trying to control the furious blush that swept her soft pink cheeks. *I am just dreadful,* she scolded herself, *when I know that I am engaged to Dieter Hellwig back in Chicago. I ought to be ashamed of myself, but Eddie Gentry is such a nice, thoughtful man, and I know how lonesome he is. And I do think he likes me a little.* Aloud, she finally said, "I mean, that's why I love being a nurse. Children are so innocent, so trusting. When they like you, it's really wonderful. And you always have to be honest with them, and never tell them *Lügen*—lies, that is."

"You know, I never thought about it that way, but I'm sure you're right, Miss Polly. It'd be a lot better all over the world, I'm thinking, if people would just tell the truth to one another."

"*Ja,* that's exactly the way I feel!" Unconsciously she reached out and touched his hand, then drew back shyly.

"It is all right if we talk a few minutes. The little ones are asleep and Mrs. Douglas said she would look after them. She's such a sweet woman, and so good to me."

"That's not hard. I mean—I can see why she'd like you a lot, you take such good care of her kids." He turned back to the reeds, then suddenly sucked in his breath and, in a low, hoarse whisper, said urgently, "Don't turn, don't move, don't make a sound now. And don't be scared, Polly. Just close your eyes, please."

"Yes—oh, what is it—I—" She instinctively obeyed, biting her lips nervously as Eddie drew his Starr .44 out of its holster and, in the same motion, pulled the trigger. Polly uttered a scream and promptly flung her arms around him, clinging to him and trembling. "Oh, Eddie, what is it, what is it? Oh, it was such a terrible noise—"

"Shh, it'll be fine now—that's all right—there's no danger now. Don't look back, Polly. Just take my hand and let's go back to the house."

"But I want to know what it was, Eddie!" Her eyes were very wide and filmed with tears, and she was staring at him intently as if trying to memorize his face and the reassuring smile on it. But his eyes were narrowed and cold, colder than she had ever seen them before.

"Don't ask questions. Come on. That's a good girl." He exhaled a deep breath and led her away from the creek.

Behind her lay the still-thrashing body of a large, grayish-black water moccasin. It had emerged from the sluggish water of the little creek, moved through the reeds, and, just as he had bent to them, had been only a foot away from where Polly had been standing.

"That's fine, Polly, you're doing just fine. Come along now," he soothed her. But, like Lot's wife, Polly could not restrain her pent-up curiosity and suddenly turned. Then she uttered a cry and clapped her hand over her mouth, her eyes huge with consternation as she saw the death throes of the water moccasin. "Oh, *Gott helfe uns*, Eddie— it was so close to me, wasn't it? And—and you saved my life—oh, Eddie, you were so brave, and I would have just died of fright if I'd seen it—oh, Eddie!" In her reaction, she burst into tears and again flung her arms around him, burying her face in his chest.

Eddie glanced furtively back at the ranch house and then gently took hold of her shoulders. "That's all right,

Polly, cry it out! It can't hurt anybody any more. And you were a brave girl to do just what I told you to. You know, Felicidad got bitten by a water moccasin just like that one—only Pablo Casares—he's the nice vaquero married to Kate—he killed it and sucked the poison out so she wouldn't get sick. Whew, that was a close call!"

"Oh, Eddie." She tearfully lifted her face to his. "You are such a good man, and I, I'm a silly German girl who oughtn't to be so bold, but I can't help saying it—I—I was so worried when you left, I prayed every day you would come back safe—there now, I am wicked to say such things—especially when I am already betrothed to Dieter Hellwig. *Ja*, it's true, Eddie, and he is working to have his own butcher shop and he thinks that maybe one day I will marry him—but now I don't think I can, now that I've met you. Oh please, I don't know what I'm saying—forgive me—"

"Don't say that—you're not silly at all—you want to know something, Polly?" His left arm round her shoulders, he gently tilted up her chin with right thumb and forefinger and smiled down at her. "I sort of dreamed that maybe you'd like me just a little. The fact is, I'm crazy about you, Polly. I never knew I could be about any girl. And maybe I haven't any right to say it—but maybe, if you're not really going to marry this fellow you just said, maybe there'd be a chance for me?"

"Ach Gott, ja, wirklich, Eddie, Liebchen!" Polly rapturously breathed. Her eyes closed, she offered her mouth to him, and Eddie, trembling in every limb, kissed her, first awkwardly and quickly on the cheek, and then, as he heard her sigh, on the mouth. For a moment, unaware of anything else in the world except each other, they stood in an embrace.

It was Polly who suddenly, almost apologetically, disengaged herself. "Oh, it was so lovely—now I think it would be wisest for us both if I went back and helped Mrs. Douglas with the *Kinder*, Eddie. I have so much to think about. I don't want to hurt poor Dieter. . . . We must talk about this again, soon, before I go back to Chicago."

"I know. Gosh, Polly, I don't want to do anything wrong—if you're stuck on him—"

"I'm not. It was just—well, my *Vater* thought it would be a good idea if I had a man because every girl should be

69

married, you know, Eddie. And Dieter was the only man I knew. But to tell you the truth, he was always so serious and I do not think he even thinks of me as a girl. Oh my, what am I saying? But I'll see you again, won't I?"

"You can count on it, Polly honey." As she turned to run back to the ranch house, Eddie stood looking after her, and all his heart was in his eyes.

The day before Eddie Gentry and Polly Behting had discovered that they cared deeply for each other, one of the newly hired vaqueros, Grigorio Salamancar, rode in with two of his companions from San Antonio, where the three cowhands had gone to purchase additional supplies and to pick up any mail or wires for their *patrón*, Lucien Edmond Bouchard. They brought a telegraph wire addressed to Charles Douglas, from his new partner in Chicago, Lawrence Harding. It read as follows:

Your house too badly burned to be rebuilt. Have located new house near Lincoln Park, yard and stable for horses. Can purchase for $5,000. Advise if interested.

Harding

Charles went directly to his wife to show her the news from Chicago. "It sounds marvelous, Charlie, dear," she exclaimed. "And I've been married to you long enough to be able to know what the look on your face means."

"Well, since you're so smart, suppose you tell me, then." He bent to kiss her and, straightening up, winked at her.

"I must say, young man, this new Texas life of yours is really changing your whole personality," she quipped, giving him an affectionate squeeze. "I can see that when you get back to Chicago, you're going to be very hard to live with. Oh yes, Mr. Charles Douglas, I was told all about what a hero you were on the trail to Corpus Christi, even though you tried to hide it from me."

"I didn't know—" His jaw dropped.

"I know, sweetheart." She was instantly solicitous. "You didn't want to worry me. You've always been so considerate, and that's why I married you, if you want to know the truth. But anyway, you're all full of energy now, and you can hardly wait to start that store of yours. Well, you won't want to have me and the children around. We'd only be in the way."

"That's not true, darling," he protested.

"Oh, yes, it is. I told you, I've been married to you long enough to read you like a book, Charles Douglas. And that's why we're going back. I want to see the new house and I want to see how they're rebuilding Chicago. That's where we were happiest, you know that. And besides, Lucien Edmond is getting ready for his spring cattle drive, and everybody's going to be busy. We'll just be in the way. So if you'd be nice enough to make arrangements for Polly and me and the children, we'll leave as soon as it's convenient."

"I'll make the arrangements, darling. You're just the most wonderful wife any man could ever have."

"So long as you keep thinking that, I can bear to be away from you until your new store is ready. And then, of course, we'll come back again for the grand opening, darling," Laurette smilingly confided as she stood up and put her arms around him. Then, lightly, breaking off the embrace, she airily added, "You know, I've got a feeling it's going to break Polly's heart to have to go back with us now."

"And why is that?"

"I know your mind's full of your store and all the goods that are going to be shipped and all the customers you're going to have," she teased. "So you haven't had much time to look around and see that Polly is head over heels in love with that nice cowboy, Eddie Gentry."

"Eddie? Yes, he's a wonderful man. Honest and straightforward. If he weren't such a Texan by birth and sentiment, I'd want to lure him away and set him up first as an assistant floorwalker in my Chicago store and then bring him along as fast as he could manage."

"Don't try to change him. He was born here, he loves this country, it's part of him. But the fact is, whether you know it or not, he's fallen in love with Polly. And you know about Polly's engagement to that butcher's apprentice. I think it won't be hard for her to break that off. They just had an understanding, that was all. But I must say, I've never seen a girl lose her heart so quickly—and I thoroughly approve of her choice, I'll have you know."

"I've never found you wrong before, especially when

71

you said 'yes' to me, darling," he chuckled and took her into his arms for a long and satisfying kiss. "Well, what do you propose to do about her?"

"Well, of course she'll have to go back with us because of the children. But I'm going to have a little talk with her this evening. I'll tell her that if she really has her mind set on Eddie, and she's very sure of him and he of her, then we can find a replacement for her once we're settled in our new house. We could send her back with all expenses paid as our wedding present to her. How does that strike you?"

"It's just another proof that I was very lucky when I proposed to you, Laurette, that's all it is," he whispered softly as he gave her a kiss.

There was a second telegram for Charles, and this was from Calvin Jemmers, to the effect that the latter had secured the site that he had mentioned to Charles as being ideal for the new store. Jemmers added that he would like to discuss this with the young Chicagoan as soon as convenient. "That makes it just perfect," Charles exulted to Laurette. "Don't you see, sweetheart? I'll ride back with you and the boys to Corpus Christi—I'm sure Lucien Edmond will lend us some of his vaqueros as escort—then we can take the boat to Galveston. You'll go on ahead to New Orleans and up to Chicago, while I ride on alone to Houston and pick up that piece of land and get things all started for my second store. I'll probably have to spend a week or so in Houston lining up some men to build the store, once I get my land."

"I'm not so sure I like the idea of your riding all the way to Houston by yourself, darling," Laurette doubtfully responded.

"I can take care of myself. Anyhow, I'm sure the other men will tell you that a single rider has less chance of being attacked than a group the way we were by those outlaws."

"But will you come back to Chicago after you've got your land? I hate to think of your being away, and so far away, from the boys and me, dearest," Laurette softly whispered.

"What I'm thinking of doing is finding a reliable man, a contractor who can hire a good working crew to build the store. And I'll have to line up some clerks for it, too. After

72

I get back to Chicago, I'll contact my suppliers and find out all I can about the cheapest way to ship my merchandise quickly on to Houston." He sighed. "Now that I'm getting into this, I can see that I'm going to have to do a little traveling back and forth. Oh well," he brightened, "it'll be worth it. We're both still young, darling, and if we have to be away from each other for a few months at a time, it won't matter in the long run. Once everything's working as planned, we'll be able to travel together and see that the children have everything they need. That's why I'm doing all this, for our family, Laurette."

"I know, Charles. I'm so very proud of you. You're a doer, and you have such ambitious plans."

"It's a big country; it's young, it's starting all over again after the war; and I just can't be happy unless I'm doing something about the future, darling. And besides, it's really you who gave me the get up and go to plan for that future, you and the boys. If I didn't have all of you, I wouldn't be so ambitious. Now you go tell Polly that we're starting back to Chicago." He patted Laurette's shoulder and kissed her on the cheek. "And see that she has a little time alone with Eddie Gentry. I'm off to see Lucien Edmond, to make the arrangements for the trip. I'll see you at dinner tonight and by then I'll be able to tell you exactly when we'll leave and who'll be going along with us."

"Are you going to let me ride a horse sidesaddle, the way I do back in Chicago, Charlie?" Laurette roguishly asked, linking her arms around his neck and giving him one of her teasing looks.

"Now just a minute, honey." He took her wrists and gently disengaged her embrace. "If you'll remember, when we came here, you and the boys rode in the wagon along with Polly, and you were comfortable, too, you know you were."

"Yes, but I'd love to ride along with you this time— can't I, please, sweetheart?"

"No, Laurette, I'd rather you didn't."

"Silly, if you think I'm pregnant again, and that's why you're saying that, you're wrong," she giggled.

He chuckled and kissed her again. "No, that's not why I'm saying it. It's kind of rough country from here to Corpus Christi. I don't want to be bossy, but I'd just as soon know that you're as comfortable as can be. I'll be riding right beside you all the way, I promise."

"Oh well, I suppose I'll have to settle for that, Charles Douglas. Just you wait till I get you back home, though." She made a saucy face at him.

"I'm right sorry to hear that you have to go back to Chicago tomorrow, Polly," Eddie Gentry blurted, nervously twisting his sombrero in his hands. "I was looking forward to teaching you how to ride. I already had a mare picked out for you before I went with your boss to Houston, you know."

"Yes, I—I know, Eddie," Polly Behting's voice was low and flustered, and she studiously looked down at the ground as she walked along beside him outside the stockade that encircled the ranch house of Windhaven Range. It was midafternoon of the day after the two telegraph wires had come for Charles. Laurette had gently broken the news to Polly about their imminent return to Chicago, and when Polly had gasped in dismay, Laurette had consoled her. "Don't fret, Polly dear. Charles and I know just how you feel about Eddie Gentry. But you have to go back and tell your fiancé that you've fallen in love with someone else— that's only fair to him, dear. After you've done that, if you still feel the same way about Eddie and he proposes to you for certain, then we'll send you back to him and pay your way—that will be our wedding present to you, dear."

The lanky young cowboy stopped and turned to Polly. "Of course," he brightened, "even if you do have to leave tomorrow morning, I could show you the mare right now and maybe put the sidesaddle on her and you could try what it's like."

"Yes, that would be very nice," she agreed, her blushes deepening as she stared down at her high-buttoned shoes, trying very hard not to show her real emotions at this moment.

"That's great! I'll bring her around right now. You just stay there now, Polly, honey—I mean—"

She turned to him then, a radiant smile on her sweet mouth, and put a hand on his wrist. "Oh, *mein lieber* Eddie, do you really think that way about me? I—I wanted to hear you say my name like that—"

"You know, Polly, I'm crazy about you. I—I'm just a cowhand and I don't make too much money, but I've got a steady job and I'd make you a good husband—that is, if you'd have me." Eddie took her by the shoulders and stared longingly at her radiantly smiling face. "You're such a sweet, nice girl, I don't know why that butcher fellow of yours back in Chicago didn't marry you before you came out here—but if there's any chance at all for me, I mean—"

"Yes, Eddie, there—there's every chance. I—I do love you, I do. I'd be proud and happy to marry you. I—I'll have to speak to poor Dieter. It's going to be hard telling him, and I don't want to hurt his feelings any more than I have to."

"I know you'll tell him in the gentlest way possible. We—we couldn't help it—I mean, I couldn't."

Polly uttered a little sob and clung to him, and their lips met. Visibly shaken, the young cowboy stammered when the kiss was done, "I'll write as often as I can, Polly. And I'll see if Mr. Lucien Edmond won't give me more work so's I can earn more money and put it away for us both." Then, as a sudden doubt assailed him, he added, "I didn't even ask to find out how you'd feel about coming to live down here in Texas. You'd be away from your father—"

"He would want me to be happy, *Liebchen*." She touched his lips with the palm of her hand, her smile tremulous and her blue eyes misting with tears. "I know I could be very happy with you anywhere, dear Eddie."

"I can't believe how lucky I am, honey!" Furtively, he rubbed his eyes with the sleeve of his jacket. "And you know, this isn't exactly going to be our goodbye. Mr. Lucien Edmond says I can ride along with the others who'll take you and the Douglases to Corpus Christi."

"Oh, that'll be wonderful, Eddie!" she beamed. Then, very primly though with the hint of coquetry in her swift glance at him, "But we must be very proper, Eddie, *Liebchen*. And—and it would not be right for you to kiss me—though I want you to, so very much—oh, my *Vater* would be very angry with me if he could hear me talk like this."

"No, he wouldn't, honey. But I won't do anything except just ride along and look at you and tell myself what a

75

lucky guy I am. And now I'd better go get that mare and show you the first things about riding. And—and I swear I'll teach you to be just as good a rider as I am, and we can go out camping and things like that—I mean—" Now Eddie himself was blushing, as he hastily turned away an ran off to the corral.

CHAPTER SEVEN

"Come in, Calvin." Arnold Shottlander rose from his desk with a vinegary smile on his thin, ascetic lips. He turned to an attractive young woman who stood on the threshold of the open door of his office and curtly dismissed her: "I'm not to be disturbed, Mrs. Fernmark. Why don't you go down and pick up a copy of the *Register* for me—and, oh, yes, go over to the recorder of deeds' office and see if they've got an up-to-date list of tax-delinquent properties."

"Yes, sir. I'll do that right away."

"Take your time, Mrs. Fernmark. Mr. Jemmers and I want to talk over a business deal and it might just take a while. If you like, when you've finished the errands, you can go on and have your lunch. No hurry about getting back. I don't have much for you to do today, anyhow."

"Yes, sir. Thank you, Mr. Shottlander." The young woman lowered her eyes and moved past Calvin Jemmers, who was already striding toward her employer's office. She made a point of not looking at him and not speaking, whereupon he stopped, turned around, and called, "Why, now, Alice, don't you say good morning to your employer's friends?"

"I'm not being paid for that, Mr. Jemmers. Good morning to you," she tersely responded and, opening the front door of the office on the corner of Bigelow and Main Streets, walked stiffly out, her back and shoulders taut as a ramrod to indicate her complete disapproval of her employer's visitor.

Alice Fernmark had good reason for ignoring the portly president of Houston Mercantile. She was twenty-eight, of medium height, with hazel eyes and dark auburn hair which she wore in a modish bun. Ten years earlier she had

77

married an affable young farmer, John Fernmark, whose parents had died the previous year and left him about four hundred acres of arable land in the Panhandle. Alice herself had been born near that region in a small settler comunity, gone to a rural school, and taught there for the year preceding her marriage. She and John, who was only two years her senior, had been childhood sweethearts.

Though both of them eagerly wanted children, their marriage was saddened by Alice's discovery that she was barren. The elderly rural doctor could not tell her why nor could he prescribe anything that would cure this sole blight on an otherwise blissful marriage. Fortunately for her peace of mind, however, her young, industrious husband loved her all the more and flatly stated that they could always adopt children when his farm really began to prosper. But just two years ago, when he had reached the goal he had set and they were beginning to discuss the happy prospect of adoption, a raiding party of a dozen Kiowa Apaches rode up to the farm, shot John Fernmark down in the barn when he tried to prevent the theft of four fine horses, and left Alice a widow.

At this time, Alice's older sister, Jeanette, was married and living in Houston, where her husband, David Perring, was a breeder and trainer of horses. He ran a profitable stable and livery, in which much of the business was the selling and renting of buggies and carriages to the wealthier gentry of Houston. The Perrings, too, were childless, but of their own volition. After the death of Alice's husband, Alice accepted her sister's invitation to come live with them for the time being. She moved into a room on the second floor of the Perrings' sturdy frame house on Dorado Street, about a mile from Arnold Shottlander's real estate office.

Calvin Jemmers, always with an eye to an attractive woman and growing increasingly bored with his dowdy, spiritless wife, Amelia, noticed Alice on the street one day, soon after she had come to live in Houston. He offered her employment at the Houston Mercantile and Alice went to work for him, not suspecting at first his motive for hiring her. Her work was that of filing correspondence and writing an occasional letter in longhand to Jemmers's dictation. When he gave her a substantial raise after only the second week of her employment, she began to question his motives. And when, at the end of the fourth week, he ingratiatingly urged her to stay after the closing of the bank to discuss some special work, she discovered exactly what those motives were. He tore her shirtwaist in a clumsy, amorous attempt on her virtue, and she scratched him with her fingernails and, bursting into tears, told him what a repugnant and odious man he was.

The next day, Jemmers appeared at the Perring house with a bouquet of flowers and a box of candy, but Alice indignantly refused to see him or to accept his peace offering. To help earn her keep, she cooked and did many of the household chores for her sister and brother-in-law; finally, since that work was tedious and depressing at best, she decided to seek an outside job so that she could regain her self-esteem. Arnold Shottlander had been recommended to her by her brother-in-law, who had had several dealings with the gloomy, taciturn speculator. She went to Shottlander's office somewhat doubtfully and found him in his way no more prepossessing than Calvin Jemmers, but he had at once coldly declared, "Mrs. Fernmark, I may as well tell you at the outset that I haven't the least interest in members of the fair sex. I have never married, and I never shall. Personally, I detest women. But you can be useful to me because a pretty face may help bring in customers, and also close deals. I'll pay you well, I expect you to be respectable, punctual, and diligent, and apart from that we shall have no association with each other. If that suits you, the post is yours."

The seventy-five dollars a month that Shottlander paid Alice enabled her to contribute her share of expenses to the Perring household and to regain her sense of independence. Her duties were certainly not onerous. Twice, to be sure, she was obliged to accompany her employer and an enthusiastic client to dinner at one of Houston's best restaurants, but all she was required to do was to grace the table with her presence, to smile, and to make a few innocuously flattering remarks about the excellence of the land her employer was offering for sale to the client. As for Arnold Shottlander himself, he could not have been more circumspect in his studied indifference to Alice's very obvious charms.

Recently, and quite by accident, Alice had finally discovered the real reason for Shottlander's coolness toward her. She had come back rather earlier from lunch than anticipated, and when she entered Shottlander's office to bring him the newpaper, she surprised him with his arm around a sturdy blond young man in his late twenties, almost at the point of kissing the latter on the mouth. She turned away quickly and coughed to indicate her presence, and Shottlander furiously exclaimed, "I told you to come back at one o'clock, not twelve-thirty, Mrs. Fernmark. If you can't obey orders, I shall have to discharge you. Please see that it never happens again!" She stammeringly apologized and left the office at once, staying on the opposite side of the street until she saw the young man leave and go down the street, away from her. Shottlander said nothing further about the incident, but he stonily glared at her and remained taciturn for the rest of the afternoon.

Then, just a few days later, when she had gone into the Del Ray Hotel to take a message from Shottlander to a customer who had come in from New Orleans and was staying over at the hotel for a week to complete the transaction, she chanced to overhear a revealing conversation. The lobby of the hotel had a side entrance opening directly into a saloon, and the jovial, thickly mustachioed bartender was laughing boisterously as he declared, "Sure, Shottlander's a queer fish. Know why you never see him down at that little house on Marbury Street on a Saturday night? He's got a yen for his own kind, that's what. Queer as a threepenny piece, if you ask me. Not that it's any of my business, mind you. But that's why you'll never hear any scandal about his breaking up a happy home, ha ha ha!"

Alice turned red and she bit her lip, as a sudden light dawned to clarify what she had seen in her employer's office. But, being a forthright young woman, she reasoned that if he truly did prefer men to women, at least she would be spared the kind of offensive tactics that Calvin Jemmers had tried on her. Surely Shottlander's attitude was preferable by far, for she knew that as an attractive young widow she was particularly open to insulting advances. She had still not forgiven Jemmers for his unspeakable behavior while she was in his employ, and it was for this reason that she spoke so sharply to him when he came to call on Shottlander.

As Alice left her employer's office on this particular day, intending to follow his instructions by remaining away until after lunch, Calvin Jemmers stared after her appreciatively, then turned to enter Arnold Shottlander's office.

"Well now, Calvin," Shottlander drily chuckled as he seated himself and waved his visitor to the chair opposite his desk. "I can tell from the look in those greedy eyes of yours that you've got yourself a prime sucker."

"I have for a fact, Arnold." The banker winked and leaned back in his chair. "He just left my office, and he's on his way back to Galveston."

"He comes from there? If he does, he might know a little more about Houston than you think," the realtor guardedly proffered.

"Oh, no, he's from Chicago. Name's Charles Douglas. Had a big department store that was burned in that fire we all heard about last October."

"Oh, yes, of course. Well, go on, Calvin. How do I figure in your acquaintanceship with this itinerant Chicagoan?" Shottlander drawled as he reached for a cheroot, lit it, then shoved the box toward the banker, who helped himself to several, which he stuffed into his waistcoat pocket, and then lit one in his turn.

"Seems he's got some kinfolk in Galveston, but he was spending time in Carrizo Springs visiting his wife's mother and such," Jemmers declared. "He showed me a letter of credit, and he's loaded. Says he wants to have a department store here in Houston, maybe one in Galveston too. Nice, straightforward fellow, but that's the kind you and I know how to work with, if we handle things the right way, eh, Arnold?"

"We've had some success in the past, yes, Calvin, I'll give you that, and I'm beholden to you. You've always had your fair reward of any profits you turned my way, and you always will. Now, why don't you give me some specifics so I can think about what's best for our ambitious young store builder?" Shottlander rejoined.

"Well, there's a nice stretch on Durwald Road, two blocks north of Main Street."

"I know all about it. Old Fred Pommering had a feed store there, went broke, owed taxes, and died just before Christmas Day. What about it?"

"Arnold, Arnold, that keen mind of yours is somewhat sluggish this morning," Jemmers playfully chided, wagging a fat forefinger at the cadaverous-looking realtor. "Have

81

you forgotten the new city ordinance that went into effect a few weeks ago—the one governing delinquent properties? And didn't you tell me last week that Mayor Scanlan is planning to pay up the back taxes and acquire the Pommering property for a nice new school?"

"Yes, I recall that," Shottlander nonchalantly responded. "But you see, Calvin, I'm way ahead of you already. What you're thinking is that you're going to offer this land—through me, of course—to this store-minded Chicago protégé of yours, and have him lay down a good deal of cash. And then, when he's ready to sign the deal, inform him that the city has taken it over and that, unfortunately, you won't be able to return his money unless he buys a different plot, because the new city ordinance you referred to provides that when delinquent property is acquired by the city itself, any previous bid by a private citizen is rendered null and void. Isn't that your drift?"

Jemmers was taken aback for a moment, then he burst into belly-shaking laughter, slapping his palm on the desk. "You're a card, Arnold, you're really a card! So you were way ahead of me all the time. Yes, that's exactly what I had in mind." Then, his face sobering, he reflectively added, "But of course, if a bid is null and void, wouldn't the bidder be entitled to a refund of his money?"

"Why Calvin, you underestimate me. There'll be legal expenses in filing the bid with the recorder's office, and then there'll be a certain number of, shall we say, gratuities, to bribe certain people on the City Council to agree to the sale of such important property to an outsider. It won't be our fault that, in the end, the sale doesn't go through—it'll be the fault of that ordinance. And finally, if he really gets obstreperous, you can always pacify him by telling him that you'll furnish the balance out of your own pocket as a down payment on another but even better piece of property that you just happen to know about—which, of course, you will purchase through me. So you see, our young Chicago friend will wind up paying four or five times what the land is really worth, and if we manage to keep our mouths shut, as I know you will and I always do, he'll be none the wiser. And, of course, we'll split fifty-fifty, as ever."

"You're positively a genius, Arnold!" Jemmers glowed as he rose from the chair. "What I'll do is wait a few days and then send a wire to the San Antonio bank where this fellow gets his messages and mail and such through a relative who runs a ranch at Carrizo Springs. Ever heard of a Lucien Edmond Bouchard?"

"Vaguely. Yes, I think he's done very well in the cattle business the last few years," Shottlander replied, rubbing his eyebrows and then the bridge of his nose as if to indicate fatigue. "It's too bad I don't have any land in that area up for sale, but it all comes out of Austin. And if memory serves me right, somebody tried to pull a real land swindle there a while back and got himself and his partner hanged for his pains. Fellow by the name of Norman Cantrell, who pretended to be a Spanish nobleman. That's so old a dodge it's worn out by now, and I personally wouldn't stoop to it. Well, Calvin, if that's all you have to say, you go on back to your office and you wait those few days and then you send your telegraph to the Chicagoan. Before he comes here, you and I will work out all the fine details."

"Understood! Say, by the way, how's Alice Fernmark working out for you?"

"She's satisfactory," Shottlander peremptorily answered with an indifferent shrug. "And I know exactly what you're thinking. I ask you, as a business acquaintance, Calvin, not to annoy me by trying to wheedle my perfectly good secretary into your bed, not on my time, at any rate. What you want to do with her after hours is perfectly immaterial to me. You know I have no use for women."

"But I do," the portly banker sniggered with another broad wink. "Well, I'll be in touch just as soon as I get that wire off to Mr. Charles Douglas."

"Don't look so downhearted, Calvin," Shottlander mockingly jested. "With the profits you'll have as your share if this deal goes through, you can visit that little house we all know about in Houston and ease your anxieties, shall we say. Except I don't care to hear about your amatory exploits, you know. And remember what I said about Alice Fernmark. Keep away from her when she's working for me. I trust I won't have to tell you that again."

"Of course not, Arnold, we're good friends, and I wouldn't do anything to sour our friendship, you know that," the banker protested with a look of hurt innocence on his fat face.

Arnold Shottlander nodded and resumed his chair. "I

hope you don't. Because if you do, there's another bank in town, and I'm a man who does business with people whom I can trust and depend upon. Have a good day, Calvin."

Lucien Edmond Bouchard had been pleased to allow Eddie Gentry to escort the Douglases and Polly Behting from Windhaven Range to the packet at Corpus Christi, and he ordered eight vaqueros to accompany the party. Lucien Edmond was of course aware of Eddie's real motivation in making the journey. He had taken a great liking to the hardworking young cowboy and sincerely hoped that Polly would be able to break her "understanding" with the butcher's apprentice in Chicago and return one day soon to Windhaven Range. It was in his mind, if that occurred, to give Eddie a substantial piece of land as a bonus for all his loyalty and industrious work.

Charles Douglas was also looking forward to the trip. After seeing his family safely off in Galveston, he planned to stop in to see James Hunter, before going on to Houston. He had promised Laurette that he would not stay in Houston longer than necessary to close the land deal, hire a contractor, and perhaps interview a few prospective employees for the store. This satisfied Laurette, who in fact had already resigned herself to the prospect of Charles's being away much of the time during the next two or three years. A practical as well as steadfastly loving wife, she understood that her husband's ambitious plans would guarantee the future of their family, and in due time cement their marriage even more powerfully. For she knew that it was for her sake as well as the boys' that he was not content with the status quo, and it secretly flattered her to know that, comfortably married though they were by now, she could still inspire him to imaginative new projects for the future.

As for Eddie Gentry, he was in a seventh heaven of delight. He was punctilious in making no overt declaration to the lovely nurse, lest he be censured for any impropriety. For him, it was quite enough to ride alongside the wagon in which she rode with the boys, occasionally flashing her a radiant smile. He was content with the soft, almost shy response he received in return, observing happily the warm glow in her lovely blue eyes. Thus, by signs and looks, the two lovers sealed their pact, and the orphaned young cowboy, who had not known close family ties since early child-hood, began to look forward to having a wife who would at last make him feel that he was wanted and that there was a purpose to all of his hard work.

When the Douglases boarded the packet at Corpus Christi, they tactfully looked the other way so that Eddie might have a few moments alone with Polly in which to say his goodbyes. He led her down to the end of the dock, where no one was watching them, and, stammering in his eagerness to assure her of his love and yet wanting to say nothing that might offend her, declared, "I guess this is goodbye for a while, Polly honey. Now you be sure to write, in care of the bank in San Antonio. Lucien Edmond sends vaqueros into town pretty regularly, so I'll be sure to get your letters. And I'll write too, you can depend on that."

"I—I want you to. But—but you won't know where to write—"

"Oh yes, I will." He brightened. "After I get your first letter, you'll have the address of the new house."

"Oh, of course—how silly of me, and how smart you are to think of that, Eddie, *Liebchen!*" She blushed violently as she stared down at the sluggish water between the edge of the dock and the stern of the packet. A covey of noisy gulls chattered in the air, swooping near them and then soaring far aloft. "Do be careful while I'm gone, Eddie, *Liebchen.* Take good care of yourself."

"I will, I promise," he whispered, grasping one of her hands and holding it in both of his as he stared into her eyes.

"Oh, I love you so, *Liebchen!* I—I do not think it will be so terribly wrong if we had a—had a goodbye kiss—after all, it will be so long until I see you again—"

"Oh, Polly!" Eddie swallowed hard, and then, glancing almost frantically back to make sure that no one was watching, grasped her by the shoulders and kissed her hard on the mouth. Then he drew back, blushing like a school-boy. "Gosh—I—I'm going to miss you something awful!"

"It will be the same for me, *Liebchen.*" Gently she drew her hand away, as he had taken hold of it again, and then stroked his head and quickly kissed him softly on the mouth. "And now I must go on board with them. You understand—I will write as often as I can, *Liebchen.*"

85

"You take care, now. And I hope—well, I sure hope that Dieter fellow won't hate me—I'm the luckiest man in the world, Polly, and I can't believe it yet. There won't ever be any other girl for me—not ever. You write me as soon as you can now, you hear?"

"*Ja, ja,* and now I must go. *Wirklich! Auf Wiedersehen, mein süsser Eddie!*" she breathed. Then hurriedly, biting her lips to fight the tears, she quickened her footsteps toward the gangplank.

"So the Houston Mercantile has found you a piece of good property for your store, Charles?" James Hunter refilled Charles's snifter from the brandy decanter and helped himself as well before settling back into his armchair.

"Yes, and I'll be riding on to Houston tomorrow. I'll follow the road that I mapped out on my first trip, just to make sure that I can carry goods over it if I have to. Here, let me show you the map I drew. It's pretty rough, but you'll be able to make out the route."

Charles reached into his pocket, pulled out the sketch he had made, and laid it on the table in front of James.

James studied the map, then nodded, "That's a good map, I can follow it easily. Hmm, yes, I see you'll need a detour there, and there, to avoid the roughest spots. Sturdy wagons will do the job. But speaking of transportation, I've found out a little bit more about the railroad we discussed when you were here last; the Galveston, Houston and Henderson line. It has a colorful history. It started up back in the early fifties, before I arrived. The Confederates used it during the war to bring in troops and supplies, and I guess it helped them hold off the Union naval and ground forces for a while. It's nothing much—just a steamer and two railroad cars. But naturally you'll want to make some inquiries of your own."

"I will," said Charles, "though the line does sound pretty inadequate. I've already learned one thing, in fact. One of the officers on the packet that brought me here told me that sometimes the Brazos River floods and covers the tracks. And there may be another problem, too. If the line starts here in Galveston, the people running it must set their own freight rates, and they could be pretty high to an outsider like me."

"That could also be true, Charles. Naturally, since I live

here in Galveston and we ship out of here by boat, we haven't concerned ourselves with the line to Houston. Besides, there's a rivalry between the two cities, and it's only human nature that the people here wouldn't really care about building up Houston trade, not if there was a chance that Houston would try to take our business away from us. Maybe it's a little of that spirit of rivalry that made me suggest you put your first new store right here in Galveston! That and the shipping problem, of course."

"Well, you may be right," Charles admitted. "But the thing is, if I can get good land in Houston right now, at a fair price, I think I should start there since the place is growing so fast. Maybe in a few years the rail lines from the Midwest will be extended as far as Houston. Then I wouldn't even have to worry about shipping goods all the way from Chicago to Galveston by boat, let alone by wagon to Houston."

"That could very well happen with an entrepreneur like Jay Gould trying to buy up all the railroads and extend and interconnect them," James agreed. "But all that's outside my province, because I've been a cotton man all my life. So you go on ahead to Houston, Charles, and size up the situation, bearing in mind that I'll back you. If Houston doesn't work out, I'll gladly back you for a store here in Galveston instead."

"I won't forget that, James, and thanks again. Well, that was a marvelous dinner, and I'm beholden to you and your lovely wife for your hospitality once again. I'll get a good night's sleep and ride into Houston early tomorrow. Good night."

"It's a pleasure to see you again, Mr. Douglas!" Calvin Jemmers rose from his chair and extended his fleshy hand with an obsequious grin. "I like a man who believes in swift action. And I think I've got the very piece of land you need for that department store of yours. Of course," here he lowered his voice to a conspiratorial whisper, "you'll have to act fast and it's going to be a little expensive—but that's only natural because it's prime property right in the middle of town where you'll get all your business."

"I'm not against paying a fair price for what I want, Mr. Jemmers."

"Call me Calvin, I like to be on a first-name basis with my clients. Now, if it's convenient for you, Charles—you don't mind, because I've a feeling we're going to be friends as well as business associates—?" Here, Charles smilingly nodded his head. "Good, good!" the banker boomed. "Now, if it's convenient for you, I want you to meet the leading real estate broker in our fair city. That would be Arnold Shottlander. As a matter of fact, I think we might conclude this transaction in a pleasingly sociable way, if you've no objection. We could all have dinner this evening at the Terrence Hotel—it's got the best restaurant in town, believe me!"

"That sounds fine. I'm here to do business, and I plan to stay on for a week or so lining up a contractor and looking after things generally," Charles affirmed. "By the way, I know there is a small railroad line connecting Houston with Galveston, but I was wondering what you think its potential might be. My goods would come in by water to Galveston, but the railroad line is so small I'm not sure it could handle what I'd be bringing in. I may have to use wagons as well."

"You won't need any wagons, you can be sure of that, Charles boy." Jemmers grew genially expansive. "When we meet for dinner tonight, you will discover that my good friend Arnold Shottlander has an inside track—if you'll pardon the pun, ha ha!—on what's being planned in our fair city. Depend on it, Charles, by the time your store is ready to open, we'll have a big railroad line all our own— maybe all the way from Chicago, who knows?"

"That certainly would be ideal. It would be faster and cheaper than shipping down the Mississippi and on to Galveston," Charles agreed.

"Then you just put your mind at ease, relax, and take in the sights of Houston until this evening. Shall we say about seven o'clock? We'll meet you at the Terrence, and I think by tomorrow you'll be able to start about the business of hiring your contractor."

"I'm indebted to you, Calvin."

"My pleasure, Charles." Jemmers energetically shook hands and offered his most engaging smile. The banker accompanied Charles to the door, and as soon as he had made certain that Charles was heading in the direction of his hotel, Jemmers made his way in the opposite direction to Arnold Shottlander's office.

"Well, Arnold, I think we can gaff our catch this evening," he declared once Alice Fernmark, ignoring his effusive greeting, had shown him into her employer's office. "I hope you haven't got another dinner engagement tonight. I've booked one for us both—and that lovely secretary of yours, too—at the Terrence at seven o'clock."

"I'm free as a bird, Calvin." The tall, cadaverous man rose from his desk and called out peremptorily, "Mrs. Fernmark, would you come in here, please?"

The auburn-haired widow entered the office, studiously ignoring the fatuously grinning banker. "Yes, sir?"

"I'll need you this evening, Mrs. Fernmark. Mr. Jemmers and I are going to close a deal. That property on Durwald Road, you remember."

"You mean the one with delinquent taxes?"

"Now that, Mrs. Fernmark, you won't have to mention this evening. As it happens, Mr. Jemmers and I are going to entertain a very important and very wealthy client from Chicago, a Mr. Charles Douglas. He's interested in acquiring that piece of land so he can build a department store."

"Yes, sir."

"So we'd like you to come along. Your presence will add a certain companionability, and it will put him more at his ease. He's a stranger to Houston, you see."

"I really—if you don't mind—"

Shottlander's lips tightened and his eyes narrowed. "If you wish to keep your present situation, Mrs. Fernmark, I suggest you accept my invitation. Please understand, you're not being asked out to dine with us with any implication that you be other than my secretary. I may wish, indeed, to have you write down a few notes as we discuss business after the repast. But that is all. I certainly hope you drew no other inferences."

Alice shrugged, and her shoulders seemed to droop. "Very well, Mr. Shottlander, if it's an order, I do need the job and I guess there's really no harm in it."

CHAPTER EIGHT

Charles Douglas spent most of the day until the proposed dinner engagement walking the streets of Houston, visiting various shops, and introducing himself to their owners, to get their views on the town's commerce and growth. He also paid a visit to the small station on the outskirts—which had once been Harrisburg—to discuss the current operating schedule of the Galveston, Houston and Henderson Railroad with the tall, old bespectacled stationmaster. What he learned was not entirely encouraging.

"You can see for yourself, Mr. Douglas," the stationmaster explained, "this is small-gauge track, and the steamer's not very big. Couldn't rightly be expected to pull big, heavy loads, not now. Oh sure, during the war they had troops on here and guns and such, but that was easy. Even so, it took about four hours to make the run from Galveston to Houston, sometimes as much as four and a half. I know, 'cause I've been here ever since January, 1860, and that's a fact, Mr. Douglas."

"I see, Mr. Skalway," the young Chicagoan reflectively nodded. "You think someday soon the railroad might lay wider track and put on heavier equipment?"

"Now that just might occur, Mr. Douglas. And there's another possibility. One of our leading citizens, T. W. Peirce, and Mr. Scanlan, our mayor, might just try to wangle a new line between these towns, maybe by next year, Mr. Douglas. But right now, from what you tell me, I don't see how you could ship all this stuff you'd need from Galveston on into Houston, not by this railroad line."

"Has anyone ever thought about the possibility of a canal, Mr. Skalway?" Charles asked.

"Well, sir, I can remember back in 1837, when I was working on my daddy's ranch, you could take a flat boat

91

through Buffalo Bayou from Galveston to Houston, and you'd spend half your time pushing aside the branches of overhanging trees and the clusters of Spanish moss. That was really a chore!" The old stationmaster chuckled reminiscently. "One of these days real soon, though I'm pretty sure the folks in Houston are going to try to dredge a deeper channel, and if they do that, then you could likely as not bring your goods in straight through by water."

"That would certainly be a blessing and it would cut costs," Charles thought aloud.

"No doubt about it, Mr. Douglas. Well, sir, what do you think of our little town of Houston?"

"I like it a lot. I like the spirit of the people I've been talking to all day. So we'll see, Mr. Skalway. Thanks for your trouble and good luck to you." The two men shook hands and Charles walked slowly back to the Terrence Hotel.

Before the afternoon ended, Arnold Shottlander had called Alice Fernmark into his office to give her more particulars about the role he wished her to play at dinner. Although he had already assured her that her presence would not involve her in anything more than a cordial business tête-à-tête, the auburn-haired young widow was not at all comfortable, especially knowing that the lecherous banker would be present. It was true that she had accompanied her employer on previous similar occasions, and the sales that had resulted had in no way been suspect. However, this time she had a curious foreboding, due mainly to the fact that the banker would be party to it. And, although Shottlander did not go into any further details about the property he planned to sell Charles Douglas, Alice knew that she had seen it in the published list of delinquent tax properties, which she obtained for her employer each week from the office of the recorder of deeds.

Many Confederates had come to Houston before and during the Civil War, and a number of them had used their last savings to buy land, to farm, ranch, or produce cotton. With the end of the war and the depletion of their own resources, and especially with the rock-bottom price that cotton was bringing on the open market, many of these investors had been reduced to penury. Some had sublet their land to others more fortunate than themselves and actually worked as employees for the latter; others had simply abandoned their property and gone elsewhere to start a new life; and then there were some who desperately clung to the worthless land in the illusory hope that somehow there would be money to pay the taxes and to resume the genteel life to which they had always been accustomed. Being alert as well as sensitive and compassionate by nature, Alice knew that her employer profited hugely by acquiring such properties through the simple expedient of paying up the back taxes and securing title, then reselling them at a very handsome advantage to himself. Yet this afternoon, after she had heard Shottlander extol Charles Douglas's business ability and optimism with that air of cynicism with which he always deprecated those whose motives were entirely honest, she began to suspect that the young Chicagoan was about to be set up for a swindle.

That was why, when he dismissed her at four o'clock and told her to dress and appear at her very best at seven o'clock that evening in the restaurant of the Terrence, Alice went directly to the office of the recorder of deeds and asked the scrawny, consumptive little grayhaired clerk for the latest delinquency list. When he handed it to her, she thanked him, expressing her gratitude for the cooperation he had shown to her and her employer. She looked at the list and found, as she knew she would, the piece of land that was about to be offered to Charles Douglas. Looking up with an appealing smile, she innocently asked, "Mr. Belton, isn't this the property that's near the city hall?"

"Indeed it is, Mrs. Fernmark. And I'll tell you something." Lemuel Belton lowered his voice and glanced around to make certain that no one could overhear him. "Just this morning, I got wind that Mayor Scanlan and the City Council are planning to buy that property and turn it into a school. Seems like we're getting so many new settlers here with families, they want an education. Well, of course, that'll mean we can charge more taxes to pay for the school. The back taxes on this piece aren't very much, anyhow. Bless my soul—in fact, if I felt like it, I could even buy it myself—though of course, I wouldn't know what in the world to do with it."

"Thank you so much for telling me, Mr. Belton. I promise you I'll keep it confidential."

93

"Glad to help any time, Mrs. Fernmark. My best to your boss, Mr. Shottlander."

"I'll tell him that this evening. There's a man from the Midwest who's having dinner with him this evening, somebody interested in starting a department store here in Houston," she confided.

"Well, now, he ought to do right well. 'Course, he'll have to pay a lot to get his goods into Houston, what with shipping first into Galveston. We Houston folks are mighty resentful of the way Galveston's treating us with their high freight and drayage rates. One of these days, you mark my words, we'll have big railroad lines all the way from maybe even New York and Chicago right through Houston and on to California. Then we won't have to worry about the port of Galveston!"

"I certainly hope you're right, for Mr. Douglas's sake— that's the man I was telling you about, Mr. Belton. Well, good night and thank you again."

"Any time, Mrs. Fernmark. Nice to see you." He permitted himself a faint titter. "Fact is, this office doesn't have nice young women like you coming in very often, so you might say I sort of look forward to it. I'm always glad to help, remember that." Then, as if horrified at his own audacity, he abruptly turned and went back to a large ledger book and pretended to riffle the pages in search of information. Alice smiled gently to herself, understanding and indulgently accepting his sudden compliment without offense—he had been a widower the past fifteen years— and went back to her sister's house to dress for dinner.

"Sit down here, Charles," Calvin Jemmers beamed, gesturing to the head of the attractively set table in a private room set off from the restaurant by a pair of thick red velvet drapes. "Mrs. Fernmark, why don't you sit at Mr. Douglas's right? That's fine. Now, we'll all be sociable and neighborly. I'll just sit here across from you with my friend Arnold." Jemmers ostentatiously seated himself at the other end of the table, thrust his napkin into his waistcoat as a kind of bib, and exhaled a sigh of sensual satisfaction, for he prided himself on being as hardy a trencherman as a philanderer. Arnold Shottlander, at the banker's right, disdainfully sniffed and edged his chair a little farther away, but this did not in the least halt the banker's exuberance.

"Now this is the way, sir, I like to do business," he boomed with another theatrical gesture which embraced the entire room and its occupants. "Good food and wine— oh yes, Charles, even here in what you might consider a backwater Texas town, we know what good French wine is, and cognac and liqueurs as well. I've asked the cook to pay particular attention tonight, because I want you to leave Houston with the very best impression possible of our culture and sophistication as well as our tremendous industrial potential."

"I've made some pretty good conclusions on that last score, Calvin," Charles smilingly responded. "I spent the day talking to a good many citizens of this town and I like what I see and what I hear."

"Excellent, sir, excellent! Now, it's my rule that we don't even breathe a syllable of business until after we've finished our coffee and brandy—I hope you won't mind, Charles?" It was obvious that Jemmers had appointed himself master of ceremonies. Nonetheless, there was a wry look on Arnold Shottlander's gloomy face, and he shot the banker a malicious glance as he carefully unfolded his napkin and laid it across his lap.

"Perfectly all right with me, Calvin. Besides, it isn't often that a simple businessman like myself has the pleasure of dining with such attractive company." He turned to smile at Alice Fernmark, who blushed and lowered her eyes. She had already been impressed by his courtesy and thoughtfulness when, after the banker had proposed that she sit beside the young Chicagoan, the latter had swiftly drawn out the chair and graciously seated her.

Alice was also pleased by the fact that, having worn her prettiest gown, designed in brown silk with puffed sleeves and bodice, she could at once see the difference between the way Charles and the lecherous Calvin Jemmers regarded her. Indeed, Charles had complimented her on the gown, humorously remarking that he hoped that his new department store in Houston would be able to offer such modern fashions, and adding that if the women of Houston were able to see her wearing this gown, they would assuredly buy him out of such merchandise. By contrast, from the other end of the table, the portly Jemmers sent her looks which made her feel as if he were stripping her garment by garment and appraising her charms in a way

95

that caused everyone else at the table to be aware of his intentions toward her.

Jemmers had spared no expense to make this a particularly memorable dinner so as to impress his supposedly naive client. As he had already confided to Shottlander, once he had seen the financial statement that had verified Charles Douglas's standing in the Chicago business community, he was more than ever determined to induce Douglas to transfer a good part of his capital into the Houston Mercantile. It was even possible, he believed, that Douglas might invest some of that capital in the project of dredging the channel to provide direct transportation by water of his goods from Chicago.

To begin the sumptuous bill of fare, there were fresh oysters from Galveston Bay, and a dry, white Graves to accompany them. There followed pompano baked in a paper bag with a rich Creole-devised sauce, a ham baked with cloves and raisins accompanied by a bottle of fine red Bordeaux, a delicate salad of shrimp and vegetables with a subtle cream dressing, and finally an overly rich pecan pie whose top was covered with melted pralines and smothered in whipped cream. There was champagne to accompany this dessert, along with a bowl of fruit, nuts, and raisins and some cheeses, and finally strong, thick black coffee, port, and brandy.

Throughout this lavish feast, Charles courteously helped his attractive dinner companion to the various viands served, and Alice's impression of him was strengthened each time he showed himself properly considerate in the social amenities. At the same time, her presentiment of the trickery that her employer and Calvin Jemmers proposed to inflict on this gracious, candid, and unsuspecting young man was intensified, particularly when she remembered her conversation with the clerk in the recorder of deeds' office this afternoon.

She herself ate abstemiously and took only a glass or two of wine and a sip of the brandy that accompanied the coffee.

Conversely, Jemmers had already loosened his cravat, and his face was florid and sweating by the time the dessert was reached. He had also imbibed somewhat more than was good for him, and he evidenced this by raising his voice, laughing at his own jokes, and occasionally inserting into the conversation a bawdy and insinuating comment on Alice's attractiveness. At such moments, the young widow bit her lips and busied herself with her knife and fork, pretending not to hear. But Charles, glancing at her, understood that she was deeply offended, and he even went so far as to shake his head meaningfully at the banker when he made a particularly improper comment.

At last, the table was cleared of its dishes, fresh coffee was poured, and the decanter of brandy was left in the center of the table. Jemmers extracted three cigars from his waistcoat pocket, tossed one to the young Chicagoan, left one beside the realtor's place, chewed off the end of his own and spat it into the spittoon on the floor beside him, then lit his and exhaled a belch. "Well, now, forgive me, but that's the best tribute I could pay to our chef, don't you agree, Charles? A splendid dinner, as good as any you'd find in your home town, I'll be bound!"

"It was really superb, and I'm indebted to you, Calvin," Charles affably responded.

"Think nothing of it, sir! Nothing but the best for one of our customers, eh, Arnold?" the banker boomed.

Shottlander visibly winced at this boisterous effusiveness. "Yes, Calvin, we both want to assure Mr. Douglas that we're interested in his welfare as a prospective future citizen of our fair city. And now, perhaps we might get down to business?"

"To be sure, to be sure, Arnold! Now, Charles, about that property you'll be wanting for your store. Arnold and I went to a great deal of trouble and expense to find exactly the place. It's admirably situated, not far from the city hall, in the center of town, a town which by now I'm sure you'll agree is certain to double its population within the next decade, if not sooner."

"That sounds attractive enough. Go ahead," Charles nodded.

"It has a thousand-foot frontage, and that's certainly all you'll need. How many stories do you plan to make the store, Charles?" Jemmers pursued.

"I'd say two, at most three. That would depend on materials, what contractor I could get, and of course the size of the inventory I'd be stocking. The one point that still bothers me is the matter of transportation, as you can easily understand," the young Chicagoan explained.

97

Arnold Shottlander was quick to interpose, with a know-ing smile: "It so happens, Mr. Douglas, that Calvin and I have prior knowledge, as you might say. Naturally, since he's the leading banker of Houston and I pride myself on being the foremost land specialist here, it's our business to glean advance information the ordinary outsider could never hope to have. I have it on good authority, Mr. Doug-las, that the railroad line will not only be expanded with heavier cars that could carry your goods once they reach the Port of Galveston, but also that the mayor himself in-tends to petition Congress to build a separate line. We al-ready have something like five railroads with a length of eleven hundred miles, but only one route to Galveston, and that one is really monopolized by the officials of that port town. Oh yes, development's bound to come. I may say also that we're reasonably sure, Calvin and I, that you'll have the channel dredged deeply enough within a year or so to permit you to ship direct down the Mississippi and on into Houston. And if that isn't enough, you'll have the rail-roads coming through here from the East, one day soon. You'll be shipping by rail straight from Chicago in ten years, at the latest, I'd say. So you see, Mr. Douglas, an investment at this moment will give you what amounts to pioneer rights in establishing yourself. And the land we've chosen for you is extremely reasonably priced."

"That sounds promising, gentlemen," Charles smilingly replied. "What price are you asking?"

Here Shottlander exchanged a quick glance with the portly banker and then, pursing his lips and stroking the tip of his bony nose, slowly answered, pontificating each syllable as if he were delivering an unforgettable prophecy: "Why sir, a paltry four thousand dollars."

"That's a little steep," Charles frowned. "I've been told that the state sells land for a lot less."

"Of course it does," Jemmers chimed in, loosening his cravat still more and quickly putting his palm over his mouth to stifle a sudden, unexpected belch, "but that's homesteader land, totally undeveloped, out in the wilds with only tumbleweed and mesquite for neighbors. Now, Charles, you're a smart businessman from Chicago, you can't expect to buy frontage near Main Street for that ri-diculous price. Heavens no! Mark my words, sir, within a year or two that four thousand dollars will seem like a mere bagatelle once your store is flourishing. Why, you may well expect to have others offer you three and even four times the value of your property, out of sheer envy, isn't that so, Arnold?"

"I shouldn't be at all surprised, Calvin." Again, Shottlander stroked his nose and scowled, assuming his most solemn demeanor. "You're really very fortunate, and we're letting you in on a piece of land that's going to be in great demand as soon as the other influential citizens of this town learn about it. Imagine, just a few blocks from our city hall—why, you'll have the mayor and his wife among your first customers. And of course, you know that word-of-mouth advertising is the best of all for a new enterprise, no matter where it's located."

"I won't argue with you there, Arnold," Charles nodded. "That is, however, a bit more than I was prepared to pay. May I think about it until tomorrow?"

"If you like. But it may not be available tomorrow," Shottlander warily proffered.

"Now that seems odd, Mr. Shottlander," Charles rose from his chair, took a last sip of brandy, and put the snifter back down on the table. "If this proposition is so secretive, how is it that there's a danger that someone else will snap it up? Granted that Houston is growing by leaps and bounds, which I'm willing to agree to, it's hard for me to believe that twenty-four hours will make that much difference. Well, gentlemen, if you've no objection, I'd like to sleep on it."

"Very well then." Shottlander sounded disgruntled as he glanced at his portly dining companion, his sunken brown eyes suspiciously narrowed. "But I urge you to come to my office tomorrow by early afternoon at the latest, Mr. Douglas, if you're still of a mind to pursue your original project."

"I think I can promise you that. Well now, I'm indebted to you both for a really splendid dinner. And to Mrs. Fernmark for being such a charming companion. You're lucky to have a secretary like her, Mr. Shottlander."

"To be sure, to be sure," the real estate operator testily agreed, again with another quick, glowering look at Calvin Jemmers who shook his head and shrugged.

99

"Perhaps you'd allow me to escort you home, Mrs. Fernmark?" Charles politely inquired as he turned toward the lovely, auburn-haired widow.

"That—that would be very nice of you, Mr. Douglas. That is, if it's all right—"

"Go ahead, Mrs. Fernmark. Just don't forget to report on time to work tomorrow morning," Shottlander replied, at which Alice indignantly flushed and again bit her lips.

Charles pretended not to notice Shottlander's maliciously sarcastic remark as he graciously held Alice's chair so that she might rise, again turned to his two hosts, and expressed his thanks again for a very pleasant evening.

When he and the young widow had left the private dining room, Jemmers furiously turned to the realtor. "You didn't say anything to her about our scheme, did you?"

"Of course not, Calvin. I thought you were more astute than that," the realtor sneeringly replied. Then his lips tightened angrily and his eyes glowed with a sudden malevolence. "Even if she did have some suspicions, she'd know enough to keep her pretty mouth shut. I'd see to that. But I don't understand what made Douglas get his wind up so quickly."

"You set the price too high, that's what. I thought you'd ask for two or maybe three thousand at the most, but you went for four. I wish you'd settled for three so both of us could have made it sound like a real bargain." Jemmers was obviously unhappy with the turn of events as he tried to straighten his cravat and put his rumpled clothes in order.

Shottland made a face. "You're really a disgusting animal, Calvin. You eat like a hog and you look like one after you've finished. And I know you want that Fernmark bitch in the worst way. Well, if we put this deal through, you can have her with my blessing. Though personally, I don't know what you see in her. She's bovine and soft—ugh."

"Each to his own, Arnold," Jemmers quipped.

That remark earned him an even more savage look of anger as the realtor snapped back, "People who live in glass houses—you know the rest of the saying, Calvin, boy. Just keep your mouth shut about my private life and I'll be obliged to you. Another remark like that, and you can go find yourself someone else for your profiteering deals. Now listen, if Douglas decides he wants this property, we'll draw

100

up a deed and take his money. Then, as I told you, when the city takes over with its priority bid for the school, we'll just substitute another piece and tell him it's even better and that we had to go to considerable sacrifice to obtain it for him. We can make ourselves look like heroes, and we might even wangle another thousand dollars out of that sucker."

"Yes, yes, I know," Jemmers replied distractedly, then added angrily, "But did you see how that Chicago rapscallion was making eyes at my Alice? Now he's walking her home, and I could tell the stupid bitch was impressed by him."

"That's because he showed some manners, which you sadly lack, Calvin," Shottlander shot back with a malicious little smile. "I'll give you another old saying for use in your extramarital courting. You can always catch more flies with molasses than with vinegar, Calvin, something you've never really understood. You don't make it obvious to a woman that you want to go to bed with her, at least not so obviously as you do, and expect her to fall swooning in your arms."

"You're a fine one to instruct me in the art of seducing women—" Jemmers began, then caught himself and gulped as the real estate operator turned on him with narrowed, evil eyes and a tight-lipped expression. "I'm sorry, it just slipped out."

"That's just about the last slip you'll ever make with me, Calvin. Be very careful from now on. And now I'm going back to my house and you go back to your fat, dowdy wife and maybe you can pretend she's Alice Fernmark. I can see you're in need of assuagement. Good night to you!"

"It's very kind of you to walk me all this long way home, Mr. Douglas. I really didn't want to give you this much trouble," Alice Fernmark apologized.

"But it's no trouble at all. I've always liked walking. I do a great deal of it back in Chicago—for the ten hours a day I'm in my department store—that is, till it burned last October in that big fire we had."

"Oh yes, I read about that. It must have been just dreadful. So many people died and so many were homeless," she responded.

"You're a very nice person, Mrs. Fernmark. I suspect,

101

too nice to be mixed up with a scoundrel like that Arnold Shottlander and that other one, Calvin Jemmers," he remarked unexpectedly.

Alice stopped, her mouth gaping, and she turned to stare wonderingly at him. "Why, whatever do you mean, Mr. Douglas?"

"I'm not exactly the country boy those two schemers think, Mrs. Fernmark. And I don't think you're in on it, either. I didn't exactly like the way Mr. Shottlander was urging me to sign on the dotted line before dinner was over, if you want to know. And, as it happens, I was walking in the neighborhood of city hall this afternoon, and I think I saw the property that he was referring to. It's really not that conveniently placed for my purposes. And I don't think it's worth four thousand dollars, either."

"It's not." Alice took a deep breath and then plunged. "And besides, you couldn't even buy it if you tried."

"Now would you mind explaining that remark to me?"

"I—I don't want you to think I had anything to do with it, honestly I didn't, Mr. Douglas."

"I'd already decided that, Mrs. Fernmark. You're a very fine, decent woman, and it's just a pity you're reduced to having to work for a scoundrel like Arnold Shottlander. We've had his kind back in Chicago. But go ahead with what you were about to tell me."

"Well, the city is going to buy up that property for back taxes and build a school there, Mr. Douglas."

"I see. Now, what do you suppose would have happened if I'd plunked down four thousand dollars tonight to buy it? Would I have gotten a deed for the property?"

"Yes, you would have, Mr. Douglas. Mr. Shottlander would have drawn up a deed and had Calvin Jemmers notarize it for you. The two of them work together. And then, when it came out that the school was going to be built on your property, Mr. Shottlander would probably tell you that it was a complete surprise to him and that, at great cost to himself, he was going to find you an even better piece of property at a sacrifice."

"I can imagine what kind of sacrifice it would be. It would probably entail another thousand dollars or so—am I right?"

Alice shamefacedly nodded, her eyes lowered, her cheeks aflame.

"Don't feel badly. Has your employer pulled schemes like this before?"

"Well, not quite like this, but others just as bad. Mr. Douglas, I really needed a job. You see, my husband was killed by raiding Indians—we had a farm quite a ways from here—and I came to live with my married sister, but I had to have something to do to support myself, so as not to be a burden to anyone."

"Of course," he said sympathetically.

"And then, well, Mr. Shottlander needed a secretary, and once in a while he wanted me to go to dinner with a customer—just the way I did tonight. But it was all very harmless. Except that, the last month or two, I began to dislike him very much."

"I should imagine so. And this Mr. Jemmers?"

"He—he's just dreadful. He—he knows I'm a widow and he thinks—well, you can guess. I think you saw how he looked at me and some of the things he said—"

"I'm quite well aware of what he said and how he acted tonight, Mrs. Fernmark. That's another thing that didn't set well with me. Come on, let's keep walking. I want to go back to my hotel and think things over."

"Please—" she quavered.

"Don't worry," he said gently, "I won't say anything that will give them any hint that what you told me influenced my decision, Mrs. Fernmark. No, what I think is that my own enthusiasm for starting a store in Houston is about to be changed in favor of Galveston. As the husband of my wife's aunt said to me, Galveston is more logical to start with anyway. And once I'm in Galveston, there's plenty of time to watch how Houston develops and to put a second store in there if there's a need for it and if I can get my goods in here without paying through the nose on freight and for the land. That's exactly what I'm going to do. I'll go back to Galveston tomorrow night. But there's another bank in town, the Houston National. Do you know anything about it?"

"Oh yes, Mr. Douglas. Mr. Dennis Claverton is the president, and he's an awfully nice and honest man. He knows about real estate, too, and he never works with Mr. Shott-lander."

"That alone is recommendation enough for me, Mrs. Fernmark. I'll see this Mr. Claverton tomorrow afternoon, then. What I may do is just arrange to put an option on a good piece of land and wait for developments, while I'm concentrating all my efforts on building a new store in Galveston. And I'm very obliged to you for telling me all this."

"I—I wanted to. You're awfully nice, and you're honest and decent—"

"Thanks. I want to stay that way. I don't think my wife would have me if I weren't, Mrs. Fernmark."

"She's a very lucky woman, Mr. Douglas. I wish—" Suddenly Alice's eyes were filled with tears and she turned her face away so that he wouldn't see them.

The young Chicagoan maintained a silence as they walked the last few blocks to Alice's sister's house, and he bade her goodnight at the door and waited until her sister opened it to let her in before, respectfully doffing his hat, he turned and walked back to his hotel.

The next morning, after breakfast, Charles Douglas set out for the city hall and requested a brief interview with Mayor Scanlan. He quickly introduced himself, then related his experiences with Arnold Shottlander and Calvin Jemmers and learned that, indeed, the City Council was planning to pay up the delinquent taxes and to acquire the property as the site of a new public school. Mayor Scanlan was a burly, bluff, genial man in his early fifties, and after Charles had related his experience of the night before, he scowled and slammed his heavy fist down on his desk with a spluttering oath. "Why, those conniving bastards! I've never liked Jemmers, he's an oily, ingratiating idiot and I've often wanted to have a look at his accounts. His bank's prosperous enough, but I don't know too much about his background. What I do know is that he's browbeaten and humiliated that poor wife of his from the very first day he came to Houston—and I haven't very much respect for a man who doesn't show consideration to his own wife. As for Shottlander, I've had wind of a couple of his shady deals, and I'm just about at the point of having the Council consider revoking his license and asking him to take his business elsewhere."

"Thanks, Mayor Scanlan. You've greatly fortified my good impression of Houston, which was just a bit blackened last night."

"I think your idea of a chain of stores is an excellent

104

one, Douglas. I for one would like to see one of them here, taking some business away from Galveston. They're too greedy down there, if you ask me. One of these days we're going to have a much better railway line, I can tell you that. Just bear with us, and maybe in a few years there'll be a Douglas Department Store in Houston. I promise you I'll be one of the first customers."

"That's good enough for me, Mayor Scanlan. Thanks again for seeing me." The two men shook hands and Charles left the city hall and directed his footsteps toward the Houston National Bank. There, for over an hour, he was closeted with wiry old Dennis Claverton, and at the end of his conference with the bank president, he had delegated the latter to act as his agent in securing a suitable piece of property for a proposed department store, to be built within a year or two. This done, he went back to Arnold Shottlander's office. Alice Fernmark, her face swollen with tears, was sitting across from her employer's desk as he entered the office. And when the realtor spied him, he snapped, "You can go to lunch now, Mrs. Fernmark."

"Why—yes, s-sir." There was a tremulous sob in her voice as she hurried out of the office, hardly glancing at Charles. Instantly, Shottlander's demeanor changed as he forced an effusive smile to his thin lips and gestured to Charles to have a seat. "Well, sir, I hope you're in a happier frame of mind this morning. Have you been touring our fair city and revising your opinion of it?"

"No, my opinion about the city is still the same, Mr. Shottlander. But I've decided to pass up that golden opportunity you wanted to foist off on me last night," was Charles's calm reply.

"I take exception to your choice of words, Mr. Douglas."

"I'm sorry, Mr. Shottlander. But you see, I went to Mayor Scanlan's office this morning, and I found out that the property you wanted me to buy for four thousand dollars is going to be purchased for about four hundred in back taxes and then made part of the Houston school system. I'm just wondering what you would have done if I'd handed over four thousand dollars last night and gotten a deed to that property? Probably tried to substitute an even choicer piece of land, I've no doubt, at a stiffer price."

"I really don't know what you're talking about—"

105

"Spare your protestations, Mr. Shottlander; I'm pretty sure of my ground, and my ground is that I don't want to do business with you and Mr. Jemmers. It's as simple as that. I'm sorry you wasted your time, and I'm sorrier that I'm indebted to you for a very fine dinner. I'd pay you back for it, if you'd entertained me in good faith. But since both of you had a swindle in mind, I feel we're about even. Good day to you, Mr. Shottlander."

"You won't get away with this—I'll see that you don't ever start a business here in Houston!" Shottlander rose from his desk, his face livid with rage.

"I'd advise you to forget these idle threats. Mayor Scanlan has had his eye on you for some little time, I gather. I wouldn't give him any more rope with which to hang you, Mr. Shottlander." Charles turned on his heel and left the office. As he did so, he glanced at his watch, frowned reflectively a moment, and then slowly began to walk back to his hotel.

When Alice Fernmark returned from an early lunch about forty-five minutes later, Arnold Shottlander beckoned her into his private office, his bony fingers gripping the edge of his desk, white to the knuckles, his face twisted in fury. "So, you bitch, you had to go and shoot your mouth off, didn't you?"

"Please, Mr. Shottlander, you don't know what you're saying—"

"Oh yes, I do! How else would that stupid bumpkin Douglas have known about the school and gone over to see Scanlan about it unless you'd tipped him off? Now don't lie, I can see it in your eyes. I'm going to teach you not to cross Arnold Shottlander, you red-haired, treacherous, sneaky little bitch, you! And when I finish with you, you know what you're going to do? You're going to go over to Calvin Jemmers and you're going to tell him that you're ready to go to bed with him—yes, you are, Mrs. Fernmark. Because if you don't, I'll have you run out of this town. I'll brand you as a whore, and I'll have the good citizens of Houston whip you and ride you out on a rail as an evil influence. Don't think I can't, I have enough power in this town. Now then, first you're going to learn your lesson."

Alice put a hand to her mouth and recoiled as he came toward her from the side of his desk, his face warped with

106

sadistic anticipation. "Please, don't—oh my God—" she sobbed as, plunging the fingers of his left hand into her thick red hair, he began to slap her face, rocking her head to and fro.

"Don't scream, there's a lot more where this came from. And you're going to get every bit of it, Alice Fernmark. And then you're going to do just what my friend Calvin wants you to; you understand me? There, you slut—you've cost Calvin and me four thousand dollars, and you're going to work it out between us, do you understand? There—" Again he struck her. Alice sank down on one knee to the floor, uttering a shriek of agony as he yanked her up by her hair and drew back his hand to strike her again.

"Let her go, Shottlander!" Charles had returned to the realtor's office, having marked away the time that he assumed Alice would be taking for lunch, and having had a presentiment that Shottlander's sadistic nature would wreak his disappointment on the unfortunate and innocent young widow.

"What the devil—you get out of here, Douglas! This is strictly a private affair—"

"Not when you brutalize a helpless woman, Shottlander! I said, let go of her!" Charles stepped forward and sent his right fist crashing against Shottlander's bony nose.

"Arrghh! My God, you've broken my nose—you bastard—oh God, I'm bleeding!" the real estate operator squealed as he stumbled back and ignominiously sat down, bumping his head against the wall. Drawing out his handkerchief, he clamped it to his broken nose, squealing with pain.

"Get up and take what's coming to you! So that's the kind of man you are, taking out your dishonesty on a helpless woman!"

"No, no, I won't fight you, you've hurt me for fair—you're a bully—get away from me or I'll have the law on you!" Shottlander whined.

"It's the other way around, Shottlander. Now listen. You're going to get out of this town and stay out. I'm going to tell Mayor Scanlan what you tried to do to Mrs. Fernmark just now. I told you he's been watching you for some little time. And he'll revoke your license, so the best thing for you is to leave while you're still reasonably healthy. And I wouldn't advise your staying anywhere in

Texas. There's no room for land swindlers in these parts."

"All right, all right, just let me be, I'll do what you want—I don't care for this goddamned town anyhow—all right, I'm going!" Shottlander babbled.

"Come outside, Mrs. Fernmark, I want to talk to you," Charles said as he helped the young woman to her feet. "Did he hurt you badly?"

"No—he—he just slapped me a lot—it—I'll be all right—oh thank God you came—" She burst into hysterical tears.

Once outside, Charles turned to her. "I've decided to start a store in Galveston right away, Mrs. Fernmark. I'd be honored if you'd come to work for me. Let me write down your address, and I'll get in touch with you when the store's ready to open. With luck, it'll be about six months."

"Mr. Douglas, I—I don't know w-what to say—" she tremulously quavered.

"I hope it'll be 'yes,'" he grinned. "Now, here's some money so you can move to Galveston when the store's ready. Also, your first month's salary of one hundred dollars and enough for room and board your first few weeks there—so you can get properly settled." He opened his wallet and took out four fifty-dollar bills.

"Oh, Mr. Douglas, that's way too much!" she gasped, drawing back.

"No, it isn't. You're going to make a marvelous sales clerk for me, Mrs. Fernmark. And I've a reputation for paying top wages for top help. Please take it."

"All—all right, t–then. I—I'd love to work for a man like you, Mr. Douglas."

"That's better." He grinned again. "I'll be in touch with you as soon as I can. And if Shottlander and Jemmers give you any more trouble, just you go to Mayor Scanlan. Well, why don't you go home now? I'll walk you back safely."

"G–God bless you, Mr. Douglas." Alice could not control the tears that flowed down her bruised cheeks. She was forlornly thinking, *Oh, dear God, if only I could find a husband like Mr. Douglas, I wouldn't be so terribly alone! And oh, what a happy, blessed woman his wife must be to have a man like him!*

CHAPTER NINE

For Luke Bouchard, now in his fifty-sixth year, life had never seemed richer or more filled with happiness and complete fulfillment. His health remained exemplary, so that he was scarcely conscious of his age and still less of the difference of twenty-five years between himself and his golden-haired wife, Laure. Indeed, last year, at an age when most men would have been contentedly anticipating the birth of a grandchild, he had fathered an exquisite little daughter, Celestine, with her mother's golden hair and gray-green eyes. And best of all, he and Laure were still ardently in love. She was completely his, and what was more, she clearly had no regrets for having given up life in the exciting and alluring city of New Orleans.

Little Paul and Lucien, Luke and Laure's older children, were thriving and a joy to both their parents. Lucien, now almost six and resembling his tall father more and more each day, was extremely articulate. The kidnapping he had endured at the hands of Luke's enemy Henri Cournier, two years before, had had no lasting ill effects. Little Paul, at three, was equally lively and showed no sign of lagging behind his elder brother. And what delighted Luke most was that both boys seemed to love the land and its beauties. In this they were following in the footsteps of old Lucien, their great-grandfather, who had found a home in the wilderness far from the bigotries and hatreds of the Old World—a place where men could live like brothers and unite in common bonds of trust and honest toil.

On a sunny morning in March 1872, Luke finished his breakfast, kissed Laure, and then lifted little Celestine in his arms and walked out to the chapel he had built to keep the vow he had made when Lucien had been returned safely to him. As he walked, he pondered the fact that some of his neighbors near Windhaven Plantation still looked askance at him, and even openly resented the black workers with whom he shared the land. Such neighbors still lived in the archaic, impractical world that had caused the Civil War. They would never accept the fact that slavery was extinct and that mankind's best hope was an open-minded tolerance which would make it possible for men to live together in harmony, regardless of their race or creed or color.

It had been seven years since the guns fell silent at Appomattox, yet a totally restorative peace had still not come to the embittered South. Here in Alabama, Luke was well aware, there was a division between the two major political parties. Worst of all, the Democrats used the detestable weapon of the Ku Klux Klan to create an aura of fear and bigotry and suspicion, as terrifying as the infamous persecution of the Holy Inquisition centuries ago. Yes, Luke knew, there were cruel excesses arising out of politics as assuredly as out of sectarian religion: each was an insidious evil because its real motivation was greed for power—power to be exercised by the self-appointed few, rather than to be shared by all the people.

Today, Luke thought with pleasure as he tenderly cradled Celestine in his arms and walked toward the chapel, he would confer with his co-owners, as he called them, and chiefly with energetic young Marius Thornton, whom he had made foreman of Windhaven Plantation. Together they would plan for the coming season. Luke planned to continue raising chickens and cattle, which he had begun last year and which had proved so profitable an enterprise. And he would plant a wide variety of crops. The markets in Montgomery and Lowndesboro would take a good deal of the crops and the meat and dairy products; the rest would be shipped down the Alabama River to Mobile. Luke would plant less cotton this year than last: the price was far too low to justify tying up too many acres in its production. Luke thought ruefully of how the arable land of the Carolinas, Georgia, and Virginia had been ruined by incessant planting of cotton and tobacco, and he was resolved not to make the same mistake here on Windhaven Plantation.

How curious it was, Luke thought as he bent his head to kiss the prattling baby girl on the forehead and to smile tenderly at her, that people so often failed to profit from the mistakes of the past. Most of the early settlers in the South had been, like old Lucien, men who were close to the soil, planters and cultivators. Surely they had learned while still in Europe that one gave the soil new life by letting it lie fallow or by rotating crops. Yet, knowing that, they had eagerly seized upon the rich, moist soil of Virginia, the Carolinas, and Georgia, and had obsessively planted only a single crop until the land was exhausted. Then they were forced to profit from the breeding and selling of human beings into bondage—a bondage that had been dissolved at last in the blazing crucible of a civil war that left the South devastated and impoverished.

What might have happened if these early planters had brought to the South the same concern they had shown to the land in Europe? What if they had also developed some kind of industry that permitted them to be self-reliant and industrious? What if they had never yielded to the luxury of forcing black slaves to do their menial work—slaves who were paid only by the lash, denied the right to an education and even to marry in a faith of their own choosing? What if there had been no Civil War—what might this young nation not have achieved as it now neared its centennial?

Deep in thought, his tall, erect figure touched by the bright rays of morning sunshine, Luke Bouchard entered the little chapel and at once knelt down, kissing Celestine and closing his eyes as he devoutly prayed. His prayer was one of gratitude and thanksgiving for the bounties of a merciful and just God, not only to Laure and himself and their children, but to all of the Bouchards. And it was a prayer, too, in memory of those who had gone on before: Lucy, his beloved first wife, valiant old Lucien, courageous Sybella, the faithful Mandingo Djamba and his wife, Celia, and Fleurette, whose life had been snuffed out tragically at so young an age. But there was in this prayer not so much sadness as thanksgiving, as he thought of those who had pioneered in the early days of Windhaven and lived lives of courage and unswerving faith in one another. These brave people were the strength of his family's heritage, an inspiration to all the Bouchards who lived now in Texas, in Chicago, and in the forsaken Indian Territory, where Dr.

Ben Wilson was beginning a new life dedicated to the memory of his gentle Fleurette.

Raising his eyes to the altar, Luke spoke aloud, "Blessed Lord, know my thanks and my undying gratitude for Your bounteous blessings upon all of us. Grant that the children of my body and Laure's and sweet Lucy's turn always to Thee in their own trials and tribulations, knowing full well how just and merciful Thou art to those who revere and abide Thy holy spirit. Grant that my little daughter, Celestine, will grow to womanhood and have her own family who will continue in Thy ways, charitable to all, willfully harming none, and bearing malice toward no one in the world, even their enemies. Forearm and guide her as you have done all the Bouchards, and hear the prayer now of one who is contrite and humble in the knowledge of Thine eternal powers. Amen."

He made the sign of the cross on his forehead and over Celestine's, and then rose and left the chapel.

After he had taken the little girl back to Laure, he went into the study where Marius Thornton was waiting. The glow on Marius's face told him that his foreman had good news to relate, and so, with a gentle smile and nod, he waited to hear Marius's news before he turned to the matter of the work to be done on Windhaven Plantation.

"Mr. Luke, Clemmie's going to have another baby by fall, she just told me!" Marius exclaimed. "I swear, Mr. Luke, back when you saved my hide in New Orleans, I never dreamed a man could be so happy and have a family like I've got—I'm just grateful to God and to you, Mr. Luke, I have to say it!"

Greatly touched, Luke nodded, turning aside so that Marius could not see the sudden mistiness in his eyes. Already his prayer in the chapel was being answered. Clearing his throat after a moment, he said, "I'm happy for you, Marius. God has truly been very good to us. And now, let's talk about how we're going to use the land this year. We may want to make some changes in the crops."

"I've got some ideas of my own, Mr. Luke."

"Go ahead, Marius. You know I'm always open to suggestions—and yours have been particularly successful over the years."

"Well, Mr. Luke, I was thinking we might start raising more pigs, and I'd clear away some of the land and build a

112

big pig pen. There's a good price for pork, at least that's what Mr. Sattersfield tells me over at his store in Lowndesboro."

"Well, he'd be a good customer for pork. And then we could have a smokehouse too, couldn't we?"

"We sure could, Mr. Luke! Pork chops and sweet yams—why, that's almost a national Southern dish, Mr. Luke, and if we have nice young pigs out of our get, we can get a fair to middling price, I'm certain of it."

"All right. Why don't you see if you can buy about four good sows and two pedigreed boars, Marius. There's money enough in our reserve fund for expanding what we're going to do this year."

"Yes, there is, Mr. Luke. We had a good year last year, and I've looked at the books—I always do that before we talk about what we're going to do next—and we're in good shape."

"Fine. And the chickens did very well last year, so we'll just let Katie Munroe take charge of them this year, too. We'll increase her flock, and that way we'll have more eggs, too. Mr. Judpath, that Montgomery butcher, will buy just about everything we can sell him."

"Judging by what he did last year, Mr. Luke, that's for certain!" Marius chuckled.

"How many head of cattle do we have right now, Marius?"

"Let's see—two bulls and a dozen cows and, right now, about fifteen-sixteen calves, I'd say right off, without looking at the ledger."

"That's very good. We'll be able to sell more cream and milk and butter, except during those weeks when the cows are freshening. And those cows that aren't producing can be sold for beef to Mr. Judpath too, and some of the meat to Mr. Sattersfield as well."

"Yes, Mr. Luke. You know, we put up a fence on the other side of the house, just beyond the creek there, because it's good grazing land for the cattle. And that way they don't take up any of the plantation acreage we're using for our melons and snap beans and yams and such."

"Well, if you build that smokehouse big enough, Marius, and Buford Phelps will be glad to help you do it, you'll be able to cure beef as well as pork, I'd say," Luke suggested.

"That's right, Mr. Luke. I'll talk to Buford about it. Weather hasn't been too bad, so far. Not as much rain as we were afraid of. What do you think about cotton?"

"I think we should reduce the cotton crop, Marius. Come to think of it, I'd just as soon not raise any cotton at all this year. The price is as low as it was just before the war, and there's hardly any profit to it once you figure your baling and shipping charges. I'd say the English mills are getting a surfeit of cotton from the West Indies, and it's cutting into our profits. Besides, I don't like the look of the money situation right now, and I'd much rather spend what capital I have for equipment and feed that would turn out a suitable profit when we're finished with our marketing."

"I'm with you, Mr. Luke. Well, sir, I'll tell all the others in the morning, then, what you've decided on."

"That's fine. I'll talk to them too, Marius. Oh, by the way, when you go into town the next time, get Clemmie something pretty. Maybe a shawl or a little bracelet or something she'd like. And be sure you charge it to my account."

"Mr. Luke, you're the most generous man I ever met. God bless you. Now I'd best get back to her."

"How's little Sheba?"

"Smart as anything, Mr. Luke, talking away and playing with the toys I make her, bright as her mother and just as sweet!"

"That's wonderful, Marius. Give Clemmie my regards. I'll see you tomorrow, then."

That evening, Luke and Laure were hosts to Dalbert Sattersfield and his charming wife, Mitzi, who brought along their twin boys, Courtney and Brandon, eight months old. Mitzi was radiantly happy, and from the devoted looks she sent her courteous and self-effacing husband, it was obvious that she adored him. From his place at the head of the table, Luke exchanged a knowing look with Laure and told himself that here again was a sign that all was well with everyone who dwelt within the sphere of Windhaven Plantation.

Shortly after breakfast the next morning, Luke Bouchard went out into the fields where Dan and Katie Munroe, Hughie Mendicott, Moses and Mary Turner, and Bu-

114

ford Phelps were already waiting for him. Hannah Atbury stood beside Hughie, whom she had married after the death of her former husband, Phineas. It was a marriage that greatly consoled her, for she found that Hughie's two lanky, teenaged sons, Davie and Louis, idolized her and gave her late in life the children she had never been able to have with Phineas.

Marius Thornton, as foreman, addressed the group, outlining the ideas he had discussed with Luke the day before, and then Luke explained his reasons for proposing them. There was unanimous agreement, and each of the workers expressed pleasure in knowing exactly what he or she was to do in the months ahead.

Luke gratefully thanked them for their vote of confidence, and as they went back to their chores, he said to Marius, "How I wish Grandfather could have been here today to see and hear all this enthusiasm for our future work! It was what he always dreamed of, working in harmony on the good land, which never betrays you if you are honest with it. Well, Marius, I'm going to ride into Montgomery this afternoon: I want to see old Jedidiah Danforth about the Bambach property. Also, I'll confess I'm anxious to find out how my adopted son, Lopasuta, is getting along in the little house Danforth was able to rent for him."

"He's sure a fine man, Mr. Luke," Marius declared as they strode back to the red-brick chateau. "Getting hisself quite a reputation as a lawyer, isn't he?"

"Yes, that pleases me very much. When he won that case for poor old Joseph Trenton against the arrogant carpetbagger, I wrote Sangrodo to tell him that I had kept my promise of friendship to help this young man with Comanche blood in his veins. I told him, too, that Lopasuta had brought great honor to Sangrodo and his tribe, and would continue to bring even more, which I'm certain of. Well, Marius, I'd be grateful if you'd saddle my horse. I'll ride out right after lunch."

"He'll be waiting for you in the stable, Mr. Luke."

"Thanks, Marius. By the way, do we need any more supplies from Montgomery? If you don't have too big a list, I can bring something back with me."

"No, Mr. Luke, we're fine, bless you. Besides, Dan and I'll be going into Montgomery the end of this week, like as not. And while we're there, we'll just mosey around and see if we can't drum up more business for the good things we're going to grow here on Windhaven Plantation."

"Now I know why I made you my foreman, Marius," Luke smilingly rejoined.

Jedidiah Danforth was in his sixty-fifth year, stooped and frail, but the unquenchable vitality of his mind and the keen look in his blue eyes belied his infirmities. He rose with alacrity from his chair as Luke Bouchard entered, and came forward to shake hands warmly with his visitor. "You're a sight for sore eyes, Luke!" was his greeting. "I'm glad you stopped by today. I have news that will please you, I rather think."

"By now, Jedidiah, each of us is able to read the other's mind," Luke smilingly quipped as he seated himself and waited for the white-haired lawyer to expatiate.

"Well, sir, I have been able to transfer the deed of the land that old Horatio Bambach had over to his daughter's husband, Andy Haskins. Matter of fact," he uttered a reedy little cackle of pleasure, "I finagled a joint deed so that both Jessica and Andy will show ownership. It'll be just about the first time in Alabama, so far as my memory serves me—and I go back a long way, as you know—that a woman's got even a sniff at title to land in her name."

"That's a fine present for their anniversary, Jedidiah. I'm very grateful to you."

"But I haven't forgotten your grandfather, Luke, don't think for a minute I have. There's less resentment now toward old-line Southerners—matter of fact, I can feel it in the wind, now that a big election's coming up. There's more Republican sentiment than I've heard around these parts for quite some time, and that's all to the good. Meaning, as your lawyer, that it won't be long before I think I can have your co-owners, as you so euphemistically call them, deed back all their plots of land to you. So then, as you see, Windhaven Plantation will be completely resored to what it was before the war."

Luke rose from his chair and walked over to the window. A sudden emotion had gripped him, and for a long moment he could not trust himself to speak. He stared out at the courthouse across the way and saw the statue of Jefferson Davis on horseback in the square. Seeing it brought back all the bitter memories of the long war that

116

had vitiated the strength of the South and decimated its youth. The cause had been gallant but tragically impractical. And yet, just seven years after, things seemed to have come full cycle: what old Lucien had achieved in the years of serene peace and growth could now be restored. And thus he, Luke Bouchard, the grandson of that indomitable pioneer, could at last fulfill the promise that he had long ago made beside the grave atop the towering red bluff that fronted the winding Alabama River.

At last he turned back to face the lawyer, who was shrewdly staring at him, half-turned in his chair to watch his client's reaction to this news. "God bless you, Jedidiah," Luke hoarsely said, "you've made a dream come true, a dream and a promise."

"I know what you mean, Luke." Jedidiah's voice was strangely gentle. "Now, as to the legal details, each sales contract will stipulate that for one dollar and other good and valuable consideration, the holder of thus and so plot of land turns over to you full title. Thus, all of it will be completely in the Bouchard name."

"They'll get much more than a dollar, be sure of that, Jedidiah," Luke declared. "I've discussed this with them many times over the last year or two. They'll go on working the land, and they'll be paid a full share of the profits that all of us glean from the total acreage. My name on the deed won't change that. All it really means, Jedidiah, is that when I die, my sons will inherit Windhaven Plantation intact, the way it was before my grandfather died. And then theirs will be the task of strengthening and developing and making the most of the assets that are bequeathed to them. Given their own will and courage and wisdom, and with God's help, they will have an opportunity to build Windhaven into a legacy for generations to come, and that is the richest gift in my power to give. So that's what your pieces of legal paper are going to do for the Bouchards, Jedidiah. It's no wonder I can't find the words to thank you."

"Come now, don't be so melodramatic," Jedidiah cackled again, but his own eyes were suspiciously moist as he turned back to his desk and shuffled the sheaf of contracts he had already prepared. "I'm just your lawyer and these contracts are perfectly routine, nothing out of the ordinary.

117

You'll find scores of them over at the courthouse any time you want to go through the records."

"You old scoundrel." Luke laughingly made a fist and brushed the lawyer's shoulder in mock retaliation. "You can call them routine if you want to, but I've a different term for them. And now, how's my adopted son doing?"

"Brilliantly, Luke. As you know, I was able to find him a little house down at the end of Ellender Road, at the south end of town. The rent's only twenty dollars a month, not too stiff for a gifted young practitioner of the law who's already beginning to attract considerable attention from his older colleagues. Jealous attention, too, I might add."

"Oh?" Luke frowned. "Care to explain that, Jedidiah?"

"Well, you could have expected it. Here's a boy, part Comanche and part Mexican, whom you adopt. That alone's enough to cause plenty of comment, in a small Southern town, with all of its hidebound traditions and prejudices—which the war hasn't entirely changed, you have to admit. Then he goes and stirs up controversy by sending a carpetbagger off with his tail between his legs and upholding the law in favor of what we used to call nigger slaves. That didn't set well with a few lawyers who would just as soon attract only carpetbagger business."

"I know. And that's the danger."

"Well, he's had a few cases in torts and done just as well as he did with his first real case. And the blacks are flocking to him because he doesn't charge them too much and because he's honest and decent. He can talk their language so they can understand the law and not be frightened of it."

"That's all to the good."

"Of course it is, man!" Jedidiah testily exclaimed. "But what I'm afraid of is that it might just get him the attention of the Ku Klux Klan. We've got a few scoundrels high in office and wealth in Montgomery who haven't forgotten how to hate, and they still hate blacks. And of course they're bound to hate a half-breed lawyer who's beating them out of business week after week. Don't worry any, I'm keeping watch over him. And he's a strong, smart young man quite capable of taking care of himself in a fight."

"Well, I'm glad you told me. Before I go back to

Lowndesboro this evening, I'll ride over there and wish him well. Not only that, I'll tell him that he's been delinquent in not visiting his adoptive parents—it's been a good two weeks since he last had dinner with Laure and me."

"Give him my best regards. Now then, who's that knocking at the door? I wasn't expecting any clients this afternoon." Jedidiah rose from his chair and, scowling at the interruption, walked over to the door and opened it. "Well, now." His manner swiftly changed to one of affability. "Come in, gentlemen. And I'll bet the fee for my next two cases that I know why you're here."

"Well, this is certainly a pleasant surprise!" Luke came forward to shake hands with the three men whom he had met at the outset of the 1870 election. There was William Blount, a portly man in his late fifties; Ebenezer Tolman, a tall, bony-faced man of about the same age as Blount; and Clarence Hartung, now in his early fifties, short, bespectacled, and nearly bald. They were the men who had persuaded him to be the Republican candidate for the Montgomery County seat in the state legislature, a debut into politics that had been unsuccessful due to the evil machinations of Barnabas McMillan. Luke would not soon forget what this sinister carpetbagger had done. He had managed to force Laure's dependable nurse into resigning her post and had put his own mistress *pro tem*, Stacey Holbrook, in her place. When Laure had found Stacey spying on the household and writing letters to McMillan, Stacey had kicked her in the belly and caused her miscarriage. Barnabas McMillan jokingly promised to marry Stacey in return for her aid in defeating Luke, but when his opponent, the black Democratic candidate, won the election, he refused to keep that promise. Stacey then came to his house, killed him, and disappeared.

"It's good to see you again, Mr. Bouchard." William Blount heartily shook hands with old Lucien's grandson. "You see, Clarence and Ebenezer and I saw your horse tied up outside to Jedidiah's rail. Fact is, we were thinking of calling on you the next day or two, but here was a golden opportunity and so we marched right in."

"You flatter me greatly, gentlemen. But why would you want to see me again?" Luke humorously asked.

"Help yourself to chairs there from the table in the library," Jedidiah Danforth waved his hand toward the adjacent room. "You make me uncomfortable, standing like that. And you make me feel older, too, dagnabit!"

"Still the same old Jedidiah," Clarence Hartung chuckled. "The sharpest and the smartest lawyer in town, that's what I've always said."

"Thank you for that much. All right, now, I'll just do my work and pretend you gentlemen aren't here, so you're at liberty to use my office to transact your business—and what it is, I can certainly guess." The old lawyer winked at the trio as he busied himself with his papers at the desk.

"You put up a fine fight two years ago, Mr. Bouchard," William Blount came directly to the point. "So good, in fact, that the three of us would like to ask you to consider running again on the Republican ticket in this year's election. Your opponent, Cletus Adams, has been directed by his Democratic bosses to step down. He certainly hasn't distinguished himself during his term in the legislature. He's taken to drink and women a little too obviously. There are plenty of good men, even if they aren't Republicans, who don't like the idea of a black man flaunting his carpetbagger-bestowed legislative powers by showing that all he cares about is dissipation. Not that they wouldn't have the same disregard for him if he were white, I hasten to add."

"Gentlemen, you can't really be serious in wanting me to try my hand at politics again. I'm flattered, as I was then, and I'm grateful that you would think of me. But I made my wife a promise that I'd never do it again." Luke's face hardened. "I also remember that my wife was needlessly and very cruelly involved—"

"I know, I know, Mr. Bouchard," Ebenezer Tolman broke in, shaking his head, "it was a damnable thing for that fellow McMillan to do, and he deserved exactly what he got in the end. But this time, things are a little different in the county. I'd like to point them out to you."

"I'd like to hear what's happening in politics these days, too, Mr. Tolman. But I'll tell you in advance that it probably won't change my mind. When I make a promise to my wife, I generally keep it," Luke replied, the directness of his answer eased with a gracious and candid smile.

"Let me spell it out for you, Mr. Bouchard, and maybe you'll see why we're so anxious to have you on the ticket

120

this time. Yes, sir, even more than two years ago. You know that since our present Democratic governor, Mr. Lindsay, took office fifteen months ago, he has got himself involved with railroad construction to such an extent that it has paralyzed the General Assembly of the state. Right now, loyal Democrats are torn between a desire to repudiate the bonds that aided the Republican-controlled Alabama and Chattanooga Railroad and the necessity to protect the credit reputation of our state."

Ebenezer Tolman paused, looked thoughtful, then went on. "I'd better give you some background—though I think it may be familiar to you already. About four years ago, a group of Boston capitalists headed by John C. Stanton got control of the old Willis Valley Railroad. There was some reshuffling and merging of lines, and ultimately the Alabama and Chattanooga Railroad was organized."

"Yes, I'm familiar with that history," Luke nodded.

"Yes, and of course you know that after the Alabama and Chattanooga was organized, Stanton—in his position as general superintendent of the railroad—persuaded our legislature at the time to raise the state endorsement of railroad bonds from twelve to sixteen thousand dollars per mile, and this helped the Alabama and Chattanooga enormously. Most of the money to build that line, in fact, came from the sale of the state-endorsed bonds."

"I read that too, in the *Advertiser*," Luke commented.

"Everyone knows it, but the sad fact is that our Republican governor at the time, William Smith, was as heedless of his responsibilities as the legislature was corrupt. He failed to block the legislature on the matter of state aid for the railroads; as a matter of fact, when his administration was over, the record shows that he had endorsed over five million dollars' worth of bonds, a great deal more than legally permitted for a completed line of two hundred and ninety-five miles."

"I hadn't realized it was that bad." Luke shook his head.

"Well, it was. The whole state government was undermined by the railroads. Let me just mention some examples. In February of 1870, Stanton got a direct loan of two million in state bonds, bribing state legislators while the bill was under consideration. Well, the Democratic railroad promoters thought they might as well get their shares, so wholesale bribery of legislators for railroad favors became an epidemic. Then in May of that year, the Alabama and Chattanooga Railroad reached the limit of all the bonds to which it was legally entitled. But Stanton persuaded Governor Smith to endorse an additional half million dollars in bonds, Stanton claiming to a firm of Philadelphia bankers that he would use the loan to pay the interest due the bondholders as of January 1, 1871. Instead, he used that loan trying to complete the Alabama and Chattanooga."

"It's unsavory history."

"Yes, it's that and more, Mr. Bouchard," Blount declared. "Right now, you see, the problem is that Governor Lindsay, in trying to deal with the situation his predecessor bequeathed to him, has made a compromise decision: to stand behind some of these questionable bonds and to make three of the interest payments. Such an arrangement satisfies no one, certainly not the schemers. And naturally, it offends honest men who want our state credit to be impeccable. Why, even people from his own party have gone so far as to accuse Governor Lindsay of selling out to Stanton and his associates, and they say that he doesn't have nerve or backbone or common sense. So you see, Mr. Bouchard, this state is ripe for a political realignment this spring. There's a new Republican organization, the Liberal Republican movement, that is working on the national level to oppose the corruption of the Grant administration. It was started by the nephew of the late Confederate General Sterling Price of Missouri, Thomas H. Price, who settled in Mobile back in 1865, and it should have some influence throughout the state. The Democrats, meanwhile, are just about deciding to nominate as Lindsay's successor another Mobile man, Thomas Hord Herndon, who was an outright secessionist at the start of the Civil War."

"I should think," Luke cautiously offered, "that all these signs point to a pretty good chance for loyal Republicans in Alabama."

"Exactly!" Clarence Hartung excitedly spoke up, half rising from his chair to emphasize his point. "And loyal Republicans will rally to a man who has always stood for honesty and fairness, without vindictiveness or secret affiliations of any kind—a man like you, Mr. Bouchard."

Luke Bouchard walked over to the window and again looked out toward the public square. Finally, he turned back to the three politicians. "I must refuse, gentlemen, though I'm deeply grateful for your trust and confidence in me. What I will do—and all I can do because of the promise I made my wife two years ago—is to agree to campaign for your candidate wherever I have the opportunity. That I will assuredly do, if of course your candidate is a man whose views and aims are compatible with my own political opinions. And I will campaign steadfastly and with all the energy I possess, because I, too, am aghast at the corruption of President Grant's administration that has spread to our own state."

"Now that sounds like a campaign speech right there!" Ebenezer Tolman smilingly exclaimed.

But Luke shook his head. "It's not that at all, gentlemen. I told my wife, Laure, that henceforth I should occupy myself with the production of food for the people who need it and with the well-being of those hardworking and loyal companions who share the land with me. I have very little vanity—perhaps if I had more, I might be tempted by your very flattering proposal. But a promise made is a promise kept, and that has always been the Bouchard credo."

The three politicians exchanged a rueful look. Then William Blount came to Luke and offered his hand. "It's a damned shame for this county and this state, Mr. Bouchard, but so far as I'm concerned, and I know I speak for Ebenezer and Clarence, I'm proud to know a man like you. And yes, we'll be only too happy to accept whatever aid you can give us to bring about a fair election of a good, sound Republican who can change the pattern of bribery and corruption and redeem the reputation of our state."

CHAPTER TEN

Luke Bouchard dismounted and tied the reins of his horse to a wooden rail outside the little frame house Jedidiah Danforth had rented for Lopasuta, whose name in Comanche meant "He who is Wise." As Luke mounted the steps to the porch, he thought to himself that the Comanches had a genius for identifying an individual with a most appropriate name. For Lopasuta, now twenty-four, the son of a Mexican mother and a Comanche father, had passed the bar in Montgomery and had already achieved a considerable reputation in the little more than a year in which he had practiced before the Montgomery courts. He had brought honor to his tribe as well as to Luke, his adoptive father. In taking legal action to make Lopasuta his adopted son, Luke Bouchard had paid tribute both to his beloved grandfather who had shared his life with the Creeks and to Sangrodo, his blood brother and his lifelong friend.

At Luke's brisk knock, the half-breed opened the door. "Mr. Bouchard!" he exclaimed—for he still often called Luke by his last name, out of respect. "Welcome to my humble dwelling. You do me great honor by your visit."

"I came, if you must know, Lopasuta," Luke smiled, "to tell you that Laure and I haven't seen much of you lately. And she asked me to invite you to dinner tomorrow night."

"I shall certainly come. Believe me, it is only that I have been very busy with the cases that are given to me—I want so much to make a good name for myself so that I can help those who need me," Lopasuta earnestly explained.

"I know that very well. I'm very proud of you, and you bring credit to my name as well as to that of your tribe. I have written to Sangrodo to tell him how well you are doing here in Montgomery and how you defend the oppressed and the downtrodden—that will please him most,

125

since he, proudest chief of an indomitable tribe, is now regarded as little more than an outlaw by our unenlightened government. But he will know, in his stronghold in Mexico, that you keep the faith and that many men of different races have already learned to respect you, young though you are," Luke gravely told him.

"You must not praise me so. I am still very young and I have much to learn. But I am trying very hard, and Mr. Danforth has been almost like a father to me," Lopasuta explained as he led the way into the kitchen. "Will you share food with me or at least some coffee? It is only right that I give you hospitality in return for all that you have given me, and I shall be always in your debt."

"Father and son do not talk of debts, Lopasuta," was Luke's candid reply. "I'll ride back to the chateau, to have dinner, but I'll be happy to have a cup of coffee with you now. Tell me, do your neighbors on this street treat you well?"

Lopasuta shrugged. "Most of them stare at me and they do not say much, but I know what they are thinking. They can see that I am dark-skinned, not black, but not white either. And they have heard about me, because they read the newspaper each day, and sometimes there are stories about the cases I handle. Sometimes I feel they think of me as a stranger in their world, and they want to shut me out."

"That's only natural. People are inclined to distrust what and whom they don't understand, Lopasuta. But you are stronger than they, you have a better mind and more opportunities to display it. You will not let such hostility defeat you, any more than Sangrodo would."

Lopasuta's eyes shone as he nodded. "To him I owe most of all, and I shall never forget this. If he had not taken notice of me and written about me to you, I should not have this chance to speak for those who have no one else to speak for them, to see that justice is done under these white-eyes laws which I am still striving to grasp. There are so many of them, and some of them seem so silly."

"Yes, it's true, Lopasuta," Luke chuckled, as he sipped his coffee. "The statute books are always in need of revision. There are old laws based on fears and superstitions and traditions, and sometimes the lawmakers forget to

126

catch up with them, and let them stand on the books. And then sometimes injustice is done instead of justice. But you will see these things, because you look for them. I've just come from Mr. Danforth's office, and he wants me to give you his best wishes."

"I wish him well. He's a kind old man, a stern teacher, but a very good one. But I think he is ill now and growing old," Lopasuta said.

"That's true. We all grow old and there's no remedy for it. Except to keep an open, youthful mind; that alone can defeat the aging of the flesh. But that's not going to be your problem for many long years, Lopasuta. Well, now, thank you for the coffee, and I'll be riding back. Remember, Laure and I expect you tomorrow night."

"I shall be there."

"One day, Lopasuta, you will feel that you belong. You will find some girl who will not care what blood is in your veins, but see in you only a good, honorable man who can bring her happiness. It will come, be patient. I myself am doubly blessed. God gave me a lovely, gentle wife in Lucy, and when she died, He solaced me with Laure. So now, when I am more than twice your age, Lopasuta, I can feel as young as you because I have a family and a young wife who will not let me think of aging and growing stodgy of mind and purpose." He held out his hand, and the tall young man earnestly shook it as they parted.

Before he rode back home to the red-brick chateau, Luke stopped at the office of the *Advertiser* for a copy of the newspaper. He read that Congress had just passed an act to establish Yellowstone National Park. That was a good omen, he thought. There were others in this country who looked upon land as a priceless heritage, to be tendered to the generation ahead and to be safeguarded against waste and usurpation. Old Lucien Bouchard would surely have approved of this investment in the future.

Through April and May, the weather was warm and pleasant in Alabama, and there were long days of work in the fields of Windhaven Plantation. Luke, as old Lucien before him, tainted by no false sense of superiority, worked in the fields alongside the black co-owners of the land that his grandfather had earned from the bounty of the Creeks. It was as if time had been set back and Luke himself were

127

in the little town of Yves-sur-lac, Normandy, working beside the peasants in the fields and experiencing the same joy of tilling the soil that old Lucien had known more than eighty years earlier. By the end of the day, Luke's shirt was unbuttoned almost to the waist, and his body was wet with the sweat of his labor. He exulted in it and it made him feel again like the young man he had been when his father, Henry Bouchard, had grudgingly appointed him as overseer on the plantation. But there was this subtle difference: he was now not an overseer of men, but a co-worker with them, grateful for the strength, at his mature age, to keep up with men younger than himself.

Then, in the evening, after he had bathed and changed his clothes, Luke would become again a father and a husband. He would visit his children in the nursery, taking delight in Laure's natural and instinctive joy in them. When the children had been put to bed, he would come to Laure's bed as her husband, her romantic wooer. Yet even in his ecstasies with the golden-haired woman, he did not forget the gentle, soft-spoken Lucy, his first love, who had shared his tribulations. He knew that, in a sense, she was a part of all his work to reestablish Windhaven as a legacy for generations to come.

The spring was warm and benevolent in Alabama this year, and Luke Bouchard was overjoyed to see that his projects for developing a versatile and profitable agricultural commune on Windhaven Plantation were moving to fruition. Dalbert Sattersfield had contracted to buy half of the eggs and chickens for his store in Lowndesboro plus a third of all the pork that could be slaughtered and cured. The butcher in Montgomery bid for most of the remainder, and Marius Thornton, thanks to his several visits to Montgomery, was able to contact other greengrocers who wanted to buy milk and cream. So promising, indeed, were these first signs of acceptance of Windhaven's bounty, that Marius was obliged to buy two more supply wagons, which could be driven to Montgomery or Lowndesboro two or three times a week to transfer the merchandise. The regular flow of weekly revenue from the merchants and Dalbert Sattersfield kept Marius equally busy with the ledger, which showed increasing profits, allocated by proportion to those who had a hand in the production and sale of each product. They sold melons and okra and snap beans as well as tomatoes and lettuce to the merchants of both towns, yet there was ample left to be shipped even more profitably down to Mobile every fortnight.

True to his pledge to the three enthusiastic Republican politicians who had urged him to run again for the state legislature, Luke wrote several letters to the *Advertiser* reiterating his views and calling for a new coalition of political forces in the state, to work toward honesty and integrity in government. He pointed out that the record of the Democrats was besmirched by their use of the sinister Ku Klux Klan and that it was essential for those who wished to preserve the rights of the state of Alabama to vote the Republican ticket as a sign of strong unity which alone could defeat the malevolent and violent forces of the illegal Klan.

On May 1, the Liberal Republicans met in a national convention at Cincinnati and nominated Horace Greeley for the presidency and B. Gratz Brown, the Missouri governor, as vice-president. At that convention, the Liberal Republicans denounced the Democratic state nominations as being a "great hindrance to the progress of liberalism" in Alabama; a vote for the Democratic ticket, they said, would really be a vote for the Ku Klux Klan.

Three weeks later, to Luke's great delight, Congress passed the Amnesty Act, which removed political disability from practically all those who had been excluded from office by the Fourteenth Amendment. This, indeed, was a definite concession to liberal and reform-minded Republicans. When the news appeared in the *Advertiser,* William Blount rode to the red-brick chateau and earnestly urged Luke to reconsider.

"No, Mr. Blount," Luke replied, "I told you what my answer would be when you and your two friends first came to me, and I haven't changed my mind. I'm going to keep my promise to my wife. Of course, I'll do all I can to campaign for this ticket by talking to my neighbors and by continuing to write letters to the *Advertiser.* But I expressly forbid my name to appear upon the ticket."

"That's a great pity, Mr. Bouchard," William Blount conceded sadly, "because there isn't a man in this entire state who's more honest and deserving than you, sir. I've read every one of your letters, and they only increase my desire to have you take a second look at this affair, to re-consider. You've already pointed out the corruption in President Grant's cabinet. Well, we here in Alabama are at the mercy of Federal patronage. Only by electing honest men to run our state can we avoid the taint of the national party."

"I'll admit that to you, Mr. Blount. I deplore the men that Ulysses Grant has surrounded himself with, and I agree that you have to have a strong and unified ticket to make sure that national party corruption doesn't take over in our state. But I'll never go back on my word, as you certainly know by now. Indeed, I see no reason why you shouldn't propose yourself for the ticket. You're as honest a man as I've ever met, and I'd be the first to support you."

"That's very flattering, Mr. Bouchard. But I am too old and tired, and I haven't the reputation that you do."

"I'll suggest a name to you. You've heard me talk about Andy Haskins, a Southerner who lost his arm in the war. I found him in New Orleans; he came with me to Wind-haven Range and he was a loyal, hard worker. Now he owns land, he's married a Southern girl, and he'll have a family. The Amnesty Act would certainly clear him for having served the Confederacy as a soldier. He's young, decent, and courageous. You could do much worse than to choose a man like that."

"Now that's not a bad idea. And there's certainly a good deal of sentimental interest in someone who was handi-capped by the war and yet managed to rise above it and to make a new life for himself." William Blount's eyes bright-ened. "Perhaps I'll have a talk with this Andy Haskins of yours."

"He's not my Andy Haskins, Mr. Blount, he's his own man. Yes, by all means, talk to him. It's true he wasn't born in Alabama, but he loves the South and he was never really on the side of slavery. He's worked hard all his life, and just like myself and my grandfather before me, he knows what can be done on the land by hard work and devotion."

And so, an hour later, William Blount tethered his horse to the wooden rail in front of the little house where Andy and Jessica Haskins lived.

He found Andy in the fields, working alongside his men,

in an ecstatic mood because Jessica had shyly told him that very morning that they were going to have a child. Andy had told her that if it was a boy, they'd name it after her beloved father, Horatio.

The young Southerner's jaw dropped as soon as Blount began to state the reason for his visit. "You must be joking, Mr. Blount!" he gasped. "Me run for the state legislature? You're joking—I'm just a farmhand, that's all."

"Not according to Mr. Luke Bouchard, Mr. Haskins," the politician smilingly corrected. "You've got a lot in your favor. You lost an arm in the war, you've settled on good Alabama land, and you're tilling it along with your workers. You have a wife and, from what you've just told me, a family coming. All those things will get votes for you, Mr. Haskins. You're young, enthusiastic, and you've got a clear idea as to what you think our state government should be—an honest one."

"That's the only kind I'd ever vote for."

"Exactly. And you can be part of it. I'm not asking for a decision today, Mr. Haskins, but talk it over with your wife, and I'll be riding out here again in a week to get your answer."

"But I haven't got any money for a political campaign, Mr. Blount."

"Don't you worry about that. My friends and I do, and if we have a winner, we'll back him. Just think about it, Mr. Haskins. Well, sir, it's been a pleasure meeting you, and you'll see me again next week."

As he rode off, Andy stared uncomprehendingly and then shook his head. He'd have to tell Jessica right away. Being asked to run for office was a wonderful honor, whether or not he chose to accept it. And yet now that Alabama was his home and Jessica was with child, maybe it made some sense, after all. Maybe he could have a hand in shaping the future of the state that had been so badly torn by war and corruption; maybe he could help make it a place where there would be lots of farms run as well as Luke Bouchard's wonderful Windhaven Plantation. . . .

The day after the Amnesty Act was passed by Congress, the Workingmen's National Convention met in New York City to nominate Ulysses S. Grant for his second term as president and Henry Wilson of Massachusetts as his running mate. When Luke read of this, he knew that Grant's own National Republican Party would almost certainly offer him the nomination when it convened in Philadelphia in June. It was disturbing to Luke that the corrupt Grant administration might be given another four years in which to undermine the national morality as well as the national economy.

But even more disturbing to Luke than the political news was a series of letters, some of them anonymously signed, which began to appear in the *Advertiser*. These letters attacked his adopted son, Lopasuta, and in so doing slurred the Bouchard name.

One such appeared in the issue of May 25 and read as follows:

It is time we free white citizens of Montgomery protested against the laws that allow an Indian to practice law in Montgomery. There is such a one here, whose origin was bypassed because of the backing of a certain scalawag who ran two years ago for the state legislature and who was properly defeated. We should like to question the motives of this scalawag in adopting an Indian whose kinfolk not very long ago massacred law-abiding, peaceful white citizens in the western part of this country. Old Andy Jackson had the right idea about getting the Indians out of Alabama, but now we have another one and he's a lawyer. This ought to be investigated because, just as the old saying goes, justice is often blind.

E Pluribus Unum

When Luke read that letter at the dinner table, his face became taut with anger and he crumpled the page with a silent imprecation. Laure understandingly put her hand on his and murmured, "There will always be small-minded people to malign anyone who's different, my darling. Lopasuta won't mind it, and you know it won't keep him from becoming the best lawyer Montgomery ever had, thanks to you. We're both proud of him—and darling, I'm very proud of you too, especially in keeping your promise that you won't run for politics again. I want you with me. I love you more than ever—and I think it won't be very long before we have an addition to our family, my dearest love."

132

CHAPTER ELEVEN

By the first week of June, Andy Haskins had come to a decision, and his wife, Jessica, had been the catalytic agent in bringing it about.

When he told her how William Blount had urged him to run for the legislature, Jessica had proudly and stubbornly declared, "Darling, just for once, won't you let somebody else be the judge of what you are and what you can do? I know that you are thoroughly honorable in such a way that even politics couldn't besmirch you. Don't you see, Andy, that's exactly what this state—in fact, this entire country—needs right now after all the scandal, corruption, and hatred that followed the war. I'm going to have a baby in November, and if it's a boy, as I pray God it will be, don't you want our son to grow up knowing his father had done all he could to bring about an honest government that would help the decent people of this state?"

"But, Jessica darling," he had protested, "I don't know the least thing about politics."

"Then I'd say you had a head start over other people who've been in politics and who look upon it as a free license to steal, cheat, and ignore their constituents."

And so, though not without many misgivings, Andy told William Blount, when he called a week later, that he would accept the honor of running on the Republican ticket to represent Montgomery County in the fall election.

During the first week of June, the Republican National Convention in Philadelphia formally nominated Ulysses S. Grant for a second term as president with Henry Wilson as vice-president. This action, which came as a surprise to no one, confirmed and strengthened Jessica's determination that her husband should enter state politics as a candidate with no taint of corruption, no axes to grind, and no favors to be repaid. At once William Blount and his two associates went to work promoting their new candidate for the legislature, and several advertisements were placed in the *Advertiser* extolling Andy Haskins's record as a soldier, a rancher, and a loyal Alabama farmer and landholder. The men who had come to work on the Haskins farm unanimously approved of their employer's decision to run for public office and, when they were not busy in the fields, spent considerable time talking to their friends and neighbors and urging them to vote for an honest, hardworking legislator.

This year, unlike 1870, gave every promise of bringing a state-wide Republican victory. A third-party movement organized by one Alexander White of Talladega, who had been concerned about the Republican Party's excessive reliance on the black vote, had dwindled away into insignificance; this left the regular Republican Party as the sole alternative to Alabama voters seeking redress against the Democratic white supremacists whose secret links to the Ku Klux Klan were known. For although the Klan was now outlawed in theory, it still thrived in the backwoods areas of Alabama. Luke Bouchard had already experienced its evils; they were to touch him again, though this time indirectly.

Late in the afternoon of the first Friday in June, elderly Judge Hosmer Dalton rapped his gavel and called the court to order. Clearing his throat, he peered through his spectacles at the tall young half-breed who sat at a table beside his client, Joshua Small, an elderly black.

Old Joshua had been a slave most of his life. For some thirty years, he had tended the azaleas, magnolias, and petunias in his master's garden. He had trimmed the hedges and looked after the live oak and cedar trees to keep them free from blight.

At the end of the Civil War, he gained his freedom, a small plot of land, and a mule. He built a small house on the land, planted some crops, and also continued to work as a gardener for the owners of various estates in the neighborhood. His work brought him the respect of everyone in the community—until one day six months ago, when he

134

had the misfortune to enter into a two-month contract to tend the garden of the estate of Mortimer Douthard, a wealthy recluse.

Before the war, Mortimer Douthard had been the owner of a prosperous Louisiana sugar cane plantation. He had married an attractive young Creole girl, and when she had died in childbirth, he had discovered to his horror and rage that the child was black. By means of hiring a private detective, he learned that his supposedly virginal young wife had had an affair with her black coachman. Douthard then engaged a gang of ruffians to track down the coachman and kill him on a deserted street at night. He gave the child away to a foundling home, saying that it was the offspring of one of his slaves who had died; and he made a generous gift to the orphange, to quiet any suspicions as well as to appear as a benevolent humanitarian.

When he saw that the Civil War was inevitable, Douthard shrewdly sold his plantation and transferred his holdings to Union banks, knowing full well that otherwise the war would destroy his fortune. He moved to Montgomery, and during the war and afterwards lived in an isolated house outside of town. He took no part in the "Confederate rebellion," as he termed it. He never remarried; however he did enjoy a succession of white mistresses, drawn mainly from the poor and uneducated class. When he got tired of them, he gave them a generous sum of money and summarily dismissed them.

Douthard had two consuming passions in life: an almost pathological hatred of blacks and a great love for the magnificent gardens that enhanced his estate. So, having heard of Joshua Small's reputation, he hired the old freedman to tend his garden, giving him specific instructions as to its care.

It was unfortunate for Joshua that two of Douthard's prize giant live oak trees had been diseased, and died despite all his efforts to restore them. Moreover, one afternoon, Joshua was unwittingly tactless enough to say something about how good it felt, to an old man who had been a slave all his life, to enjoy freedom now and be outdoors in God's creation. This simple remark drove Douthard to a frenzied attack on the black race, and in particular Joshua's abilities and intelligence. The upshot of it was that at the end of the two months he refused to honor his contract with Joshua and pay the fee agreed upon. Moreover, he warned Joshua that it would do the black no good to seek redress, because "who would take the word of a stupid old nigger like you against an upstanding citizen like myself?"

A friend of Joshua who had heard Lopasuta defend Joseph Trenton against the carpetbagger Clarence Mathewson urged the gardener to tell his story to Lopasuta. Lopasuta, after listening carefully to Joshua, had decided to bring suit against Mortimer Douthard for breach of contract.

All during this long afternoon, Lopasuta had argued eloquently that there was more than reasonable doubt that the blight of the live oak trees was attributable to the negligence of his client. At a table across the aisle of the courtroom, Mortimer Douthard sat, perfectly dressed, a sneer on his face as he glanced now and again at Joshua Small, then bent to whisper to his attorney, Vernor Markwell. The latter nodded and whispered back, "Don't worry, Mortimer, Judge Dalton is a sensible man. You certainly don't think he's going to find for the plaintiff, not when it's a stupid nigger defended by a half-breed with Injun blood in him, do you?"

"I certainly hope not, Vernor. I'm paying you enough to get this stupid suit dismissed. That nigger ruined my trees and, in fact, I'm thinking of asking for damages from him."

"Now, don't be hasty, Mortimer," his attorney swiftly retorted. "That wouldn't be too wise on your part. Just walk away from this without having to pay him a cent, and the right folks in this town will say you're the kind of smart Southerner we want in these parts. Besides, Small hasn't got any money. It ought to be enough for you that he's worked for two months without any pay."

Douthard shrugged and leaned back in his chair. "All right, if you say so, Vernor, but you'd better be right."

Markwell adjusted his cravat with a smug smile. "I usually am," he whispered back. Then he turned to look at Lopasuta with a condescending smile, before turning to watch the judge attentively.

Vernor Markwell was forty-three, the son of a wealthy plantation owner in Tuskeegee. He had married one of the town belles there eighteen years ago and, after his father's death, had sold the plantation and moved to Montgomery where he had set up his legal practice. When the Civil War

136

came, he arranged to pay for a substitute to serve in the army for him—for physically he was a coward.

In addition to being a coward, Markwell was a philanderer, and he indulged this tendency more and more as years went by. When his wife, Alexandra, finally learned of his many infidelities—two years before the present trial—she made up her mind to leave him. But there was an even more urgent reason for her decision. While looking in her attic one day for some clothing, she came across the white hood and robe of a Klansman and a sheaf of parchment which designated Vernor Markwell as Grand Dragon empowered to call a klavern of the faithful to punish the oppressors of the fair South.

When Alexandra confronted Markwell with this damning evidence of his nefarious activities, he simply laughed and said, "Alexandra, you're behaving like a child! Yes, I'm a member of the Klan and I'm proud of it. What other weapon do we have against the niggers who would otherwise run riot in our streets and attack our women?" When Alexander sarcastically retorted, "I suppose that's why you have license to seek out so many other women away from the marriage bed, Vernor," he slapped her and viciously retorted, "Perhaps if you were better in bed, my dear, I shouldn't find it necessary to seek my rightful pleasure elsewhere." With that, Alexandra quickly packed and left the house.

Looking like an aristocrat as he sat in the courtroom this afternoon, Markwell was nattily dressed, with a flowered cravat, a ruffled linen shirt, and a ruby stick pin. Six feet tall, slim and athletic, with a mane of wavy black hair, a trim Van Dyke beard, and a waxed moustache on his upper lip, he looked like a veritable Creole dandy. He had had a fair success before the Montgomery courts, mainly representing rich carpetbaggers and affluent Southern landholders who, like Mortimer Douthard, had been ingenious enough to preserve their fortunes against the depredations of war. He sat back confidently now as Judge Dalton again pounded his gavel, awaiting a verdict which he was certain would be in his client's favor.

"Will the court please come to order!" Judge Dalton ordered. Then, clearing his throat, he declared, "This court finds for the plaintiff, and orders that the defendant pay the full amount owed under contract agreed upon between him and the plaintiff, in addition to all legal fees and court costs attendant upon this case."

"Your Honor——" Vernor Markwell was on his feet, a stupefied look on his face. Mortimer Douthard's jaw dropped, and then he grabbed at his lawyer's wrist and hissed, "For Christ's sake, Vernor, I thought you had the judge in your pocket!"

"I have made my decision, Mr. Markwell, and you and your client will abide by it or suffer the consequences," was Judge Dalton's reply. Then, with great dignity, he rose from the bench and left the courtroom.

Across the aisle, Joshua Small clasped Lopasuta's hand in both of his, tears falling down his cheeks. "God bless you, Mr. Lopasuta—I never thought in all my life I'd live to see the day that a poor ol' nigger like me would git justice from a rich white man like that Mr. Douthard!"

"Thank God instead, Joshua, for the justice of the law, which even here in the South has to recognize right and wrong, regardless of the fact that you're black," Lopasuta replied. "You'll get your money, and the fees for my services will be paid by Mr. Douthard, as Judge Dalton ordered. That means you don't owe me a cent, Joshua. Besides, I wouldn't have taken a penny from you anyway."

"I won't ever forget what you've done for me, Mr. Lopasuta, sir." Joshua could hardly speak for emotion, and again he wrung Lopasuta's hand. "If ever you has a nice garden or trees you want looked after, you just call ol' Joshua. He'll do the work for you and won't charge you nothin', not ever!"

"No, Joshua, if I'm lucky enough to ever have a house with a garden and trees you can tend, I'll pay you a decent wage for any work you do for me. I'd never have it otherwise. Now, I'll take you home."

As the old black walked beside the young half-breed, Vernor Markwell stepped away from his chair and hissed, "You dirty half-breed, you haven't heard the last of this, you mark my words!"

Lopasuta turned and coldly scanned the hate-contorted face of his legal adversary. "I'm sure I haven't, Mr. Markwell. But I think you ought to advise your client to abide by Judge Dalton's decision. My client will expect his money by the end of next week, at the very latest. I trust that's understood. Good day to you, sir."

Fifteen miles west of Montgomery, on the other side of the Alabama River, was a strip of land that had once been prairie, framed by tall, gnarled oak, cypress, and cedar trees. In November of the year 1789, when the land was still ruled by the Creeks, the trees on this plot of land were cut down, their stumps uprooted, and the soil leveled. A quadrangle some ninety yards wide by a hundred and fifty yards long was laid out, and two poles were placed six feet apart at each end of the field. Thus did the unfledged braves of the Creeks, the *atac emittla*, prepare the land for the competition of *tokonhay*, a game played by rival villages. Old Lucien Bouchard had participated in one such game, and by scoring the winning goal for his team he won the right to ask the *mico*, Tunkamara, for the hand of his beautiful young daughter, Dimarte.

Now this ancient playing field, the scene of such honorable combat, lay abandoned and desolate. Trees grew again more profusely than before, and tall grass as high as a man's waist. Superstition had it that the ghosts of Creek warriors visited this isolated locale at midnight, and the townspeople of Montgomery avoided it. When they needed to ride past on business, they skirted it by several miles, fearing the hostile spirits who held dominion over the place where once the mightiest Indian warriors had played their noble games.

On a calm night in June, a sudden chilling breeze blew through this sinister, abandoned glade. The full moon hid behind a thick, dark cloud which portended a storm by morning, and from a distance there was the faint sound of thunder.

But now, at almost midnight, the rumble seemed closer. It was more than thunder: the sound of horses' hooves, following an obscure path through the tangles of briars and tall grass, a trail almost obliterated and used only by those with clandestine business. There were a dozen riders, all of them wearing white hoods and robes save for the leader, whose hood was red and in the shape of a bishop's miter, with a black cross sewn near the peak.

The men halted their horses at last, tethered them by the reins to the trunks of nearby trees, and then moved into a partly cleared space in that glade—near, indeed, where the goal of the rival village had stood and across which young

Lucien Bouchard had scored the goal that gave Econchate the victory and brought his beloved Dimarte to his nuptial bed.

Two of the men took from their saddles crude wooden crosses, and two others smeared these with pitch and then lit them so that they burned furiously, sinister beacons to illumine the glade . . . driving away the ghosts of the Creeks and substituting the spectrally clad members of the Ku Klux Klan.

The eleven men took their places, standing with their right hands pressed over their hearts, as their leader in the red hood faced them and intoned: "Brothers, I have summoned you to this klavern to right a wrong that must not go unpunished. Despite our valiant efforts to liberate the downtrodden South, we are still beset by the blacks, those apes and gibbering animals who now walk upright and call themselves free men and the equal of us whose lineage goes back through the centuries."

There was a low mutter of "Aye!" in chorus from the eleven listeners, and they nodded so that their hoods bowed toward their leader.

"What is even worse, my brothers," the leader continued in a mellifluous voice which he raised to impress his hearers, "is that we are now menaced by a half-breed who sides with these black apes against the finest of our citizens. He has Indian blood, and to make matters even more vile and contemptible, he has been adopted as a son by a white man. And this white man, Luke Bouchard, is one whose grandfather settled here, and who should know better than to bring into his family the dregs of other races."

The sound of a kind of growl rose from his listeners, and he waited a moment for dramatic effect before continuing: "Yesterday afternoon, this half-breed defended an old, worthless nigger in open court before a white judge, who dared to bring in a verdict for this black ape against one of our most illustrious citizens, Mortimer Douthard, whom all of you know and respect as I do."

Once again, the chorus of "Aye, that is so!" rang out in the desolate glade. The flickering light of the torches, fanned now by a gentle and warmer wind, cast grotesque shadows on the hooded figures as they stood waiting to hear the judgment of their leader.

"This judge, this foolish white man who had a distinguished record and who should never have dreamed of returning such a verdict, will be dealt with later. The one we must punish now and drive forth from our community is this half-breed, this Indian who poses as a lawyer and who speaks so sanctimoniously of serving the oppressed—by whom he means the illiterate, stupid rabble of blacks whom we must suffer in our midst. But, my brothers, we shall not suffer them in silence, nor shall we forget their arrogance and their pretensions. Not till the sun sets in the east and the moon rises in the west shall we of the Klan forget the threat this rabble poses to us all, to our very existence, and to the chastity of our wives and daughters."

There came a chorus of "Never!" from his spellbound hearers.

"I pronounce the sentence of the Klan on this half-breed Lopasuta, this dirty redskin who dares to protect the animal Africans against illustrious white Southerners of gentle birth! Do you agree, my brothers?"

"Yes!" the chorus thundered.

"We shall not kill him—unless, of course, he ignores our first and final warning, my brothers," the leader continued. "We shall punish him as we used to in the old days—by the lash. We shall strip him of his fine clothes and show his dirty Indian hide to the moon. We shall tar and feather him and tell him to go from our midst and never let his face be seen in Montgomery again."

"And this Bouchard who you say is his foster father—what of him?" one of the white-robed men spoke up.

The leader permitted himself a sardonic laugh, which echoed in the glade. "He will be punished sufficiently for now when his fine adopted son disappears and when he learns how the Klan dealt with him for his arrogance. Then Luke Bouchard will know that we of the Klan are not to be trifled with and that if he persists in defying the rules whereby decent Southern whites live, he may have his own turn at the whipping tree and feel the scorching heat of the tar and the feathers. Now, are we all agreed?"

"We are!" came the shouted chorus.

"My brothers, I am proud of you. Tomorrow night—Sunday—will be quiet in Montgomery. This Lopasuta lives in a little house on the outskirts of town. He will have no

141

friends or protectors. It will be easy to take him and bring him here for his punishment. Let it be done. I, your Grand Dragon, so ordain."

And softly came the answer, "Let it be done—let it be done—let it be done!"

"Thank you, my brothers," the red-hooded leader unctuously declared. "Now we ride back to our homes, but first I will pass among you and choose eight who will accompany me, your Grand Dragon, to administer this punishment. We shall let the crosses burn. If there be solitary riders going near this place of our meeting, let them be warned that, though a craven legislature tries to outlaw us, we shall exist so long as there is oppression to any one of our number. This I so swear!"

"And so do we, all of us!" came the chorus once again.

The leader touched this man and then that one on the shoulder. Each so designated bowed his head and murmured, "By the oath I have taken, I shall carry out the deed as judged at this klavern, so help me God!"

When the eight had been chosen, all of them turned back to their horses and rode out of the glade, leaving the crosses burning. There were grotesque shadows on the field where once Lucien Bouchard had found the joy of brotherhood that transcended all races, all creeds, all colors.

Old Emily Cantwell, who had served Jedidiah Danforth as housekeeper for the last seventeen years, had been visiting her dearest friend, the widow Clara Moseby. Clara lived in a white-painted frame house about a quarter of a mile from Lopasuta's house. Jedidiah's health had been failing for the past six months, but he was still as spry and cantankerous as ever, and he had snorted at Mrs. Cantwell's suggestion that she not take her free day this Sunday so that she might be there to tend him if need be. "Woman, it'll be you who will be the death of me yet, not my infirmities," he had declared. "I'm fine. I take the tonic Dr. Medbury gives me, I watch my diet, I don't drink or smoke more than I should. Besides, when my time's up and the good Lord decides he needs a lawyer up in heaven, even your being here won't make a particle of difference. No, Mrs. Cantwell, you go on and enjoy yourself, I'll be fine. I want to read some Blackstone today. Now that my protégé is doing so well in the courts, it behooves his

142

teacher to brush up on his own legal technique before that young stripling puts me to shame."

Clara Moseby, like Emily Cantwell, had been widowed long before the Civil War. She earned a modest living as an expert seamstress and often made wedding dresses for the fashionable society beauties of Montgomery and Lowndesboro. Her husband had left her the little house in which she lived and a modest inheritance which she had frugally guarded and invested wisely—thanks to Jedidiah Danforth's advice. Her only companion was a shaggy collie now ten years old whom she had named Bruce as a poignant reminder of the stillborn son who had been her only child.

This evening, Clara and Emily had played a little whist after their supper and then sat in the parlor chatting, oblivious to the lateness of the hour. As Clara herself often facetiously remarked, "I maintain, Emily, an old body doesn't need too much sleep. Besides, what I miss now, I'll make up for when I'm dead, because then I can sleep for all eternity. So why waste time now when there's things to talk about and things to do that keep a body spry and happy."

So it was nearly midnight when at last Clara stifled a yawn and, glancing at the old grandfather clock in the hallway, remarked, "Gracious me, would you ever look at the time—it's just about midnight, Emily!"

"Oh, my goodness! But that's how time flies when good friends get together, isn't it, dear? My, what's that?"

"It's Bruce barking in the yard. Now whatever would make him do that? I didn't hear anything, did you?"

"No, not really."

"I'll go have a look-see," Clara offered. Emily, mildly curious, followed her down the hall to the kitchen and out the back door to the porch. The old collie stood barking, and only at the sound of his mistress's sharply raised voice did he desist and reluctantly turn back toward her, wagging his tail.

"That's a naughty boy, Brucie," she chided as she stroked his head. "My goodness, waking up all the neighbors at midnight on a Sunday night—whatever can you see, boy, a rabbit? Oh, maybe it was Mrs. MacGruder's tabby cat—she lets it run loose so often and then she wonders why it has another litter of kittens, the silly woman. Wait now—what's that?"

"I don't see anything," Emily dubiously observed.

"I thought I did just now, off there to my left, some riders on horseback. It's so dark and there's hardly any moon—maybe that's what Bruce was barking at."

"Riders," Emily slowly repeated. "But that's where Loapsuta lives, a few blocks in that direction—oh my gracious, oh heavens, I've got to get back to Attorney Danforth right away."

"Why, what's the matter, dear?"

"I've got the most dreadful feeling, Clara!" Emily exclaimed. "You know, when Lopasuta won that case against Mortimer Douthard on Friday, there was a great deal of grumbling, and there's been bad feeling in the community for some time. Some very nasty letters in the *Advertiser* the last few weeks have been making slurs about that fine young man. Those riders could be from the Ku Klux Klan!"

"Good heavens—do you really think so?"

"Yes. Mr. Danforth said that the Klan is still around here, even though it's forbidden by law to meet any more—oh, how can I get to Mr. Danforth's house right away?"

"That's easy, dear, we'll hitch up the horse to the buggy. You can drive it, can't you?"

"Oh yes, my husband and I used to have a buggy, and I drove it all the time on errands," Emily said.

"Maybe you're mistaken," Clara tried to soothe her friend. "Maybe you shouldn't wake Mr. Danforth so late tonight. He's been ill, you've told me—"

"I know, I know, Clara, but if that was the Klan, I'd feel awful the rest of my life if I didn't do something to help that nice young man—and Mr. Danforth would know exactly what to do. He hates the Klan worse than poison."

"So do I. All right, let's go out to the stable and you'll be there in a jiffy."

The nine riders slowly circled Lopasuta's little house from the eastern side and drew their horses to a halt. Dismounting, the red-hooded leader put his finger to his lips and whispered to the stocky, bald-headed Klansman nearest him—the owner of a bookstore in Montgomery and an obsessive racist—"The redskin's home. See that kerosene

144

lamp in the living-room window? This should be easy. There's no one around here, and the other houses on this block are all dark. Besides, anyone who sees us knows that we mean business, and they're not about to interfere with the holy work of our righteous society!"

"Aye, Grand Dragon," the stocky man respectfully murmured as he adjusted his hood to conceal his features. "You call him out, we'll take him back to where we had our klavern and there, for sure, nobody'll trifle with us when we administer punishment."

"That's exactly what I had in mind. Now quiet, all of you!" the leader hissed as he tiptoed up the stairs to the porch and then, raising his fist, hammered on the door and called out in a stentorian voice, "Redskin lawyer who sleeps with niggers, come out and hear the judgment of your betters!"

Young Lopasuta had been unable to sleep. In nightshirt and moccasins, he had brought a new book on torts Jedidiah Danforth had given to him to the living-room table and was assiduously studying it, when he was startled by the hammering blows on the front door. Instantly alert, he moved swiftly and soundlessly to the edge of the bay window, which was thickly covered with chenille curtains provided by Clara Moseby. Very cautiously lifting away the edge of the curtain, he peered out into the darkness and saw the robed and hooded riders sitting silently astride their mounts. Tied to the pommel of one of the saddles he could see a coiled rope and a vicious-looking blacksnake whip. He understood. At that moment the leader again banged on the door with his fist and thundered, "This is your last chance, else you'll have worse punishment than is already due you, nigger-loving redskin! Come out now, let's see this dirty breed who pretends to be a lawyer and who would put down honorable white men just because he boasts a little more education than the niggers he defends!"

Jedidiah Danforth had given Lopasuta a Starr .44 revolver about a month ago, insisting that the young Comanche keep it to defend himself in the event that any of the embittered racists in town attempt any kind of personal attack upon him. He had hidden it in the drawer of a little sideboard across the room, and he hurried now to get it, prime and cock it, and make certain that its chambers were filled with cartridges. Then, as silently as before, he

145

hurried back to the edge of the bay window and again peered out.

"Break down the door!" he heard one of the riders shout. And then he heard the thudding of a man's boot against the door, making it creak and shudder with the impact. Very carefully, he sighted along the revolver and squeezed the trigger. There was the explosive sound of the shot and the tinkle of glass, and the stout book dealer, with a gurgling cry, toppled from his horse and sprawled lifeless on the ground.

There was a hoarse cry of rage from the other riders and, from the red-hooded leader, a violent and profane tirade: "Why, you goddamned dirty redskin, you've murdered a Klansman! Now it won't be just a whip and tar and feathers for you, breed, but we'll give you the whip first and then we'll burn you on the cross as an example for all the niggers to see! You won't be defending them in court any more, you murdering redskin!"

Lopasuta, who had drawn back away from the window, now peered out again and saw the other riders yank at the reins of their horses and move them around till they were out of view. But before they could move out of range, he fired again, and grinned with a savage kind of satisfaction to see another rider stiffen, drop his reins, and slide off his horse till he lay sprawled on his back, his arms flung out in a grotesque cross.

"We'll burn him out!" the leader cried in a frenzy of rage. "That's two Klansmen he's murdered, the filthy, nigger-loving savage! Back into the yard, boys, set fire to the house! If he's too scared to come out and take his medicine, he can just as well stay in there and burn!"

One of the hooded riders had attached to the pommel of his saddle a half-filled bucket of pitch. Dismounting in the yard behind Lopasuta's house, he hurried with the bucket to the back steps and emptied its contents on the old, weatherbeaten wood. To this, he added dry twigs and leaves which he scooped up by the armful from the yard, until he had made a highly combustible heap on the porch. Then, with a tinderbox, he started a fire and, stepping back, watched it begin to blaze. An exultant cry rose from the other five riders who by now had dismounted and, crouching low, were circling the back of the house, trying to peer through the curtained windows.

146

Thick black smoke filtered through the chinks of the back door and into the house. Lopasuta sniffed the pungent odor and knew what it was. Bending low, he hurried toward the back of the house, as a red tongue of flame licked round and up the side of the back door. His eyes narrowed, his face hard with anger, he drew aside the curtain of the window nearest him and fired another shot. A howl of pain indicated that he had wounded one of the Klansmen. Then, out of some sixth sense, he flattened himself on the floor just as a fusillade of shots rang out. The leader and the other five uninjured Klansmen had drawn their rifles and pistols and begun to fire at the curtained windows. There was a crash of glass, and Lopasuta crawled quickly back to the living room. Hurriedly, he ransacked the little drawer of the sideboard in search of more ammunition, but the box contained only six more cartridges. He must make every shot count, he knew.

"My God, Mrs. Cantwell, I never though they'd come into town here—the scurrilous, yellow-livered bastards—I beg your pardon, Mrs. Cantwell—but that's what they are, every mother's son of them!" old Jedidiah Danforth spluttered. "I'm beholden to you for bringing me this news. And I know just what to do about it."

"But Mr. Danforth, you mustn't go out in this cold night air—"

"Poppycock, woman! What good's a man's life if he can't stand up to cowards? Especially on the side of a fine young man who's going to be one of the best attorneys Montgomery ever had, you mark my words! Now I'll just put my coat on, and then you'll drive me in that buggy of yours over to Mrs. Elliott's boarding house. Happens she's rooming four or five veterans from old Jeb Stuart's regiment, and they haven't forgotten how to ride or shoot, either! Hurry, woman, we've got to get there in time to save him!"

A few minutes later, Jedidiah was impatiently pulling the bell rope at the door of a stately old mansion that had seen better days, which old Elfrida Elliott had turned into a boarding house after her children had married and her husband died. The door was opened and the old woman began to shake her fist at this unwarranted interruption of her slumbers, but Jedidiah cut her short with an angry:

147

"Time for me to apologize later, Mrs. Elliott! Now you get Sandy Murray, Ben Posthwaite, and Harvey Brandreth out of bed on the double, tell them I need them to rout a bunch of cowardly Klansmen—that'll fetch them! Hurry now, woman! Like as not those Klansmen'll burn the poor fellow's house down and drag him out and burn him too, if you don't get a move on!"

"Good Lord, Mr. Danforth—I'll just be a minute—I'll get them, never fear!" she called as she hobbled up the stairs and began, with a voice amazingly sonorous for a woman of her age, to call out the names Jedidiah Danforth had cited.

The three ex-Confederate soldiers hurried down the stairs, in breeches and jackets and boots, each carrying a Whitworth rifle, that weapon which, in the hands of an expert marksman, had wrought such deadly havoc among the Union ranks.

"Oh, some action at last, Mr. Danforth," Sandy Murray greeted him. He was a tall, gangling, light-brown-haired man in his mid-thirties, personally decorated for valor by Jeb Stuart himself and now the top clerk in a drygoods store in Montgomery. "Klansmen, is that what it is? Let me at them! And my buddies here have been itching for a good fight for much too long. Let's go!"

"Then get in the buggy and not so much talk out of you, Sandy. You and your friends still owe me a fee, as I recall, for legal services I did for you some years back, but I never reminded you of it. I'll mark the debt paid in full if you save this young Indian attorney I sponsored before the bar—he's the adopted son of Mr. Luke Bouchard."

"Then that's good enough for me, Mr. Danforth. Anybody Mr. Bouchard thinks well enough of to take into his house is a gentleman. And he's a good lawyer, too. Reckon we all might need his help in case any of those dirty skunks try to go to court."

"Not likely," Jedidiah drily retorted. "Into that buggy, less talk and more action! All right, Mrs. Cantwell, use the whip and don't spare the horse, not when a man's life is at stake!"

The Klan leader and one of his henchmen had moved to the front of the house and were directing their fire into the living room windows, while the four others, as well as the Klansman whom Lopasuta had wounded, continued their

148

fire into the house from the back yard. Meanwhile, fanned by a northeasterly wind, the fire began to spread. The back door crashed to the floor with a shower of blazing embers, and the kitchen was soon engulfed in flames. "We've got him now!" cried one of the hooded riders as he leveled his pistol at the open entrance to the back of the house and fired three shots at random. "Come on out, you red sonuvabitch, or you can burn with the house—this is your last chance!"

Lopasuta, lying on his belly on the floor of the living room, aimed his revolver at the window through which the shots of the leader and his compaion were coming, but from an upward angle the balls had no chance of finding a mark and whistled harmlessly over the Klansmen's heads, which they greeted with derisive laughter. "The Injun can't even shoot—he's scared, he's probably wet his britches like as not!" Then, in a bawling, menacing tone, the leader shouted, "We'll give you just one last chance, Injun! Come on out with your hands up and maybe we'll be kind enough to give you a quick death instead of the fire! Hurry up now, we haven't got all night for scum like you!"

At this moment, with Emily Cantwell breathlessly plying the thin carriage whip over the exhausted horse's flanks, the clatter of the buggy wheels came down the street. The red-hooded leader turned to his companion. "Who the devil is that? Go find out and tell them to be about their business—tell them this is the Klan who judges and punishes here!"

The middle-aged grocery clerk who stood beside the red-hooded leader nodded and moved out toward the sidewalk. Cupping his hands, he boomed out: "Stay away from here, stay clear! Or else you become the enemy of the Klan! We are here to judge and punish—be off!"

"Says you!" Sandy Murray called back as he cupped his hands to his mouth. Then, nimbly rising to his feet in the crowded buggy, he put his Whitworth rifle to his shoulder, squinted along the sight, and pulled the trigger. With a shriek, the grocery clerk spun round, his eyes rolling in their sockets, and then toppled to the ground. With an angry oath, the Klan leader hurried round the side of the house to join his companions in the back yard.

The two other ex-Confederates leaped out of the buggy and followed their companion, crouching low, their rifles ready. Jedidiah Danforth piped up as loudly as he could, "Lopasuta, Lopasuta, come on out through the front door, we've got them cornered in the yard!"

With a gasp of relief, the young Comanche sprang to his feet, unlocked the door, and ran out to greet his elderly sponsor. "Thank God you brought help, Mr. Danforth! I couldn't have held out much longer—the back of the house is in flames, and the smoke was just about choking me!"

There rose the sound of shots and cries of pain. Two more Klansmen had fallen dead to the accurate fire of the Whitworths, and the leader himself had pressed his left hand against a shoulder wound, his eyes bloodshot with pain and frustrated rage.

"Mr. Danforth, we're done! Come around here and see who this leader of theirs is!" Ben Posthwaite called out.

Lopasuta and Jedidiah hurried around the side of the house to the back yard. Five of the Klansmen were dead and two wounded, including the leader, who, panting, wincing with the pain of his wound, stood defiantly facing the ex-Confederate soldiers.

Jedidiah stepped forward and yanked down the red hood. Lopasuta uttered a cry of amazement. "It's Mr. Markwell!"

"So it is," the old attorney grimly assented. "Well, Markwell, this just about ends your days as a lawyer here in Montgomery. I'll see Judge Henley tomorrow morning and draw up disbarment papers right off."

"No—I—we're beaten. Look, Danforth, I'll leave town, if that'll satisfy you!"

"Well, Lopasuta, it's up to you." The white-haired attorney turned to the young Comanche. "Personally, I'd like to ride this skunk out of town on a rail and put some of the tar and feathers on him that he and his dirty, cowardly friends have been inflicting on innocent, helpless people all these years. But what do you say?"

Lopasuta shrugged. "Now that he's known for what he is, his fangs are drawn, as we Comanches would draw the venom from a rattlesnake. Let him go." He moved forward to face Markwell, staring silently at him until the beaten man's eyes lowered and he finally bowed his head in total defeat. "Get out of town, because if I ever see you again, I'll challenge you to a duel Comanche style: the two of us in a circle, a single knife thrust in the middle, and whoever gets the knife kills the other. Yes, even if he steps out of the circle to escape the knife—that's Comanche law."

"I—I'll leave in the morning, I promise."

"We'll notify the undertaker to bury your dead. Get your wounded friend to a doctor, and he and the other two had best leave town too," Jedidiah Danforth curtly directed.

Vernor Markwell stumbled toward his horse, as the three other Klansmen slowly mounted theirs, and the four of them rode off whence they had come. Their hoods were down, they had been unmasked at last and their power had vanished. The smoldering blaze of Lopasuta's house cast a ghastly light on the usually quiet street.

"Well, Lopasuta, I'll have to get you a new house, I can see that."

"The worst thing, Mr. Danforth, is that new book on torts you gave me—it's a wonderful book—"

"Never mind, with the fame and the money you're going to make as the best lawyer in town, son, you'll be able to buy all the new law books you want. Come along now, you can stay at my place again. Poor Mrs. Cantwell is dying for some sleep—but if it hadn't been for her, God knows what might have happened."

"And Markwell? What do you think will happen to him?" the young Comanche gravely asked.

"He'll go somewhere else and bully and bluster until his day is done. There'll be a reckoning for all who try to live by the sword. God sees to that, even if sometimes He takes time to do the judging. But it's better judging than any Klansman could ever do," was Jedidiah's solemn answer.

Vernor Markwell kept his word. He rode back to his house, hurriedly packed what gold he had stored away, and rode toward the river to take a packet down to Mobile early the next morning. From there, he took the ferry to New Orleans, hoping to seek a new fortune in the Queen City. But by the end of the year, he would die ignominiously, shot by a faro dealer for trying to cheat at cards.

CHAPTER TWELVE

Although this winter was the harshest that Dr. Ben Wilson had known in all his thirty-eight years, it was in many ways the most rewarding and fulfilling. The thick snow and the howling, bone-chilling wind that swept across the barren plains of Indian Territory were surely more uncomfortable than the worst winter he could remember from his youthful days in Pittsburgh. Here, on an isolated reservation, the once-powerful Creeks of Alabama—the descendants of those who had welcomed old Lucien Bouchard to their lands—lived in poverty and desolation. The United States government had brought these few hundred people to an unfriendly land where there was neither hunting nor fertile soil for the planting of life-sustaining crops, a land with no other inhabitants for many miles in every direction. And then, as if to remind these poor souls of how much of their former freedom and dignity they had lost, a rickety wooden fence had been erected to enclose the few tepees and rude huts that housed them. Over the years, the fury of the elements—snow, rain, and oppressive heat— had rotted away sections of the fence, and one could easily walk out of the enclosure through any of these gaps. Nevertheless, the message of the fence was clear to every young brave, old man, and squaw: "Remember always that you are a prisoner here; henceforth this shall be your world until you die. Even though the ravaged fence allows you to walk out of this prescribed enclosure, you must not think you can flee beyond the boundaries that we in our official wisdom have imposed upon you. Therefore, forget what your forebears once were, and humbly and peacefully accept your lot."

Friar Bartoloméo Alicante, a friend to everyone at Windhaven Range as well as to every member of this oppressed tribe, had spent much of the preceding year ministering to the Creeks. Now that he had taken his leave and gone on his self-appointed pilgrimage to the villages of other Indian tribes, Dr. Ben Wilson remained as the only white man who had voluntarily attached himself to the Creek reservation. He dearly loved Elone, his young Aiyuta Sioux wife, whom the Creeks had taken in and sheltered as one of their own. Many times, late at night, when she was fast asleep, Ben would walk through the village and through one of the gaps in the fence to ponder his situation, and the strange and unpredicted chain of events that had brought him to this place. All around him was desolation and flat prairie and the savage cold of the biting wind, which tugged at him as if to draw him onward to some abyss.

There were moments when, in the great isolation of this land, Ben felt an agonizing loneliness and a yearning for the past. Added to this yearning was a sense of helplessness, for gentle Fleurette, his first wife, had died despite all his efforts and his advanced medical skill. Ben did not question the will of the Almighty in so ordaining his destiny; rather, with tears on his cheeks and his face lifted to the dark winter sky, he thanked his Maker both for his enduring memories of Fleurette and for the gentle and tender Indian girl whose life was now merged undeviatingly with his own. And he often said a prayer of gratitude: "I who believe in peace and abhor all that is evil and violent and ugly in men grieve for my Fleurette. I thank God for the two children she gave me, that they are well and strong. And in spite of my mourning, I thank God for the peace I now have with Elone. I know that Elone somehow was brought here by the will of God so that I might find in her the same kind of dedicated and inspiring love that I knew with Fleurette. Oh, blessed Lord, Thou hast given me such solace as I could not know would be vouchsafed to me, in the hours of my darkest agony when she was taken from me. I shall be eternally grateful to Thee for letting Elone share my life and my purpose in trying to do good unto those who need it most and who, though some men call them heathen and savages, are as much Thy children as are all of us, and perhaps even more."

Thus he communed with the Eternal Spirit whom the Creeks called Ibofanagā, the Giver of Breath. And his prayer was not blasphemy or heresy, for he truly believed in the oneness of all religions which speak in many tongues and with many different images of one God who judges all men, not by the particular form of their creed, but by the honesty of their souls.

On this particular night in late January, Ben stood outside the fence looking toward the east. It was after midnight and gentle Elone had been asleep for hours. Two weeks earlier she had given birth to their son, whom he had named Bartholomew in honor of the Franciscan friar. As a boy, he had often thought that priests and friars practiced an unrelentingly harsh faith, but all such thoughts had been dispelled when he had met the genial, self-effacing Friar Bartoloméo, who had resigned his post in Santa Fe because his rich parishioners had complained to the Bishop of Madrid that he spent too much time with the poor and the Indians. Friar Bartoloméo's credo was like Ben's own: he believed in a loving God who held out the hope of salvation to all who earnestly repented of their sins and atoned for them through their efforts to live a good life.

Ben thought again of Elone sleeping in the tepee and of their son whom he himself had delivered. In one sense, he had violated the principles of his calling, in caring for her. Down through the centuries—ever since doctors had first taken the Hippocratic oath—it had been accepted tradition that no physician should tend his own kin, lest his emotional concern for his loved ones affect his objective judgment as a physician. But circumstances had forced Ben to attend to Elone, and he had given her the same dispassionate and objective care that he would have given to anyone in need—even an enemy. He had always done this. He recalled again the occasion on which he had performed a tracheotomy on Fleurette, trying to save her life from diphtheria. He had performed exactly the same operation on the corrupt and vindictive Benjamin Hardesty. He had shown the same skill with the man who had hated him for wanting to establish a free clinic for the city's poor as he had with the sweet wife who had nursed him when he had been wounded during the Civil War. And, ironically, Hardesty's life had been spared and hers taken. But now he understood God's divine restoration: he had been granted the boon of delivering his own son by her who was God's solace for his loss.

155

Although the wind gathered in force and its cold bite reminded him that even the elements seemed to direct their hostile force against the abandoned Creeks, Ben sank to his knees in the snow and, bowing his head and clasping his hands, fervently thanked God. His eyes were blurred with unashamed tears as he remembered that tomorrow morning the new Indian agent would visit the reservation. Then, rising, he looked at the sky and saw a star which had been dim suddenly glow with an unusual brightness, like the star of Bethlehem. He turned, strangely comforted, and went back to Elone and the newborn child. As he drew aside the flaps of the tepee, he saw Elone's first-born daughter, Tisinqua, in the small bed which one of the old men had made as a gift to the "white-eyes shaman," and at that moment, she stirred in her sleep, opened her eyes and, with a happy little laugh, held out her arms to him.

"The soldiers come with the wagon for us, my brother." Emataba pointed toward the northwest as he stood beside the Quaker doctor on this frosty January morning. "It is good that they come. For many moons now, we have had no Indian agent to help us—ever since the evil one who tried to harm Elone was sent away. During that time we have had but few visits from the soldiers. I am glad that your great chief in Washington is at last sending us the agent he promised us."

"I too am glad, for I have never been able to understand the long delay in his coming," Ben Wilson replied. "Ever since I wrote to President Grant and had that thieving Matthias Stillman discharged, I have been expecting his replacement. I am glad that in the months that have gone by your blood brother Lucien Edmond and I have been able to do something to supply the needs of your people. A reliable agent will be able to do even more."

"It will be good," Emataba slowly replied, "for the old men and women of this village to see a white-eyes—sent by your great chief—who will remember that we were once proud and strong. Yes, it will be good for them after all these years when they are now ready to die, believing themselves worthless and scorned. But, even better, there will be hope for the young men and the children who will see that a white-eyes besides yourself can keep his word and deal with us fairly."

156

"That is what I have prayed for, Emataba," Dr. Ben Wilson responded as he watched the wagon approach, flanked by two mounted soldiers on each side and a fifth man, dressed in civilian clothes, riding ahead.

The foremost rider spurred his horse and cantered up to the reservation, dismounted, tied the reins to the top rail, and came forward to extend his hand to the tall *mico* of the Creeks. "I am your new agent, Emataba," he declared in a resonant voice, a pleasant smile on his lean, weather-beaten face.

The agent, Douglas Larrimer, was nearly as tall as Emataba, with a short, trimmed beard; clear, honest brown eyes that did not waver or shift when they looked at the Creek chief; and a high-arching forehead. He wore a beaver coat, and the end of the left arm of his suit coat beneath it had been neatly rolled and pinned back. His left arm had been amputated at the elbow after a minié ball had shattered it at the Battle of Five Forks. That battle had taken place eight days before Appomattox, and Captain Larrimer had watched as General Grant had gone into the tent to meet with General Lee and sign the terms of surrender. He had worn a medal, having been decorated for valor at that first battle. President Grant had appointed him as Indian agent for this territory not only because he showed valor on the field of battle, but also because his great-grandmother had been a Cherokee. One who had Indian blood in his veins would surely not seek to cheat those who had so many times in the past been deceived by the white man's treaties and promises.

"I bid you welcome to our stronghold," the *mico* said without the slightest inflection of irony, moving forward to extend his hand, which Douglas Larrimer heartily shook. "Perhaps you will stay with us and share our meal, for I should like to have all of my people meet you." Then, glancing at Ben, he added, "This man is our shaman, or doctor as you call him, Dr. Ben Wilson."

"I am glad to meet you both. From your letter to Washington, Dr. Wilson, I know you are a Quaker, and thus have infinite compassion for the downtrodden and the needy—a sentiment I wholeheartedly share." He turned back to Emataba. "I would like very much to share your meal, Emataba. Do you know that when men of strange faiths and different races break bread together, somehow

157

there is always a beginning of friendship between them. It is easier to talk and to listen to a stranger and to believe in him, if one first shares food with him."

"That is what I have always felt," Emataba nodded as he turned toward the entrance of the reservation. "Come, then."

"I shall have the soldiers unload the supplies I've brought you for this month, and then I shall be privileged to sit with you," the new Indian agent answered.

With this, he turned to the four soldiers who had escorted the large, heavily burdened wagon from the fort, and gave swift, terse orders. Ben could see at once that here was a man who commanded obedience, yet without pompousness or arrogance. And he thought to himself that Mr. Larrimer would comprehend the gentle Quaker faith, which held that a man of courage and honesty need only speak simply and declare his intentions without being ostentatious and blustery—the way Matthias Stillman, the former Indian agent, had always been.

Raising his voice, Emataba called out to several young braves nearby, and they hurried to aid the soldiers in unloading the wagon. Douglas Larrimer turned to Emataba. "I have brought you extra flour, molasses, salt pork, beans, coffee, and many blankets and smallclothes to keep the children warm. This is a very bad winter, and I promise you I'll do everything I can."

"May Ibofanaga look down upon you with favor for this kindness," Emataba solemnly responded. "And yet I am saddened in my heart."

"I understand you, my *mico*," the agent replied.

Ben looked sharply at Douglas Larrimer and saw in his lean, weatherbeaten face not the slightest hypocrisy: his words were frank and swiftly uttered, as if the agent understood at once the sensitive pride of the Creek leader. And in his own heart, Ben felt considerably cheered, as he had not felt since he had come with Friar Bartoloméo to the village in Indian Territory.

"Yes," Douglas Larrimer repeated, "I know what you must be thinking and I cannot blame you for it. You think that because we whites, who have driven you from your land in the South, bring you food and blankets, we wish to think of you as beggars. Believe me, this is farthest from my thoughts. So long as I am assigned here to care for you

158

and your people, Emataba, I regard this as only a small part of what my government owes your people for usurping your land."

"Now this is new to me and very strange," the tall Creek chieftain said wonderingly as he turned to look at the Indian agent. "Since my father and his tribe left the land where we once ruled in dignity and honor, I cannot remember having heard a white-eyes ever admit that his leaders were guilty of wrongdoing against us. Yet the first time you speak to me you tell me this. Truly it is a strange thing."

"Understand me, Emataba, I do not come here to make you false promises or to speak with a forked tongue. So long as I have this authority as Indian agent, I give you my word that every penny given to me will be spent to buy you and your people all the supplies it can. I do not put into my pocket money that belongs to you—I give you my word of honor as a soldier and as a man."

"And I believe you and I trust you. How strange it is that the first time we meet, I should feel already that you are my friend," the *mico* solemnly declared.

By now the squaws had prepared a simple meal and Emataba, Ben, and Mr. Larrimer seated themselves tailor-fashion in front of the cooking fire. Emataba took a piece of meat from the bubbling pot and gave it to the agent, who smiled and nodded.

"This is very good, Emataba," he commented.

"It is the jackrabbit of our plains. There are many of them here and they are easy to catch. We do not often see deer and still less the buffalo which our northern brothers use for food," Emataba explained.

"Are there any other supplies I can bring you before my visit next month? I have in my warehouse many goods, and I suspect, after Dr. Wilson's letter to the government in Washington, that these things were bought by my predecessor and never given to you. If you are lacking for anything, you have only to speak, and I shall see that you receive it."

"Perhaps some salt, and—but this is of no consequence —" the Creek leader began.

"No, speak from your heart. There should always be honesty between us, with nothing hidden one from the other," Douglas Larrimer assured him earnestly.

"You have great kindness. I trust you now as I trust this good white-eyes shaman who has dwelt in our midst so long that we respect him as one of us." Emataba gestured toward the Quaker doctor. "Well, since you say I may, I will tell you—it is the old people for whom I most fear. They are ready to die. They think that your people have abandoned us and look down on us with scorn as if we were dogs near a compfire trying to grab at a bone and run off before we are scolded for it. But if you could give us hats, such as these men who drive the cattle wear, they would protect us from sun and rain."

"Sombreros," Douglas Larrimer interposed with a chuckle. "I see no reason why I can't bring you a dozen or more sombreros the next time I come here. You shall have them. Anything else?"

Now it was Ben who spoke up, out of his own concern and a sudden yearning to make a home for himself and his new family. "I am here as a doctor, you understand, Mr. Larrimer. Elone and my newly born child, as well as her first-born daughter, Tisinqua, will be better off if I could find a place for them in a town, perhaps Wichita."

"Yes, I know that. I'm aware that there's quite a flourishing Quaker society in Wichita. There's no reason you can't go there if you wish. You see, I've obtained authority to send an army doctor here at least once a month. Emataba, when the man comes, you will have your people assemble. You will tell them that this shaman, as you call him, will examine every one of them and give medicine that will cure their sickness."

"That is very good. I am in your debt, as I am to this good man who has stayed with us so long." Again Emataba gestured toward the Quaker doctor.

"I understand you, Emataba," Mr. Larrimer nodded. "And the doctor that I have myself chosen from the military staff at the fort that has jurisdiction over this reservation is a good and considerate man. He will work as hard as Dr. Wilson to cure your sick and to give comfort to those who have lost their belief in themselves."

Ben stared wonderingly at the one-armed Indian agent. "You begin to give me new hope, Mr. Larrimer. I could not and I would not leave these people so long as they need me."

"I can believe that, coming from you, Dr. Wilson. You

160

see, what you don't know is that when Washigton received your letter criticizing the corruption of my predecessor, someone in authority there took the trouble to look up your record in Pittsburgh. You're a fine doctor, and quite a man in your own right. You're conscientious and obviously devoted to these people, and I give you my word that they will not be ignored or cheated ever again so long as I am the agent. I only wish I could have come to join you sooner. Shortly after President Grant issued the original order for me to come here, someone in Washington changed his mind for him, and I was sent to Kansas instead. I served there among the Tonkawas and the Kiowas for more than a year. Then—again unexpectedly—I was ordered here. Such is the way of Washington. The upshot is that I am here now, and if you are thinking of settling in town to resume your practice—and there's no reason for you not to do so—you may make your preparations whenever you wish. Dr. Brenton will be as conscientious as you have been here."

Dr. Ben Wilson drew a deep breath. It was incredible how this wise man comprehended his deepest desires. For some months now he had thought of moving to a place like Wichita. There was a Quaker society there, headed by good-natured, honest Jacob Hartmann. That was where he had been married, and if he were free to leave the Creek village, he could begin a new life with Elone, Tisinqua, and the baby, Bartholomew, and bring little Thomas and Sybella to their permanent new home. It would give him and his family a greater sense of belonging than they could ever achieve in this desolate and abandoned village on the plains. When he raised his eyes to look at Douglas Larrimer, he flushed to see a gentle look of understanding on the other man's face.

"I thought that might please you, Dr. Wilson. I'll see to it that Dr. Brenton comes here soon. Meanwhile, do you have any serious illnesses to report, cases you yourself are treating?" the agent inquired.

"No, thank God, in the main everyone's healthy, Mr. Larrimer."

"In that case, Dr. Wilson, I thank you on behalf of the United States government for what you have done here, and I tell you that you are free to seek your own practice wherever you may choose. I understand why you have

161

shared your life with all its hardships with these good people. I should be proud to shake your hand and also to give you my pledge that your work will be continued to the best of my ability and Dr. Brenton's."

"Thank you—God bless you, Mr. Larrimer!" Ben said hoarsely. "I believe you, and I will confess to you that for some time I have wanted to take Elone and our children to Wichita. Once we are settled there, I can return for my dead wife's boy and girl—I left them, you see, with her mother in Texas. Now her mother is dead, and other members of Lucien Edmond Bouchard's family at Windhaven Range are looking after them."

"Once you've settled in Wichita, Dr. Wilson, I'm sure you can make any necessary arrangements to bring the boy and girl to you. Well, you'll pardon me a moment, Emataba. I must go make sure the soldiers have distributed all the supplies I brought."

CHAPTER THIRTEEN

In the days following Douglas Larrimer's first visit to the Creek reservation, Ben Wilson conferred often with Emataba. They talked about the new agent and about Ben's plan to take Elone, Tisinqua, and Bartholomew to a new home in Wichita.

"I would not have asked this of you, O *mico* of the Creeks," he said to the tall Creek leader, "if I had had the slightest doubt that this new agent is far better than the evil man who cheated you and pocketed the money that our government said should be spent for your neglected people. But in my heart I know him to be a good, decent man, and now that he has promised to send a doctor regularly to this reservation, I feel that perhaps I can be of service in this city of the white-eyes where there are so many new settlers and so few doctors."

"It is your calling, it is the will of the Great Spirit in whom you believe, that draws you away from us, my brother," Emataba gravely replied. Putting his left hand over Ben's heart and clasping the latter's right shoulder with his own right hand, he solemnly added, "I feel in my own heart that we do not lose you forever. This is why, though it saddens me to see you go from us, I have the hope that you will one day return. And since I trust you, I agree that this new man who has lost his arm in battle and who has shown courage and honor will treat us as you have treated us in the past. How fortunate it is that the people in my village have learned that at last they can trust a white-eyes who speaks with a straight tongue. You and I both know, as we have said so many times before, that your Great Spirit and our Ibofanaga watch over all men in this world and that there is no difference in us."

"Yes. But not all those of my own race understand this,

Emataba. That is why I sometimes worry about your village—that one day, if I am no longer here and Douglas Larrimer is transferred for some reason, things will go badly with you. I pray it will not be so."

"I too, my brother. But even if we are destined to endure still more suffering, at least we will have within our hearts the remembrance of what you did. It will be a good feeling. It will warm the heart even if the belly is empty."

"So far as it is in my power, Emataba, I will see that no belly is ever empty in your village," Ben promised. "And if you should need me, you have only to send one of your braves to Wichita and I'll return with him to aid your people. This I pledge you as your brother, and doubly so because I am sworn to the white-eyes oath to tend those who are in need."

"My father told me that there were some of your race who did not look down upon us with scorn," Emataba slowly answered. "I did not doubt the elders, but I waited, and for long I did not see or meet such a man. But already in the span that the Giver of Breath has bestowed upon me, I have known one who is called Lucien Edmond Bouchard, and I have lived with you to see truly how what we are is of no importance to you, except that we are suffering and turn to you for help. This you have more than generously given, my brother. And for it you will forever be blessed, I know."

"My brother does me too much honor. I am not worthy of it. Yet I repeat, if ever the time comes when you need me, send for me and I shall return because there is a bond between us," the Quaker doctor earnestly declared.

"I shall not forget what you have said today. Nor will any of my people when I tell them," Emataba replied. He added with a soft irony in his voice, "Isn't it strange, my brother, that here you and I stand as friends, you far from your people and I countless miles away from the land where the Creeks were once proud and free? If this were known to all throughout the land, would it not be easier for the white-eyes to make peace at last with all of us? We mean you no harm, even though the white-eyes have cast us out. We live because of your goodness, and we know hope which had never been known to us until you came."

"Yes, Emataba. Perhaps because it is such a simple lesson, it is all the harder to learn, at least for many of my people. They have never lived with you as I have, they do not understand you, they think that you plot to attack and to kill and to avenge what wrongs we have done you. Truly it is a sorrowful thing that there is not better understanding among all races."

"This is so, I have long thought on it," the *mico* answered. "And because it is so, because there are those who have nothing but hatred in their hearts, I would send an escort of my strongest braves with you and your wife and children to Wichita."

But the Quaker doctor shook his head, a gentle smile on his homely face. "There is no danger. We shall go in a small wagon. We are peaceful, we are Quakers, and we trust in our God to watch over us."

"All the same, my brother, I would be easier in my mind if you would arm yourself. You will recall that once before, when you went to Wichita to bring us supplies, you were attacked by evil men who would have killed you and taken the food and the clothing you were bringing back to us. Surely, since it happened as it did, you will not be foolish enough to leave us without some protection?"

"If by that you mean take weapons, Emataba, I cannot." Ben soberly shook his head. "I have told you of the Quaker faith. It does not admit of violence and the bearing of weapons. It is a faith based on love and trust, not suspicion and hatred."

"I understand this. I have often told the elders of my council how wisely you speak of love among all men. But you know better than I that there are some of your own race who think only of making themselves strong and taking what they wish from those who are weak. I urge you to take with you one of the guns my younger braves own." Here the tall Creek leader permitted himself a wry smile and swiftly added, "I tell you that we plan no war against the white-eyes. It is only that when the soldiers brought us here, they did not search all of us for weapons. These weapons are old, it is true, but they will still protect you against evildoers."

But again Ben shook his head. "No, Emataba. I would offend against my faith if I took with me anything that could kill or wound or maim. We must resist evil with our faith in God."

The tall *mico* uttered a long sigh. "I know that you be-

165

lieve truly in what you tell me, so I will not argue with my brother. But if, when you are ready to depart from us, you have in your heart the feeling that there may be danger on your journey, do not be too stubborn in your pride. Take a weapon and regard it as a token of our great concern for you and for Elone and the two little children."

"Again I thank the *mico* for his thoughts of me. But we shall arrive safely in Wichita and we shall take no weapons from your braves, Emataba. Now, I will go to pack what I shall need on the journey. May our Lord watch over you and all of those in your village. When I reach Wichita and join the congregation of our Quaker society, I give you my promise that all of us will pray eagerly that your lives will be bettered by this agent who will, from now on, look after you as I have tried to do."

On Monday morning of the first week of February, Dr. Ben Wilson prepared to take his leave of Emataba and the young braves who had taught him the Creek language and were his most stalwart friends in the village. The *mico* had two of the best horses hitched to the supply wagon which the Quaker doctor had often driven to and from Wichita to purchase supplies. Ben held Tisinqua in his arms, smiling at her from time to time and speaking affectionately to her. Elone, having already packed their belongings and placed them at the back of the wagon, now came with little Bartholomew in her arms, her eyes shining with love as she kissed the infant and murmured reassuringly to him.

There had been a sporadic blizzard the previous week but today, despite the frosty cold, there was hardly any wind. Both Tisinqua and Bartholomew wore little coats of cloth to which Elone had sewn thick pieces of beaver and muskrat fur she had secured the previous fall from a half-breed trapper. She had made her husband and herself similar coats, as well as fur-covered mittens, as protection against the penetrating winter cold of the plains.

Seeing that Ben was engrossed in speaking with the young braves, Emataba left them talking and quickly approached Elone. "Do not raise your voice, he must not hear," he whispered with a quick glance over at Ben. "Your man is good. I respect him as I do his faith. But between here and Wichita may be many dangers, brought about by evil men. You who have entered his life to share

166

it are still new enough to this faith he so fervently practices, that it is you who must protect him."

She nodded, not speaking, but her dark eyes questioningly sought his. With another glance over at Ben and the group of braves, Emataba put his right hand under the folds of the thick blanket he wore like a cape and handed her a six-shooter. "Hide this. I have loaded it, and here"— again his hand disappeared into the folds of the blanket and emerged with a small pouch—"are more cartridges to load it if it should be needed. I pray to Ibofanaga that your journey will be a safe one, without danger."

Again Elone nodded. Transferring Bartholomew to the crook of her left arm and hugging him snugly against herself, she took the six-shooter and the pouch and swiftly concealed them beneath her belongings in the back of the wagon.

"That is good," Emataba murmured. "Remember, you are not yet bound by his faith, for he has said that when the two of you reach Wichita you will both join this church which preaches kindness even to one's enemies. Do you understand me, Elone?"

Once again she nodded, then bowed her head in respect to a tribal chieftain. At this moment, Ben turned from his Creek friends and genially called, "Come, my dear one, we begin our journey. God has given us a good sign—the sky is clear, there is no snow or wind."

"I come, my husband," Elone murmured. Once again she made the sign of respect to the *mico* by bowing her head low before him. As she straightened, she sent him a look of grateful understanding and, aloud, exclaimed, "I thank you, chief of the Creeks, for the kindness you and your people have shown to me and my little Tisinqua, and now so greatly to my husband and his first-born of my body. I will pray to the Great Spirit to guide all of you here, and I will think of you often." Then she clambered into the wagon with Ben's help and laid the baby boy in a sturdy little crib one of the older men had fashioned. Ben helped Tisinqua into the wagon; then, taking up the reins and clucking to the two stong, snorting horses who seemed eager to be off, he waved farewell to Emataba and the others. The wagon moved on with creaking wheels till it reached the level plain about a quarter of a mile beyond the fenced-in reservation. When the village was out of sight, Ben turned to Elone and said in a regretful tone, "I have prayed, my dear one, that this time my judgment of a man is correct. But I do not think that Douglas Larrimer will break his word once he has given it. He will see that these people are well and fairly treated and that a doctor replaces me to look after their ailments and protect them through this harsh winter."

"I feel as you do, my husband," Elone murmured, her eyes downcast. And then, looking up, she met her husband's earnest look, smiled, and leaned toward him, closing her eyes and resting her head against his shoulder as he drove the horses on at a steady pace.

He had quickly discovered that the gentle young Aiyuta Sioux girl had an alert mind and surprising powers of retention. Stolen from her native village by Kiowas and forced to a life of virtual servitude as the squaw of a Kiowa chief, she had made the best of her cruel situation, learning something of the Kiowa tongue. When she had been taken in by the Creeks, she had learned enough of their language to speak eloquently and with more subtlety than might be expected of a young squaw. After Ben arrived at the village and cured both Elone and her daughter of the deadly croup, he was able to converse with her, for he had learned much of the Creek language, from Sipanata, a man of the village. In time, Elone had become remarkably proficient in English. Together, she and Ben practiced the languages they knew, each encouraging and inspiring the other.

In the course of their exchanges, Ben had often pondered the true meaning of the parable of Babel, wherein many people spoke with many tongues, and were not understood. It was a miracle that here, in this abandoned wilderness, he had found understanding with a gentle Indian girl, and all barriers of language had been overcome. He perceived that his own spirit had been regenerated. This rebirth lay at the heart of the Quaker faith, which taught that through the exchange of love and peaceful deeds one communicated with God and was strengthened against life's greatest adversities.

The weather continued obdurately cold, and after twenty miles the wind suddenly grew louder and stronger. To make certain that little Bartholomew would not fall ill, Ben made frequent stops during the day, while Elone fed the baby and bundled him in fresh, warm swaddling clothes. The natural simplicity of her maternal tasks filled him with wonder: he could see how ably she nursed and cared for the little baby. As a man of unswerving tenderness and honesty, he was often moved to tears, which he tried not to show her.

To distract her from the cold, he found himself telling her of his boyhood, of his parents, of his hopes as a young intern, and then, finally, of the struggle to adhere to his deep-rooted convictions against the tyrannical and wealthy executive Benjamin Hardesty. Elone listened attentively, her soft eyes fixed on his, and she nodded from time to time to show him that she understood what he was saying.

Ben did not often talk of Fleurette. When he did, it was with a kind of quick allusion, because he did not wish to suggest to Elone that he thought more of Fleurette than of her. And Elone did not speak, except perhaps to murmur some soft assent when he halted, groping for words as the remembrance of his happy days with his first wife struck a chord of memory he thought had been silenced. When at times his voice broke and his eyes grew misty, Elone put her soft hand on his shoulder and leaned closer to him, pressing her cheek against his shoulder while she crooned to little Bartholomew. Then Ben was swept with a warm wave of tender joy, and gratitude for Elone's presence swelled in him.

On the third night out, Ben made camp within the protective shelter of a clump of cedar trees. Just a few feet east of the edge of this natural barricade against the wind was a stretch of thick buffalo grass touched only lightly by the winter snow. Here he built a cheerful little fire and cooked the evening meal of broth for Tisinqua, and beans flavored with molasses, dried jerky, and strong tea for Elone and himself. While he tended the fire before preparing the meal, Elone fed little Bartholomew in the wagon. Then she joined him, going back to the wagon to feed Tisinqua the nourishing, hot soup and a tidbit or two of the jerky, which she had dipped in the broth to make it easier to chew and more palatable.

As he continued to prepare the meal for Elone and himself, Ben spoke of what lay ahead for them in Wichita. At length, she asked timidly, "When will you bring the children by your dead wife to Wichita, my husband?"

"Soon, my dear one. But first, as you know, good Jacob Hartmann must find us a place to live that will be suitable for all of our family. And it will take some weeks before Tisinqua and Bartholomew are comfortable in the new home. Then I will return to Windhaven Range to bring back Thomas and Sybella."

"That is very good." Her face shone with a smile that brightened the melancholy of her dark eyes. "You know that I will love them as much as if they were mine, my husband. I have heard you say so much about her, I know that I would love her if she were still alive. And you know well that among our people, a brave takes more than one squaw, yet both are dutiful and have no jealousy one for the other."

"Yes, Elone. But you know also that even if she were alive, the law of the white-eyes would not allow this. Yet I know what you say to me, and I am very grateful to you for saying and thinking it. God has blessed me in leading me to you. I will be a good husband to you."

"Oh no, that you need not say, because I have known it already for these many moons," she gently corrected him, putting out her hand to touch his cheek, then shyly drawing it away and lowering her eyes. "It is I who am blessed to have found you and to have won favor in your sight. When the Kiowa chief took me and made me his squaw, I prayed to the Great Spirit that if he gave me a child, I would have love for it, though I could not love its father. But the Great Spirit answered my prayers and more than I had dreamed of asking, because, as you see, it is the child of the husband I love to whom I give the milk of my breast. Truly am I fortunate in this."

He cupped her face in his hands and kissed her forehead, as the tears blurred his eyes. The exquisite tenderness of her avowal had stirred him to the very depths of his soul. To hide his emotions, he casually remarked, "For certain it will be more comfortable for all of us in Wichita than in the village of Emataba. Though he and his people have been very kind to us, we cannot forget that we and our children had to live in a tepee and to think of food and blankets and shelter against the wind, rain, and snow. And, for our little ones, it will be so much better; they will be healthy and strong once they have a comfortable home. Of course, this is selfish, for I wish your people could have such comforts as we go to now."

"That is what I think also, my husband," Elone murmured.

Quickly he turned back to the cooking pot and busied himself with the rest of their meal. He ladled beans and jerky onto tin plates, giving Elone the larger portion. "There is more, if you are still hungry, my dear one. And while you eat, I'll go back to the wagon to look after the little ones."

"Thank you, my husband. But Bartholomew is already asleep. I fed him, and he will sleep for a long time."

Ben sat down beside her. They ate in silence, until at last Elone—not looking up at him but frowning as she strove to put her thoughts into words—said, "All this day, as we rode toward Wichita, my husband, I have thanked the Great Spirit for the joy I feel with you. And yet I have thought also that in a town where there are many scores of white-eyes, it will be hard for you when you bring me among them."

Startled, Ben looked up and asked, "Why do you say this, my dear one?"

"Because," she frowned again and abstractly traced the tines of her fork over the surface of her plate, "I have heard what it is that the white-eyes call one of their own who takes an Indian girl to be his squaw."

"His wife, you mean," Ben gently corrected.

"His wife, then," Elone amended. "But I fear what they will say of you when we are in Wichita—that you are a squaw man because you have married an Indian girl and not one of your own kind."

"What people say about someone who lives his life by the teachings of our dear Lord will not change my feelings for you, Elone. We have been married in the faith of the white-eyes, to use your word for my people. The Society of Friends excludes no one because he or she has a different color of skin or a different faith or comes from a different land. Many of those who go to Pastor Hartmann's services have known what it was like to be persecuted for their beliefs. No, my dear one, they will welcome you and be kind to you. As for those who may say bad things about me, my faith makes me strong enough to ignore them."

"I understand what you say, my husband. But if ever I

171

should lose favor in your eyes, you must send me away."

"I will never do that, and you must never say such a thing to me again, my sweet wife. It distresses me when you say that you are not worthy. For, you see, that is what I feel about myself, that I must strive harder to be a good husband to you."

Now there were tears in her eyes as she turned to him. She stroked his cheek and his forehead and tried to smoothe out the lines of concern and anguish she saw there. "You are so good, so kind, there could never be any other man for me. Believe that, my husband, for I say it with a straight tongue and with love in my heart for you. I say to myself that the Great Spirit has been very good to me, because a man who gives so much of himself to strangers and to the poor and needy, as you have done, could surely find many women worthier of you than I am."

"No, please do not say such a thing ever again, Elone. I would not have married you if I had not thought that you were the worthiest of all women, and this you are. Come, the fire is nearly out. Let us make it warmer in the wagon for the children, before we go to sleep." He lifted her up gently, kissed her again, and then led her back to the wagon.

During the next day, the weather was unexpectedly warmer, and Ben and Elone took advantage of this by making several stops to walk and stretch their legs. True, they did not go very far, since Tisinqua and Bartholomew were alone in the wagon, but at least it was an opportunity to walk hand in hand and to commune with each other. Once again the Quaker doctor was struck by the uncanny resemblance between Fleurette's demeanor and Elone's ways. When he and Fleurette had first been married, they had often walked out into the garden of the little house in Pittsburgh and had been content to hold hands, exchanging occasional glances that amply substituted for words. Indeed, during these periods of silence, he had always had the impression that there was more intense and direct communication between them than if they had spoken—and so it was now again with Elone.

He found himself marveling as never before at simple, elemental things: the brilliant reds and rich purples of the sunset, the luster of the sun as it touched with glistening brilliance the snow that covered the plain. Or the sudden chatter of a jaybird, which swooped out of nowhere to land upon a crooked branch, its weight making the snow drop softly to the ground below, and the bright, keenly scrutinizing eyes of the bird as it turned toward them, marking them as aliens in a world where there were only birds and four-footed animals. The smell of burning twigs and the crackle of a fire, and then the aroma from the cooking pot that heralded a simple and yet hugely satisfying meal. It was as if Ben had come to life for the first time, had cast away the impersonality of scalpel and bandage, and was observing a thousand insignificant things that now seemed momentous and vital. He watched Elone, too, the way she carefully plaited her braids, or raised little Bartholomew to her breast—and now it seemed to him that he could feel all these things and sense them as a man and not as a physician. And because there was silence all around them, and no one in sight, he had the eerie sensation of being either the first man with the first woman, or else the last, going on to discover whether there was anything left—and, if there was not, to begin life on earth all over again.

They had come perhaps fifteen miles this fourth day, without haste, for their supplies were plentiful and Ben did not wish to tax his family with the rigors of a rapid journey in winter weather. But now the sky was suddenly clouded and there was no moon, so he built a larger campfire than before, not only for the evening meal, but also to provide greater warmth for Elone. Before seating herself tailor-fashion in the thick blanket, she had gone to the wagon to make sure that the children were warm enough, and she had pulled together the canvas flaps tightly at the back. Seeing that Ben was occupied in tending the fire and preparing the evening meal, Elone had swiftly taken the six-shooter and the pouch of cartridges out of their place of concealment and put them under a nearly empty burlap sack where they would be swiftly accessible in case of danger. As she did so, she looked up at the cloudy, morose sky and murmured a prayer to the Great Spirit to let them arrive at Wichita without violence or harm.

They ate in silence, exchanging tender glances, and Elone reflected that she had never felt so much at ease, so much at peace, not even with her own father and mother back in the Aiyuta village when she had been a little girl. She had been a virgin until the Kiowa chief had abducted

173

her and taken her to his blanket. At first she had resisted, only to be told that she had the choice of being a degraded slave to all of the tribe or else to submit, and so she had. When she had known herself with child by her savage mate, she had resolved to live for the child and to take what joy she could from its birth and thus to diminish the anguish of her loneliness with so brutal a mate and his callous companions.

Innately chaste, she had come to the homely young Quaker doctor virginal in spirit, if not in flesh; and in his tenderness with her when they lay together after their marriage in Wichita, she had known for the first time the exquisite joy that can exist between a man and a woman who are considerate of each other. Tonight, out in the wilderness, as she looked around at the darkness and up at the gloomy, clouded, moonless sky, she felt herself wishing that he would take her in his arms.

Their meal finished, Ben put out the campfire and came to take her hand and lead her back to the wagon. "It has been an easy day, my dear one," he told her. "In another three days, if all goes well and there is no more snow or wind to hinder us, we shall reach Wichita."

"I am glad of that, my husband," she murmured.

Then suddenly she drew back, for she had heard the pounding of horses' hooves, and a sudden fear assailed her. "There are riders coming to us," she whispered.

"Perhaps they are the couriers from the cattle market going to tell my good friend Lucien Edmond Bouchard that they await the bringing of his herd," he replied. "Do not be afraid. If they should be evil men, perhaps fleeing from the law, we have nothing they desire. Come, let us go into the wagon and prepare for bed. They will pass us by, I'm sure of it, Elone."

Carl Gronauer reined in his black mustang and pointed toward the southeast with a pudgy forefinger. "See that glimmer of light over yonder, Matt boy?"

" 'Course I see it, Carl. It's a campfire, that's what."

"Sure. And I can make out just one wagon and a couple of horses. Settlers, maybe. They're going to Wichita for supplies from wherever they live, most likely."

"I'll give you that, too. So what does that mean? Hell, Carl, we've got to put distance behind us. Like as not, the posse's after us, and our horses are winded already," Matt tensely declared.

"Not so fast, dummy. I gotta do all the thinking for us, seems like. And it's all your fault, too, that we've got the posse after us."

Matt Tinsley, in his late twenties, lean and tall, his black sideburns hiding the ugly, jagged, purplish scar of an old knife wound, glowered at his companion. "Now jist what the hell do you mean by that?"

"I'm saying to you, when we robbed that grocer in Wichita and he tried to pull a gun and I shot him, you had to go and get jittery and shoot up the stairs when you heard someone coming. You damned young fool, couldn't you figger that anybody coming down the stairs from that store had to be the wife or the kid of the storekeeper? So you shot a fifteen-year-old girl and that's why the posse's chasing us so hard."

"Now you hold your water, Carl, I don't like that sort of talk. S'pose it'd been his partner with a gun—"

"Jist shut your mouth. Now you listen real careful to what I'm saying. There's two horses tied to that wagon, and they're jist putting out the fire now—there's a man and a woman there. We'll take their horses and whatever else they've got."

"And maybe the woman too, huh, Carl?" Tinsley hazarded.

"Now you look here, boy, we're not going to waste time while you haul your ashes over some chippy. Besides, my share comes first and don't you forget it—I was the one who watched this old man in his store and figgered he was ripe for taking. But if I take a fancy to her, I guess we'll bring her along with us. The posse won't be looking for three riders, jist two, get me?"

"Yeah, that's right!" Tinsley breathed with a bawdy snigger. "All right, I'm with you, Carl. Let's go see what we've got there before they get back into their wagon."

"Now jist you keep your mouth shut, Matt, and let me do the talking," the older man warned.

Carl Gronauer was forty-two, without family or kinfolk. Of medium height and stocky, with thinning brown hair and a fat, moonish face, he had become an outlaw six years earlier when a Missouri trail boss discharged him for cowardice in the face of a stampede. Since then, he had robbed

175

several banks and stores in little towns. He had met Matt Tinsley in a Lawrence saloon and proposed a partnership which, thus far, had been highly profitable. One reason for Gronauer's willingness to make such an alliance was that he himself was not only a coward but also a poor shot. Although he had killed three men during the course of his robberies, he had shot all three of his victims in the back. Tinsley, however, had a quick draw and no conscience, and thus could furnish him with dependable aid.

At Gronauer's sign, the two men rode slowly toward the wagon, dismounted, and tethered their exhausted mustangs to a tall, isolated birch tree about five hundred yards from the little supply wagon. Both men strolled casually toward Elone and Ben Wilson, just as the latter was helping the young Indian girl into the front of the wagon.

"How you be, folks?" Carl Gronauer affably greeted them as he sauntered up to the wagon. Matt Tinsley, his right hand lowered toward the holster of the pistol, which he wore unusually low on his right thigh, stood by, watching intently.

"Oh, good—good evening." the Quaker doctor stammeringly greeted the two outlaws. "My wife heard you riding by, and I thought you might be from the cattle market, riding down to Texas to tell the ranchers about the market."

"You thought wrong, friend," Gronauer grinned, revealing crooked, yellowish teeth. "Where're you from and where're you headed?"

"To Wichita, with my wife and two children in the wagon. I'm Dr. Ben Wilson."

"Glad to know you, Ben boy," Gronauer grinned, again. "So you're headed for Wichita? We just came from there. And we've been riding mighty hard the last couple of days. That's why, when Matt here saw your horses, he thought we might jist maybe switch."

"Switch? I—I don't quite understand—" Ben doubtfully began.

Gronauer drew his pistol and his younger companion instantly emulated him. "You don't have to have much brains to understand, friend. I'm drawing on you. Now you jist be nice and peaceful, and we'll take the horses. Ours are about done in, savvy?"

"I—I can't stop you, if that's what you want to do."

"Now that's showing sense. Hey, now, this your woman?" Gronauer had just seen Elone peer down from the driver's seat in the wagon and his beady, watery blue eyes glinted with a sudden lust.

"Yes, this is my *wife*," Ben calmly responded.

Matt Tinsley eyed Elone with a crooked grin, then winked at his companion. "Damn if she ain't an Injun, Carl. Well, lookee here now, we got ourselves a squaw man, seems like. Now you can't tell me, Carl, that a man up and hitches an Injun girl the way he would one of his own kind, in a church, I mean in front of a real, honest-to-God preacher?"

"I catch your meaning, boy," Gronauer chuckled. He and Matt pointed their guns at Ben while they leeringly appraised Elone. She stood, eyes lowered, arms at her sides, in an attitude of meek submission, as if she sensed that she could make no decision and that, whatever these two armed men might decree, she must abide by it.

"There is no need to keep your guns on me," Ben said mildly. "I carry no weapons. I'm a Quaker, and it's against my faith."

"Well, now, that's right obliging, mister," Gronauer sneered. "Oh yeah, Matt, seems I heard tell of folks like this. Slap his face 'n he'll turn the other cheek—ain't that right now, mister?"

"I don't believe in violence, that's true. But we've nothing to give you, we mean you no harm, and there are two little children in the wagon, one an infant—I'd be grateful if you'd ride away and leave us in peace," Ben declared.

"See what I told you?" Gronauer grinned at his younger partner. "Real streak of yellow down his back. Figgers. When a man can't git hisself one of his own kind to go to bed with, he picks an Injun squaw 'cause she feels easy, beds down with any man who hankers after her." Then, turning to the Quaker doctor, he drawled, "Now then, mister, here's what Matt 'n me're gonna do. We're gonna take your purty squaw along with us and fooferaw her good. 'N we'll jist take your horses, 'cause ours are jist about done in."

"Ain't you fergittin' one thing, though, Carl?" Tinsley picked at his nose and then sniggered, with a sidelong glance at Elone, who seemed to shrink away when she heard herself being discussed so rudely and callously.

177

"Oh, yeah, that's right, Matt. I see whatcher drivin' at. Well, mister," as he contemptuously looked Ben up and down and waved his gun meaningfully in the air, "guess we'll hafta kill you. Not that we got anything personal against you, you understand. Back in Wichita, where we come from, we hadda shoot a fellow that ran a store we robbed, jist to keep him from talkin' to the law about where we was headed. And then his fool young daughter hadda come in where she had no business bein', so naturally she had to git it too. Now she was a right purty young thing—only right now, 'peers to me this squaw of yours is a heap purtier. That's why we ain't gonna kill her—not right off, anyhow."

So saying, he slowly lowered his gun, his eyes narrowing, till the muzzle pointed at Ben's forehead.

"No, wait!" Elone quickly gasped, turning and putting her hand on Carl Gronauer's left shoulder. "He can do you no harm. That one," she made a derisive face at the Quaker doctor as now she stared intently into Gronauer's glinting eyes, "he is like a woman. But I, Elone, will go willingly with you because you are strong and have much spirit, which this one does not."

"Hey now, Carl," Matt Tinsley excitedly spoke up. "You hear what that purty Injun gal jist said? I do believe she'd rather have us fooferaw her than that yellow-livered Quaker man of hers."

"It is true," Elone spoke breathlessly, almost pleadingly as she saw Gronauer continue to hold the gun leveled at her husband's forehead. "He is a coward, as you say. It would be better than killing him to let him go back alone so that everyone would know he could not even fight for his wife. And besides, I will tell you where he has hidden his gold to buy goods in Wichita."

"Yeah?" Tinsley moved toward her, his eyes greedily narrowed. "Where's he got this gold hidden, honey? Carl, reckon we might jist let this spineless skunk run fer his life like this purty Injun pokemeat wants if she buys him off. Not a bad idea having everybody laugh at him fer bein' such a coward, I'd say."

"Well now, honey," Gronauer at last lowered the gun till the muzzle pointed at the ground, "suppose you jist show me where this gold is stashed away. Then we'll talk about it, huh?"

"In the back of the wagon. The papooses are sleeping—you promise you will not hurt them?"

"Naw, whaddya think I am?" the older man contemptuously sniffed. "Jist be quick 'n git that gold for me, then we'll do some palavering."

"Tell her she can do it on her back in the wagon to show she's not lyin'," Tinsley lewdly prompted.

"I will do whatever you want. Come, I will show you where the gold is," Elone murmured. Coquettishly, she turned to look at both outlaws, while a soft, beguiling smile curved her mouth. Both of them lowered their pistols as they followed her to the back of the wagon.

She drew aside the canvas flaps. "There, you see where the papooses sleep," she murmured. "I have hidden the gold right here under the blanket. Do not come so close and do not talk—you will wake them."

"All right," Gronauer snarled. "Jist git it out quick as you can, honey, before I change my mind."

"Yes, I will do what you want. And then, if you let that man walk back where he came from, taking the papooses with him—for I do not want them any more, fathered as they were by a man with little spirit—then I will show you how an Indian girl can love men who are strong and brave," Elone murmured alluringly.

"Hot damn!" Tingsley ejaculated, holstering his gun and licking his lips in lubricious anticipation.

Elone delved her right hand under the folded-over top of the burlap bag, gripped the butt of the six-shooter, and in the same swift movement turned and fired point-blank at Carl Gronauer. He staggered back, his eyes huge with incredulity, as a red stain blossomed in the center of his forehead, and then fell like a dead weight at her feet. Before Matt Tinsley could reach for his holstered gun, Ben had come up behind him, circled his waist with his left arm, and pulled the gun out of its holster with his right hand.

"Hey, you killed Carl, you dirty Injun bitch!" Tinsley's voice was choked with fury.

"Be careful, or Elone will shoot you too. Don't make a move. I'm going to throw your gun away, and then I'm going to teach you a lesson," Ben panted. Moving back, he flung the outlaw's gun with all his might toward the north, while Elone backed away from the wagon, keeping the six-shooter leveled at Tinsley's belly.

179

"Turn around now and see if you can defend yourself in a fair fight without weapons," the Quaker doctor challenged.

"Oh yeah, sure," Tinsley hoarsely jeered, "and have your Injun bitch gun me down the way she did poor Carl—fat chance. Go ahead, have her finish the job—you're too yellow to do it yourself."

"No." Ben shook his head. "Elone, put the gun back into the wagon—do not let him get it, but you are not to use it against him, do you understand? It will be just between the two of us with bare fists."

"As you wish, my husband," Elone murmured, and put the six-shooter back in the place from which she had taken it.

Matt Tinsley glanced around, and then a wicked smile warped his thin lips. "Why, now, that's more like it. Know what I'm gonna do, Quaker? I'm gonna beat you to a pulp 'n then I'm gonna poke yer Injun bitch jist like Carl 'n I was goin' to. You wanna fight? Let's see if you got gumption enough to take jist one punch!" So saying, he lunged at Ben with a sweeping blow of his right fist. The Quaker doctor ducked under the flailing attack and countered with a solid punch to Tinsley's belly, which staggered the younger man and drew a grunt of pain from him.

"Hunnhh! Well, you got in a lucky one, that's all, and that's the last one! I'm gonna kill you, you weaseling sonuvabitch!"

Now, more cautiously, crouching a little, he came forward with both fists clenched and the right hand leading as he circled his adversary. Then suddenly he kicked out with his booted right foot, catching the Quaker doctor in the thigh just above the knee. The ruse took Ben by surprise, and he winced and hobbled to one side just as Tinsley, with a hoarse chuckle of delight, came at him with both fists flailing. One of them bruised Ben's cheek, but he doggedly stood his ground and retaliated with a punishing right uppercut to the jaw.

Tinsley slowly got to his feet, his eyes murderously glinting and narrowed. "Well, Quaker, you've been real lucky so far. Gotta give you credit, but now it's my turn, savvy?" This time, he lowered his head and charged Ben as a bull charges a matador. Wrapping his arms around his opponent, he flung Ben to the ground and then tried to knee

180

him in the groin. But Ben agilely twisted to one side so that
the knee only bruised his hip and, extricating his right arm
from the bear hug of his opponent, he drove his fist with
all his strength against Tinsley's Adam's apple.

The young outlaw uttered a gurgling shriek and vomited, going limp and sprawling across the Quaker doctor's
body. Ben pushed him onto his side and stumbled to his
feet. "Get up and take what's coming to you!" he hoarsely
demanded.

But his young opponent rolled back and forth, a hand
clasped to his throat, his face greenish and his eyes bulging
with the unspeakable agony of that punishing blow.
"Aaarrgghhh—lemme be—you've fair done me in—
goddamn Quaker—oh, Jesus, you killed me—"

"Hardly," Ben contemptuously retorted. "Quakers don't
kill. Your friend there, who seemed to know so much
about them, should have told you that. Get on your feet."

"No—oh, Gawd, it hurts—I've had enough—I quit—
aagghh!" The outlaw coughed and vomited again, sprawling
onto his back and continuing to rub his throat.

"Very well. Get on your horse and head for the Mexican
border. You've boasted about what you and your friend
did in Wichita—I've no doubt lawmen are riding after you
right now. If they catch you, they're sure to hang you. Get
on your horse and ride, and be thankful I don't believe in
killing."

Matt Tinsley got to his knees, his face still contorted
with pain. Slowly, he staggered to his tethered mustang
and mounted it. Then, with a last vindictive look, he rode
off to the south.

"Oh, my husband, my dear husband!" Elone burst into
tears as she ran toward Ben and clung to him, pressing her
tear-stained face against his heaving chest. "Forgive me,
forgive me!"

"But, my dear one, there's nothing to forgive," he protested.

"Oh yes. Did you not hear me tell them that I would
like to be with them in the wagon, did you not wonder
why I said such evil things about the man who is dearest to
me in all this world? I did not mean those words, you must
know that, my husband!"

"I understand. You saved us all, Elone. I understand
now. Emataba gave you that gun."

"Yes, my husband," she whispered, her face still pressed against his chest as she feverishly clung to him and burst into uncontrollable sobs.

"How wise he was," Ben mused. "He knew that you had not taken your final vows in my faith, even though you had been married to me by a Quaker pastor. And that was why he gave you the gun I would never take."

"Yes, my husband. I could not have let them kill you—even if I had the final vows, I could not, I could not. I love you more than life itself. You have given me life, you have given me love, you have made me a woman; I have borne your son and I am yours always."

Gently he cupped her trembling chin and lifted her tear-stained face, and there were tears in his own eyes as he bent to kiss her. "Your God and mine, Elone, will, I'm sure, forgive this one transgression against His commandment, 'Thou shalt not kill.' Because, my dear one, even if they had killed me and taken you, what would have become of our Tisinqua and Bartholomew? Assuredly, evil men like them would have killed the innocent children too. Truly I am blessed by having such a wife as you, my Elone."

They stood together in the stillness of the night, clinging to each other, as they wept in the joy of their salvation and the discovery of their heroic love.

CHAPTER FOURTEEN

By the middle of March 1872, it was already warm in Carrizo Springs, unseasonably so, and it was time, Lucien Edmond Bouchard decided, to plan the year's cattle drive. This year, the drive would have a new destination, for thanks to a mounted courier sent by Joseph McCoy from Abilene, Lucien Edmond knew that the farmers near Abilene had forced the town to close its doors to the ranchers' herds.

That was the topic of discussion this warm, humid evening as he, Ramón Hernandez, Simata, and Joe Duvray finished dinner in the spacious dining room of the ranch house and walked into the living room to continue their discussion over brandy, coffee, and cigars.

"I have to give Joe McCoy credit for being a gentleman," Lucien Edmond said as he unfolded the printed circular the hard-riding courier had brought two days before. "If I hadn't had this news, we'd have gone on to Abilene as we've done in the past, only to find ourselves turned away."

"Well," Ramón replied, "judging from last year's prices, I for one would just as soon look elsewhere. With the interbreeding that you and Joe have done, it seems to me that you should be able to get a much better price than the ten dollars and seventy-five cents you got last year from the new Armour buyer."

"I agree, Ramón." Lucien Edmond frowned and meditatively drew on his cigar to get it going. "Remember, when we got to Abilene last fall, we heard that the Santa Fe had reached Newton, about sixty-five miles south of Abilene. The last time I rode into San Antonio to do business at our bank and to get more supplies, I sent a telegraph to the station operator at Newton to ask him if the Santa Fe was equipping itself to take on cattle, and the answer was yes."

"Then that's where we'll go this spring," Ramón eagerly declared.

"I think it's a wise move. But we're going to hold back about five thousand of our cattle this time. We've got too many yearlings, for one thing, from crossing our Brahmas with the Herefords."

"That makes sense," Joe Duvray nodded.

"What worries me, too, is that President Grant is almost certain of reelection," Lucien Edmond continued, his frown deepening. "In my opinion, that will mean he'll continue to be surrounded by corrupt weaklings who look upon their political situation as an open license to theft. We're headed for a major economic crisis, and that means a slump in the prices for cattle and agricultural products and just about everything else."

"Do you really think so, Lucien Edmond?" Joe anxiously inquired.

"I do indeed, I'm sorry to say. I think the wisest course for us is to get what we can for just part of our stock this summer at Newton, and really start building our herd. Next year, we'll hold back even more. I wouldn't be surprised if we sold just in local markets like San Antonio, Santa Fe, and maybe some of the army posts in Kansas and Indian Territory. After that, we'll see which way the wind is blowing. The next few years will be rough, but I can foresee booming prices once the slump is over, just because everyone else will also hold back supplies for a decent price and people who want the beef we're raising now will be willing to pay more for it. Yes, it's very likely that, within three or four years at the most, we'll be getting as much as twenty dollars a head."

Ramón Hernandez uttered a low whistle and grinned. "No reason that you and Joe couldn't build up a herd of about twenty thousand head by that time. At twenty dollars a head, we'd all be rich!"

"Exactly. Meanwhile, we've all done very well here. We've met our expenses, we pay our vaqueros a good wage and keep them well and happy, we've banked a good reserve for the lean years. Best of all, like Father, I'm very happy to work on the land, to enjoy my family, and to have the companionship and friendship of men like you and all our workers. I think, in a way, that's what Great-grandfather Lucien wanted us all to realize—the material reward doesn't count so much as the satisfaction of a life of meaningful work, with good friends and strong family ties to carry one through the difficult times."

"Yes," Ramón mused aloud. "We've survived bandits and landgrabbers. And now, because you were smart enough to buy that Caldemare land next to ours and deed it over to Joe, the two of you are forming a ranch that one day will be one of the biggest in all Texas, supplying quality beef to the entire country."

"As soon as the railroads reach here and finish their cross-continental development, that's for certain." Lucien Edmond smiled as he lifted his brandy goblet. "A toast, then, to this year's drive to Newton."

"Is Abilene really dead then, Lucien Edmond?" Joe asked.

"I'm afraid it is. When I talked to Joe McCoy last fall, he told me that the small farmers—the cowmen call them 'nesters'—have been pushing steadily westward along the Kansas Pacific. And, of course, to a farmer, a cattleman is a natural enemy: his herd tramples down the wheat and corn and vegetables, takes the drinking water the farmers' animals need. No, this note from McCoy is dated from last month, and it orders ranchers to stay away from Abilene. Listen, I'll read it to you—Jim McCoy didn't write this, but the newly organized Farmers' Protective Association did." He cleared his throat, unfolded the sheet he had pulled from the pocket of his waistcoat, and read aloud:

We, the undersigned, members of the Farmers' Protective Association, and officers and citizens of Dickinson County, Kansas, most respectfully request all who have contemplated driving Texas cattle to Abilene this coming season to seek some other points for shipment, as the inhabitants of Dickinson will no longer submit to the evils of the trade.

"Evils of the trade, my behind!" Joe irreverently guffawed. "Why, it was herds like yours, Lucien Edmond, that made Abilene boom and brought it cowhands with money to spend there in all the saloons and the dance halls."

"Well, you can be certain that Joe McCoy, the man who started Abilene as a cattle town, is shrewd enough to move somewhere else when his own profit is at stake," Lucien Edmond retorted. "There's a postscript to this note, and it says that there are already twenty buildings in Newton. Of course, you can expect them to be the usual false-front structures, but Joe McCoy is building a second stockyard, large enough to hold four thousand cattle. And his Newton yards are located a mile and a half from the original business section, so there won't be any cattle stampedes into town to disturb the citizens of this new metropolis."

"Four thousand, eh?" Joe repeated. "Well, the trains will be busy shuttling back and forth to Chicago, if McCoy gets all the cattle this year that he got last year in Abilene. So how many do you plan on taking?"

"I'd say about three thousand prime. Say we get eleven dollars a head—I don't really look for much more this year—that's thirty-three thousand dollars, a third of which is for our vaqueros, and the rest split between you and me, Joe."

"Wait a minute, Lucien Edmond, that's being much too generous and you know it," Joe protested. "You sold me the Caldemare land for a dollar and other valuable considerations, you know, and you already gave Margaret and me quite a wedding present last year."

"You've earned your share by helping me with the interbreeding, and by the way your men are patrolling our combined acreage and making it a unified ranch so that no landgrabbers or rustlers can bother us this year," was Lucien Edmond's smiling reply. "All right, let's get some sleep and then tomorrow we'll start picking out our cattle. And you, Ramón, choose your vaqueros and the horses you want for the remuda."

In Chicago, the third week of March brought unseasonably warm weather, interspersed with long hours of steady rain. That rain would have been a blessed boon in October of the previous year; it might have prevented the devastating fire. And yet, only five months after that staggering disaster, the Windy City was in the throes of an energetic rebuilding program. Charles Douglas's partner, genial Lawrence Harding, had met Laurette, Polly Behting, and the three little boys at the railroad station and escorted them in a bright new phaeton to the new house near Lincoln Park. Laurette had fallen in love with it at first sight.

There was a big yard for the children to play in, plenty of space for her own projected gardens of flowers and vegetables, and she was already planning to put up a gazebo for the summer. The two-story brick and wood house was certainly more solid and durable than any of their previous abodes. And Lawrence had gone so far as to furnish the house; after her first quick inspection, Laurette had profusely thanked him for his admirable taste. What amused her was that he was a bachelor of thirty-eight and yet knew what a family would need in the way of conveniences. She had already made up her mind to invite some eligible and attractive young women to dinner in whom Charles's partner might become seriously interested.

What with shopping for food and buying clothes for the boys and for herself as well, Laurette was happily busy, which distracted her from anxiety over her husband's protracted absence. She had already received a letter from him detailing his unsatisfactory attempt to buy land and begin his first new store in Houston, and he had told her that he was going back to James Hunter in Galveston to plan for an opening there instead. He indicated that if all went well, and if he could find a trustworthy construction boss who would carry out his orders without his having to be there, he might be home toward the end of April.

In return, Laurette was able to write to Charles that the rebuilding of the Chicago store was going well and that a reopening was scheduled for late April. Here again Lawrence Harding proved himself to be tireless and dedicated in his association with her husband. A week after she had settled in the new house, he called for her and took her downtown to see the progress of that restoration. Moreover, he was beginning to hire qualified sales clerks, and from the conversation she had with this black-haired, tall, courteous Easterner, she was certain that he would know how to choose employees who would be a credit to the Douglas merchandising creed.

She thought then of Carrie Melton Haines and murmured a prayer for that young woman's soul. She remembered all too well how Carrie had once tried to seduce her husband, been discharged, and then made social overtures to her once she had married that fatuous old fool of a banker, Dalton Haines. She remembered with deep contrition how she had taken a horsewhip to Carrie in the bank where the latter worked, a punishment motivated by her own jealous anger at a girl she believed to be nothing more than a cheap adventuress. Yet that same girl had commandeered a buggy during the panic of the great fire, put her and the boys and Polly into it, and paid for that act with her own life when ruffians, seeing the money she carried in her reticule, stole it and knocked her down to be trampled to death by the fleeing mob.

But on this unusually warm and sunny Saturday, Laurette was able to banish such mournful thoughts. She was bustling about in her new kitchen, preparing for a five o'clock dinner to which Ezekiel Benderson and his gracious, gray-haired wife, Doris, were invited, as well as her new next-door neighbors, William and Elmyra Young. Ezekiel Benderson held the post of city treasurer, and he had been working long hours after the great fire to help restore the city's economy. William Young was the alderman of the ward in which the Douglases now resided, a man in his early fifties, jovial and florid-faced as the result of his fondness for rich food, but scrupulously honest. He was to bring his niece, Sylvia Cross, an attractive reddish-blond schoolteacher in her early thirties. And Lawrence Harding had agreed to come for dinner also—Laurette smiled to herself as she began to set the elaborate dining-room table and arrange the place-markers that would seat her husband's handsome partner and the attractive schoolteacher side by side this evening.

Polly Behting appeared at the dining-room doorway, her blue eyes eager as she remarked, "Excuse me, Mrs. Douglas, but the weather's so nice outside, I was just wondering if you'd like me to take the boys for a walk this afternoon?"

"Why, that's a very good idea, Polly dear." Laurette turned from the table to smile at the pretty young German governess. "Just be back in plenty of time to get the children ready for our early dinner tonight. The children will be at our table, and they'll be able to have a few minutes with the grownups before it's time for bed."

"*Natürlich.* I'll make sure they're tucked in bed when it's time," Polly promised.

"You like this new house of ours, don't you, Polly?"

"Oh, *ja, wirklich!* It's so big, and such a beautiful yard!" Polly eagerly replied.

"Yes, I think Charles will just love this place when he comes back from Galveston. There's a big room upstairs he can use as his study, and there are enough guest rooms so that if he brings any of his traveling business associates to the house, we'll be able to offer them hospitality. But tell me now, dear, have you been able to tell Dieter yet about your intentions back in Texas?"

"*Ja,* I have." Polly blushed and lowered her eyes. "I was really afraid—poor Dieter, I knew he was planning to open his own butcher shop soon and then, of course, he would want to get married. But—well, I finally did tell him yesterday, and he understands, and he wishes me well."

"It sounds to me, dear, as if while you were away in Texas your hardworking butcher found himself another girl. You know, that would be a perfect solution. That way, he wouldn't really ever hold a grudge against you for breaking off the engagement," Laurette gently commented.

"But that is true!" Polly looked up, her eyes shining with happiness. "That is just what happened, and it is *unglaublich!* When I saw him, I was trembling and afraid to say what I had to—that is, about dear Eddie—and all of a sudden it was Dieter who was starting to apologize and saying that he had something to tell me that I wouldn't like and that he hoped I would understand. *Jawohl,* while we were down in Texas, his brother Ludwig moved here from St. Louis and is going to go into partnership with him in the butcher shop. Ludwig is married, and he brought along his sister-in-law, Marlene, to live with him and his wife for a time until she can find a job here in Chicago. And—well, Dieter says he fell in love with her."

"I'm so glad, darling!" Laurette quickly moved to the blushing young governess and gave her a hug and a kiss on the cheek. "I tell you what, why don't you sit down right now and write Eddie a letter and tell him that everything's all right? I know he'll be very happy to get it. And then you can mail it when you go for a walk with the boys."

"*Ja,* I will do that—with your permission, *natürlich,*" Polly excitedly exclaimed.

Laurette smiled and nodded. "There's lots of time. Write him a nice long letter, dear. And send him my best wishes." She turned back to the table, her mood now totally euphoric, anticipating the pleasant sociability of the evening and her own debut as a matchmaker.

189

*   *   *

"How beautiful it is outside, in the warm sun!" Polly Behting exulted as she left the new house with the three little boys. She had made them dress warmly, for there could often be sharp winds in March. Yet now the sun was high and the sky was clear, except for some small white clouds that looked like a herd of young lambs jauntily parading, so that it seemed more like mid-May than March.

Kenneth and Arthur, the twins, now six and a half, had already learned to dress themselves carefully and were quite proud of their appearance. Polly never failed to praise them both for their conscientious grooming. As for little Howard, now three, he still needed help, but was always most cooperative. Her heart went out to him, and as she hugged him when she had finished putting on his little coat, she stood for a moment and closed her eyes with a serene inner rapture. She was thinking of Eddie Gentry. She wondered what he was doing this very moment out there on that vast range where already the weather was so very warm. Was he thinking of her? She had already received two letters, short ones, with guardedly prosaic expressions—but she could read between the lines. A man like that, she knew, would not pour forth his heart in a letter: no, he would wait until they could be together. And perhaps he wouldn't use fancy, poetic words, but when he held her and kissed her, she would know that wonderful feeling of belonging entirely to someone, of entrusting her life to his keeping. Oh, how happy, how wonderful it was going to be when they could finally be together! And now that she'd written this letter and told him that he didn't have to worry about Dieter any more and that, if he still wanted her, she would really like to have him say so, she could hardly wait to post the letter. "We shall go to Lincoln Park today, boys," she announced. "Now then, you, Kenneth and Arthur, walk on my right side, and be very careful. And you must be sure to stop when we come to the end of the street and not go forward till I say so, *versteht ihr*? Now you, dear Howard, you will be at my left and you will give me your right hand—that's a *Liebchen*! And now, we shall go see how nice it is outdoors. Maybe, if you are all very good, there will be someone selling candy when we come to Lincoln Park, and you shall all have just a little—not too much, though, because dinner will be early this evening. Come along now, boys!"

They proceeded down the street, Polly looking radiant as she breathed in the clean, sweet air. The fire, although a catastrophe, had purged Chicago, and already the city was beginning to surpass what it had been and to set a standard for the rest of the world to admire. Laurette Douglas had told Polly about William D. Kerfoot, a real-estate dealer whose shack was to be the origin of the city's Kerfoot Block. A few days after the fire, he had nailed a sign to the top of his makeshift office, and what it said had become part of Chicago's folklore: "All Gone but Wife, Children, and Energy." And less than a week after the fire, Field, Leiter and Company had put up signs notifying their cash boys where to get their back pay, and still other signs announcing resumption of business in their temporary headquarters on the Near South Side. Then there was the Nixon Block at LaSalle and Monroe Streets, which would be touted for years as the "only structure in the Chicago Burnt District not damaged by flames." It had only been partially built at the time of the fire, and its floor surfacing and wood trim were consumed by the flames. Yet the damage was so slight that the building was rushed to completion one week after the fire, and it was to serve for decades as an office building for architects and businessmen.

Yes, Polly Behting loved Chicago, and for a moment, as she looked around the newly rebuilt street with its houses, she felt a touch of regret at the thought of going back to Texas. Perhaps, she thought, Eddie might be induced to come here. Surely such a smart young man could make his fortune in Chicago as had so many others. No, that was selfish. She would go wherever he wished, because she loved him.

Yet how wonderfully energetic this city was! Joseph Medill had won the mayoral election last November on a "fireproof" ticket, urging a host of measures that would prevent a recurrence of the great fire. There were to be no more false fronts, and there would be greater emphasis on fire-resistant materials like brick, stone, and iron, as well as an improved water system. On the South Side, thirty-four million dollars had already been spent in new construction, on the North nearly four million dollars, and on the West Side two million dollars. On streets only a few months ago

191

stripped of all trees, saplings now grew. Where once there had been only ashes and rubble, one could now see patches of verdant green park. And Chicago had a great new hotel, the Grand Pacific. Three even larger ones were to follow within the next three years, with the majestic Palmer House already advertised as revolutionary with its large rooms, magnificently proportioned dining hall, and a barber shop that would have silver dollars imbedded in the floor . . . a hotel that would win the unrestrained praise of sophisticated Europeans for its tessellated marble and gold trimmings.

She would miss all this, she reflected. But then, looking up at the bright sky, remembering how it looked in Texas and how the vastness of the horizon awed her, she smiled again and was content. Out there, she and Eddie would have true *Freiheit*—freedom. Perhaps he would have a little farm and raise cows and horses, and she could raise a flock of chickens. The children could be outdoors all the time, playing—their children. She blushed again at such thoughts, for they were not even married yet. She could hardly wait to have his letter back answering hers. Her father had already resigned himself to her absence, when she had told him in such glowing terms how beautiful Windhaven Range was and how honest and good the men who worked on it were. She had also told him about Eddie. "You'll love him like a son, *mein Vater,* I promise you will."

The three little boys walked along eagerly, chattering to each other like aggressive little chipmunks who took in everything and were impatient to see and do more. She urged the twins not to go too far ahead of her. Howard's hand was tightly clasped in hers, and she turned to smile at him. Here was a corner; they would have to stop and wait.

"Kenneth, Arthur, wait for me," she urged. "Very good. Now you see there are people coming along in carriages— *mein Gott*—oh, the poor woman—"

Across the street, a shabbily dressed woman had stumbled on the rude curb, and her little boy, as she let go of his hand, had walked out into the street. From Polly's right came a lumbering horsecar, drawn by three dappled Percherons. The little boy was oblivious to its approach, and the mother uttered a shriek of terror as she saw the horses bearing down upon her child.

"Wait here, don't move!" Polly called to her three charges. Gathering her skirts in her hand, she swiftly ran toward the child, bent and scooped him up, and cast him toward his mother, crying out, "Here, catch him, *Gott helfe dich!*"

She straightened, for by now the horses were almost upon her. But the street was muddy and her shoe stuck, and then the terrible shock struck her, and she had just time to say, "Oh, *mein* Eddie, oh *Gott*, please no—" and then all was darkness.

It was the last day of March, and on the morrow Lucien Edmond Bouchard, Joe Duvray, Ramón Hernandez and twenty vaqueros would begin to drive three thousand head of cattle toward the new market of Newton. Santiago Miraflores, one of the vaqueros whom Ramón had hired last year, rode in with his *compañero,* Nacio Lorcas, another of the new vaqueros who had been recruited in Nuevo Laredo. They had come in from San Antonio with a supply wagon and with messages from the bank. Santiago hurried to the ranch house, carrying the letters and a telegram for Lucien Edmond.

In the living room, Lucien Edmond was leaning back on the settee, his eyes closed, a smile on his handsome face as he listened to his beautiful wife, Maxine, playing a Mozart sonata on the spinet. The elegant grace of the music drove out all thoughts of the hazards that might await him on the arduous cattle drive, which would take three months and hold incalculable risks.

He sprang to his feet when he heard Santiago Miraflores timidly knock at the door, and opened it. "*Mi patrón,* there is this from the bank. And there is a *telegrama—es muy importante.*"

"*Gracias,* Santiago. Tell the men to turn in early tonight. We start at dawn tomorrow."

"*Sí, mi patrón.* I will tell them at once. *Gracias.*" Santiago bobbed his head and backed away with a broad grin. He already knew that he was in great luck to have found such a fine *patrón.* And Nacio shared his feeling. It was indeed the best job he and Nacio had ever had. He was looking forward eagerly to tomorrow. Even though both of them had been assigned to ride behind the herd, which

193

meant eating the dust, it did not matter. It was an honor to work for so distinguished an *hombre* as Señor Lucien Edmond Bouchard.

Maxine Bouchard ended the sonata in a whirlwind coda and rose from the spinet, her eyes shining. "It's such wonderful music, isn't it, my darling?" she murmured. "It almost makes me forget that you're going to be gone from me for at least three whole months." Then, seeing the scowl on his face, she hastily gasped, "What is it? Is it bad news?"

He had torn open the telegraph wire and now uttered a heavy sigh. "The very worst possible. Oh God, I'd give anything not to have to tell poor Eddie."

"Eddie?" she wonderingly echoed.

"Yes." He stared at the crumpled piece of paper in his hand, wadded it into a ball, and flung it on the floor with a solemn imprecation. "At all times, to have to tell him such dreadful news. He's been so happy, whistling and singing and helping Ramón with the horses for the remuda. And now this, on the eve of the drive. I hope to God it won't break him to pieces."

"What is it, my darling? Please, what is it?" Maxine was almost in tears.

"You know that sweet German governess, Polly Behting, who came with the Douglas children?" he said in a hoarse voice.

She nodded wordlessly.

"She was killed a week ago. She tried to save a little boy who had wandered out into the street. A carriage was bearing down on him, and Polly ran out and caught him and tossed him in the air to his mother who had stumbled and lost her balance. She couldn't escape—it was a muddy street and—"

"Oh dear God, no!" Maxine sobbed and covered her face with her hands.

Lucien Edmond went to her, put his arm around her, and kissed her. "I wish to God I didn't have to tell him. But I must. And he's got to go on that drive. It's the only thing that'll keep him from breaking."

"I know. He's such a good man, so kind. And he's strong, too."

"I know. I'm counting on that to see him through this

dreadful time. Well, Maxine darling, I'm going to tell him now. He was looking forward so eagerly to her coming down here. And I was going to give him some land so they could have a little ranch of their own. Damn it, why do things like this have to happen to nice, decent people?"

CHAPTER FIFTEEN

Eddie Gentry walked slowly down the steps of the ranch house, twisting his sombrero in his hands, his face drawn. He hardly heard the friendly greeting of Lucas, who, with one of the vaqueros, was busy replacing several of the posts in the stockade fence.

Just a few minutes before, he had stood in the ranch house, his friendly grin changing to a look of pain and incredulity as Lucien Edmond painstakingly broke the news received in the telegraph message from Chicago. He had ground his teeth and blinked his eyes furiously to hide the sudden rush of tears. He tried to tell himself that somehow there had been a terrible mistake, and perhaps this was a kind of test of courage on the eve of the cattle drive on which he was to ride. Lucien Edmond had said, "I want you to ride the right point again this year, Eddie, because you did so well at it last year. You're a born leader, and the men all like and respect you. And she'd have wanted you to continue in your work, you know."

That last phrase had been too much for Eddie. He had mumbled something unintelligible, turned tail, and strode out of the ranch house. It wasn't rudeness, it was just that suddenly he wanted to be by himself to understand this dreadful, impossible thing that had happened so far away, something over which he could never have had any control at all. Oh God, if he'd only been there with her—he could have saved the child and her, too—how could you expect a young girl to do all that and not lose her footing in the muddy street. . . .

It wasn't fair. It wasn't fair at all. Polly was such a good person, not a mean bone in her body, only thinking of the Douglas children and wanting to please everyone. And the miracle of it had been that she had fallen in love with him and, for the first time, made him feel what it could be like to be wanted by someone who cared, someone who wanted to share her life with him. He had been thinking about all the little things that never seemed to matter before, like what kind of furniture to have in the house they lived in and even what kind of curtains and . . .

He turned abruptly and walked toward the corral. Ramón Hernandez had gone out riding southeast a couple of days ago just for the sport of it and come upon a herd of wild mustangs, the kind the Kiowas and Comanches rode. He'd picked one of the herd and roped him and brought him back to a special stall in the corral. He was something like Pablo Casares's gray stallion, Fuerza Torda. So far, when any of the vaqueros came near him, the mustang reared in the air with an angry snort, pawing with his hooves, his eyes rolling wildly, baring his teeth in defiance.

He'd been downright rude, walking out on Mr. Lucien Edmond that way. But Eddie figured that he'd understand. He just couldn't have stood there any more, listening to what Mr. Lucien Edmond had to say. He'd have to go back and apologize later—yes, and thank Mr. Lucien Edmond, too, for making him point rider again this year. That was really an honor. He didn't know if he was up to it this season—right now, he had to work things out in his mind, think things over. There was such a numb feeling in him, he couldn't tell what he wanted to do right this minute. Except come hell or high water, he was going to break that mustang, even if it broke him in the process.

When he got to the stall, the mustang reared again, and one of its hooves clattered on the rail near his face. He grinned, understanding. There was a challenge here, and you either met it or you walked away less of a man. He had to do it. And there wasn't time to take a saddle or reins and bit to a horse like this. This horse had been born on the plains, had galloped free as the wind with the rest of the herd, had never known the weight of a man on its back. Right now, Ramón was in the bunkhouse giving the vaqueros he'd chosen to ride with him some pointers on how Newton would be different from Abilene and how they were going to drive the herd this time. Ramón would probably want to beat the living daylights out of him for touching the mustang, but he just had to.

Very carefully, he climbed over the wooden rails of the stall, waiting for his chance. The mustang lunged at him, its teeth bared, trying to nip his leg. Swiftly, he turned and leaped astride it, gripping it by the neck, one hand grasping the thick, beautiful mane. The beast lunged furiously against the entrance to the stall, and Eddie leaned over and quickly threw aside the two topmost rails.

Now the mustang began to buck, trying to throw him, but Eddie grimly held on, his sombrero long since dropped to the ground and trampled by the thudding hooves of the infuriated horse. As it turned and tried to back against the lowered entrance to the stall, trying its best to unseat him, Eddie reached back with his right foot and kicked off first one and then another rail. Then, tugging at the mustang's mane, he turned its head toward the entrance. With a bound, it cleared the two low rails that remained and galloped wildly out toward the southeast, where Ramón had found it. It would join its fellows, Eddie knew; it would follow them no matter where they had gone. Only, this time, he was going to ride it until either the mustang or he was finished.

Twice the powerful gray mustang reared in the air, whinnying angrily, and then bucked and veered off toward the north. By sheer tenacity, Eddie clung to his perilous bareback hold, both hands twisted in the thick mane on the superb horse's arching neck. Its eyes were wild and it snorted furiously as it raced at full speed over the verdant plain, lurching near huge clumps of mesquite and sometimes veering toward a clump of trees in an attempt to dash its rider to the ground and be free again.

Eddie's sun-bronzed face was twisted with desperate concentration. There was nothing now in the world except the mustang and himself, nothing in his mind save the all-consuming determination to stay on the horse to the very end of this primal duel between them.

The sun was warm and there was a mild wind from the south drifting across the Mexican border and stirring the branches of mesquite all around him. But all Eddie could feel was the agonizing stress in the tendons of his thighs as his legs gripped the mustang's flanks, and the aching of his fingers as he clutched the mustang's mane. Now the gray horse galloped at full stride, whinnying shrilly as if calling to its companions to return, to aid it in vanquishing this outrageous human intruder upon its hitherto unchallenged freedom. Bending low over its neck, Eddie let the mustang go where it would. It seemed to him that he and the horse had become an inseparable unit, each welded to the other by a stubborn resolve to conquer or be conquered.

They had been traveling toward a low, arid canyon, two miles north of the sluggish, winding Nueces River. Here the soil was sandy, and the land was desolate, with no human habitation in sight in any direction. Now there were only the mustang and its rider in this barren landscape whose very loneliness and sterility recalled that prehistoric era when man first had to fight against the beasts to survive.

Yet there was also beauty, for the mesquite was thick and grew as tall as a full-grown man. There were beds of wild yellow roses, drawing nurture from some mysterious underground source of water that belied the crumbly, sun-baked earth. Far to the north lay a fanciful pattern of winding canyons and arroyos. They were barren and had been so for untold eons, and it looked as if some whimsical finger had idly traced furrows in the yielding earth at the moment of creation. Overhead and behind the galloping mustang with its crouching, panting rider, a dozen long-feathered black crows appeared, cawing mockingly, then soaring high overhead and turning back to the south across the winding river.

The mustang's maddened pace had begun to slacken. Now and again, it turned its head to one side and then the other, as if looking back in wonderment that this audacious, two-legged creature should still dispute its mastery of the plains. It whinnied and its eyes rolled, bloodshot and raging, but by now its sides had begun to heave and there was foam on its muzzle.

Then, suddenly, the mustang slowed to a walk, its great head lowered, and Eddie felt against his constricting thighs the violent shuddering of its flanks and belly. It stopped dead in its tracks, and again there was an even more violent and prolonged shudder as it acknowledged defeat. It waited, submissive now in the recognition of the unyielding tenacity of its rider. Eddie slowly let go of its mane, flexing his numb and swollen fingers, his contorted face damp with sweat. He remained with head bowed over the horse's humbled neck, gulping in air to ease the constriction of his lungs. After a long moment, he murmured soothingly to the mustang: "Good boy. We're all right now, aren't we? You're fine, you're the strongest horse I ever rode and that's no lie. I had to do it, you know that. If it'd been up to me, I'd have let you go back to the herd, to run free for the rest of your life. But I had to do this, feeling the way I did. I'm sorry."

As if the mustang understood, it slowly lifted its head and whinnied softly. With a groan, Eddie slid off the horse and sprawled on all fours on the sun-baked earth. Then, and only then, did he burst into racking sobs, as a surging wave of terrible grief and hopeless loss possessed him.

"Oh my God, oh my sweet girl, my poor Polly—God rest your sweet, gentle soul—I wanted you so, and now you'll never know how much you meant to me. Oh Polly, Polly, what am I going to do without you now?" His words came tumbling out, choked back by the sobs of inconsolable grief that exhaustion had finally allowed him to release. The mustang turned slowly now, regarding him with eyes no longer wild but glazed with exhaustion. It sensed that it was bound to this creature who had dared to ride and master it. Lowering its head, it nudged Eddie's shoulder.

He slowly got to his feet and stood gazing toward the east. He was remembering how he had been a penniless, unemployed cowhand when Dr. Ben Wilson and his two little children had landed at the port of Corpus Christi. He remembered how proud he'd been when Lucien Edmond had taken him on in the outfit: He who had been an orphan had at last found a home and friends among the vaqueros who shared the simple life of a cattle ranch. And then, when he believed himself to be secure, he had met Polly Behting, and known her for so pathetically brief a time.

He turned back to the mustang, gently stroking its neck and crooning to it just as every cowboy soothes the horse on whose reliability his very life depends. When he got back to the ranch, he would ask Ramón to sell him the wild mustang. As a stallion, it couldn't go on the drive. But he wanted to ride it when he got back. He wanted to re-

Newton because that was his job. But he wouldn't ever forget her, no matter how long he lived, he knew that.

"Let's go back home now," he murmured, and the mustang patiently waited for him to mount and then docilely turned back toward Windhaven Range.

member Polly that way. Tomorrow he'd go on the drive to

CHAPTER SIXTEEN

At dawn on the already warm first day of April, Lucien Edmond Bouchard went with the men and women of Windhaven Ranch into the chapel the men themselves had built to pray for the success of the cattle drive. Maxine Bouchard, holding her youngest child, Diane, now sixteen months old, knelt beside her husband and children, glancing occasionally at Lucien Edmond, for it would be long months before she would see him again. Ramón and Mara Hernandez were there with their children and Lucas and Felicidad brought their son, James. Simata took a place in the row behind Lucien Edmond's family. Pablo Casares, who had volunteered to be the cook of the outfit on this drive, was there with his beautiful wife, Kate, and their daughter, Catarina, who was just Diane's age. Like Mara and Felicidad, Kate was expecting a child in the summer, perhaps even before her husband returned from the drive.

Joe and Margaret Duvray were also present, Margaret carrying her four-month-old son, Robert, whom Joe had urged to name after her father. "Honey, he was all you had, and when you were a young girl, he stood for all that was good," Joe had said, "And our son will have the same name. He'll have the best of your father and, I swear to you, the best I've got to give him."

Eddie Gentry took his place at the very back of the chapel, his face haggard and worn, for he had not slept well last night. After he had returned the gray mustang to its stall, he had eaten a quick supper at the bunkhouse and then walked along the little creek where he and Polly Behting had exchanged the first shy words that had led to a pledge that could never be fulfilled. When the service was over, he abruptly rose and left the chapel. Ramón Hernan-

203

dez followed after him quickly and, putting an arm around his shoulders, murmured, *"Es tu caballo, amigo."*

Eddie turned and stared at Ramón's sympathetic face. "I didn't have any right—I just had to ride him—" he began in an unsteady voice.

Ramón nodded. "You don't have to tell me, Eddie. I've had one of the men put him into a separate corral all by himself, with plenty of room, to wait for you until you get back. He'll be a good companion to you. And that's not a bad name to call him, either, come to think of it."

"Compañero—yes, that sounds fine. Thanks, Ramón. I won't forget this."

"Everybody knows how you feel, Eddie. Words don't mean anything at a time like this, but all of us prayed for you in there and for your girl." Ramón tightened his grip around the lanky cowhand's shoulders. "Best not to think about it. The hard work of the drive will be a relief, you'll see."

"Yes." Eddie had to turn away because his eyes had begun to water, and he impatiently rubbed them with the back of his hand. "It's a big job, riding the point."

"I told Lucien Edmond there wasn't a better man in the outfit for that post. I mean it, Eddie. And Simata will blaze the trail for us, as he always does. I don't have to tell you anything, you know your job already."

Ramón gave Eddie's shoulder a last compassionate squeeze and walked away, leaving the young cowboy to his own anguished thoughts. Eddie turned to look back at the chapel, from which the vaqueros were now emerging. He knew them to be friends, good companions who would share the hardships and often monotonous work of the long cattle drive. He took a deep breath and straightened his shoulders. It wouldn't do any good to show them that he was sick inside with grief. Ramón was right: he'd lose himself in his work, because riding the point was one of the toughest jobs a cowboy could draw. It meant three months or more of leading the herd through heat, dust, sudden storms, and the ever-present danger of attack by rustlers or bushwhackers or hostile Indians.

He moved toward his gelding, made sure the cinch straps of the saddle were good and snug, and then mounted. Ramón, mounting his own gelding, caught his eye and waved to him, and Eddie waved back. He swallowed hard to down the lump in his throat as he headed his gelding out of the open gate to the stockade, to take his place ahead of the lowing herd which the vaqueros were now beginning to move into some semblance of order.

Lucien Edmond, at the same time, was taking up his position. Watching with satisfaction as his vaqueros readied the herd for the march, he let his mind wander. He thought of Emataba, whose blood brother he had become three years before on the way back from Abilene. He remembered how he and his outfit had been attacked by the Reedy gang when they were only thirty miles from the Kansas market and how they had driven the outlaws off with heavy losses. The survivors of that gang had raided the Kiowa camp where Elone was living as a captive squaw and had slaughtered all but Elone and her daughter, Tisinqua. Lucien Edmond had found the two huddled in the ruins of the camp and had taken them to the Creek reservation for shelter.

After the ceremony that had united him in spirit with the tall *mico*, Lucien Edmond and his men had resumed their journey back to Windhaven Range, only to be attacked by those same outlaws, who desperately needed horses and ammunition. It was during this raid that Pablo Casares had saved the life of Kate Strallis, when she was attacked by the outlaw Ed Harschmer. Though wounded in his right arm by a revolver bullet and having his own defective six-shooter explode to maim his left hand, Pablo had summoned all his strength and flung his hunting knife with unerring aim into Ed Harschmer's back, killing the last survivor of the murderous bushwhacker gang. Thus he had won Kate as his loving, devoted wife, and her two little boys who likewise adored him.

It would be good to have Pablo along as cook this year, Lucien Edmond reflected. He would take the place of Tiburcio Caltran, who had held the job for the previous two years, and who had announced last month that he was going back to work on his cousin's farm. He would be missed, but Pablo would be an able replacement. The men always liked whatever he prepared.

Yes, all signs were good for the coming drive. In addition to the three thousand head of cattle, which had been carefully selected to bring top prices at the new market in Newton, Lucien Edmond had added another fifty head, which included six cows, two young bulls, and the rest steers, so that Emataba and his people would have meat and milk through the fall and early winter. He had also brought a large supply of vegetable and fruit seeds that one of his vaqueros had purchased in San Antonio. Friar Bartoloméo Alicante had suggested that the women and children of the Creek village might start their own gardens, and thus provide fruits and vegetables to supplement the meager diet that the former Indian agent, Matthias Stillman, had constantly depleted by diverting government money into his own pocket and purchasing only the poorest quality of supplies with the rest.

He was anxious, too, to see Dr. Ben Wilson again and to tell him that Thomas and Sybella were asking for their father. His own wife, Maxine, along with Maybelle Belcher, had become a kind of foster mother to the young Wilson children, and she showed them as much care and tenderness as she gave to Carla and Hugo, Edwina and Diane. Although he greatly respected the Quaker doctor's selfless dedication to the forsaken Creeks, Lucien Edmond sincerely hoped that Ben would ultimately move to some civilized town where he could have a house and some of the benefits of civilization. Certainly an Indian reservation was not the best place for Thomas and Sybella during the years when they should be getting regular schooling. Indeed, he meant to speak about this—though he knew it was really none of his business—when he met Ben Wilson in Emataba's village.

After the first few days of travel, Lucien Edmond was considerably heartened by the progress he and his men were making. They were averaging twelve to thirteen miles a day, and there were no mishaps. There were no buffalo herds to distract his cows as had happened several times in the past; there were no violent storms to stampede and scatter the herd over the plains. By the time the herd had crossed the surging Colorado, Lucien Edmond and his men were already eight days ahead of the schedule he had laid out before leaving Windhaven Range. It was indeed a good omen.

Yet, because he was now Emataba's blood brother and felt the same kinship with the Creeks that his great-grandfather had felt, Lucien Edmond was painfully aware that the absence of the buffalo spelled the end of the Indians upon the plains. The railroads were bringing hordes of buffalo hunters who killed for bounty and left scores of carcasses to rot instead of furnishing meat for hungry tribes of the plains. Those once powerful tribes—the Kiowa, the Comanche, the Sioux—were being driven farther to the north into land where there was little hunting and where the harshness of the climate brought illness and starvation. It amounted to a seemingly calculated policy of genocide, Lucien Edmond reflected, and it had all begun when President Andrew Jackson had vowed to drive the Creeks, the Cherokees, the Chickasaws, and the Choctaws from the South. Far to the west, the Apaches remained unconquered, and there were some bands of roving Comanches and Kiowa Apaches. Sangrodo, most powerful and feared of all Comanche chiefs, had found a new stronghold in a little Mexican village where he and his people had been able to begin a peaceful, agrarian life unique in the history of his people. But these were exceptional cases; elsewhere, Indians were dying out. Once all Indians had been killed or driven off their land, a ruthless, amoral struggle would begin among unscrupulous land sharks and profiteers. It was indeed wisdom to have given Joe Duvray the Caldemare land so that he and Joe, working side by side, could expand their holdings and merge them into a single powerful cattle ranch. Together, they would be capable of withstanding both enemy attack and the machinations of the landgrabbers.

Along the trail, the men were in high good humor. Pedro Dornado had brought along his guitar, and he regaled his companions with sentimental love songs and ballads of adventure in the olden days. Such music lulled the drowsy herd at nightfall and eased the outfit's task. There were, to be sure, occasional problems. Swarms of heel flies attacked the herd several times before they reached the Colorado River. And the day after they crossed it there was a brief thunderstorm and drenching rain, and half a day was lost to rounding up the several hundred head of cattle that had scattered during the storm. Yet in the main it was surely the easiest drive that Lucien Edmond, as trail boss, had ever managed. There was only one somber note: despite the camaraderie and the warmth of his companions, Eddie Gentry held himself apart, moody and silent, grieving for his lovely fiancée. By contrast, he rode point with a dogged determination and vigilance that made Lucien Edmond shake his head at the young cowboy's merciless compulsion.

Even Ramón noticed this and, one evening at the campfire, remarked to his brother-in-law, "There isn't a man in the outfit who doesn't want to go up to Eddie and tell him how sorry he is for everything that's happened. But he'd snap their heads off if anyone tried that, Lucien Edmond. You and I know why he's the way he is. I told you how he rode that mustang as if he didn't care whether it killed him or he killed it. In my country, they would say that he was being ridden by the devil himself."

"Yes, I know that, Ramón," Lucien Edmond philosophically observed. "And that's exactly why no one can help him. He'll do it himself. You mark my words, something will happen before this drive is over to take the devil off his back and to give him a new outlook. Maybe a girl."

"Do you really think so, Lucien Edmond?" The handsome young Mexican looked wonderingly at him.

"Remember how Ben Wilson found Elone to take Fleurette's place? I've often thought that God takes pity on our grief and, if we believe in Him, knows how to compensate for our losses. You've only to read the Bible story of Job."

"*Sí, es verdad,*" Ramón mused.

Dr. Ben Wilson had reached Wichita in twelve days, twice the time it had taken when he had ridden alone on horseback to procure supplies after having voluntarily appointed himself as doctor-shaman to the abandoned Creek villagers. Elone and the two children had borne the discomforts of the trip with its wintry weather extremely well, and kindly Jacob Hartmann, the pastor of the Quaker group in Wichita, had found a little frame house with a large fenced-in yard located three-quarters of a mile from his general store. The Quaker doctor had deposited half of his savings in the main Wichita bank and so was able to buy the little house at an extremely low price, since he was paying hard cash for it. Once again, Jacob Hartmann was responsible for Ben's good fortune, since the owner of the house was an ailing friend of his who wanted to leave for San Francisco to spend his last days with a spinster sister and was willing to take only four hundred dollars for the property.

On the first Sunday after their arrival in their new home, Ben and all his family attended the Quaker services presided over by Pastor Hartmann, where they were introduced to the members of the society. This warmed the doctor's heart, for such expressions of fellowship had always been for him one of the more endearing attributes of the Friends. He responded deeply to the communication with his fellows and the warm exchange of good wishes, as well as the offer of aid in the event of crisis. It seemed to Ben that the Quaker congregation in many ways was more than a religious body; it was a community of people helping each other, such as once existed in the little towns of New England when this young nation had its beginning.

Wichita had only one other doctor, an elderly man who was more experienced with veterinary work than in treating human patients and who, because of his subsequent failures with those seriously ill, took to the bottle to console himself for losing them. "Wichita needs you badly, Dr. Wilson," Jacob Hartmann said at the end of the service. "Poor Dr. Hatfield tries hard, but he just doesn't have the experience you've had. He wouldn't know what to do if we had an outbreak of measles or whooping cough or chicken pox, you see. And I'll tell you one thing more, Dr. Wilson. Running a store as I do and keeping up with my trade, I feel that the Santa Fe is going to run its line through here before very much longer, and then you'll see a cattle boom and hundreds of cowboys coming into Wichita. Yes, there'll be violence, alas, as there always is in a cattle town— gunplay and men wounded and killed. Your God-given skill will save many lives that would otherwise be lost. Truly, God has sent you to us, Dr. Wilson."

"I only hope," the earnest young doctor solemnly responded, "that in coming here, I shan't have neglected those helpless Creeks who ask so little and receive even less."

"Don't fret yourself, Dr. Wilson." The pastor put his hand on the younger man's shoulder. "From what you've told me of this new Indian agent, I have the feeling, as you do, that he will keep his word and that he will send the doctor to visit the reservation at least once a month. But now, we shall enjoy some refreshments that my good wife has prepared, and tomorrow the two of us will help you pick out such furniture and clothing as you will need for your new house and family."

"Do you think, Pastor Hartmann, that the people here will look down upon Elone because she is an Indian?"

"Have faith," Pastor Hartmann replied. "The people who already live here, and especially the members of our society, are compassionate and understanding. They have met Elone and seen what kind of person she is. She is now one of us. No, Dr. Wilson, the only trouble that may arise will come when Wichita begins to expand. Then, of course, you will see to it that she stays in the house and is not seen by the rowdy, godless men who drive cattle herds. But all of us will look after her—that is our way, as well you know."

"Yes, it comforts me, Pastor Hartmann. As soon as Elone and the little ones are settled, I want to go back to Windhaven Range and bring back my other children, Thomas and Sybella."

"My wife and some of the other women will be happy to stay with Elone and the little ones while you make your journey, Dr. Wilson. It will be our pleasure."

"God bless you. With such friends as you and your wife and all these others who believe as I have been brought up to believe, I feel at last that I can start a new life with purpose and inspiration."

"Of that I was certain the first moment I met you, Dr. Wilson," the pastor beamed as the two men shook hands in a bond of deepest friendship.

During the second week of March, some three weeks before Lucien Edmond Bouchard and his men began the cattle drive to Newton, Jacob Hartmann visited Dr. Ben Wilson at the latter's little frame house to bring him news that would strengthen his desire to make Wichita his new home. "After you left the services yesterday, Dr. Wilson," the storekeeper declared, "we voted to offer you the post of deacon at our church. All of us look upon you as a welcome addition not only to our society, but also to our town, and you will help us grow in the right way. It would honor us, Dr. Wilson, if you would accept this post and preside at our meetings."

The young doctor bowed his head and closed his eyes, and finally responded, "I accept joyously, Pastor Hartmann. Though I have known the members of the society here in Wichita only a short time, already I feel comfortable with them, accepted as one of them. To me, it is a sign that my coming here was perhaps destined. Yet I ask you to bear with me for a short time—I am still troubled in my mind over those Indians with whom I lived, who needed me. I ask you to allow me to visit them first to make certain that the new agent has kept his promise in providing a doctor for them. And as you know, I must also go back to Windhaven Range to bring back Thomas and Sybella."

"To be sure, all of us wish you and your family to be reunited and to remain with us, Dr. Wilson," the bearded storekeeper replied. "I have told you that my wife, as well as Mrs. Coulter and Mrs. Davies, would be overjoyed to look after your wife and the little girl and your baby son in your absence. But it is a long journey back to Texas. Will you not need an escort?"

"No, Pastor Hartmann. God will watch over me as He has always done. I shall go alone on horseback to the Creek village and stay there till I am assured that all is well with them. When I get back to Windhaven Range, I will borrow one of their wagons to bring back Thomas and Sybella."

"But that return journey by wagon, which will take far longer than on horseback, may have more danger for you, alone as you will be with your children, Dr. Wilson."

"I would not ask any of your members to accompany me. They are Quakers as I am, and we should not carry weapons. It would only endanger them unnecessarily to go with me. No, I shall pray to the All-Merciful to watch over us till we can return to you."

"As you will. Our prayers go with you, then, Dr. Wilson."

Shortly before noon on the eighth day after his conversation with Jacob Hartmann, Dr. Ben Wilson rode up to the fenced-in Creek reservation and, dismounting and tethering the reins of his horse to the side of the gate, was joyously welcomed by Emataba, who had emerged from his tepee and seen the lone rider approaching from the north.

"My heart warms to see you again, beloved shaman," the *mico* exclaimed as he clasped Ben's hand and warmly shook it.

"And I am glad to see you again, Emataba. How goes it with your people?"

"Very well. This new agent, Douglas Larrimer, has indeed kept his promise. Shortly after you left, the new shaman he promised came to us. He is called Dr. Thomas Brenton. He is older than you, and most concerned about our people. He walks among them as you did, respecting what they were and the dignity of their past; he does not look down upon them, and they have confidence in him. Last week, he gave medicine to old Disyangata, who was ill with fever, and stayed with her all through the next day until she was better. And one of the young braves had broken his arm, and the new shaman made a splint and set it back into place." Emataba's somber face was suddenly lightened by an almost whimsical smile. "Besides, he had filled his pockets with store candy, and he gave it all to the children. They flocked around him, and it was good to hear their laughter again. Truly, though there is no one to my mind who can take your place, this new shaman will be welcome here."

"That is good to hear, Emataba. All goes well with the village, then?"

Emataba's face darkened and he shook his head. "Since you left us, one thing has happened that fills me with anger. There is a white-eyes trader, who is named Joe Hampton. He visited our village about ten days after you and your family left for Wichita. He brought with him trinkets for the women, beads and looking glasses and such. But for the men he brought whiskey."

"Whiskey?" Ben incredulously echoed. "But that is forbidden. And besides, your people have no money. How could they pay for it?"

Emataba scowled. "From what I have learned, it is some of the young braves here who are restless with the peaceful, dreary life they lead. They remember that their forebears were great warriors and that the white-eyes feared them and did not take away their land. And those forebears passed on rich wampum belts, adorned with precious stones. It is these mementos of our time of glory that my foolish young men have given to this Joe Hampton in exchange for his cheap whiskey. I know this because only two days ago I found Imanisay in his tepee, sodden with drink. And I saw that the old calumet his grandfather had

212

given him, a calumet set with precious stones, was no longer in his tepee. When he wakened and I asked him where it had gone, he said that he had traded it for three bottles of the whiskey."

"And no one tries to stop this trader?"

"I myself told him the last time he came that I, as *mico*, forbade him to come here. He laughed and said that I could not stop him, that he had a license to trade, and that if some of those in my village wished to trade with him, it was their business and not mine. Also, he wears a gun, and he makes big talk how important he is. He says that if one of our braves should kill him, the white-eyes soldiers would take us from here and hang us all."

"The lying scoundrel!" Ben angrily exclaimed.

"Sipanata and his friends Nimasike and Bentijo have told me that if I give the command they will take him out into the prairie and bury him where not even the coyotes will find him. But I say to them, there shall be no killing. Evil though he is, he is a white-eyes, and if any of my braves is guilty of his death, then I know in my heart it will go badly with us. We are already despised by those powerful white-eyes who make the treaties with us and our brothers throughout this land."

"Not all white-eyes are evil; this you know already, Emataba. And I pray to my God each day that He will grant justice to you and your people and to all the tribes who were here upon the land before my own people came upon it, Emataba."

The tall *mico* smiled gravely and touched Ben's heart with his right palm. "If all men were like you, we should live where we once did and there would be no war between Indians and white-eyes. You see, I cannot blame my young men too much. They came here as striplings, unfledged braves, and instead of hunting and playing the games to prepare them to become warriors and take their place in the council, they have known only contempt from the white-eyes and the fencing-in to make us believe ourselves to be little better than wild animals feared for treachery."

"I understand," the doctor compassionately murmured. "I will stay here for a few days, and if I see this Joe Hampton, I will tell him that I had the previous Indian agent sent away by writing a letter to the President. I will tell him that a new agent is here now to look after your interests, and that if he does not stop selling whiskey, both the agent and I will see that he does not come again."

"I respect you, my shaman," Emataba sighed wearily. "But you are a man of peace, you carry no gun. I remember how Sipanata and his two friends rode after you when you went to bring us supplies and the cows, and how you would have been killed if they had not defended you."

"I remember that also, Emataba. God sent them to aid me, and that is why I pray to Him eternally. He is my weapon, He is my right hand."

"As is our Ibofanaga, my shaman. All the same," Emataba observed with a wry smile. "When we went into battle against our enemies, we prayed to him, but also we bore weapons. We prayed that Ibofanaga would give us skill and cunning to defend ourselves against those who would slay us."

The Quaker doctor looked at Emataba for a long moment of silence and then gently said, "The one God who watches over all of us, Emataba, acts in many ways to answer our prayers. I know how it happened that Elone saved me when we were on our way to Wichita. She was very brave." And Ben quickly told Emataba about the outlaw attack, and how Elone had foiled it.

"I knew you would not have taken the gun, my shaman," the *mico* said, when Ben had finished his story. "I had a bad dream before you left, and that is why I gave it to her. Have I offended you and your God in what I did?"

"Surely not, Emataba. You acted out of your own faith as seemed best to you. Thus you saved my life, and yet it was my God who answered my prayers for safety. Do you not see in this how we are bound as men of all faiths and origins to the devotion of Him who reads our hearts?"

"I see it well, my shaman. And now you must rest. Tonight we shall hold a feast in celebration of your return to us, even for this short time, and we shall talk some more."

Early the next afternoon, two little boys played catch near the gate of the Creek village with a ball made of deerskin and filled with twigs and straw, very much like the one used in games of *tokonhay* back in Econchate nearly a century before. One of them threw the ball so vigorously that it sailed over the gate toward the north. His playmate angrily remonstrated with him, then agilely climbed over

214

the gate to retrieve it. Then he stopped, shading his eyes from the bright sun, and called in Creek, "Riders come to us—hurry, Misaka, tell the *mico* they ride toward us!"

Emataba and Ben Wilson came out to meet the riders. To the doctor's joy, he recognized Douglas Larrimer riding at the head of a group of six soldiers and a wagon drawn by two sturdy dray horses driven by a sergeant. "He has brought supplies with him—I'm glad I came in time to meet him and talk with him again," Ben eagerly exclaimed. "I'll tell him about this whiskey-selling traitor who's been plaguing your village, Emataba!"

As the riders came closer, the doctor could see that Douglas Larrimer was wearing a buckskin jacket and breeches and the sturdy winter moccasins of the Plains Indians. Over this, the coat of a Union cavalry officer was draped around his shoulders. He waved, and the Indian agent, recognizing him, waved back as he spurred his bay into a canter to ride up beside the *mico* and the doctor.

"It's good to see you, Dr. Wilson!" Douglas Larrimer exclaimed as he dismounted with the precision of a cavalry officer, despite his handicap. "I decided to come a week earlier than usual, because we've reports at the fort that there's a spell of bad weather coming in from the north. This time, Emataba, I've brought an extra supply of warm, thick blankets, salt, molasses, flour, beans, and several sides of bacon. Also, when I heard that your new doctor had become a favorite overnight by bringing the youngsters candy, I brought along an extra supply. I want to be your friend, too, you see."

"That you are already," Emataba replied as he extended his hand in friendship. Then, turning to Ben, he added, "You see for yourself what your letter has done. This is a good man, with kindness in his heart toward the needy. He does not look upon us with eyes of scorn because our skins are red."

"That would be to look down upon my own ancestors, Emataba," the Indian agent promptly answered. "In olden days, the Cherokees and the Creeks had the richest culture of the South. There were looms, there was industry, there was honesty, and there was peace. No, I shall never forget the blood in my veins. It reminds me of the importance of my duties as Indian agent."

"But your heart and your mind remind you most of all,

and we who have not greatly loved the white-eyes who came upon us when I was a boy are learning the much-needed lesson that when there is a straight tongue and an honest heart, the white-eyes can once again become our friends," the *mico* said to him. "Will you and your men not stay and share our food and our lodging?"

"I'd like that. We rode hard to reach you, and my men wouldn't mind a good night's rest before we head back," Douglas Larrimer averred.

Emataba watched the soldiers enter the reservation and begin to distribute the supplies. The burly, genial sergeant who had driven the wagon took the sack full of store candy and, standing in the center of the village, called out a few words in Creek to signify what he had for the children. Almost at once the boys and girls of the village came running, their eyes shining with pleasure. Ben Wilson turned questioningly to the Indian agent, who chuckled and nodded. "I've handpicked my detail for our visits, Dr. Wilson. I know a little Creek myself, you see, and I taught Sergeant Burton what to say. You can tell how he's enjoying it—he's got a wife and five children of his own back in Iowa, so he was just the man for this job."

"I'm very pleased, Mr. Larrimer, more than I can tell you. These people will be in good hands from now on. And I've had good reports from Emataba about the doctor you sent here."

"Yes, he's a fine man. You can confidently start your own practice in Wichita, knowing that I won't let you down," the Indian agent declared.

The cavalry escort, having dismounted and tethered their horses, followed the sergeant into the center of the village. To Ben's pleasure, a few of the men began to converse in sign language with the women and old men and the younger braves. Again he turned to Douglas Larrimer, saying, "You don't know how something like this boosts their morale, Mr. Larrimer. Treatment like this will go a long way toward making them forget how harshly Matthias Stillman dealt with them in the past."

"I've got some good soldiers with me," the Indian agent said. "I personally went over the duty roster at the fort and I chose as many men as I could find who had some Indian blood in them. You'll find Kiowa, Comanche, and Kiowa Apache in their antecedents, and I suppose that years ago

216

all those tribes were not always the best of friends. But the main thing is, they're good soldiers, and they understand what I want to do here. So far as it's in my power, they'll come with me every time I visit here to bring supplies or to palaver."

"Speaking of palavering, Mr. Larrimer, Emataba just told me about a serious problem he's had. There's a white trader who comes here frequently and sells the young braves whiskey. Emataba has told him to stay away from the reservation, but this man laughs at him and says he has a perfect right to go wherever he wants because of his license."

"That's not true, Dr. Wilson. I don't want anyone to harass the Indians here. What's his name?"

"Emataba tells me that he's known as Joe Hampton. Apparently, since the Creeks obviously have no cash money, he's trading trinkets and beads and the like to the women and rotgut whiskey to the young braves in return for some of their heirlooms, like jeweled wampum belts," Ben responded.

The Indian agent nodded, his lips thinning in contempt. "I think the description fits a deserter who used to be in my regiment some nine years ago. He ran away before a big battle, as I recall, and some of my men tried to track him down, but lost him. Apparently he went to Missouri and hid out under an assumed name. But I've heard of him from time to time, most recently when he sold some defective Whitworths to a tribe of Penateka Comanches in the Panhandle. That was about eighteen months ago. Of course, I can't prove anything, but the description fits, and the way he's acting here makes me certain it's the same man. In my outfit he was called Dick Hamden. You'll find, Dr. Wilson, that when a criminal changes his name, his alias is almost invariably based on either the same initial or a derivative of the original name. Hampton—Hamden— pathetically obvious, I'd say."

"But the problem, Emataba tells me, is that he's boasting that he's got a gun and can't be touched, but he has a perfect right to trade here if he wants to."

"That's an obvious bluff, too. Look, he might come back any time. If he turns up while I'm here, I'll show you how I get rid of scum like that. From what I've heard, the Penatekas are looking for him to find out why he took their

217

buffalo hides and horses for defective rifles. One of these days, go where he will, he's bound to run into some of the people he's tricked so shabbily—then he'll vanish from my agenda."

"That's a comforting thought, Mr. Larrimer. I'm just afraid that some of the older braves may get so angry at him they'll try to kill him—and you know they'll be blamed and punished out of proportion for the crime."

"I can promise you I can handle that deserter once and for all, Dr. Wilson. But now let's talk of more pleasant things. If I can manage it, and if the funds from Washington hold out, I'd like to continue and extend the educational program for the youngsters here, which you began a couple of years ago. I'd like to bring a retired schoolteacher to give the Creek children lessons in English and something of our history. Also, this fellow, Seth Grafton, is getting a reputation for some of his watercolors. He's very eager to discover artistic talent in these Indian children. Now we know that the Creeks as well as the Comanches and Sioux make picturegraphs to pass on their legends and their history to the next generation. Grafton has a cousin with an art gallery in Philadelphia. And he told me, last time I saw him, that he'd like to send on some of the efforts of these Creek youngsters as proof that there's plenty of creativity and skill to be found on Indian reservations. I needn't tell you that something like this will redound to my own credit and, more importantly, I want to see achievements."

"I'm very comfortable talking with you about things like this, Mr. Larrimer," Ben smilingly confided. "Anything you can do to show the people of this country that Indians are imaginative people who contributed to our culture a long time before the white man came is sure to overcome some of the dreadful prejudices we've set up against all Indians."

"I quite agree. Look, Dr. Wilson, you're a man after my own heart. I've brought along a bottle of good French wine in my saddlebags. Why don't we continue this useful conversation in your tepee and share a drink or two while we're having it?"

Ben Wilson and Douglas Larrimer talked enthusiastically throughout most of the night and, with the wine a relaxing stimulant to their discussion, both slept till almost noon. As the one-armed Indian agent was preparing to return to the fort, Sipanata hurried to Ematabá's tepee, his face grave and concerned. A moment later the tribal *mico* emerged and went to find Larrimer, who was assembling his gear with Ben's help.

"Sipanata says that the whiskey-seller has just come to the other end of the village and is selling his whiskey against my wishes," he angrily announced.

"Come along with me, Dr. Wilson," the Indian agent proposed. "If I get rid of this scoundrel for you, you'll have to admit that your former charges will be in good hands from now on."

The doctor nodded his assent and followed the agent out to the eastern end of the village. There, about a hundred yards from the broken fence, stood a supply wagon drawn by two Percherons. A black-bearded, portly, middle-aged man had descended from his wagon and, going to the back, had drawn out several bottles of cheap whiskey. As Larrimer and Ben watched, they saw two of the younger Creek braves vault the low fence and hurry toward the wagon.

The Indian agent walked out toward the bearded driver and called out, in a stern voice, "Dick Hamden, get down off that wagon and come here."

"Who the devil's calling me Dick Hamden?" the whiskey trader snarled with a shrug of his shoulders.

"Your former commanding officer, that's who. Now front and center, you dirty, yellow-livered deserter!"

"Now jist a minute—who the hell do you think you are, talking to me like that? Hell, man, the war's been over seven years, and even if I did have brains enough to light out before things got bad, you can't do a damn thing about it. I've got a license to trade and I'm using it."

"Not to sell Indians whiskey, you're not. For your information, I'm the Indian agent in this territory. And this territory is out of bounds to you from now on. Pack your stuff up and head your team a good ways away from here, if you know what's good for you," Douglas Larrimer declared angrily.

The bearded trader put down the whiskey bottle he was holding and ambled toward the Indian agent, a grin on his ugly face. "Now, Mr. Larrimer, sir, I do remember you used to be my captain. But that was a long time ago. Now why can't you be sensible, Cap'n? What the hell do you care if some dirty redskins get likkered up and the soldiers shoot 'em down—why, you'll be able to hold back your supplies for this crummy village and pocket the money all for yourself. That's the way Matthias Stillman used to handle things, and nobody was any the wiser."

"I'm not pulling rank with you at this late date, Hamden. I'm just telling you, for your own good, get the hell out of here and don't ever let me see your ugly face in these parts. I'm the Indian agent, and I'll have no dirty whiskey-dealers like you bothering these poor people. Can you get that through your thick skull?"

"Now, jist a minute, Mr. Larrimer, sir," Joe Hampton's tone was heavily sarcastic. "My motto's live and let live. Now jist you wait till I finish my business with these bucks, and I'll be off and not bothering you any."

"That won't do at all. I told you to pack up and get out, and I meant it."

"Think you can make me, Cap'n, sir?" Hampton's right hand edged toward his holster.

Ben Wilson's mouth gaped as the one-armed Indian agent, with a lightning-like movement, dropped his right hand to his own holster, drew out his Starr .44, and fired just as the bearded trader went for his gun. There was a howl of pain as Larrimer's bullet smashed the knuckle of Joe Hampton's middle finger.

"Arrghh! Goddamn, what did you have to go and do that for? You've fair broken my hand!"

"Pull that gun out of your holster real slow now, and throw it to the ground. That's it. Now here's mine. And now, though I'm not going to turn you in for desertion at this late date, I've never forgotten how you ran away like a scared rabbit from guard duty the night before the big battle." Douglas Larrimer clenched his right fist and moved menacingly toward the bearded trader.

With a bellow of anger, Joe Hampton flung himself forward, flailing out with his right fist despite his wound. The Indian agent ducked and sent a right uppercut to Hampton's jaw, staggering him and making him flounder backwards, waving his arms in the air as he strove for balance.

Suddenly Hampton darted his left hand down to his boot and drew out a hunting knife, and in the same movement lunged forward at his opponent. Ben's shout of alarm was drowned out by a sardonic laugh from Douglas Larrimer who swiftly came forward and delivered a brisk kick with his right boot, knocking the knife out of the trader's hand. Then, in almost the same motion, he smashed his right fist against Hampton's cheekbone, felling the trader.

"Cut it out—you bastid, Cap'n, lemme be!"

"Now look here, Hamden. You're going to get back in your wagon and you're going to drive away from here as fast as you can, you understand? When I get back to the fort tomorrow evening, I'm putting you on report as a suspected renegade and a deserter from the Union army. And I promise you, Hamden, if I ever see you around here again, I'll beat the living hell out of you."

"All right, all right, I'm going. Goddamn you anyhow, Cap'n. Spoiling a man's living, that's what you're doing. All right, I won't come back. Those other redskins will pay plenty for what I've got in my wagon."

"I don't doubt that. But if any of those Indians happen to live in the territory I'm assigned to by the government, I'm serving notice on you here and now that you're in real trouble, Hamden. Now get, before I give you some more!"

With a wail of fright, the bearded trader stumbled to his feet and hurried to the wagon. Picking up the reins, he clucked his tongue and, with a venomous glance at his conqueror, vanished into the dusk.

Ben turned to the one-armed Indian agent, his eyes bright with admiration. "Thank God for a man like you here, Mr. Larrimer. These Creeks will be well taken care of, I have no further doubts. Tomorrow morning, I plan to ride back to Windhaven Range and bring back my boy and girl to my new home in Wichita. And I'll pray for you Mr. Larrimer, next Sunday. I'll pray that more people will remember what Edmund Burke once said, 'The only thing necessary for the triumph of evil is for good men to do nothing.' I pray God that Washington will let you stay here many years to look after these people who, thanks to you, can now have hope."

CHAPTER SEVENTEEN

Despite Ben Wilson's protestations that he could ride to Windhaven Range and bring Thomas and Sybella back to Wichita himself, Emataba ordered Sipanata, Nimasike, and Bentijo to accompany the doctor to Carrizo Springs. They arrived about two weeks after Lucien Edmond Bouchard and his outfit had begun their cattle drive to Newton, and that night Maybelle Belcher and Maxine Bouchard cooked a festive dinner in honor of the occasion.

To Ben's delight, Maxine told him that his seven-year-old son, Thomas, had learned to play several simple pieces on the spinet, and he sat enthralled as he watched his sturdy young son seat himself and, with a self-conscious and loving glance at his father, proceed to play one of Mozart's earliest sonatas, which he composed at about the same age as Thomas was now. As he listened, little Sybella sat in his lap, her arms entwined around his neck, whispering excitedly of the happy times she and her brother had had and how the vaqueros had made toys for them and even let Thomas ride a pony back and forth in a small section of the corral. "You'll have your own pony one day, my little darling," he raptly told her, as he hugged her to him.

As never before, Ben felt himself bound in spirit to Sybella, Fleurette's mother, for whom his little girl was named, and he remembered fondly all that Fleurette had told him about her. He knew himself to be inextricably linked to the Bouchards and he felt no conflict between the unswerving Catholic faith that all of them followed and his own creed. For most of the Bouchards had always manifested a compassion that transcended all narrow boundaries of religious denomination or sect.

The next day at seven in the morning, before the sun rose

223

high to send down its blazing heat upon the plains that loomed to the north, Ben Wilson lifted Sybella and Thomas into the wagon to sit on either side of him. He took the reins of two sturdy young mares, which Felipe Hermanos, youngest of the new vaqueros recruited in Nuevo Laredo, had hitched to the small wagon, a gift from Maxine Bouchard. He had protested and assured her that he would have the wagon returned, but Maxine had smiled and shaken her head and told him, "My husband would want you to have this wagon, Dr. Wilson. It's little enough we can do for you. Besides, we're hoping that you and your family will come visit us again some day. In the meantime, may God grant you and your family in Wichita a happy new life. I envy what you're doing as a doctor for people who need you. Please do send us a letter as soon as you reach Wichita safely, because we want to keep in touch with you always."

The journey back to Wichita took nearly six weeks, but it was peaceful and, for Thomas and Sybella, an absorbing adventure. Their father was grateful that Ematala had insisted that the three young Creeks accompany him. Sipanata, who had once looked upon him as an enemy because he had been white, but who had learned to admire and respect him for the devotion he had shown to the Creeks, acted as a kind of friendly uncle and informative guide along the journey. When they stopped at noon for a simple meal and at sunset to make camp, he took upon himself the role of commentator on the wild and primitive beauties of the landscape through which they passed.

He showed Thomas and Sybella plants and berries and trees, relating stories from the Creek folklore, pointing out to them roots and leaves and bits of wood whose medicinal and nutritive qualities made up the resources of his people. And his friends Nimasike and Bentijo, who had learned to speak English almost as well as he did, made little toys and dolls to divert the children during the tedious hours when they rode in the creaking wagon toward the north.

For Thomas and Sybella, the countryside that was blossoming in this warm spring was like a magical world. Indeed, this journey both intensified and augmented all they had learned during their stay at the Creek reservation. Moreover, it was vastly and excitingly different from anything that Thomas could remember from their home in

Pittsburgh. There were flowering dogwood, the bright green pods of mesquite, clumps of wild elderberries, blackberries, and brilliant cornflowers. There were the sounds of distant animals, from the rabbit to the coyote, from the whinnying of wild mustangs to the lowing of a wild young bull who guarded the cows of his herd and defied any interloper to lock horns with him. There were the birds, bright-plumaged, with their curious, inimitable sounds and calls. The three Creek braves had many stories to relate to the fascinated children of how these birds and animals were once demigods, when the world was young, and how the Great Spirit, Ibofanaga, delegated magical powers to them, long before man set foot upon the earth.

When at last, toward the end of May, Dr. Ben Wilson drove the wagon into the outskirts of Wichita and turned to bid farewell to his three Creek friends, it seemed to him that Thomas and Sybella were even closer to him in spirit than they had been back in Pittsburgh, where he and Fleurette had struggled so valiantly for survival. They were closer to him even than they had been during their months of living on the Creek reservation. For in Pittsburgh they had known a life without flora and fauna, and on the reservation their horizons had been limited by the poverty of the land the Creeks had been given, and by the fence around it. During the weeks of travel, Thomas and Sybella had deepened their appreciation of life as it had been in the early days, an appreciation that could not have been granted to them otherwise. Moreover, Ben found it singularly appropriate that their new mother should be a gentle Indian girl who could savor the natural phenomena of a life that had already begun to disappear as the American frontier was pushed back by the unrelenting tide of progress.

On the first Sunday after his return to Wichita, Ben sat in a Quaker meeting with his entire family, earnestly listening to Pastor Hartmann as he spoke on a passage from St. Matthew:

And Jesus called a little child unto Him, and set him in the midst of them. And said, "Verily I say unto you, except ye be converted, and become as little children, ye shall not enter into the kingdom of heaven. Whosoever, therefore, shall humble himself as this lit-

225

tle child, the same is greatest in the kingdom of heaven. And whoso shall receive one such little child in my name, receiveth me."

The young doctor smiled at Thomas and Sybella, his arms around their shoulders, and then turned to look lovingly at Elone, who cradled baby Bartholomew against her, while her right hand clasped that of little Tisinqua. He saw in their shining eyes a revelation of innocence and truth and honesty, and he saw it as a sign that this new life had been ordained. He sensed, also, that there was a kind of mystic symbol in beginning his new life in Wichita with two children in whose veins there flowed the blood of the pioneer Bouchards and these younger children whose Indian origin linked him inextricably with old Lucien Bouchard, who had understood from the very outset that where there was love and faith, it did not matter what blood was intermingled.

A week before Lucien Edmond Bouchard had set out for Newton, Amelia Jemmers, now in her mid-forties and looking ten years older because of her unrewarding life with her lecherous husband, Calvin, paid a visit one Saturday afternoon to an elderly widow who had done some sewing for her. The widow, Mrs. Hepzibah Tolliver, nearing sixty, was a gentle little woman with stooped shoulders, horn-rimmed spectacles, and a perennially apologetic air. Since she and her deceased husband had been childless, Hepzibah Tolliver had turned her starved affections to stray animals and had recently taken in a spaniel bitch brutally kicked out of a saloon by its drunken owner. The bitch had had a litter of puppies, only two of which had survived. Hepzibah had kept one of them for herself; the other, she insisted that Amelia Jemmers adopt on the very afternoon of her visit.

With an almost pathetic eagerness, Amelia took the puppy home and hid it in the cellar so that her husband would not find it. Then, for the first time since she and Calvin Jemmers had moved to Houston, she began to enjoy the delights of true companionship. Jemmers hardly ever took her to social functions any more, glibly explaining that his wife constantly had the "vapors." As his illicit passion for Alice Fernmark had grown, he had rele-

226

gated his wife more and more to a background of oblivion and neglect. He rarely spoke to her any more, except to address a perfunctory order to prepare his breakfast or his supper, or to make denigrating comments about her ineptitude as a wife. Amelia bore these remarks with a meek silence, as she had learned to do over the years since she had first discovered that her husband had married her only to gain control of her dowry.

The puppy was the first secret Amelia had ever kept from her husband, and it filled her with a guilty joy, after he had gone to the Houston Mercantile Bank, to hurry down each morning to the cellar to tend to the puppy's needs. It was a female, much less sturdy than Hepzibah's thriving young male. Yet its very meagerness and pathetic efforts to please provided Amelia with the greatest happiness she had ever known. Against the ever-present fear that her husband would discover the puppy and forbid her to keep it, there was the ecstatic joy of feeding it and cuddling it and talking to it for long minutes on end. And when the puppy seemed to fix her with its expressive brown eyes as if it understood, Amelia felt an outpouring of emotion that had been stifled in her almost since her wedding night.

Thanks to her unflagging efforts, the puppy began to put on weight and to gain in spirit. Often it barked, and Amelia was terrified lest the sound come to the attention of her overbearing husband. Whenever the puppy's yips came faintly to her ears while she was serving him his dinner, she sought to conceal them by talking more loudly than was her wont, or by rattling dishes and silverware. Then he would turn and upbraid her, his mouth curving in a sneer as he detailed to her the faults that made her so distasteful to him. At such moments, Amelia would lower her eyes and meekly submit to his tirade, praying that the spaniel would not bark again.

One Friday evening in mid-May, the puppy began to bark repeatedly, and Amelia's attempts to drown out this canine clamor failed. His brows arching, a look of reproof on his pudgy features, the banker demanded, "What, pray tell, is that noise downstairs, Amelia? It sounds very much like a dog. Don't tell me you're keeping one in this house. You know how I detest animals."

"Oh, Calvin, I really—oh heavens—" The spaniel's bark grew louder and more insistent.

"So!" he gloatingly observed as he rose from his chair. "You've gone against my wishes again, haven't you, Amelia? You know, I've put up with a great deal from you, but this I absolutely shan't tolerate. You're hiding a dog downstairs, aren't you? And you're lying and sneaking around to hide it from me. Very well, madam. I'm going to put an end to it this minute."

"No, Calvin! What—what do you mean?" she hysterically exclaimed, clenching her fists, her eyes shining with sudden tears.

"You can follow me and see for yourself, my dear," he sneered as he strode toward the cellar door. Opening it, he took a kerosene lamp from the kitchen counter and, holding it high above his head, carefully descended the narrow cellar steps.

The little spaniel bitch, hearing footsteps, set up a frantic barking. Jemmers turned back to glower at his wife. "Disgusting, madam. And the worst of it all is that you tried to deceive me. Well, it's time you had a lesson. I've let you have your own way far too long in this house, but it's over now, do you mark my words?"

"Calvin, I beg of you—it's only a little puppy—Mrs. Tolliver gave it to me—" she stammered, a hand clutching her breast, her face flushed and tearstained.

"And don't snivel. Really, Amelia, you're becoming detestable." He reached the landing of the cellar and strode over to the basket in which the spaniel puppy lay. His lips curled back to bare his yellowing teeth as he bent down and, savagely seizing the little spaniel bitch by the neck, he strangled it.

"There, you see? I don't ever want you to bring an animal of any kind to this house again. Is that understood, madam?" he drawled at her, turning and holding up the lifeless puppy clutched in his right hand.

Amelia uttered a shriek of horror. Then she flung herself at him and slapped him across the mouth with all her might.

Calvin Jemmers staggered, his eyes bulging, a wave of red suffusing his face and forehead. Dropping the lifeless puppy, he put his hand to his heart and fell headlong, dead.

Amelia clasped her hands in prayer and burst into hysterical laughter mingled with agonized, wracking sobs.

She groped toward the inert body of the dead puppy and picked it up tenderly. Then, holding it against her breast, she crooned to it, as the tears streamed down her face.

CHAPTER EIGHTEEN

By June 1872, those vaqueros who had worked for Lucien Edmond Bouchard on Windhaven Range for several years enthusiastically agreed to a man that this year's trail drive was turning out to be the easiest of all. Five years earlier, it had taken them two and a half months to drive the herd to the mighty Red River, through dusty plains, dry gullies, and treacherous ravines, till at last they had reached verdant, higher land where the herd could graze. This year, they had covered the more than four hundred miles in two months and three days. True, the herd was smaller than it had been the past two or three years, but even taking that into account, Lucien Edmond reckoned they had made exceptionally good time. Their luck continued to be good, with no stampedes and no sign of hostile Indians, bushwhackers, or rustlers. Just past Mineral Springs, the herd had been able to travel as much as thirteen to fourteen miles a day. Now it had slackened its pace and was traveling a steady nine or ten miles a day. The vaqueros' spirits were high: they had plenty of provisions, they were well armed, and their work—so far—was easy. And the bonds of friendship among them were stronger than before, thanks to previous drives which had taught them all the value of reliance one upon another.

Simata had found a better route this year, leading the herd a few miles to the northeast instead of directly north. Thus the outfit avoided some of the little towns and farm communities where they had had to endure delays in the past. In years gone by, many of the settlers had ridden out to gossip with them and, in some instances, to haggle with them over the price of a side of beef. Lucien Edmond Bouchard did not like to make these quick, small sales; they wasted too much time, and the prime cattle that individual

231

buyers would invariably select would be lost to the big market buyer. The absence of just those three or four head of cattle might detract, in the buyer's eyes, from the overall quality of the herd. And because he had decided this spring to limit the size of the herd and hold back a reserve, Lucien Edmond was particularly anxious to avoid casual sales and to save the entire herd for the market at Newton, where he would get the best price.

At night, when they made camp, Lucien Edmond would move among his vaqueros, pausing to talk with each man, to ask him about his family, to learn more about his particular hopes and dreams and problems. This closeness brought about a unity and solidarity among the men, vital to the success of any cattle drive through hundreds of miles of unoccupied territory. A less cohesive group might panic at the first sign of trouble, whereas these men were trustworthy, not easily taken by surprise, and resourceful when danger threatened.

What concerned Lucien Edmond most was the continued morose silence of Eddie Gentry, who rode right point with all the skill his boss had expected him to show, yet with a dogged, even exaggerated bravado. It was as if the lanky young Texan sought to punish himself for Polly Behting's tragic death. He stayed longer in the saddle than any of the other men, and he exhausted himself each time he went after strays. Galloping after them, he would slap his sombrero against his gelding's side, bawling out at them in a hoarse, angry voice, driving them back into line. His face was grim, his eyes narrowed, his lips compressed: he had not yet been purged of the anguish that the news of the young German nurse's death had inflicted on his innermost being.

Ramón and Lucien Edmond often commented on this behavior. The night before they reached the Red River, Lucien Edmond's brother-in-law anxiously declared, "You know, Lucien Edmond, that I saw my father flogged to death as a peon. I can't help thinking now, when I see poor Eddie riding himself to exhaustion every day of this drive, that he is doing the same thing to himself as was done to my father. I know why, as you do. Is there no way we can reach him?"

Lucien Edmond shook his head. "No, Ramón. You saw yourself last week how Santiago Miraflores tried to cheer

232

him up by borrowing Pedro Dornado's guitar and asking Eddie if he could remember some of the old Texas songs he learned when he was a boy. And Eddie just shook his head, mumbled something, walked off by himself into the darkness and stood there for a long time. No, Ramón, he's young and he's proud, and he doesn't want to break down and show his feelings. He's got to work it out for himself, it's the only way. Maybe when we get to Newton, he'll meet someone, or something will happen to make him stop all this terrible brooding."

"I hope you are right, Lucien Edmond." Ramón sighed and got to his feet. "I feel so sorry for him. But I can't reach him, any more than you or any of the other men can. And yet, he does his job. You have to admit that nobody could ride the right point better than he's done on this drive."

"I think he's working extra hard because he wants to lose himself in his work," Lucien Edmond said. "Well, he proved himself as point rider last year, and he's even better at it this year. I've let him know that the few times I've had a chance to say anything to him. No, we'll just have to wait till we reach Newton to see what happens."

"We've made wonderful time, Lucien Edmond, the best I can ever remember. I hope our luck holds out, and then I hope you get a decent price for these fine cattle. I've never seen better, ever since I first rode for you."

"I'm not putting my hopes too high, as I told you before, Ramón," Lucien Edmond responded. "That's one of the main reasons I held back so many head this time. And somehow I don't feel that Newton is going to be a steady market for us. I shouldn't be surprised if next year there'll be another boomtown where Joseph McCoy will make his headquarters and attract Midwestern buyers. Well, let's turn in early. And let's hope that tomorrow the Red River will be at low ebb, the way it was five years ago."

"I remember that. Still, even with the water as low as it was that year, it took us nearly two whole days to get the herd across," Ramón replied.

But the next day, when the vaqueros neared the thickly grassed banks, Lucien Edmond's hopes were dashed. Simata shook his head and spurred his gelding back to his boss to report, "The water is high, and the current too swift to cross. I will ride to the east to see if I can find shallower water for the fording."

"And I'll ride westward," Eddie Gentry volunteered, his weatherbeaten face glistening with the sweat of the burning sun.

An hour later, Simata and Eddie reported that there was no possibility of crossing today. Nor was there for the next three days, till at last the current slackened and the high level of the water began to drop. Simata found a bend in the river some three miles eastward, and Lucien Edmond gave the signal for the vaqueros to drive the lowing cattle across. Before the last young steer plodded doggedly into the water and, almost floundering in trying to swim to the other side, at last was drawn up with the aid of a lariat, seven full days had been spent in the crossing.

Now came the deep buffalo grass and the ascending plains of Indian Territory. What weight the herd had lost in the arduous crossing was almost at once replaced through bountiful grazing. Lucien Edmond, his tension easing at last, watched the procession of cows, bulls, steers, and sturdy yearlings moving to the north, toward a horizon that seemed endless, beneath a nearly cloudless sky.

Eight days later, moving lazily to let the cattle graze all they wished, the outfit neared the desolate reservation of the Creeks.

Emataba hurried out to welcome Lucien Edmond Bouchard, his blood brother, and the two men shook hands warmly and then embraced in the Creek fashion. Emataba exclaimed, "It is good to see my brother again. I have good news for him—this time, things go much better for us. And this is due entirely to the white-eyes shaman who came to live with us and who is now in Wichita reunited with his entire family."

"Yes, I was going to ask you for news about Dr. Ben Wilson, Emataba."

"Three of my braves, good friends of his, accompanied him to your Texas ranch to help him bring back the children of his dead wife," the Creek *mico* replied. "He is a proud man and his faith does him credit, but I insisted that my braves go with him to prevent any danger to him and the little ones. Besides, if I had not given a gun to Elone, when they left to go to their new home in Wichita, evil men might well have slain him and taken her to be their

234

woman—and perhaps the babies would have died as well."

"I'm grateful to you for that, Emataba. We certainly don't want to lose Dr. Wilson. After I've sold my cattle in Newton, I'll ride over to Wichita and visit with him."

"That would be a good thing. Tell him that the white-eyes shaman who took his place is very kind and is liked here, and that the new Indian agent has kept his word. We are comfortable for the first time in many years—we are being cared for now as Dr. Ben Wilson cared for us, and we can ask no more."

"I know what you say and also what you do not say, Emataba," Lucien Edmond compassionately observed. "I see this fence, and I know its meaning for you. Yet, you have withstood the shame of it, showing that you and your people are indeed stronger of heart than those who fenced you in. And I pledge to you, my blood brother, that I and my children will see that your people do not starve and are not neglected. As proof of my pledge, I have two fine bulls, some cows, and steers for meat so that you will have plenty to eat and have milk for the children when the snows come. My vaqueros will help build a special corral to fence in these cattle so that they cannot run away."

"My brother is kind, as always. The Creeks will never forget him. But perhaps," Emataba could not help adding with an ironic smile, "the vaqueros could repair this old fence, which tells us what our boundaries are, as ordered by our white-eyes keepers. There is temptation, with the fence nearly rotted away in many places, for some of the restless young braves to flee and to taste—if only for a few hours—the joy of freedom."

"You know you do not mean that, Emataba. If I had my way, I would tear down the fence completely. But do you not see that it is another kind of symbol? The fearful among those high in power in our land wished to shut you away. But the fence that they put up is almost useless now—yet you remain here in peace. That gives the lie to their fears and proves how much weaker than you they truly are."

"Ho, what you have said has much meaning. Yes, I examine it, and it will give us more heart and courage. Before you leave, I shall tell my people what you have said. Perhaps it will free them from this black thought of despair

235

which is always with them when they come outside their wigwams and tepees and see that ugly fence surrounding us here in the midst of nowhere. The white-eyes soldiers used to say to us, we must stay here under their protection as otherwise we should ride on the warpath. Yet how could we do this? Some of the younger braves have guns, but they are old and few in number. What could they do against all the bright new guns of the soldiers that would be sent against us if we rebelled? No," Emataba sadly shook his head, "we shall spin out our lives here. If Ibofanaga wills it, we may be moved farther to the north so that there is even less danger to fearful white-eyes. There is no strength left in us, not for war. There never was strength for war, save to protect our land. And as for what was taken long ago, we knew even then that our numbers could not equal those of the white-eyes who had come always against us with better weapons than we could devise and with more greed than we had for our own land. We loved our land because it was our birthright. Those who wished to take it from us envied us, and this envy gave them strength, the kind of strength which an enemy has when he feels hatred for you. No, my blood brother, I see the end of our days stretching before us like these endless plains. But we shall keep our heads high and we shall remember our heritage, thanks to friends like you and Dr. Ben Wilson and this new Indian agent."

Lucien Edmond Bouchard was deeply moved and could not speak. He put his left hand over the heart of the *mico* and nodded, to show that he understood. Then, side by side, they walked through the village as Emataba gave orders for the feast to welcome them.

Eddie Gentry was one of those who helped build the corral in which Lucien Edmond's gift of cattle to the *mico* would be penned. The lanky, towheaded young Texan watched the villagers, seeing the brightening faces of the Indians and the eagerness of the young children who ran to greet the vaqueros. And he understood the bond of friendship between red man and white. That night, walking far out into the plains, certain that he was far enough from the campfires that no one would see or hear him, he knelt down and wept for Polly Behting and his tears eased his own despairing loneliness.

* * *

236

Lucien Edmond Bouchard's herd would not be the first to reach the new cow town of Newton. Amanda Burks, one of the few women ever to experience a trail drive, accompanied her husband, W. F. Burks, from Nueces County, Texas, to Newton five months before Lucien Edmond commenced his drive from Windhaven Range. She drove a buggy most of the way, and she endured lightning and hailstorms. She witnessed fights with rustlers and hostile Indians, a prairie fire, and a stampede. Before the Burkses reached Newton, cattle prices had dropped alarmingly, so they had wintered their herd at Smoky River, a considerable distance north of Newton. Then they sold their cattle in the spring, made the return journey by rail to St. Louis and New Orleans, thence by water to Corpus Christi. But Lucien Edmond Bouchard had vowed that never would his beautiful wife, Maxine, endure the harrowing experiences of the arduous cattle drive from Texas to Kansas.

Already, Newton had its "Hide Park," the name given to a shambling collection of dance halls and saloons south of the Atchison, Topeka & Santa Fe railroad tracks. One of these saloons, owned by a gawky and loquacious Missourian, Perry Tuttle, had already become a popular rendezvous for trail drivers.

Grass still covered the streets of this new cow town, and there were prairie dog colonies on every side. Indeed, wild animals were so numerous that the newly created city council was forced to pass an ordinance prohibiting the running at large of buffaloes and other animals. There was constant gunfire almost daily, but little bloodshed. As Texas and Missouri trail outfits arrived in the booming market town, they gave vent to their pent-up spirits by flourishing their guns and firing into the air. Lucien Edmond Bouchard had always put a damper on such exuberance; he believed in the maxim that one should never draw shooting irons unless intending to use them. Moreover, as he had often told Ramón, "Even if you shoot off your gun just because you're happy you finally got your cattle to market, somebody may misunderstand and start a real shootout with you. And then innocent men will die, all because of what some people call high spirits. I, for one, won't let my vaqueros use their guns to announce their arrival."

237

It was the evening of June 10, a few days before Lucien Edmond's arrival in town. In Perry Tuttle's dance hall, Jack Martin was glowering over the poker hand that Hugh Emory, English remittance man turned house gambler, had dealt him. He had been playing all afternoon, and the chips on the green baize tablecloth represented his very last stake. Beside him sat the Mexican renegade Benito Tonsado, a man in his mid-forties, with a heavy, drooping moustache, twitching eyelids, and a bulbous nose. Tonsado was wanted for three murders in Nuevo Laredo and suspected of another in Austin.

Hugh Emory, the supercilious Englishman who had drifted from New York to St. Louis to New Orleans and, finally, to Newton, eyed Jack Martin. Emory had spent five years as a gambling wanderer after his patrician father had driven him out of England forever, promising to send a monthly allowance on condition that his son never return.

"Cards, Mr. Martin?" Emory said in a high-pitched, faintly amused voice.

Jack Martin was thirty-six, wiry and of medium height, with a hawklike nose, squinting, cold blue eyes, and a jagged purplish scar on his left cheek, the ineffaceable mark of a fight over cards four years ago in a Sedalia gambling den when his assailant had slashed at his face with a broken bottle. He had knifed the man, but not fatally; two weeks later, seeing his assailant on the street at night, he had shot him in the back and turned outlaw. He had met Benito Tonsado two years ago in Nagadoches and formed a partnership with him, and the two men had engaged in rustling, bushwhacking, cheating at cards, and a dozen robberies of small banks and stores throughout the Texas and Kansas territories.

The newly appointed marshall of Newton, Mike McCluskie, was an easygoing man who did not bother with outlaws unless they challenged his rule of the town. Knowing McCluskie's reputation for ignoring wanted posters, Martin had unerringly chosen Newton as his present theater of operations, and he and Tonsado, both down to their last few dollars, had determined to stage a spectacular coup to regain their dissipated stakes.

Scowling at Hugh Emory, Martin squinted at his cards

and then growled, "Gimme two, and none of your fancy dealing off the bottom of the deck, either."

"Sir, you offend my integrity with a remark like that," the Englishman drawled. But, with another faint smile, he methodically dealt two cards off the top of the deck as slowly as he could. "There, I trust that meets your specifications?"

"It better had, or by God, I'll cut your tripes out," Martin grumbled as he reached for the cards, discarded the two worthless ones in his hand, and studied the luck of the draw. A flicker of interest made his cheekbones redden, and impulsively he shoved forward the last of his chips. "I'll just raise this much."

"I'll stay," a pudgy, nearly bald railroad man said as he shoved forward the requisite number of chips from his own modestly stacked pile.

"I'll guess I'll stick with what I have," Emory declared with a casual glance at his hand, then folded it and laid it down on the table with the back of his hand covering the cards.

"Two sixes and a pair of jacks," Martin announced, spreading his hand on the table.

"I'm sorry, Mr. Martin. Four kings," Emory replied indifferently as, lifting his hand, he spread his cards face up for the scarfaced gambler to see.

"Sonuvabitch—of all the goddamn luck! Englishman, you're too lucky to stay alive!" Martin growled as he rose unsteadily from the table. But the remittance man had already drawn a pearl-handled derringer and now aimed it squarely at Martin's heart. "It was a fair deal, all the rest of you saw it. You're just a bad loser, Mr. Martin. I'm sorry, but I think you'd best take your custom elsewhere."

"You can betchyer lousy life on that, Englishman. Come on, Benito, let's get the hell out of here!" Martin snarled. As he reached the swinging doors of the dance hall-saloon, he turned to send Hugh Emory a venomous look. "I'll be back when I've got some *dinero*, and then I'll take you for every cent you've got, Englishman. You just mark my words—but not the cards, get me?"

Outside in the dark warm night, he turned to the renegade Mexican. "Amigo, we've got to get us some *dinero* or cash in our chips for good. But this town's dead. There isn't much cattle here yet, and nobody's loaded for bear. They're all waiting for the trail herds."

"*Sí, es verdad*," the Mexican agreed. "And that is the way we shall earn our *dinero, mi compañero*."

"I get your drift, Benito." A crafty grin curved Martin's thin, small mouth. "We'll just get some boys together and bushwhack ourselves one of the herds coming in."

"*Sí,* that is exactly what I meant, *mi amigo.* Now, I have heard this Joseph McCoy talking to one of the Chicago buyers just the other day. As I remember, he has said that he expects a large herd coming in from Texas. There is a *hacendado* there who has come to Abilene each year and done very well. He should be on the way by now. And if we were to ride out to meet him and take him by surprise, we could take his cattle and turn them into *mucho dinero*."

"You're damned right, Benito. Let's go over to the Bull's Head Tavern. I know at least four or five of the boys drinking there right now, and they'd be glad to ride with us. They're on their uppers too, the way we are. And they'd like a little acton."

"They are *pistoleros*?" Tonsado demanded.

"You're damned right they're *pistoleros*. And they don't care who they kill so long as they get paid for it. Hitch on to two or three thousand head of cattle, Benito, and we've got ourselves a nice big stake, even if we have to split it ten or twelve ways. Well, are you with me?"

"I know some *hombres* too who would ride with us."

"Well, what are you waiting for? You go find your men, I'll get mine. Tell you what—we'll meet out near McCoy's cattle pens at midnight and we'll talk this over, get me?"

"*Sí, comprendo.*"

Jack Martin and Benito Tonsado had recruited a dozen ne'er-do-wells from the saloons, all of them men who lived either by the gun or their wits and, like the two leaders, were temporarily down on their luck and eager to recoup with one quick stroke. Seven of the men were white renegades who, after coming to terms with the leaders, had gone back to their lodgings to pack their gear. The other five were Mexicans; these Martin and Tonsado invited into a saloon, to conclude their discussion and to seal their agreement with tequila.

Two of the Mexicans, Luis Calera and Francisco Yradier, had been recruited by Benito Tonsado. They had been vaqueros for a wealthy *hacendado* in Durango, discharged for trying to steal some of their *patrón*'s cattle, and had drifted across the border, living as best they could by rustling cattle and robbing small groups of homesteaders who were journeying into the Texas Panhandle. Calera, a small, deceptively friendly man in his early thirties, had killed five men and women with the Bowie knife he wore in a leather sheath strapped to his right thigh, and he was also an expert pistol shot. It was he who, when Martin and Tonsado outlined their plan to bushwhack the expected Bouchard herd, offered a practical suggestion which the leaders had not thought of: "Señores, if I may be permitted to offer a piece of advice, it will be necessary to change the marks of these *ganado* before you try to sell them to the Señor McCoy's buyers. He is not a fool. He would recognize the brand on these cattle."

"Hombre, usted tiene razon," Benito Tonsado's sly grin revealed blackened teeth. Turning to Jack Martin, he added, "It will mean *mucho trabajo, mi amigo.* But it will be worth it. From what I overheard the Señor McCoy say, this *hacendado* Bouchard should be driving at least three thousand head of cattle. From this, one could expect at least thirty thousand dollars. Perhaps more. For such *dinero,* I for one do not mind a little work."

"And also, Señor Martin," Francisco Yradier spoke up with a crafty grin, "there will be the horses we shall take and the supplies and also, since it is a bad thing to waste what dead men have in their pockets, whatever *dinero* we shall find when we have put all those vaqueros to sleep forever." A big, heavy-set man in his mid-thirties with a handlebar moustache, which he waxed daily with the vanity of a narcissist, he held out his big hands, spreading the large, thick fingers and then clenching them slowly. He had boasted that he had strangled or broken the backs of at least ten men since he and Luis Calera had fled Durango with a price on their heads and their *patrón*'s threat that he would hang them on sight.

Jack Martin chuckled and nodded as he eyed his Mexican crony. "Looks to me, Benito, like you picked some men with brains for this job. I'll go along with the branding idea. But first things first. We'll ride out at dawn, all of us, savvy? I'd say that Bouchard outfit ought to be some-where in Indian Territory right now, heading for here. We'll go after them, and once we scout them, we'll pick ourselves a likely spot for an ambush at night, that's the best time. We'll wait till they're bedded down for the night, and when we attack, the gunfire'll stampede their cattle."

"It is a good plan," Benito Tonsado agreed. "In addition to Luis and Francisco here, the men you found, Jack, ob-viously have been vaqueros too, and they know how to round up cattle after a stampede. Especially when there are no other men alive to ride after them, *no es verdad, ami-gos*?" At this, the three other Mexicans, who had been re-cruited by Martin, eyed one another, then grinned and nodded, breaking out into voluble Spanish to declare their capabilities as *gran vaqueros*.

"Then that's it," Martin decided. "Get your horses, all the guns you can muster and be sure they're loaded, and bring plenty of extra ammunition. We'll meet at dawn with the seven other men, just beyond Joe McCoy's big stock-yard. And in a couple of weeks, we ought to be able to fill that stockyard, eh, Benito?"

"Pero sí, mi compañero," the Mexican outlaw laugh-ingly agreed.

CHAPTER NINETEEN

This late June night held the threat of a storm, for late in the afternoon, Simata had seen dark clouds gathering to the northeast and had been sure that he had heard, if only once, the faint rumble of distant thunder. As Pablo Casares busied himself with the preparation of the evening meal and Santiago Miraflores shouldered his Spencer carbine and trudged off to stand his shift on guard at the northern-most point of the camp, two hundred yards away from the bedded-down herd, Ramón and Lucien Edmond conferred in quiet tones.

"We were making good time till we hit the Red River," Lucien Edmond averred. "So far, thank God, we haven't lost any cattle and, best of all, not a single vaquero has had so much as a scratch. But we're short one supply wagon which we lost in the river. It's too bad we couldn't salvage anything."

"Do you think we'll have enough supplies, Lucien Edmond?" Ramón anxiously demanded.

"Yes, if we can make good time from now on. Just the same, since Wichita is in our direct line to Newton, it wouldn't do any harm to send two or three of the vaqueros on ahead to pick up some extra sacks of flour, beans, some coffee, and a side or two of bacon. Matter of fact," Lucien Edmond brightened, "I'll ride in with them when we get that close. I'm anxious to have news of Dr. Wilson and see Thomas and Sybella again."

"I've been thinking, Lucien Edmond," Ramón suddenly proposed, "that because we took about ten more horses than we need, we might add a little to our profits by selling them in Wichita. There are several good-sized stables there, and prime horses such as we have ought to bring a premium."

"We'll see. That's not a bad idea, though." Lucien Edmond grinned boyishly. "I could use a little extra money to bring back presents for Maxine and Diane, as well as the others in my little brood. Besides, I'd like to buy that sweet Elone a new dress or a bracelet or something she'd like. You know, Ramón, it was a wonderful thing that Ben found her and fell in love with her. After losing Fleurette, he was on the way to making a martyr of himself with his work at Emataba's village. Say what you like about spiritual inspiration, there isn't a man living who isn't the better because of the love of a woman who respects and helps him. I'd be nowhere without my Maxine. And the wonder of it is, Ramón, she was a brilliant intellectual from Baltimore who was visiting the South for the first time, when I met her. Yet just see how she's adapted herself to being a rancher's wife, a mother, a defender of the ranch when all of us are out here, far away from home."

"And I can say the same thing and even more about my beautiful Mara." Ramón turned to look southward, his eyes soft and gentle with remembrance, his lips curving in a lover's smile. "It is hard to believe my good fortune. I, who was the son of a peon and who rode with that bandit Diego Macaras, was given a second chance at life by the good Señor Dios, when he sent me to warn you that Diego Macaras would attack Windhaven Range. Thus I met you and your beautiful sister, the joy of my heart. She has given me my new life. And now, she will soon give me another little one—perhaps even before we return home."

"You are too modest about what you have accomplished, Ramón." Lucien Edmond put a comradely arm around Ramón's shoulders. "You give Mara all the credit, and you forget that, when she came to Texas, it was in a mood of black despair and cynicism. It is you who have given her new life and hope and love. And for this I'm deeply grateful. You see, our lives are bound together. And if I were a very superstitious man, I should say that all of this was part of some plan that began in the days of my great-grandfather."

"I understand you, my brother-in-law," Ramón softly murmured. "I, too, am not a superstitious man, but there are many things that have happened to us both which cannot be explained by the mind alone. The heart tells us what we are to do, very often. And I think that often the heart is the best judge of a man, not the mind. I know when I first met your father, I saw at once how wrong I had been to think that Diego Macaras was the patriot who would lead us all toward *libertad*. No, Lucien Edmond, it was your father, and his grandfather before him, who truly knew the meaning of freedom and who worked to earn it."

"And now," Lucien Edmond said with an embarrassed little laugh, for the conversation had unexpectedly become emotionally compelling, "I suggest we think of such practical things as Pablo's cooking. I, for one, am as hungry as a starved wolf."

The vaqueros were especially hungry tonight, perhaps because of the exhausting work they had had to do in crossing the Red River and then, by emotional contrast, the two days they had spent with the forlorn villagers of the Creek reservation. Many of those vaqueros had been either peons in their youth or the sons of peons and thus had known how dreary life could be without freedom. Mingling with the welcoming villagers at that lonely reservation, they had been poignantly reminded that here were once free, proud men who were now in many ways far worse off than the lowliest peon of their homeland. So Pablo Casares was kept busy in his chuckwagon doling out seconds of beef and dumplings, beans with molasses, and strong, black coffee, beaming with pleasure at the compliments heaped upon him by his compatriots.

By ten o'clock, most of the men had spread out their bedrolls and were fast asleep, except for Pedro Dornado, who, strumming his guitar and singing softly to keep the cattle at rest, took up his guard position at the farthest southern point behind the herd. Lucas remained on guard also, inspecting his Spencer carbine and making sure it was loaded and that replacement ammunition was within his reach. Pablo, having tidied up the chuck wagon at last, dozed in the back, smiling as he dreamed of his wife, Kate, and their little daughter, Catarina.

They had made camp this evening about twenty miles south of the Kansas border. About a mile west, there was a small creek where the herd had watered its fill. Directly east of them was a large forest of spruce, oak, and short-needle fir trees, standing out on a slightly rising series of little hills that looked like Indian burial mounds, with an average height of about three feet. Between the trees chokeberries, wild flowers, and thick buffalo grass grew profusely. There was only a quarter moon, and its faint light was intermittently covered by dark clouds. The warm June wind, which had raised clouds of dust at the drag points of the milling herd that afternoon, was suddenly cooler and stronger. It blew from the northeast, rippling the grass and making the fir cones bobble from the tips of the angling branches. In the distance, there was the mournful howl of a lone coyote. Lucas instinctively crouched and moved nearer to the dark forest, peering into it, his senses keen with sudden foreboding. He was thinking of his heroic father, Djamba, and he glanced up at the brooding sky and murmured a prayer for Djamba's soul.

Fernando Reyes, one of the three young Mexican vaqueros recruited by Jack Martin, had ridden ahead of the band of bushwhackers to determine the location of Lucien Edmond Bouchard's oncoming herd. He had reined in his stallion about two miles north of the Bouchard campsite, uttered a joyous exclamation as he made out the dark mass of the herd, and then veered the stallion toward the east to make a wide circle and to judge the terrain. When he caught sight of the rambling forest along the succession of mound-like low hills, he jerked the reins savagely and turned the protesting stallion to the north to gallop back to the outlaw band. Jack Martin, at the head of the bushwhackers, spurred his horse to meet the oncoming young Mexican. "Well, Reyes, did you find them?"

"*Sí*, Senor Martin! *Caramba*, they will be very easy to attack. There are many trees and little hills to the east of them, where they camp. We can hide there and surprise them late tonight."

"Good work, Reyes!" the scar-faced outlaw chuckled. Turning to his Mexican partner, he declared, "Benito, we'll make a wide circle to the east. Nice and slow, mind you. We'll tie up the horses, and then, when the men are all sound asleep, we'll attack. We'll have cover from the trees and the grass and the darkness. With any luck, we should be able to wipe them out to the last man before they know what hits them!"

Benito Tonsado nodded and, turning to his compatriots, gave orders in a quick, low voice. The fourteen riders turned eastward, moving slowly, as the shadows of night deepened. Deliberately, they rode about five miles east-ward to avoid detection by any scout the Bouchard outfit might have sent out. There they paused beside a winding creek with only about two feet of water in it and let their horses drink their fill. Dismounting, they made a quick meal of jerky and hardtack, but lit no fire for coffee, lest it be seen by a Bouchard scout. When they had finished, Martin gave another order: "We'll walk to the edge of that hideout, *hombres.* You will lead your horses—that way, those Texans won't hear us coming. And we'll wait till there's not a sign of life stirring before we take them. Now let's get moving!"

Dismounting, he took an empty flour sack from his saddle bag, pulled it over his horse's head, and wound and knotted a rawhide throng in the middle to blindfold and silence his docile mount. The others followed his example, and then, leading their horses by the reins, they walked slowly toward the easternmost edge of the sprawling forest. There they tied the reins to the branches or trunks of trees and, spreading out, began to creep forward toward the west, to reach the edge of the forest nearest the Bouchard campsite.

The five Mexicans of the band were armed with knives, old Belgian pistols, and rifles dating back to the army of Marshall Bazaine, which once had kept Maximilian on the throne of Mexico. Jack Martin wore two holstered Starr .44s, while Benito Tonsado was armed with an old Sharps single-shot rifle. The seven white renegades who had been recruited out of the Newton saloons had three six-shooters, a Confederate Whitworth long-range rifle, two derringers, and a Starr .44 among them.

It was after midnight, and they heard only the chirping of the cicadas and the soft rustle of the wind through the grass and the trees. The Bouchard campfires had long since been extinguished. Here and there a heifer or a steer lifted its head and lowed softly to the soothing sounds of the guitar strummed by Pedro Dornado. Simata, the half-breed scout, who would take his post as guard at about four in the morning, had been unable to sleep. Leaving his bedroll, he walked slowly toward the chuck wagon to see if Pablo Casares was still awake and had any coffee left.

Santiago Miraflores, whose turn it was to stand guard, walked slowly past the sleeping heifers and steers who sprawled on the eastern edge of the bedded herd. He was only a few yards away from the edge of the forest, and he did not look at it as he moved slowly toward the south end of the camp. He would have a word with Pedro Dornado to see how things were going at that end of the herd.

Luis Calera grinned savagely as he inched forward. Drawing his sharp Bowie knife out of its sheath, he gripped it by the finely honed tip. Getting to his knees, he took careful aim, then flung the knife forward with a quick snap of his wrist. Santiago stopped dead in his tracks, his eyes bulging in horrified surprise as the Bowie knife buried itself in his back. He took a step to the left, then his knees buckled under him and he fell heavily, his right hand feebly reaching back to try to pluck out the weapon. His body shuddered twice and then lay still.

Jack Martin nodded his approval and patted Calera on the back. Then, drawing the Starr .44 from its right-hand holster, he raised it and pulled the trigger. The loud report shattered the stillness of the night, and at once the heifers and steers lumbered to their feet and began to move. He drew the other pistol and fired again. With frightened bellows, the herd began to run.

"Now, boys!" Martin cried hoarsely.

Simata whirled after hearing the first shot and, kneeling down at the rear of the chuck wagon, leveled his Spencer carbine at the forest from which the sound of the shot had come. He saw the flash of fire from Martin's second stampeding shot and answered it by triggering the carbine in the direction of that light. One of the white renegades a few feet away from Martin slumped dead, a bullet through his forehead. A second man, in the act of shouldering his Whitworth and bringing it to bear on Simata, uttered an agonized cry, stumbled to his feet, and then sank down onto his side, his hand pressed over the profusely bleeding wound in his hip.

Lucien Edmond Bouchard sprang to his feet, grabbing his Spencer carbine, and called to Ramón beside him, "Bushwhackers, Ramón! Have the men stretch out on the ground so they won't give our attackers any kind of a target. It's coming from those trees—they must have ridden up from the east and led their horses on foot so we couldn't hear them—get some of the men to lie under the

248

chuck wagon and the supply wagons and keep peppering those trees!"

Ramón nodded and began to crawl toward the bedrolls of the vaqueros, whispering Lucien Edmond's instructions. Four of the vaqueros, seizing their carbines, crawled on their bellies to the chuck wagon and the largest supply wagon standing beside it and took their positions under them, firing their weapons into the trees whenever they saw flashes of gunfire.

The placid calm of the warm June night had suddenly turned into a nightmare of chaos and noise. There was the thunderous sound of the cattle's hooves as the frightened beasts ran off in all directions, heads down, eyes glassy and maddened. There were the cries of the wounded and the hoarse commands of Jack Martin, shouting from his hiding place behind a fir tree. There were the excited cries of Ramón and Lucien Edmond as they called out to their vaqueros to remain where they were and to concentrate their fire wherever they saw the flashes of gunfire from the bushwhackers.

Pedro Dornado, dropping his guitar, had hurried to retrieve the Spencer carbine he had laid on his unpacked bedroll. Just as he reached it, Fernando Reyes, profiting from the sudden light shed by the quarter-moon as it emerged from behind a cloud, cradled his Belgian rifle against his left shoulder, sighted, and squeezed the trigger. Pedro straightened as if propelled by a invisible hand, let go of the carbine, his right hand shakingly moving up as if to touch the red hole in his right cheek, then pitched forward and lay lifeless over the bedroll. Lucas, crouching behind the wheel of one of the supply wagons, saw the fire that sprang from Reyes's weapon and, lofting his Spencer carbine, triggered three shots in that precise direction. The young Mexican outlaw uttered a soft groan, dropped the rifle, bowed his head, and lay still.

By now, the fleeing herd had left the campsite in half a dozen different directions, and the drumming of their hooves was fading away. In its place there came the agonized groans of one of Lucien Edmond's vaqueros who had been trampled by the stampeding cattle and who lay dying near the chuck wagon. Then, as if mercifully to drown out those dreadful sounds, came the rapid, desultory gunfire from the forest answered by Lucien Edmond's men.

249

Jack Martin swore under his breath. "It's not working out the way I figgered, Benito. Damn it to hell, I'd hoped the stampede would've knocked off a lot more of their men than that bastard moaning out there! Now we're pinned down here."

"But so are they, *amigo*," the Mexican outlaw counseled as he reloaded his Sharps, then took careful aim and fired at the shadowy outline of one of the younger vaqueros who had crawled out from under one of the supply wagons and, crouching, was trying to run to the chuck wagon to join forces with one of his friends there. A shot grazed the vaquero's thigh; he stumbled, but reached his goal safely and, swearing under his breath, rolled over onto his side so that Teobaldo Armenguez, one of Lucien Edmond's most recently engaged vaqueros, could stop the bleeding and bandage the wound. "*Es muy estúpido*," Armenguez scolded his friend as he improvised a tourniquet from a torn piece of his shirt. "You should have stayed where you were."

"You're an old woman, Teobaldo! *Ayudame*, that hurts—but I can still shoot. See there, toward the center of the big oak trees, there are shots coming—watch this, *amigo*!" So saying, he rolled over onto his belly, adjusted his carbine, and sent seven shots toward the area he had pointed out. There was a gurgling cry from one of the white renegades, a scream from another, and a third rolled over dead with a bullet hole in his skull.

Enraged by these losses of his men, Jack Martin, baring his teeth in a rictus of venomous hatred, unholstered his Starr .44s and commenced firing at the chuck wagon. One of the bullets grazed Pablo Casares's left arm, but, nothing daunted, he leaped down from the chuck wagon, carbine in hand, flung himself out on the ground, and began to fire into the woods. Another of the white renegades, who was crawling on all fours toward a tree with a thicker trunk, took the bullet in his left side and, with a scream of mortal agony, rolled over and over, thrashing and arching until at last he lay still.

But to counter this, Benito Tonsado's well-aimed ball from the old Sharps killed another of Lucien Edmond's vaqueros. Simata and Lucas, with a simultaneous cry of anger as they saw their companion roll over and lie sprawled with his arms crossed, leveled their carbines and pumped the triggers to empty them. Tonsado, who had squatted to one side of the tree behind which he had been hiding and was hurriedly reloading the Sharps, let out a shrill scream of pain, rolled over onto one side, then slowly turned and lay with his face against the humid earth.

Luis Calera did not want to lose the Bowie knife whose haft rose from the middle of dead Santiago Miraflores's back. The moon disappeared behind a large dark cloud, and he scrambled forward toward the corpse of the vaquero, reached down, and plucked out the razor-sharp blade. But as he turned to run back to his hiding place, Lucien Edmond killed him with rapid-fire shots from the Spencer carbine he had just finished reloading.

Jack Martin swore again as he saw his ranks decimated by the greater fire power of the Texas outfit. Two of Fernando Reyes's companions survived, as did Francisco Yradier, who, stretched out on his belly and hidden in the thick buffalo grass, had flattened a clump ahead of him so that he could see to aim his old Belgian rifle at the campsite. Of the seven white outlaws who had been recruited, three were dead and three were fatally wounded. The seventh had collected some of the guns of his dead companions and coolly, despite a scratch on his arm from the graze of a carbine bullet, kept up a continuous fire at whatever targets he could make out in the eerie darkness.

Lucien Edmond had observed the lack of intensity of the outlaws' fire and rightly calculated that at least half of them were out of action by now. In a low voice, he muttered to Ramón, "Get word to the men under the wagons to concentrate all their fire right into the center of the woods there. I'll flank them from the south."

"It's too dangerous, Lucien Edmond; I'll go with you," Ramón protested.

"Well, I'll admit I can use some help. Pass the word now, then we'll wait till the moon's hidden again behind one of those big clouds," Lucien Edmond impatiently urged.

Cupping his hands to his mouth, Ramón called softly to Teobaldo Armenguez, who nodded his understanding and whispered to his wounded friend. Then, crawling carefully under the next wagon, he informed Simata and Lucas and two other vaqueros of the trail boss's plan of attack.

All of them now began to concentrate their fire on the

woods, while Lucien Edmond and Ramón, crouching low, waited till the moon went behind a thick cloud. Then they ran swiftly in a flanking maneuver toward the south and dashed to the edge of the woods, flung themselves down into the thick buffalo grass, and cautiously began to crawl forward.

Earlier that evening Ramón had securely tethered the extra horses brought along in the remuda, and it was well that he had. The noise of the stampeding cattle, the continuous sounds of rifles and pistols and carbines had terrified the animals, and they were rearing in the air, pawing with their hooves, whinnying shrilly, their eyes rolling in their fright. Only one of them, a gray gelding, had managed to break its tethering and gallop off to the west.

Eddie Gentry had been unhurt during the furious battle and now, lying beside Pablo under the chuck wagon, he squinted at the wooded area and made out a dark shadow moving through the grass. Raising his carbine, he triggered it, and one of the two remaining Mexican vaqueros who had worked with Fernando Reyes stumbled, grabbed at his belly, and fell dying. His companion brandished his fist and swore in virulent Spanish, then aimed his Belgian rifle at Eddie. But from his vantage point within the woods, Lucien Edmond snapped off a shot from his carbine and the young vaquero dropped his rifle and fell back dead, his lifeless eyes staring up at the branches that obscured the sky.

Francisco Yradier was firing at the men under the chuck wagon with two Belgian pistols. One of them exploded in his left hand, and with an oath, he flung it away and drew out a sharp hunting knife from the sheath strapped to his left thigh. He had heard the shot from the perimeter of the woods to his left and seen the young Mexican fall, and he began to crawl now toward where Lucien Edmond and Ramón lay in hiding.

Now only Yradier, the red-bearded white renegade, and Jack Martin were left of the fourteen men who had ridden out to bushwhack Lucien Edmond Bouchard's herd. Martin snarled like a cornered animal as the lessening sounds of gunfire from the woods told him that most of his men had been killed. He too began to crawl toward the southern end of the woods, ready to make a run for his horse and put an end to this ill-fated adventure. He had reloaded his Starr .44s and, holding them in front of him, crawled on his belly from the opposite side of where Francisco Yradier was already moving forward toward the attackers who had entered to cut them off.

The red-bearded renegade, who had used up nearly all of his ammunition, now crouched to search the body of one of the Mexican vaqueros and to draw out a derringer. With a frustrated oath, he turned and sent a useless shot whistling above the chuck wagon just as Eddie Gentry, having reloaded his carbine, sprayed the bullets in the direction of that tiny flash of fire. The red-bearded outlaw dropped the derringer, fell backwards, arched his shuddering body from the ground, then slumped in death.

Now for a moment there was silence, more terrible in its intensity than the constant thunder of guns. Jack Martin, clammy with sweat, grinding his teeth, inched forward. As the moon emerged again, the filtering rays down into the woods let him see Lucien Edmond lying on his belly about twenty feet away. With an exultant cry, he lifted himself up and fired one of the pistols. But the cry had warned Lucien Edmond just in time to let him roll to one side, taking the bullet in his thigh instead of in his head. Ramón, ignoring his brother-in-law's writhing and groans of pain, steadied his carbine and pulled the trigger. Martin gasped, tried to lift the other Starr .44, his eyes glazing, then rolled over onto his side, his face frozen in death.

"That must be all of them by now, Lucien Edmond," Ramón whispered. "Are you hit badly?"

"No, no, just in the leg. See if you can stop the bleeding some—just patch me up for the time being, then we'll go back to the men," Lucien Edmond panted.

At this moment, Francisco Yradier rose up from his hiding place—his hunting knife held high in his right hand—and lunged at Ramón. The young Mexican had just time enough to see him out of the corner of his eye and wheel, the knife brushing his jacket. In the maneuver, however, Ramón dropped his carbine and, in a desperate reflexive movement, clenched his fist and smashed it against the bushwhacker's cheekbone, felling him to the ground. Then he flung himself down upon the outlaw, both his hands gripping Yradier's wrists, twisting away the gleaming, deadly sharp knife the outlaw tried to force against him.

253

"Give up, *hombre*! All your friends are dead by now, don't make me kill you!" Ramón panted.

But Yradier shook his head and, hawking and spitting into Ramón's face, redoubled his efforts to break loose and to drive the gleaming blade into Ramón's belly. His face taut and cold, Lucien Edmond's brother-in-law twisted his adversary's right wrist until the point of the knife turned back against its owner and then lunged downward. Yradier stiffened, raised his head, his eyes bulging with horrified surprise, then sank back dead.

"I didn't want to kill him, Lucien Edmond, but it's over now. Lie still, you're still bleeding," he ordered. Then, ripping away part of the dead man's shirt, he wrapped the cloth tightly around Lucien Edmond's thigh, inserting a thick twig in the cloth to make a tourniquet. This done, he stooped and lifted Luke's son to his feet. "Can you make it back to the wagon, do you think, Lucien Edmond?"

"I'm sure I can. You saved my life, Ramón."

"You have saved mine many times, *mi hermano*. Now let's get you into one of the wagons where you can rest."

"The men will have to round up the cattle. God knows how long it'll take," Lucien Edmond weakly protested.

"As long as it takes, that's how long. Don't worry, we'll get them all. Just you rest."

"I will. But tell the men what I think of them. We were taken by surprise, our cattle were stampeded, yet we beat off their attack. There'll be a special bonus for all of them when we get to Newton. God, my leg's beginning to throb."

"I might just have to cut that bullet out of you, Lucien Edmond. But we'll wait until you've rested, and see how it looks tomorrow morning. There we are, just a few steps more. All right, Pablo is going to help you inside and so am I."

CHAPTER TWENTY

At dawn the next morning, Lucien Edmond Bouchard led the funeral services over the bodies of the valiant vaqueros who had given their lives. Santiago Miraflores and Pedro Dornado were buried near the little creek, and after they had been covered, their mourning vaquero friends hewed wooden crosses from the timber of the nearby woods where the bushwhackers had hidden, and inserted them in the ground to mark the graves of men who would not be forgotten.

After the service, Ramón insisted that the trail boss allow the removal of the bullet in his leg. Reluctantly, Lucien Edmond submitted after swallowing a stiff drink of whiskey and clenching his teeth against a strip of tarpaulin to withstand the pain of Ramón's probing. The bullet came out easily, leaving a clean wound which Ramón swabbed with whiskey. Then he added a splint to strengthen the muscle when Lucien Edmond would make his first tentative steps.

This done, Joe Duvray, Eddie Gentry, Simata, and Ramón each took charge of a group of vaqueros and rode after the stampeded herd. It took six days to round up the panic-stricken cattle and bring them back to the original campsite. By this time, Lucien Edmond's wound had almost healed and he was able to walk, though with a slight limp. After the cattle had been rounded up, he made his tally, which would be given to the highest bidder at the Newton market. Sixty-seven head of cattle were missing, some of them found dead from foundering or exhaustion far along the trail, others having outdistanced their pursuers and merged with the waning buffalo herds which still traversed the plains of Indian Territory.

Then, having realigned the herd, the vaqueros—now

more vigilant than ever at the drag and point posts—headed the nearly three thousand cattle toward the market at Newton.

As they were passing Wichita, Lucien Edmond rode into town with Simata, Joe Duvray, and two other vaqueros to replenish their supplies and sell their spare horses. They rode up to Jacob Hartmann's general store, tethered their horses, and entered. The kindly Quaker pastor greeted them, and Lucien Edmond introduced himself and asked for news of Dr. Ben Wilson. To his delight, the genial storekeeper assured him that Thomas and Sybella had been brought safely back from Windhaven Range and were now living in Dr. Wilson's new house. Half an hour later, Lucien Edmond and Joe Duvray rode up to the house, ascended the steps of the front porch, and knocked energetically at the front door. It was opened by Elone, who bade them welcome. Her husband, she informed them, was attending a woman about to deliver her first child on the southern edge of town, and the two men asked if they might wait until he returned.

Three hours later, weary to the point of exhaustion, the young Quaker doctor rode up to the house and tethered his horse to the rail. His eyes widening with surprise to see the other two horses, he strode to the door of his house and entered it.

"Ben!" Lucien Edmond sprang to his feet and came forward with an eager grin to welcome the doctor. "Pastor Hartmann told us where to find you. We're on our way to Newton, but I had to stop by to see if you made it safely."

"We did indeed," Ben replied, shaking hands with Lucien Edmond and Joe. "The three Creek braves who went with me to Windhaven Range and accompanied us back watched over us, and our journey was uneventful. But come, let us have some coffee, if you have the time."

They continued their conversation over refreshments, talking animatedly of their plans for the future. At length, Lucien Edmond and Joe rose to take their leave.

"It's been good to see you again," Lucien Edmond said. "We both wish you the very best, and we'll keep in touch with you, be sure of that."

"I wish you Godspeed, Lucien Edmond. I can never repay you for your hospitality at Windhaven Range," Ben earnestly avowed. "Elone's prayers and mine go with you,

256

and may you return safely home. I ask one favor of you—plant roses on Mother Sybella's grave, in memory of my dead Fleurette."

"I'll see to it, Ben. God bless you and your family. Well now, Joe, let's get back to the outfit."

On July 9, 1872, Lucien Edmond Bouchard and his men drove the herd into the Newton stockyard. Joseph McCoy was on hand to welcome them as he had in Abilene.

"Seems like to me you brought more cattle last year, Mr. Bouchard," he commented as he watched the heifers, cows, and steers being driven into the pens.

"You're right, Mr. McCoy. I'm holding back much of my herd to finish my interbreeding and also to wait for better prices, to be frank with you."

"Well, Mr. Bouchard, it's our economy, that's what it is. Right now, there's a glut of meat, and that's why the Midwestern buyers aren't offering the really good prices they did when you first drove your herd to Abilene," Joseph McCoy philosophically explained. "Talking price around here these days is about ten dollars a head for prime."

"That is less than last year. But I'm not surprised, I was expecting it. I'll still have a good reserve to meet expenses and payroll and a little something extra for developing my ranch. Mr. McCoy, I'd like you to meet Joe Duvray, who's taken over the acreage to the west of mine and who's working with me to consolidate Windhaven Range." Lucien Edmond introduced the genial young Southerner.

"Glad to meet you, Mr. Duvray. You could do a lot worse than by teaming up with Mr. Bouchard here. Well now, let's go find you a buyer."

The final tally was 2928 head, and a fussy, overdressed St. Louis buyer took the entire herd. As was his custom, Lucien Edmond asked for several thousand dollars in cash and the rest in a bank draft, so that he could pay off his riders and give them a bonus, as at least token reward for the hardships they had endured under fire from the bushwhackers.

When the transaction was over, Lucien Edmond turned to the stock man and said, "I'll be back next year, Mr. McCoy. Will I see you here in Newton?"

"Step over here, Mr. Bouchard." Joseph McCoy glanced nervously around, then took Lucien Edmond by the arm and led him away from the pens. "I'd say, just off the record, you ought to be planning to drive your herd to Ellsworth. You see, the Kansas Pacific Railroad has already pushed westward there. It's a town lying right on the treeless banks of Smoky Hill River. There's a huge prairie of grama grass all around it, and as you know, grama grass fattens cattle real quick. I've a notion that next season most of the Texas ranchers will be heading there. There's another good reason for this too, Mr. Bouchard. The Kansas Pacific sees that it's got a fight on its hands for the cattle trade with the new Santa Fe line. So it's going to go all out to back Ellsworth with its financial support. I hear they're already surveying a new cattle trail from Ellsworth southeast to the old Chisholm trail. One of the Kansas Pacific men told me just yesterday that they're going to publish a guide map and distribute copies all through ranching country."

"That sounds impressive," Lucien Edmond agreed.

"Yes, sir, it certainly does. We've had a few herds already in the Ellsworth pens this summer. But I'll see that you get a copy of the guide map, and you can just plan to start a little earlier next spring so you can get the top price."

"That sounds encouraging, Mr. McCoy," Lucien Edmond retorted, "but I'd say that price is going to depend on a lot more than just an available market. What worries me is this election. If President Grant is reelected and doesn't do something about his weak-kneed cabinet and the greedy financial advisors he surrounds himself with, the price of cattle and everything else might just drop out of sight next year."

"I sure as hell hope you're wrong about that, Mr. Bouchard. Well, I've got to go back to my hotel and stand treat to one of the ranchers who came in yesterday ahead of you. Join me for a drink, Mr. Bouchard?"

"Thank you, Mr. McCoy, I'll accept your hospitality. Let's go, Joe. Ramón"—he turned to the young Mexican—"do me a favor and pay off the men with this gold. See that they don't get into too much trouble in the saloons and dance halls. We'll pull out tomorrow afternoon after we've all had a good night's rest."

"I'll take care of it, Lucien Edmond. Glad to see you

again, Mr. McCoy," Ramón shook hands with the enterprising stock man.

After they had been paid, several of the vaqueros headed for the local barbershop to get a haircut and have their moustaches or beards properly shaped and blacked, then visited a clothing store for new outfits. Invariably, they bought hats and boots embellished with Texas stars. Light Stetson hats were going for ten dollars and brand-new pants cost twelve. Some of the vaqueros purchased fancy boots with red and blue-colored tops, decorated with a half-moon and star.

Eddie Gentry paid two bits for a haircut and four for a bath. His face sober and drawn, he walked slowly down the main street, at a loss as to how to spend the time until they headed back to Windhaven Range. Nacio Lorcas, Lucas, and Simata hailed him as they stepped out of the barbershop and saw him walking along ahead of them.

"Hey, Eddie, come along with us," Nacio bawled. Simata and Lucas eyed him and Lucas softly proffered, "Won't do any good to him, Nacio. He's still suffering over his sweet girl, Polly."

"But the drive's over," the vaquero insisted with a wide grin. "Me, I've always had a hankering to see what a dance hall looks like. Won't do him any harm to join us. We're all *compañeros*, aren't we?"

Eddie turned, his face blank as if he did not recognize the trio. Then, listlessly, he shrugged and walked back toward them. "Might as well," he said in a dull tone. "Nothing else to do till we head back tomorrow, I suppose. What've you fellows got in mind?"

"Why, *amigo*, Simata and Lucas and I were heading for that brand-new saloon at the other end of the street. See the one with the sign *Texas Queen*? *Caramba*, maybe we could have a drink there of good tequila or whiskey, and look at some pretty two-legged heifers for a change, after all the four-legged, dust-raising critters we've played nursemaid to on the trail," Nacio cheerfully explained.

"I'm not much of a drinking man, but I'll buy you all one to start off with," Eddie offered. He looked back down the street, already crowded with noisy cowboys, some of them lifting their guns in the air and firing to express their high spirits at the end of a hard trail drive. "At least it'll be safer inside than out here on the street. Some of those loco riders might just shoot their guns the wrong way. All right, let's go, then."

The four men pushed through the swinging doors of the dance hall, and Nacio let out an admiring "¡Qué linda!" as he spied, over the ornate rectangular mirror behind the bar, an oil portrait which depicted a naked, golden-haired nymph of sumptuous endowments reposing on a grassy knoll, her head pillowed on her arms, while a leering Pan peeked from behind a tree to ogle her.

At the back of the spacious hall, a little man in a bowler hat with a cigar stub clamped between his lips played dance tunes on an old spinet. Booted and spurred cowboys stood at the bar, some of them boisterously loud in recounting the harrowing adventures of the cattle drive they had just finished. Others sat at tables, drinking absorbedly, paying little heed to the calico-clad, bespangled, painted girls who weaved through the crowd to solicit drinks or to hint at more intimate favors for a price. There were three bartenders at the long bar, all feverishly busy.

A tall, henna-haired woman approached the table at which Eddie and his three friends were sitting. She was in her early thirties, wearing a low-cut red calico dress that descended only to mid-calf. Planting her palms on the grainy wood of the table and bending low so that the four men might observe the lushness of her bosom, she winked and inquired, "You boys just in from the trail? How about some refreshment? My name's Lily. If you'd like I can keep you company."

"Gracias, señorita," Nacio Lorcas gallantly doffed his sombrero. "For me, tequila. For my friends, the best whiskey in the house."

"Glass or bottle?" the henna-haired hostess inquired. "Whiskey's three bucks a bottle here, boys. Else it's four bits a shot. You'd be better off with bottles, take it from me. And besides," this with an arch smile, "that way you'd have a glass for little Lily. I get awful thirsty on a night like this when we're awful busy."

Lucas chuckled and shook his head. "We're not really drinking men, Miss Lily. Suppose you bring Nacio here a glass of tequila to start with, and just one bottle for the three of us."

"I see. Cheapskates, huh?" Lily flounced off in high

dudgeon, glancing back over her shoulder with a contemptuous curl of her painted mouth as she hurried to the bar. Threading her way through the men at the bar, who stopped to whisper to her or pinch her, and deftly avoiding the cowboys who were dancing with other hostesses, she came back with a tray and set Nacio's tequila before him, then three glasses and a bottle before Lucas. "That'll be four bucks, boys," she announced, holding the tray out in both hands in front of Lucas. Then, as if to explain the reason for the tariff, she brusquely added, "Jim has us charge four bits extra for glasses when a table only orders one bottle, see? It's not my rule, I just work here. Sure you don't want me to keep you company, boys? Later on, when it thins out here, those rooms upstairs—you know." She put one hand to the back of her garish pompadour and arched her bosom out by way of provocative suggestion. Eddie Gentry stared at her, then turned away and reached for a glass, his face taut and disconsolate. Lily shrugged, gave them a withering look, and walked away.

Nacio Lorcas lifted his glass of tequila, smacked his lips, and took a lusty swig, then set the glass down with a clatter on the table. "*Es bueno,*" he proclaimed. "I drink to our good *patrón*, and to all my *compañeros* on the drive. Come now, Señor Lucas, tell me how the whiskey is."

Lucas had uncorked the bottle and poured liberally into the three glasses. Eddie mechanically took hold of his, his eyes straying to the oil painting above the bar mirror, and then grimaced with distaste. Simata chuckled softly. "It is very funny, is it not, that here I am with Kiowa blood in me and being allowed to drink whiskey in a Kansas saloon. My father, who was chief, would roar with laughter if he knew. But of course they are too busy here and too greedy for money to look at me closely."

"And I am black, and the color of my hide would make some Southern folks in the Panhandle downright unhappy," Lucas jested in his turn, as he lifted his glass and took a tentative sip. "It's rotgut. A man would have to have a cast-iron stomach to finish this bottle. But at least we'll spend some time here and see how other folks amuse themselves after their work's done. Eddie," he turned to the lanky young cowboy, "don't drink too much of this. Maybe that girl Lily was right—let her have the rest of the bottle."

261

"Sure," Eddie mumbled as he put the shot glass to his lips and took a sip, then grimaced again and set the glass down with a clatter. "Now I know why I'm not a drinking man." He leaned back in his chair, his eyes fixed on the carpeted stairway which led to the second floor of the dance hall. He could see several tipsy cowboys staggering up the steps, their arms around painted hostesses who smiled and whispered as they made their arrangements for the night. He stared moodily down at his glass and uttered a heartfelt sigh. Nacio Lorcas caught Simata's eye and nodded sympathetically, then put a finger to his lips. Suddenly there was a shrill scream from upstairs, and everyone turned to look.

From the second-floor landing, a slim, black-haired young woman who could not have been more than twenty, her hair coiffed in an extravagant topknot that left the nape of her neck bare and showed off her dainty ears, hurried down the stairs, grasping the bannister and glancing tearfully back over her shoulder. She wore a green silk gown that left her shoulders bare and exposed the cleft of her closely set, high-arching, proud young bosom. The skirt revealed trim, chiseled ankles in black net hose. Her feet were shod in red satin slippers with gaudy rhinestone buckles. "No, Señor Jim," she sobbed hysterically. "*¡Por favor, por piedad!*"

Behind her came a tall, bearded, gray-haired man in black frock coat, white ruffled shirt, and gleaming new boots. In his right hand he carried a brown leather quirt with split tip. Raising it high above his head, he brutally slashed it across the back of the young woman's shoulders. Again her agonized scream rang out, and she sank down on her knees, clasping her hands, turning back to look up at him as the tears streamed down her face. "I cannot do it—have mercy—please, Señor Jim—"

Eddie Gentry, electrified by what he saw, sprang up from the chair and, shoving his way through the crowd, ascended the steps with a bound.

"Now you just put that thing down, mister!" His voice was hoarse with anger. "That's no way to treat a woman, not where I come from, anyhow."

"Stay out of it, cowboy," the bearded dance-hall owner curtly retorted. "This new bitch won't earn her keep on her back, and she needs a lesson. I run this place, mister. Jim Bradshaw. Happens you've heard who I am?"

"Not till you told me your monicker just now. And it doesn't cut any ice with me, either. Now you put down that quirt or I'll take it away from you." Eddie's face was pale with anger and he had begun to tremble. But his eyes fixed on the saloon-keeper's face and his right hand edged toward his holstered Starr .44.

Jim Bradshaw shrugged. "Mebbe you'd like to buy her time, cowboy. So long as she earns money for me, I won't have to use this."

"All right! Here—here's twenty dollars, Mr. Bradshaw." Eddie dug into his pocket and tossed a gold piece into the air. Bradshaw deftly caught it, bit it, then nodded. "All right. You've got an hour with her. There's rooms back down the hall upstairs. But you better tell her to make it worth your gold, cowboy, or she'll get another lesson after you leave, get me?"

"Come along, miss." Eddie bent and lifted the sobbing young woman to her feet. "Let's go have ourselves some fun for an hour, anyhow." But even as he spoke, he sent her a covert smile and put a finger to his lips to indicate that he was gaining her a respite, rather than buying her body. Slowly she rose to her feet and nodded. "Yes, señor, I will show you where to go."

"That's more like it, honey," Bradshaw roughly declared as he twisted the quirt between his hands and stepped to one side to allow the two to go upstairs. Then, quickly descending, he harshly commanded the bowler-hatted piano player, "Who the hell told you to stop playing, Professor? These men want to dance. Bartenders, a free round for everybody. Jim Bradshaw treats his customers right!"

CHAPTER TWENTY-ONE

The black-haired young woman, her head bowed, trying to control her sobs, led the way to a room at the far end of the second floor, opened it, and meekly turned to nod to Eddie Gentry that he should enter ahead of her. He did so, and she followed, closing the door behind her.

There was a chaise longue in one corner of the room, a huge, four-postered, canopied bed in the other, and a little dressing table and two chairs. Thick, elegant Oriental rugs covered the floor, and near the false window, covered with chintz curtains, there was a mahogany-framed long mirror hanging from a peg set near the ceiling.

"He hurt you," Eddie said, his voice still unsteady, as he saw the darkening welts the quirt had left on the olive-sheened skin of the young woman's shoulders. "Do you have to work for a man like that, miss?"

She turned away, suddenly covering her face with her hands, and began to weep.

"Oh please, miss, I'm not going to hurt you—I just wanted to talk to you and see if something could be done about that fellow—a man who'd use a quirt on a woman ought to be shot down like a dog!" he angrily declared.

"You—you are very kind, señor. But—but I have no choice. I—I belong to the Señor Bradshaw."

"What the hell do you mean? What's your name?" Eddie stared uncomprehendingly at her, his fists clenched, his body taut with anger at the saloon-keeper.

"I—I am Maria Elena Romero, señor. And what I say, *es verdad. Mi padre* wanted me to marry an old *hacendado* back in San Luis Potosí to whom he owed money, and I would not. He—he was fat and ugly—and—I knew that he whipped his *criadas.*"

"His servants, you mean. My God, I wouldn't blame

you for not wanting to marry a man like that—he sounds worse than this fellow Bradshaw," Eddie exclaimed.

"Yes, señor, that is what I thought too. And so—and so I told *mi padre* I would never marry Don Felipe Velasco. But our family was very poor. And Don Felipe owned the little farm where we lived, you see, señor." She moved over to the chaise longue and sat down on the edge of it, bowing her head, with her soft fingertips trying to brush away the tears that flooded her eyes. After a moment, she resumed, "Then one day a *gringo* came to see my father, señor. And he told my father that he would give him *mucho dinero* if I would come to the *Estados Unidos* to work for his friend."

"My God—you mean your father actually sold you—and that's why you're here? Oh my God! I've got to get you out of this, Señorita Romero!" Eddie resolutely declared.

"I have prayed every night since I came here, señor. The Señor Bradshaw wanted me to come upstairs here with any man who would—who would—"

"I know. You don't have to tell me. That damned animal!" Eddie fiercely broke in. "Look, Señorita Romero, I'm going down and have a talk with this fellow Bradshaw. I just got paid—I work for Lucien Edmond Bouchard in Texas, and we just sold his cattle today. I'll see if I can't buy you away from Bradshaw so you can go home where you belong. A nice decent girl like you—I can't let you stay here—I won't. Now you wait right here till I get back, *comprende*?"

"*Sí.*" Slowly she raised her sensitive, oval face, her large dark-brown eyes wonderingly searching his face. "You are very kind to do this for somebody you do not even know, señor."

"My name is Eddie Gentry, Señorita Romero. I don't have to know any more than I do. I saw the way he was treating you. My God, to force a decent girl to go with any man who wanted to buy her, to live off what she made that way—I'm going to talk to Bradshaw right now. I'll be right back."

He turned back to look at the young Mexican woman, saw her staring at him, her lips trembling as they formed a pathetic little smile of gratitude, and he was deeply moved by it. He strode to her and awkwardly patted her shoulder. "Now don't you fret, Señorita Romero. I swear I'll get you

266

out of this, no matter what it takes. You just wait here. I'll come back as soon as I find out what Bradshaw wants, you hear me?"

"Sí, Señor Gentry," she quavered.

He opened the door, took a last look at her, and then closed it and went down the stairs to seek out the bearded saloon-keeper. Jim Bradshaw was at the bar, expansively greeting his regular customers, slapping them on the back, his mood patronizingly jovial. Eddie's eyes narrowed as he pushed his way through the crowd around the bar and stood behind Bradshaw.

"Mr. Bradshaw, I want to talk business to you. Can we get out of this noisy place?" he demanded.

Bradshaw turned, a lazy smile creasing his shrewd, angular face. Then he nodded. "We'll go back upstairs, cowboy. Now what's on your mind? Don't you fancy that Mexican heifer?"

"I have a business proposition for you, Mr. Bradshaw, but I don't like talking business with people all around me and that damn piano player tinkling out of tune," Eddie retorted.

"I'm at your service, cowboy. Excuse me, gentlemen. Bartenders, another round for my good friends here. All right now, let's go see what's on your mind, cowboy."

Halfway up the stairway, Eddie turned to Bradshaw. "How much do you want to let her go?" was his blunt question.

"What—do you mean for good, cowboy?"

"That's exactly what I'm driving at, Mr. Bradshaw. How much?"

The saloon-keeper insolently looked Eddie up and down, a sneer on his lips. "How about three hundred in gold? Is that too much for you? From what I hear tell, Texas cowhands get about twenty a month. 'Course, you might be the thrifty kind, but I think three hundred in gold will do fine."

"And if I give you the money, you'll let her walk out of here free as a bird, right?"

"I generally keep my word, cowboy."

"My name's Gentry, Eddie Gentry. Now you wait here a second, Mr. Bradshaw. I'll go see my boss. He'll lend me what I need. And mind you, don't you send any other man

267

up to Miss Romero's room till I get back, or you'll have me to deal with."

"Well now, since you're so fierce and romantic about it, *Mister* Gentry," Jim Bradshaw sneeringly emphasized the title, "I'll see that the little heifer isn't mounted by any other bull. But don't take all night. That'll cost me too much money, and it's high time she started earning her keep."

Eddie shot him a murderous look, turned on his heel, and strode out of the saloon. Nacio Lorcas, Simata, and Lucas looked up from the table and watched him go, then conferred among themselves.

"What's got into Eddie?" Lucas wanted to know.

"It's that pretty Mexican girl," Simata explained. "It riled him to see that fellow who runs this place taking a quirt to her."

"As for me, señores, I would not allow that *cobarde* to whip that *muchachita linda*, either," Nacio Lorcas proudly averred.

Eddie made his way to the hotel where Lucien Edmond Bouchard was staying, knocked on the door, and was told to enter. Quickly, he explained his mission. Lucien Edmond smiled and nodded.

"I'll be glad to give you three hundred dollars, Eddie. We'll consider it a loan. You keep your wages, you earned them and more. I wouldn't want you to be short of cash when you get back home." Then, seriously, "Do you know anything about this girl? It isn't just a gallant fancy, I hope. Though I'd understand that, you know."

"No, Mr. Bouchard. It's just that—well, when I saw that fellow Bradshaw lay a quirt on her bare flesh, I sort of saw red. And then when she told me that her father sold her to go to work in a place like that just because she wouldn't marry a fat old ranch owner her father owed money to, I just couldn't stand by and not do anything."

Lucien Edmond reached for a leather pouch, loosened the drawstrings, and counted out three hundred dollars in gold pieces. "There you are, Eddie. Good luck to you, But watch yourself, a man like Bradshaw can be tricky."

"He said he'd let her go, Mr. Bouchard, for three hundred. I aim to make him keep his word. Thanks a lot. I—I'll work this off, I'll pay it back as soon as I get back to the ranch, I swear it."

"Sure, Eddie. When it's over, come tell me how it worked out. And good luck."

Eddie Gentry, his face grim with purpose, strode back down the street, pushed open the doors of the saloon, and made his way up to the bar where Jim Bradshaw still stood. "I'm ready to talk business now, Mr. Bradshaw," he called out.

"Well, that was fast work, cowboy—excuse me, I mean, *Mister* Gentry," the saloon-keeper drawled as he turned to smirk at the fuming young Texas cowboy. "I take it you have the three hundred in gold we discussed?"

"In my britches, Mr. Bradshaw. But I'd like to give it to you upstairs, where there won't be anybody crowding in on us and maybe trying some gunplay."

"Of course. I can see that you've some gentlemanly instincts, Mr. Gentry. By all means, we'll go back upstairs to the young lady's room. Then she can see for herself to whom she owes her freedom, shall we say."

Bradshaw leaned across the bar to whisper something to the bald, moustachioed bartender, and the latter nodded. Then, turning, he followed Eddie up the stairs and down the hall to Maria Elena Romero's room. Eddie knocked, then opened the door and went in. The young Mexican girl sprang to her feet with a frightened little cry, a hand at her mouth as she saw Bradshaw enter behind him.

"It's all right, Miss Romero," Eddie smilingly exclaimed. "I've persuaded Mr. Bradshaw here to let you go. Now then, here's your money. Count it all to make sure it's there." Turning, he plunged his hand into his pocket and drew out the gold pieces, which he dropped onto Bradshaw's cupped palms, flushing with resentment over the insolent smirk on the saloon-keeper's face.

"There. I think you'll find three hundred in gold, just like you said. Now, if you've no objection, I'm taking Miss Romero out of this dirty dive."

"You really wound me with an insult like that, Mr. Gentry," Bradshaw drawled. "Why, even Joseph McCoy himself tells me I've got the liveliest place in all Newton. And certainly the prettiest dance-hall girls—as you yourself have just proved. All right, the three hundred is in my pocket now, so go ahead."

"Thanks," Eddie curtly shot at him. "Come on, Miss

Romero. Never mind your clothes or anything, let's just get out of here."

"You mean that—that I may go with you? Is that true, S-Señor Bradshaw?" She turned, her eyes wide with incredulity, to stare at the bearded saloon-keeper, who nodded, an amused smile on his lips. "Oh, Señor Gentry, I'll never be able to thank you enough—the good *Señor Dios* will bless you, and I will pray for you every night of my life for what you have done—thank you, a thousand thanks, Señor Gentry—"

"That's all right," Eddie awkwardly mumbled, flushing with embarrassment at the young woman's effusive praise. "Here, take my arm, we'll go out together. Nobody's going to bother us, I promise you that, Miss Romero."

Hesitantly, the young Mexican girl took Eddie's arm, and they began to walk down the hallway to the staircase landing. Jim Bradshaw followed, swaggering, his smile deepening.

Perhaps because the fat, bald bartender had been relating what was going on, the patrons at the bar had given up their noisy talking and drinking to watch what was taking place. A sudden hush fell on the saloon as Eddie and Maria Elena started slowly down the stairs. He whispered to her, "Keep your chin up, Miss Romero. Don't let on you're scared, not even a little bit. I'll take care of you. Everything's going to be fine, just fine."

Then suddenly, from behind him, came Bradshaw's jeering voice. "You stupid bastard, d'you think I'd sell a fancy heifer like her when I can make that much a week out of her once I teach her how to work for me? All right now, Mr. Gentry, you've had your fun. Get the hell out of my place, and be thankful I don't shoot you down for causing all this ruckus!"

With this, he thrust his right hand inside his frock coat. Maria Elena had looked back with a frightened little cry as she heard his words, and she saw him draw out a pearl-handled derringer. "Look out, Señor Gentry!" she had just time to cry out, then disengaged her arm from Eddie's and gave him a slight push.

The young Texas cowboy stumbled, but quickly regained his balance and, instantly divining what the saloon-keeper intended, darted his right hand down to his holster, drew out the Starr .44, and fired. At the same instant, the

270

derringer spat fire, and Eddie uttered a cry and leaned heavily against the bannister as the bullet took him in the left shoulder, near the collarbone. Jim Bradshaw dropped his derringer and took a step forward, his head tilting back and his eyes wide and unseeing, as a red stain spread on the ruffled white shirt. Then he fell forward, rolling down the stairs, and lay sprawled at the foot of the staircase.

The fat bartender suddenly dived under the bar and came up with a shotgun. "Just put that down, or I'll blast you!" Lucas cried out in a stentorian voice as he lifted his Spencer carbine from where he had leaned it against the table and aimed it at the bartender's head. "Drop it! You heard me, drop it, or I'll give you all seven shots right where the barrel's pointing!"

"Sure, mister, sure—I wasn't aiming to do nuttin'—" the bartender gulped, as the shotgun clattered to the floor behind the bar.

Nacio Lorcas, Simata, and Lucas stood, their carbines ready, and Lucas called, "Come on, Eddie, we'll see you safely out of here. Are you hit bad?"

"It—it's not too bad—I can make it—hold on to me tight, Miss Romero—we'll manage!" Eddie panted.

The crowd around the bar and on the dance floor moved back, transfixed by the drama that had just taken place, to let the wounded young Texan and the trembling Mexican woman pass. Outside, in the cool night air, Maria Elena Romero knelt down in front of Eddie and, tears streaming down her face, seized his hand and brought it to her lips. Then, looking up at the kindly face of Nacio Lorcas, she sobbed, "Please, señor, he's bleeding badly—don't let him die—he's saved me—such a good, kind man, don't let him die!"

"No, *linda*," Nacio gently answered as he helped her to her feet. "Simata, Lucas, take hold of him. We'll find a doctor. We'll take him to the hotel where the *patrón* is staying—he can ask Señor McCoy to find us a doctor for Eddie."

CHAPTER TWENTY-TWO

Charles Douglas had stayed away from Chicago longer than he had originally estimated. After his disenchantment with Calvin Jemmers and Arnold Shottlander, and his more encouraging conversations with Mayor Scanlan and Dennis Claverton of the Houston National Bank, he had ridden back to Galveston to confer with James Hunter. As he related his experiences, the tall, gray-haired Southerner chuckled and, pausing to fill two goblets with fine old French cognac from a sideboard decanter, handed the young Chicagoan one of them as he lifted his in toast.

"Frankly, Charles, I'm glad things worked out that way—or rather, didn't work out, to make a very bad joke. Because, you see, ever since you visited me and told me about your desire to start another department store, I'll have to admit to you that the idea has captured my imagination. I told you before, I'd back you. It will be a good change from the cotton business, which I'm beginning to find a bit tedious. Year in, year out, watching the crops grow and get harvested, praying for good weather to make the yield of prime quality, then praying even more earnestly that the price won't dip and leave you with a loss to show for your year of hard work—it's an old story. Even a decade before the Civil War, we in the South saw cotton prices drop till it seemed to me that even the stupidest large plantation owners would realize that they just had to diversify, if they wanted to have any money at the end of the year."

"I could see that myself, even in Tuscaloosa, when I was just a clerk in a store wishing I could be my own boss," Charles confided as he sipped his cognac and exhaled a sigh of physical gratification.

"Precisely." Again James chuckled. His wife, his daughter Melinda, and the latter's little son, Gary, were visiting a neighbor, and James was secretly delighted to have the entire evening to himself for a conversation which, he sensed, was part of an adventurous new way of life for him. For some little time, now that he had become affluent as a cotton factor for his cousin Jeremy, he had been assailed by many misgivings. Though he was nearly a partner in Cousin Jeremy's business, he felt he was contributing very little to the resurgence of what was practically a new state of the Union. He felt he was simply going through the motions of holding a job—one for which he was handsomely paid, it was true, but which did not tax his imagination, intellect, or innate vitality to the extent he wished. Also, since he and Arabella had reached a happy and serene stage in their marriage, wherein they were enjoying a kind of second honeymoon, he had begun to see new, rewarding qualities in his wife. He wished to savor these to the fullest, and in order to do so he needed to feel part of something new and important, too. The thought of engaging himself in a new enterprise which would require not only capital investment, but also new ideas and new business methods, was an extremely stimulating prospect to him.

"Well, James, I think I know what you're driving at. Just the same," Charles made a rueful face as he took another sip of his cognac, "maybe I was being obstinate, but I really wanted to start my first store in Houston. I like that town, for all you here in Galveston thumb your noses at it."

"But we don't," James laughingly protested. "The mere existence of Houston only fifty miles away from us keeps us on our toes and make us determined to increase our commerce, particularly that of our seaport. If that mayor in Houston and several of his city administrators weren't so damnably efficient and imaginative, we might be inclined to lean back and consider that we had nothing to do but count our profits at the end of the day without a lick of work." He leaned forward in his chair, his eyes sparkling with interest. "No, Charles, what I meant to say was that, as a working partner in this scheme of yours, I definitely want you to build your first new department store right here in Galveston. Since you left, I've been talking to Mason Elberding. He's not only one of our leading bankers,

274

but also a very civic-minded man who wants to see Galveston grow by leaps and bounds. Not only that, he has connections with some honest realtors, not like that fellow Shottlander you were telling me about. I'd like you to meet him tomorrow morning. Then we'll all have lunch at the Crescent. It's one of the finest restaurants in town, and I think you'll find it can even rival some of the great New Orleans culinary establishments."

"I'd like that very much, James."

"Now, as I understand it, you mentioned that you'd like to find a trustworthy contractor, a man who could handle a good, hardworking crew and carry out your orders to the letter so that you wouldn't have to linger here and leave that beautiful wife of yours and your children pining away in Chicago, is that right?"

"You hit the nail on the head, James," Charles smiled as he finished his cognac. "No, no, no more tonight. I'm feeling lightheaded enough already, just thinking about this new store of mine. And I suppose I'm twice as anxious because of the time I wasted in Houston. Of course, I'm still not going to rule Houston out—as I told you, Dennis Claverton of the Houston National Bank is looking at properties for me."

"No reason why you shouldn't continue to explore Houston. Once your store here is booming, you can build a subsidiary there. Believe me, that Mayor Scanlan will go all out to help you, if only because he wants to catch up with what we're doing here. But first things first. How much cash do you think you'll need for your land and your store in Galveston? What sort of merchandise do you figure you're going to stock and what will it cost you to transport it here? I can be of some help to you in that direction, Charles. I've got a tariff statement from the Galveston harbormaster—the fact is, the day you left for Houston, I went down to see him and picked it up, just on the chance that you'd want to refer to it when you got back here."

"I see I underestimated you, James." Charles flashed his boyish grin. "But let me ask you another and even more direct question—would you be willing to be a kind of overseer, once I hire my contractor and crew?"

"Of course I would. That's what I've been getting at. I'd like nothing better than to tell Cousin Jeremy that I'm taking a sabbatical, as it were. Besides, he owes me several months' vacation, considering all the time I put in during the first few years after the war. I think I can persuade him to give me at least three months. And I'll devote every day to going down to the site you pick and making sure this contractor and crew of yours keep working."

"James, all I can say is, I'm sure glad I came to Texas. You and I are going to have fun being partners, I can see that already." Charles rose from his chair and offered his hand, which James cordially shook.

Charles Douglas liked Mason Elberding at their first meeting. The banker was a man of forty-six, with thinning, slightly graying dark-brown hair, of medium height, and with a frank, genial face that was, remarkably for the period, clean-shaven. He had a wry wit and a thorough practical knowledge of business affairs, not only in Galveston, but also in most of Texas. Over an excellent luncheon at the Crescent, which Charles had to admit was as good as any restaurant in New Orleans, Elberding acquainted him with the cost of land and the availability of several excellent sites for a general department store, and even went so far as to recommend a man who could capably carry out the young Chicagoan's building plans.

"I've known him for at least eight years, Mr. Douglas," Elberding declared. "His name is Max Steinfeldt. He's of German descent, came from a poor farming family in Iowa. He served in the Civil War as a sergeant and was decorated for valor beyond the call of duty. While he was in the army, his wife died, so after the war he came out to Galveston, because he had a cousin here. When he was still in the army, he had to do a great deal of carpentry work for the engineering corps and you might say that he learned by doing. He's worked here with some of our best architects; he doesn't spare himself, but he treats his men the way diligent workmen ought to be treated. That's to say he gets the most out of them without browbeating or driving them like a Prussian."

"That sounds like the sort of man I'd like to have build my department store."

"You couldn't do better than Max Steinfeldt, believe me, Mr. Douglas. Not only that, he's very popular in town. He gives a lot of money to charity, to poor widows and orphan children and the like; he's given jobs to men on their up-

276

pers and turned them into good, law-abiding citizens. He's even advanced the money out of his own pocket when there wasn't a chance they'd repay it, but somehow they did so just because they liked the cut of his jib."

"You've already sold me on him, Mr. Elberding. When can I meet him?"

"Tomorrow morning, if you like. But now let's talk about the amount of land you'll want. You'd like to be near our main street, obviously."

"Yes, of course."

"As it happens, there's about a quarter of a block available for a storefront on Demmering Avenue, which is about three blocks from our main street. I think you could buy it for about twenty-nine hundred dollars."

Charles let out a low whistle. "That's certainly in line with what I was thinking, Mr. Elberding. Right now, after just a few minutes' conversation with you, I feel that my store's already built and will be ready for the Christmas trade."

"Now I like optimism like that. And I've known Jim Hunter here ever since he came from Alabama. You'll have a good partner. He's a most respected man here in Galveston," Elberding declared.

Max Steinfeldt impressed Charles Douglas just as much as Mason Elberding had at the very first meeting. He was stocky, forty-two, with a youthful cowlick in his fading blond hair, but the solidity and geniality of his features, his bright blue eyes and frank mouth at once made Charles feel that here was an honest man who gave a full day's work and would never think of ways in which to cheat an employer or to cut corners so as to line his own pockets. After half an hour's conversation with the energetic, friendly German widower, Charles suggested that they go to a lawyer's office to draw up a contract whereby Steinfeldt would be engaged as a contractor for the Douglas Department Store, with full powers to hire a working crew and to report directly to both Douglas himself and James Hunter.

This done, James proposed the name of an architect who could work with Charles and draw up plans for the new store. It would be two stories high, large enough to accommodate an extremely wide variety of merchandise. "With concentration on the woman shopper, James," Charles explained. "To my mind, it's the wife who makes the real decisions about buying merchandise. And she influences her husband, even though we haven't got full emancipation for the sexes yet. The fact still remains, I'd rather have a woman in my store than a man, nine times out of ten. She'll spend more, she'll tell more friends about what she likes and doesn't like in my place, and she'll wind up bringing me more business than any single man could do."

"That's sound thinking," James smiled. "Knowing Bella as I have all these years, I'm inclined to go along with your merchandising ideas, Charles. All right, let's go find Edwin Folsum—he's the architect I had in mind. Matter of fact, he was the one who designed Mason Elberding's bank, and you'll have to agree it's an attractive structure."

"I do indeed. If that's a sample of his work, I shan't have to look any farther for an architect," Charles beamed.

By the end of the week, the energetic young Chicagoan had met with the architect and indicated his own ideas for the construction of the new department store, with Max Steinfeldt present to contribute practical suggestions on the materials needed for construction and the most feasible schedule for their procurement. Remembering the terrible Chicago fire, Charles urged the architect to use stone and brick wherever possible, with a minimum of flammable wood.

A week later, Folsum presented his first draft, which Charles enthusiastically endorsed. Brick would present no problem, since there was a kiln not far from the port; the stone would be shipped from a quarry near New Orleans, as well as sturdy wood for beams.

Charles then wrote a draft on his Chicago bank, which he presented to Max Steinfeldt as the first outlay of wages for the construction crew that the affable contractor had already begun to recruit. He also paid the architect for his services thus far; he was confident that Folsum would be able to solve any technical problems that might arise during construction. Steinfeldt estimated that, if all went well, the department store could be ready to open for the Christmas shopping season, a prospect that greatly heartened the enthusiastic young Chicagoan. James, who was present at all of these meetings, promised that he would act as proxy for Charles, maintaining a constant liaison between the architect and the construction boss.

"Well, gentlemen," Charles declared at the last meeting,

"I feel that everything is in good hands, and it's time I was getting back to my family in Chicago and my new house and the work that's piled up now that my burned-out store has been rebuilt. James, there aren't enough words to tell you how grateful I am. You just wire me after things have gotten off to a good start, and I'll make it back down here as fast as I can. Meanwhile, I'll be talking with my suppliers so that they'll be able to ship the goods I'll need for the new store here in time for the Christmas opening. And you, Max, I'll see that you get a bonus if you keep that date—you too, Mr. Folsum."

So Charles Douglas began the return journey to Chicago in the middle of April, excitedly anticipating both the exhilarating work of creating the new store and of regaining his business foothold in the city he had come to love as his permanent home. He told himself that he would try to express his gratitude to his Chicago partner, Lawrence Harding, in a tangible way, since without Harding's help, this prolonged trip to Texas and its successful conclusion would not have been possible.

Laurette Douglas had arranged for Polly Behting's funeral and seen to it that a marble headstone was erected with an inscription that paid tribute to the young German girl's supreme self-sacrifice in giving her own life to rescue the little child. Polly's father, a frail middle-aged man, dazed and bewildered in his grief, had attended, and Laurette had done all she could to attempt to ease his grief. It was an excruciatingly trying ordeal for her, for the unfortunate man kept repeating, as he shook his head, "If only *meine Tochter* had stayed home and married Dieter—*ach, Gott,* if only she had done that . . ."

Once again, it had been Charles Douglas's new partner, Lawrence Harding, who had come to her rescue in this trying situation. He had paid a visit to Heinrich Behting at the latter's little house on North Avenue and, during the course of the sympathetic talk, had discovered that Polly's father was thinking very seriously of returning to Germany and spending his last years in his homeland. Lawrence then offered to pay for and arrange Herr Behting's passage to Frankfurt-am-Rhein, saying that this was the Douglases' way of showing him how much Polly had meant to them. Heinrich Behting broke down and wept, tearfully accepting

279

this benevolence, and a week later Lawrence Harding and Laurette Douglas saw him off on the train that would take him to New York, where he would board the steamer for Germany.

Laurette had been greatly heartened by the receipt of a telegraph wire from her husband, jubilantly announcing that he had found a site for his new store in Galveston instead of Houston and that James Hunter would supervise construction as an active partner in his new enterprise. With fresh enthusiasm, Laurette turned her mind back to the immediate task of adapting herself and the children to the new home and, most specifically, of finding a replacement for Polly Behting. So, the day after she had received her husband's wire, she visited the Aznoe Nurses' Registry on LaSalle Street for the purpose of having the agency screen several candidates for this post. Her friends the Von Emmerichs had recommended the agency, for it had recently helped them locate a governess for their two adopted children.

The Aznoe agency was quickly able to find three promising candidates for Laurette, and she spent an hour interviewing each one. The third and last interviewee was a handsome, dark-brown-haired woman in her mid-thirties named Agnes Strion. Laurette was impressed by her neat attire, her modest behavior, and particularly by her obvious affection for children. During the interview, Agnes Strion mentioned that she herself painted watercolors and that, in her previous posts, she had attempted to instruct her young charges in the art. Laurette found that a most engaging idea, since she had felt for some time that the boys ought to have some practical and artistic form of expression to round out their creative growth.

When she asked for references, Agnes handed her a letter on the impressive letterhead of a Chicago business executive. It stated that the governess had worked for his family for three years, that he had found her invaluable with the children—cheerful, imaginative, devoted, and industrious—and that he did not hesitate to recommend her with the very highest praise as an ideal governess or nurse for young children. It was this letter that decided Laurette to choose Agnes over the two other, somewhat older candidates.

What impressed Laurette about this letter of recommendation was that it was signed by Frederick Mulvaney, a man who was known to her. He had established an extremely prosperous catering business to go with his elegant greengrocer shop at Rush and Goethe Streets. Indeed, on several festive occasions, Laurette and her husband had enjoyed a supper provided by Mulvaney's caterers, delivered in a smart new phaeton by two frock-coated young men wearing tall silk hats and white gloves. The use of their service was a mark of prestige, and less affluent neighbors would gawk at the Mulvaney phaeton drawn up before a fashionable house, watching while doily-topped wicker baskets of tasty provender were delivered to the mistress of the household.

It was because she recognized Mulvaney's name on the letter that Laurette impulsively engaged Agnes on the spot. When the amiable young woman said she was quite ready to live in and did not even bother to ask about days off and other privileges, Laurette urged Agnes to come to her house the very next day.

At eight o'clock the next morning, the new governess arrived with all her possessions packed in a single valise, promptly apologized for disturbing Laurette so early in the morning, and at once offered to help with the children's breakfast. This further won Laurette's favor, since at that very moment she was scurrying about to prepare breakfast for her three hungry boys. Setting her valise down in the foyer, Agnes doffed her bonnet and cape and hurried into the kitchen with Laurette. She insisted that Laurette seat herself at the breakfast table and then proceeded to serve all four of them with great skill. Not only that, she washed the dishes and put them away in such neat order that Laurette's eyes shone with delight. It seemed that a kindly Providence had replaced the treasure that had been Polly Behting with another of perhaps even greater solicitude and efficiency.

Only after Laurette had had her second cup of coffee did Agnes consent to eat her own breakfast, and this only at Laurette's almost pleading insistence. As she ate, Laurette had an opportunity to study Agnes in detail and found no obtrusively annoying flaw. She was of medium height, her face gently rounded, her dark-brown hair drawn back from the temples and fixed into a prim, heart-shaped bun at the nape.

There was no sign of garish makeup, not even rice powder or the slightest touch of rouge to the cheeks, which many younger domestics employed, particularly when their skins were pale and suggested anemia, in order to convey the impression of robust health. Her gently arching eyebrows were not plucked, and they surmounted large, rather narrowly set dark-brown eyes between which was a daintily sculptured Roman nose. Her mouth was firm and incisive, but not sensual in its ripeness. Best of all, she wore a decorous dress of gray bombazine, which gave her an appearance of both propriety and modest awareness of fashion. Also, Laurette's critical eye detected, she wore nononsense high button shoes with solid, low heels, exactly the type of footgear that a hard-working governess should select. In all things, therefore, she more than justified Laurette's selection, to such an extent that the latter was beginning to congratulate herself on her good fortune as well as her wisdom of choice.

In the application by which she registered herself with the Aznoe agency, Agnes Strion had avowed herself to be thirty-five and a spinster. These statements were true—but other facts far more significant had been intentionally omitted. For neither the agency nor Laurette could know that the letter signed by Frederick Mulvaney rhapsodizing over Agnes Strion's virtues as a governess had been written by a man whose secret mistress Agnes had been for the previous five years.

Agnes was indeed a spinster; she was also an orphan. She had been the illegitimate daughter of a woman who had come to Chicago as an Irish immigrant to work for a rich, influential family. There, her mother had been seduced by the oldest son and had borne Agnes in a foundling home. A few months later, she had abandoned Agnes, leaving the girl to be brought up in the home and eventually to earn her own livelihood as best she could.

While in the foundling home, Agnes had been adopted by one foster family, at the age of sixteen: but here again fate stepped in to obliterate all her hopes for identity and security. Just as had happened with her mother, Agnes was ravished by the fourteen-year-old son of her foster parents. When the mother discovered her son in Agnes's room, she blamed the girl and turned her out of the house. When Agnes went back to the foundling home, she learned to her dismay that the irate mother had already sent a note by messenger denouncing her as a young trollop; as a consequence, the stern, puritanical director refused to take her back.

Agnes then went to work in a book bindery, then worked in a small department store where she was a clerk for five years. At the age of twenty-two, she was hired by a saloon-keeper to be a hostess in his outdoor beer parlor, and she fell in love with him. Naively, she became his mistress for two years in the hope that he would eventually marry her. When he married instead a rich, dowdy German girl who brought him a handsome dowry, Agnes left his employ and went to work as a waitress in a cheap little restaurant off Division Street. About six months after she had begun her job, the cook was taken ill and Agnes was pressed into service. It was then that she discovered her flair for cooking and experienced her first real happiness. The restaurant owner was a hardworking, honest German in his fifties, faithfully married for over twenty years, with absolutely no amorous interest in this attractive young woman whose culinary skill had already begun to attract new customers. Thanks to Agnes, it was becoming known that Fritz's Eatery had the best and the cheapest *sauerbraten*, cottage-fried potatoes, and lentil-prune soup in town.

Three months after she had switched from working tables to toiling in the stiflingly hot kitchen, Agnes was given a raise that practically doubled her previous wages, and the effusive praise of her employer indicated to her that she would have a job as his chief cook so long as the restaurant existed. Two years later, he opened a second restaurant, this one much more spacious and located on Dearborn Street near North Avenue, and Agnes was put in charge of it. She was able to rent a decent room with bath, to buy a new wardrobe, and to open a modest savings account.

After the ill-fated liaison with the saloon-keeper, Agnes had steadfastly avoided any amorous ties with the opposite sex. But, a week before her thirtieth birthday, her employer died of a heart attack and his ailing, aging widow decided to sell the two restaurants and return to her relatives in Berlin. Agnes thus found herself out of a job, with a month's wages and a glowing letter of recommendation.

By then, she had already heard of the virtually city-wide acceptance of Frederick Mulvaney's catering service and the excellence of his greengrocer shop. By now, too, the material success she had achieved over the past several years had made her almost desperately eager to continue in a way of life that would fulfill her creative talents and, at the same time, provide her with a comfortable living. That was why, with a letter of recommendation from Fritz Biemann's widow in hand, she walked to Mulvaney's greengrocer shop and asked the insolent young manager to announce her to the founder of the establishment.

Frederick Mulvaney was then forty-six, married for seven years to a society belle of whom he had begun to tire because of her exigent demands for clothes and jewels and her perfunctory response to his lovemaking. He was tall, with graying sideburns and piercing dark-blue eyes, and was something of a romantic. When Agnes Strion was ushered into his cluttered office at the back of the shop, she was almost awed by his animal magnetism and his exuberance.

In his turn, Frederick Mulvaney examined Agnes and saw in her a latent beauty who had been thwarted and stifled during most of her life. Indeed, the poetic quotation, "Full many a flower is born to blush unseen and waste its sweetness on the desert air," leaped into his mind as he listened to her somewhat stammered explanation of why she was applying for a job with his catering concern and why she believed that she could give satisfaction.

Mulvaney hired Agnes for two reasons. First, he had known about her culinary skill first-hand, having on several occasions eaten at Fritz's when business took him to that part of town. And, second, he sensed in her the potential for becoming a thrillingly satisfying mistress who would, unlike his shallow and selfish wife, be genuinely grateful for affection and reciprocate with all the pent-up emotion that he divined she had long suppressed.

Within a week of hiring her, Mulvaney was convinced that Agnes would increase his business; not only did she cook with exceptional ability, but she had a talent for improvised baking, as she soon proved by experimenting with tarts and cobblers and deep-dish pies which were the best he had ever tasted.

Three weeks after she had gone to work for Mulvaney, Agnes became his mistress. The staff had worked late that Saturday night to deliver rush orders to a number of his

284

best customers. By ten o'clock, the catering shop had closed down, and only Mulvaney and Agnes were left. Exhausted from nearly twelve hours of work, she bent over the kitchen counter, her face flushed and perspiring, her neat bun of hair disarranged and straggling. Yet to him she had never looked more alluring, more desirable. Jauntily, he told her that he would lock up the shop but that he would appreciate her remaining for a moment, because he wished to give her a bonus for the extra hours and hard work she had contributed today. He went around to draw the blinds at the front of the shop and then returned to her, as she wearily turned and forced a smile to her curving lips.

"Agnes, forgive me—I can't help this—I've wanted you since the first moment you walked in here looking for a job," he said in a low, hoarse voice. Then, his hands gentle on her rounded shoulders, he drew her to him and kissed her lingeringly on the mouth.

With a little sob of wonder and delight, Agnes closed her eyes and, locking her arms around him, surrendered herself to this rare and unexpected pleasure. No lover had ever shown her such tenderness, nor had she ever been kissed in the gentle yet persuasive way in which Frederick Mulvaney kissed her just then. His hands caressed her, never showing haste or grossness, making her thrill and quiver to his slightest touch. For himself, Mulvaney was almost feverishly amorous: a sensualist by nature, well-read and cultured, he had devotedly tried to remain faithful to his wife during their loveless marriage. But now, at once comprehending how passionately Agnes was ready to yield to him, he summoned forth all the imaginative and solicitous attention that a romantic lover brings to his beloved. Swooning in his arms, Agnes was hardly conscious that he was undressing her, nor did she experience any deterrent shock of false modesty to find herself naked in his arms. Their coming together was ecstatic, almost blinding in its unleashed fury because each had such a burning need for the other.

When it was over, as he lay beside her on the thick carpet of his office, stroking her firm, round breasts, he murmured, "My God, darling, I dreamed it would be like this, just like this. Agnes, I want you as my love, but I also want you to go on working for me. I'm only wondering how we can manage it without letting everybody else in the shop know our secret?"

"Oh Frederick, dearest," she breathed, turning to cup his face in her hands and kiss him ardently, "I swear I won't give it away. I'll be so happy just to be near you, and I love my work."

"I know you do. And you're very good at it, Agnes. You've already gotten me compliments on my business, and my reputation for catering was quite good even before you came to me. So you see how valuable you are to me—and more than your work, you're given me the first love I've ever truly known. I mean it, my dearest. Yes, I'm married, but my wife, Virginia, hasn't the slightest interest in me—she never really did have, to be truthful."

"I don't ask anything of you, only to let me work and to love you when we can, dear Frederick," she whispered.

Thus it had begun. Agnes managed to find a little house several blocks away from the greengrocer and catering shop, and paid the rent herself, though to be sure the funds were furnished by her lover. In this way, she averted suspicion. Moreover, the house had a back yard and a rear entrance to an alleyway. It was easy for Frederick Mulvaney (whose wife was used to his staying late on many a night to look after his business) to close up the shop early and to go by a circuitous route to the alleyway and thence through the kitchen of the little house where Agnes eagerly awaited him.

He had told her that he and his wife were childless, and one night, after their transports had been particularly rapturous, Agnes whispered, "Oh, my dearest one, how I want to give you a child—now don't say no, Frederick! Even if you could never acknowledge it, I'd have it, I'd bring it up, it would be yours, made of our flesh and blood, our love together—and it would be the dearest, most wonderful gift you could give me."

She was to repeat this theme many times, and yet, for all their lovemaking, she did not become pregnant. After two years, she visited a physician, giving an assumed name to avert suspicion. There she learned that an obstruction of the womb prevented her from conceiving. The elderly physician stroked his beard and guardedly remarked that he had known of such cases, and that sometimes—though the operation was not without great danger—it was

286

possible to correct the condition so that the woman could conceive. But the doubtful way in which he spoke of the possible success of such an operation terrified Agnes, so she resigned herself to barrenness.

On the night of the great fire of October 8, 1871, Frederick Mulvaney closed his shop and, having sent all his employees to the city limits, hurried over to Agnes Strion's house. He had managed to procure a horse and buggy, and in this he drove her to the edge of the city at Fullerton Avenue where they both watched the awesome spectacle of the flames against the dark night.

Virginia Mulvaney meanwhile had fled from their house, driven by a servant. Amid the hubbub and the terror of that night, she saw her husband sitting beside Agnes in the buggy, his arm around her, soothing and comforting her.

Ordering her servant to maneuver the buggy near her husband's, Virginia Mulvaney demanded, "Why didn't you come home and save your wife, Frederick? Who is this woman? How dare you sit there with your arm around her—have you no respect for me? I demand to know who that woman is!"

Though guiltily startled at the unforeseen chance that his wife should have found him among all the thousands of refugees from the dreadful fire, Mulvaney kept his wits about him. He explained that Agnes Strion was the best catering cook in the entire city of Chicago, that she had been very nearly trapped in her house, that he had come by and rescued her and brought her out here. Finally, he said, he had been certain that the servants would look to the safety of his wife, since the streets had been blocked with hundreds of panic-stricken people fleeing northward and it would not have been possible to have gone back to the house for her. Virginia Mulvaney seemed satisfied by this explanation, and even went so far as to express solicitous concern for the tearful, exhausted young woman.

But, a week after the fire, she hired a private detective to investigate Agnes Strion's background. It took another week for the detective to learn that Agnes's house had been rented as a love nest, and that Agnes was not only Mulvaney's catering cook, but also his "fancy girl."

Armed with this evidence, Virginia Mulvaney confronted her husband in the shop before all his clerks and female employees, denouncing him as a philandering scoundrel, and then turned her jealous rage on Agnes. When she had finished, she turned to her husband and indignantly ordered, "You will discharge that slut at once, do you understand, Frederick? And you're never to see her again, is that understood? Just you keep your word, and if I find that you've got rid of her and put her out of your mind forever, I may take you back—but that's up to you. Now, which is it to be?"

For all his romantic tenderness, Frederick Mulvaney was a moral coward. It was true that he loved Agnes Strion deeply, but the thought of divorce made him reflect on the ensuing scandal and the harm it could do his prospering business, particularly among Chicago's elite who, he was sure, would never countenance doing business with a man whose wife had divorced him for infidelity. Consequently, he stammered out, "Miss Strion, I've no choice. Your position is ended here, and I shall give you two weeks' pay in lieu of notice. I'm sure that with your skill you'll have no trouble finding a good job in some restaurant."

"Oh yes, or in some other man's bed," Virginia Mulvaney spitefully added. Agnes turned crimson with mortification, burst into tears, and ran out of the shop.

When it was all over, Mulvaney had a change of heart, knowing himself to have acted like a despicable coward. He stealthily visited Agnes, trying to propose some other way in which they could still be lovers, even going so far as to suggest that perhaps he could talk his wife into separating from him. But by now the unfortunate young woman considered herself betrayed and shamed, and the bright, hopeful love she had nurtured these five years was extinguished. Coldly she told him that she would never resume their relationship.

"All I ask, Frederick, is that you give me a decent letter of recommendation. I want a job; I'll need one now for certain." Then, with a bitter little laugh, she added, "You know how once I told you I wanted your child? Well, I found out that I can't ever have any. But at least I think I'd like to be around children. I could be good to them. It would be almost like having my own, if I were to work at some house and help bring them up. So all I want of you is a letter saying that I've done that—for you. I'm sure no one will know. I wouldn't go looking for a job among your fine society friends—because they'd probably know that you and your wife are childless. But there are lots of others who don't know anything about you, I'm sure. I'll go to a placement agency, and a letter from you could help a good deal."

After two weeks, Laurette Douglas was boasting to her neighbors that she undoubtedly had the most devoted and considerate governess any Chicago mother could ever have. To be sure, she tempered this adulation by soberly adding that nobody could really replace poor Polly Behting, but all the same, Agnes Strion was certainly a Godsend in this time of need. The three little boys appeared to be equally delighted with their new governess, particularly little Howard. Agnes, for her part, showed him slightly more attention than she did the twins, Kenneth and Arthur. Laurette had often noticed, with a tender smile of maternal approval, how the pleasant, soft-spoken woman would take the little boy on her lap and tell him stories, or gently urge him to finish all his breakfast—something he appeared to do for Agnes which he had not done for either Polly or Laurette herself. That in itself was a blessing, Laurette happily thought.

Also, the new governess bought toys out of her own wages, and most of these were showered on Howard. On several occasions, when it was the children's bedtime, Laurette stood on the threshhold of the room to watch Agnes cradle Howard in her arms, tell him a last fairy tale, and then gently lay him down in his little bed and tuck the covers up to his chest. At such moments, Laurette observed a look of profound devotion in Agnes's eyes, and this too enhanced her opinion of so dedicated a governess.

What she could not know was that Agnes had begun to experience the agonizing aftermath of her separation from Frederick Mulvaney. She had concealed her grief from him when he had come to her to beg for a renewal of their affair, and almost icily had told him that she wanted nothing more than that letter of recommendation which would give her entry into homes with children where she could, in some way, realize a few of the joys of the motherhood that would forever be denied her. Many a night, after she finished her duties with the twins and little Howard, she went to her room and there wept hysterically, muffling the sound in her pillow, as she relived the exquisite hours with her lover, remembering their tender moments together and her having urged him to give her a child even if it meant that she could never legitimize its birth.

There was something more that Laurette could never have surmised: each time Agnes looked at little Howard, she saw her lover's dark-blue eyes, and she began to tell herself that, if their child had been born, it would have been about the same age as her youngest charge. By the end of the third week of her employment, it was obvious even to Laurette that Agnes was beginning to favor Howard over his older twin brothers to an unhealthy degree, and late one Friday afternoon she gently remonstrated with the new governess.

"I think it's just marvelous the way Howard takes to you, Agnes. But, if you'll forgive my saying so, there's bound to be a great deal of rivalry between children growing up in the same household. And you do seem to like Howard more than Kenneth and Arthur. They're bound to notice that, Agnes, so perhaps you shouldn't make it quite so obvious—I know I'm saying it very badly, but I'm sure you understand what I'm driving at."

"But of course, Mrs. Douglas. Good heavens, I wouldn't think of offending you—I like my job here so much, and I just adore your children!" Agnes almost tearfully exclaimed, clasping her slim fingers and twisting them till the knuckles whitened. Laurette did not see in this act anything more than a sign of contrition on the part of a governess who still believed herself on probation and wished to prove her worth to her employer. So, almost chattily, she interposed, "I didn't mean to upset you, Agnes, truly I didn't. And of course, I want you to stay on—you're doing wonders with the children. Especially the way you get them to enjoy their food and tell them stories and take them for walks—my goodness, they come back telling me how many things you've shown them. I know that when Charles comes home, he'll be just as delighted as I am to have you here. Now please don't worry about what I said; I would just try to even out the attention you show the three boys, that's all. Thank you so much for understanding."

Agnes nodded, her eyes welling with sudden tears, which of course made Laurette self-consciously aware of having blundered in her tactics, of having said more than she meant to say. She tried to change the subject by suddenly suggesting that Agnes could mail a letter for her to her mother, Maybelle, at Windhaven Range when she took the boys out for their afternoon walk. She winced inwardly as the new governess, with an almost pathetic eagerness, responded, "Of course, Mrs. Douglas, I'll be happy to mail it for you! Please, I'm very grateful you pointed all this out to me—I don't want to make any mistakes here. I'm so anxious to be of service with these sweet little boys!"

With the news, announced by a telegraph wire, that Charles was on his way back to Chicago, Laurette's attention was happily diverted from what she had already concluded was only Agnes Strion's affection for her young charges. Looking forward to Charles's return, Laurette concluded that she had overreacted. There was no doubt, after all, that three-year-old Howard, now beginning to want to "catch up" with his older twin brothers, was particularly appealing as he strove for recognition. A younger child, she understood, would instinctively seek more expressions of love and kindness to fulfill his need for complete security.

Moreover, there was something else to divert Laurette's attention. To her great delight, it appeared that Charles's new partner, Lawrence Harding, was beginning to hit it off with Sylvia Cross. She had had them both to supper last Sunday, and the evening had been a great success. Only yesterday, Sylvia's uncle, Alderman Young, had dropped by to tell Laurette of a new fireproofing ordinance he was introducing in the city council for the purpose of preventing a recurrence of the October fire. He casually mentioned that Lawrence Harding and his niece had been out to dinner two nights previously and that Sylvia had reported she found him a most fascinating and considerate man. Laurette smiled to herself: she was sure that Charles would be as pleased as she was to learn that his efficient partner was finally thinking about marrying and settling down with a nice girl.

Charles would be back tomorrow, Sunday, she had estimated from her knowledge of the time it would take him to come by rail from New Orleans to St. Louis and thence on into Chicago. And today was an exceptionally busy one. She was having the Von Emmerichs to dinner and also the pleasant couple from across the street, Mr. and Mrs. Jennings Marlowe. Marlowe owned a bookstore on Dearborn Street and his wife, five years older than Laurette, was a teacher at the nearby elementary school. The Marlowes were childless, which Laurette thought a great pity, because they so obviously loved children. Harlene Marlowe was a particularly devoted teacher, and Laurette had heard her praises sung by many of her neighbors down the block whose children were enrolled at that school. Both of them always made such a fuss over the twins and little Howard. Yes, tonight would be a very delightful evening, a fitting preface to her husband's long-awaited return. As she worked in the kitchen, Laurette felt a warm glow of anticipation; not only had she missed Charles, but also she had so very much news to tell him!

It was three o'clock. Gracious, how the time flew when one was busy! She would serve a fine baron of beef, boiled potatoes in their jackets, a tossed salad, tiny lima beans, and peas mixed with pearl onions, and right now she was putting the finishing touches on a three-layered chocolate cake. She lifted the wooden spoon out of the bowl and giggled as she carefully laid it on a large dinner plate. The boys always insisted on licking the chocolate-cake spoon, and even if it wasn't the most hygienic thing in the world, they had so much pleasure out of it that she didn't have the heart to deny them.

Come to think of it, they should be home by now. They had all gone out for their customary Saturday afternoon walk. Laurette was glad she had insisted that Agnes take the children out, in spite of Agnes's offer to cook a big company dinner. It was such a beautiful afternoon, and besides, Laurette had wanted to put her own personal stamp on tonight's festive meal.

There, the cake was ready, and the beef was doing very nicely. Perhaps, she thought to herself, it might have come from one of Lucien Edmond Bouchard's herd. Then she corrected herself; no, he'd just be starting his cattle drive to market, and, of course, what he'd sold last year had long ago been slaughtered. Just the same, it gave her a warm feeling to think about the Bouchards because they had been so hospitable to Charles and her and the boys at their ranch. For herself, though, she didn't think she'd care to live in Texas permanently; the weather was dreadfully hot so much of the time. Chicago's summers weren't exactly paradise, but at least there was exhilarating seasonal change.

There was a knock on the front door, and taking a last look at the beef and the cake, Laurette hurried into the living room. When she opened the door, she was startled to see Kenneth and Arthur standing there. "Boys, where are Howard and your governess?" she gasped.

"Mama, she said she had to do an errand and that we were to come home now," Arthur volunteered with an uneasy glance at his twin brother.

"An errand? I don't understand. I didn't send her out for anything that I recall," Laurette doubtfully replied. "Are you sure that's what she said?"

"Oh yes, Mama," Kenneth contributed, energetically nodding his head. "She said you weren't to worry, everything was going to be just fine now. Really, Mama, that's what she said."

"But where did she go, boys?" Laurette could scarcely conceal her growing dismay.

"Well, Mama," Arthur piped up, "we went to the park like we always do, and then Howie got tired, so she said they'd sit on the bench and rest a little. Then she said she would take him for an ice cream, but we were to go home and tell you so you wouldn't worry, and then she said she'd take good care of Howie and you weren't to worry at all."

"We didn't really want to come back without him," Kenneth explained, with another nervous glance at his twin brother, "but she said it was all right and that she wanted us to."

"But that's so strange!" Laurette wonderingly exclaimed. "Well, come in then. I've saved the chocolate-cake spoon for you, but don't you dare eat it all up, be sure to leave some for Howard, now."

"Yes, Mama," they dutifully chorused as they scampered off to the kitchen.

Laurette seated herself on the settee, lines of worry creasing her smooth, high-arching forehead. "Oh dear," she said aloud, and then abruptly rose, biting her lower lip in indecision. It was a chilly afternoon for late April; the wind had already begun to rise, and she could hear it against the windows now. If Howard was tired, why didn't Agnes bring him right back? And she didn't at all like that business about her not worrying and that Howard would be all right.

She hurried to the kitchen and found the twins arguing over who was to lick the spoon first. "Boys, I'm going out to look for Agnes and your brother," she nervously announced. "Now, then you two, stop arguing—Arthur, let go of that spoon, you'll get your clothes all sticky! There's time enough for that later. Please"—her voice broke with sudden unreasonable dread. "Now please, boys, I'm going out for a walk to find Agnes and your brother. Be nice, go to your room and play, and I promise you'll have an extra large piece of chocolate cake at dinner tonight."

Reluctantly, they relinquished the spoon and set it back down on the plate, eyeing each other, not without a certain amount of hostility. Then they nodded obediently and went off to their room, while Laurette swiftly drew a cape over her shoulders and left the house.

When she returned nearly an hour later, she was hysterical. There was no sign of Agnes or Howard anywhere in the park or its environs. She had asked several people seated on park benches if they had seen the governess and the little boy, and one of them had said that he had, and that they had walked westward toward Clark Street and then turned south.

By five minutes to six, when the Von Emmerichs and the Marlowes were due to arrive, she was hysterical. When the Marlowes arrived she burst into tears and related what had happened, asking them if they would stay in the house and watch the children and also let the Von Emmerichs in while she went to the police station to report that little Howard and his governess were missing and perhaps had met with foul play.

CHAPTER TWENTY-THREE

"Laurette, please, dearest, try to get hold of yourself—I feel the way you do, but we've got to think clearly about this." Charles Douglas held his hysterically sobbing wife in his arms and tried to soothe her with a calmness he himself did not really feel. He had come from the railroad just before noon the next day, Sunday, to find his wife in a state of hysterical shock and the Von Emmerichs and Marlowes doing their best to try to calm her.

Hans von Emmerich, whose imported fabric and leather goods shop had been burned in the great fire and who had relocated it on Clark Street near Fullerton, quickly filled Charles in on the events of the preceding day. He and his wife had come for dinner, only to learn that Laurette had gone to the police station to report that Howard and the governess, Agnes Strion, were inexplicably missing. The Marlowes had insisted on staying overnight with the distracted young mother, and this morning, the Von Emmerichs had returned. Both women had taken care of the twins, Kenneth and Arthur, while the men had already gone back to the police station this morning to learn if there was any news.

"Oh, Charles, it's just so awful!" Laurette sobbed as she clung to him. "I've no idea in the world where they could be—poor little Howie! Oh, Charles, whatever possessed her to send the twins back home and take him on by herself when she knew he'd be tired by then? Maybe—oh God, I don't even want to think about that—maybe there was an accident, you know, like the one poor Polly was in!"

"Now sweetheart," he murmured as he gently stroked her tear-wet cheek, "Hans and Jennings told you they'd asked the officer in the station if there'd been any reports of accidents turned in by the hospitals, and there's nothing like that. We have to look on the brighter side. And now, I want you to think very carefully—do you know anything about this Agnes Strion's background, whether she had any friends?"

"No, that's the most awful part about it!" Laurette sobbed as she clung to him with a desperate urgency, trembling convulsively as she fought to control her sobs. "In all the time she was here, she never said a word about any friends or family. And Aznoe's is closed till tomorrow, because I already thought of that. Don't you think the agency would have a record of her past employment and maybe the names and addresses of people she'd worked for?"

"I think we can assume that, darling. But maybe we can find a clue in her personal effects."

"Oh my, I—I never thought of that!" Laurette confessed as, catching her breath, she looked hopefully up at her young husband.

"Well, why don't we do that right now? Let's go to her room, Laurette darling. Maybe we'll find some letters or papers or some identification that can give us a lead as to where she might have gone."

"But why, Charles?" Laurette's voice broke with anguish. "Whatever could have made her take Howie away and just—just disappear? Do you think—oh God, please let it not be that!—do you think she—she kidnapped him? And what reason could she have for a thing like that?"

"Now you mustn't get upset, sweetheart. Please try to calm yourself. Let's you and I just go to her room and see if we can find anything that can help us locate them both," Charles gently repeated.

He led her to the room which Agnes Strion had occupied in the Douglas house, trying to conceal his own mounting anxiety. Yet both Jennings Marlowe and Hans von Emmerich had told him that they had met Agnes and that she seemed to be totally dedicated to the little boys. And so far as he himself knew, he had no enemies who would attempt to strike at him by kidnapping his son.

Methodically, he opened the drawers of the large mahogany dresser in Agnes's room, but found nothing. In the closet, there were only two dresses and an extra coat. Turning to Laurette, he asked, "Didn't she bring a bag or trunk with her when she moved in here, darling?"

"Let me try to think—oh, Charles, every minute that passes, I'm worrying how Howie is—"

"I know, sweetheart. Try hard to think—what did she have when she came here the first day?" he compassionately prompted her.

Laurette sniffled and frowned, forcing herself to think back. Then, brightening, she volunteered, "Now I remember—she had a valise. That's absolutely all, Charles, just a valise, and the clothes she was wearing."

"Well then, let's look for this valise. Here it is, way up on the top shelf of the closet," he exclaimed as he looked upward and saw the handle on the top part of the valise protruding from over the topmost closet shelf. Reaching up, he lifted it down and brought it over to the bed, then opened it. "It seems to have been emptied out—wait a minute, what's this?" Having observed a small compartment sectioned off by elastic ribbon against the inner side of the bottom of the valise, he passed his hand into it and produced an envelope. "It's a letter—maybe this will help us."

"Oh Charles, what is it? Oh please, please, God, let it be something that'll bring poor little Howie back right away!" Laurette burst into tears and, covering her face with her hands, gave vent to her despair.

"Please don't, Laurette darling. Let me read this—wait, this is a real stroke of luck!" he suddenly exulted. Laurette, struck by the confidence in his voice, straightened, dropping her hands slowly and staring tearfully at him. "It seems to be a letter from some friend of hers in Indianapolis."

"What does the letter say, Charles? Read it to me, oh please, read it to me quickly! Oh, Howie, Howie, darling, I pray God you're all right and not hurt!" Laurette sobbed.

"Now listen," Charles excitedly ordered. "It's from a woman by the name of Ella Harley. It was written last August to this governess of yours. She mentions that she and Agnes Strion used to work together at Fritz's Eatery— did you know anything about that?"

"No," Laurette quavered, shaking her head, her eyes wide and fixed on her husband, clasping her hands at her heaving bosom in her agitation.

"Well, at any rate, this Ella Harley says that she'd love to see Agnes and that, if Agnes ever decided to take a vacation, she'd be very welcome at this Ella Harley's boarding house. And the envelope has the woman's address—719 Davidson Street. Hm, I've been to Indianapolis quite a few times, to do business with David Porter, the furniture manufacturer, but I don't remember that street. It must be in one of the outlying sections of town that I've never visited. Well, it's easy enough to find out."

"You mean—you think that maybe Agnes took Howie to that woman's boarding house, Charles? But why ever would she do a think like that? Couldn't she imagine how terribly upset I'd be without having a word from her all this time? Why, she—she's as good as kidnapped him, if that's true, Charles."

"Well, let's not jump to conclusions. I'll tell you what, sweetheart. The Marlowes and the Von Emmerichs are wonderful friends, and they told me they'll stick with you until this is all over. As for myself, I'll have a bite to eat and a quick nap, and then I'll go down to the station and get the first train to Indianapolis."

"Oh Charles, you're so tired from that terribly long trip from Texas—"

"That's not important at all. I want to find Howie just as much as you do, sweetheart. And since I know that you'll be taken good care of by our friends, and time is important, I'll leave right away. Now you go lie down and rest. I'll ask Minna von Emmerich to stay with you." He chuckled goodnaturedly. "She's a card, that Minna is! Why, would you believe that she's just as much interested in baseball as Hans? Not only that, she boasts about how well she can ride a velocipede. Though personally, I think I'd try to reduce a little if I were she before I got on one of those contraptions."

Laurette, despite her anxiety, found her husband's humor contagious and reassuring, and began to giggle through her tears. "That's just awful of you, darling! I do hope poor Minna never hears you say a thing about that—she's very self-conscious about her weight. Oh, thank God you're back, you always know what to do, Charles!"

"No, not always, sweetheart," he soberly corrected. "But it's all I can think of doing right now. Besides, Hans and Jennings will go to the police station again tomorrow morning and also call on that nurse's registry where you got Agnes Strion. I've got a feeling that, between us all, we'll find Howie real soon. Now you do what I told you to, Laurette, you go to bed and rest."

"Yes, Charles. You're so wonderful to me, so dependable—" She began to sob again. Charles took her in his arms and kissed her eyelids, soothing her. Then he led her to her bedroom, and Minna von Emmerich, who had come down the hall to inquire after her, caught his sign and nodded.

"Come on, *Liebchen*." She put her arm around Laurette's shoulders and talked to her as she would to a child. "Minna will put you to bed and bring you some nice hot soup after you've had a little rest. Everything's going to be all right, you'll see. That's a good girl, dear."

"God bless you, Minna. I'm going to Indianapolis after I've had a bite and a catnap," Charles quickly explained. "Your husband and Jennings can check the agency where Laurette got Agnes from tomorrow, and maybe we'll get a few more leads. You see, I just found a letter in Agnes's valise which mentions a friend who runs a boarding house in Indianapolis. It's just a chance, of course, but I'm going to take it."

"I'll pray for you, Charles. Come along now, Laurette, all of us are going to do just everything we can. Howie will be back very soon, you can depend on it," Minna reassured the sobbing, red-haired young woman.

It was midnight when Charles Douglas got off the train at the Indianapolis station and boarded a hansom cab to take him to the Cass Hotel, where he usually stayed on his business trips. He had brought with him a daguerrotype of little Howard as well as the boy's birth certificate to verify his own identity as the child's father. The picture was an excellent likeness; it had been taken six months earlier, and it showed Howard's curly hair and strikingly large eyes, as well as the unmistakable curve of his firm little mouth. Charles also had taken the precaution of bringing along a loaded six-shooter, in the event that he ran into trouble. After talking with the desk clerk at the Cass Hotel and learning the location of Ella Harley's boardinghouse, he was glad that he had the revolver; the boardinghouse was in one of the most disreputable areas of the city, where the police were constantly being summoned for robberies, rapes, and other crimes of violence.

He spent a sleepless night, debating with himself whether he should ask his furniture manufacturer's aid; the two men had become fast friends, quite apart from their business relationship. He finally decided against it. It would be much better to go to Davidson Street during the day and take up a vantage point near the boarding house, in hopes that Agnes would emerge with the little boy. He hoped to persuade her to give back the abducted child. There was, he knew, always the possibility that this had been a kidnapping for ransom. The thought chilled him, but he determined to try to handle the situation by himself. If he could take Agnes by surprise and if she were alone with the child, he was sure that he could get Howard back without too much difficulty.

After a hasty breakfast, he left the hotel about eight in the morning and had a hansom cab drive him to Davidson Street, letting him off about three blocks from the address of the boarding house. Then, very calmly, he strolled down the dingy street, observing the squalor of the ramshackle frame tenement buildings, the cheap restaurants and saloons, the noisy, badly dressed children playing in the streets and shouting obscenities at one another.

He walked to within a few doors of the boarding house and, acting like a casual passerby, entered one of the cheap saloons and asked for whiskey. The bartender, a surly, short, potbellied man in his late fifties, glowered at him and, as he shoved the glass across the badly scuffed and dirty bar, growled, "Lookin' fer one'a Daisy's girls, mister? Yer a mite early fer that. Her house don't open till noon. That'll be two bits."

"Thanks. Here you are. No, I'm not looking for one of her girls. Tell me, do you know Ella Harley's boarding house down the street?"

"Sure. Ella herself comes in regular fer a gin now and again. Why, she don't keep no girls—not that I know about, anyhow. Where you from, mister?"

"Chicago."

"Thought so," the bartender triumphantly sneered with a humorless little laugh as he took a dirty cloth and began to scour some of the empty glasses remaining on the bar from the night before. " 'S'matter, all the sluts in Chicago leave after that big fire you had down there?"

"I don't think so." Charles managed a cheerful smile he

didn't feel. "Besides, I said I wasn't looking for that kind of girl. Now about this Ella Harley—she's got a friend, a pleasant-looking woman in her thirties, I'd say. And a little boy, with curly hair and dark-blue eyes. Maybe you might have seen them—they just came to Indianapolis, I'm told. Probably yesterday."

"Now listen, mister." The bartender leaned across the bar, elbows planted, his surly face menacing, his eyes narrowed. "I run a respectable place. No little brat gets in here. Think I want trouble with the law? We've got enough law around these parts at night and I want no truck with 'em, get me? Now, I'd like it fine if you'd finish your drink and take your business elsewhere. Too early for questions like you're askin'."

"I'm sorry to have troubled you. There"—he put the glass on the counter, having taken only a perfunctory sip— "that's not bad whiskey. Well, I'll be going now." Nodding companionably to the glowering bartender, he left the saloon.

He walked slowly till he found himself opposite the boarding house, a two-story white frame building with a rickety porch of eight steps. There was an iron gate guarding the narrow cobblestoned walk to the porch. The curtains were drawn and there was no sign of life in the house. He had put the six-shooter inside his coat pocket, and self-consciously he patted the coat, somewhat apprehensive over the suspicious bulge. Then he took up his vigil.

The moments seemed to drag by like hours, and some of the children playing in the dirty street pointed at him, for it was not usual for someone so well dressed to come down Davidson Street even in quest of the carnal pleasures to which the bartender had referred. Charles ignored them and eventually they tired of their sport and moved farther down the street, to his great relief.

Several times, during the seemingly interminable wait, Charles was tempted to go for a policeman, but each time he reflected that, if he left the scene, Agnes Strion and his little son—if, as he suspected, they were both in that house across the street—would have ample opportunity to leave and go somewhere else where he would not be able to find them.

Now, to his left and on the same side of the street where he waited, a handsomely buxom but coarse-featured woman in her early thirties approached, wearing a red lisle skirt and matching shirtwaist, over which a threadbare cloth coat was draped, but with only one button made fast so that he could see the garments beneath. She stopped to eye him, and then her lips curved in what was meant as a provocative smile.

"Dearie, want to come along home with me? It's so early in the day, t'won't cost ye much—jist four bits. 'Course, if you're a man wut likes to take his time, then I'll charge you only a dollar."

"No, thank you, miss," Charles politely declined. The smile left her face and was replaced by a sneering frown. "Oho, think yerself too good fer the likes of me, do ye?" she jeered. Then, seeing that his gaze strayed across the street to the boarding house, she uttered a short, derisive laugh. "Hah! So yer waitin' fer Ella, are ye? Whoever told ye she took fancy men on was a liar. Why, all Ella does is rent rooms to whores. She's got her own steady man!"

"I—I wasn't waiting for that, miss. I—I'm waiting to see someone who's staying there," Charles stammered. The coarse-featured woman stared at him a moment, then shrugged and contemptuously spat as she walked on down the street, turning back to send him another mocking glance.

The sky was gray, and now suddenly a few drops of rain fell. Charles impatiently ground his teeth and shook his head with annoyance. If Agnes was in there with Howard, she certainly wouldn't be likely to take the child for a walk if it were raining. And now, as if to plague him, the rain began to fall so violently, driven by a northeast wind, that he was obliged to take refuge inside the narrow doorway of an indescribably squalid four-flat frame building whose drab gray paint had long since been effaced to expose the rotting wood beneath. A few minutes later, he heard steps on the stairway behind him and turned to see a heavily set, black-bearded man with a cap pulled down over one side of his face.

"Hey, whatcha you doin' here, you fancy toff?" the man grumbled. "You don't belong here nohow. Who you lookin' fer?"

"Why—it's just started raining—and I came in so I wouldn't get wet," Charles lamely explained.

"Raining, is it? Hell, and I hafta go to work at the tannery. Well, mister, git out of my way. I'm late enough already, see?" the bearded man indignantly demanded.

Charles suppressed a groan of weariness as he opened the door and stepped out onto the sidewalk. The bearded man moved warily outside, swore volubly at the rain; then, tugging his cap down even more, he began to run down the street, not without a backward, suspicious glance at this unusually well-groomed stranger.

The rain ended as suddenly as it had begun, and Charles breathed a sign of relief as he stepped outside. The fetid odors from the rooms above and the almost inky blackness in the narrow entranceway had depressed him. He resumed his post outside, his eyes fixed on the front door of Ella Harley's boarding house.

Half an hour later, the sun made a bleak appearance in the sky, and here and there, along the wretched slum street, shabbily dressed men and women began to come out of the tenement dwellings and the rickety frame houses. Some of them headed for the saloon where he had just been, and all of them stared curiously at him, clearly suspicious of anyone so obviously better off than themselves. The group of children who had been playing in the street, and who had disappeared with the advent of the rain, now returned, their shrill cries and their oaths making Charles wince. He had known of the dreadful Bridgeport slum in Chicago, but he had never visited it. Now he found himself in a terrible, alien world which aroused both distaste and the utmost compassion for those compelled to live in such abysmal poverty.

His temples were already throbbing with a sick headache from the intense concentration and the prolonged, seemingly hopeless wait. He began to tell himself that he would have done much better to have gone to the nearest police station, informed the sergeant in charge, and enlisted aid, rather than venturing into this dangerous, inimical neighborhood by himself. Yet doggedly he waited, breaking the agonizing monotony by walking slowly down the sidewalk to one end, then retracing his footsteps till again he stood opposite the boarding house.

Then he suppressed a cry of joy when he saw the front door open and two women come out. One of them was brown-haired, with pleasant features, wearing a bonnet and a black dress; the other, at least ten years older, was plump

303

and gray-haired and carried a reticule. Between them, each of the women holding one hand, was Howard, dressed shabbily, a cheap cap pulled down over his curls.

"Howard!" he called out hoarsely, and ran across the street, oblivious to the fact that a cart drawn by an old dray horse was approaching from his left. The driver cursed at him, then applied his carriage whip viciously over the flanks of the old horse, which stumbled, whinnied in protest, and then with a bound of energy produced by the lash, began a slow trot down the cobblestoned street.

The two women, hearing him call, turned as if to go back into the house. Little Howard protestingly dragged at their grip on his hands and was about to cry out, "Daddy!" when the younger woman—Agnes Strion—clapped her other hand over his mouth and bent down and whispered fiercely to the child.

"Wait—that's my son! You're Agnes Strion—you've kidnapped my boy!" Charles shouted as he pushed open the iron gate and hastened up the rickety wooden steps of the porch.

"Mister, you must be daft'" the older, plump woman hissed at him. "This tyke's name's Frederick—ain't that right, dearie?" she said to Agnes who at once energetically nodded, her eyes very wide and glassy.

"Madam, I assume you're Ella Harley." Charles, his heart wildly pounding, tried to control his distraught nerves and to reason logically. "This is my son Howard, and that woman there is Agnes Strion, whom my wife, Laurette, engaged as governess in Chicago. I've proof that this boy is my son—I've a picture of him and his birth certificate. His name is Howard Douglas."

"You're dead wrong, mister," the fat woman indignantly retorted. "This tyke's name's Frederick, like I told you, see? It's Agnes's boy all right, by Mr. Mulvaney, and that's a fact. Now you just be off and don't go bothering decent people this early in the day, you hear? Or I'll have the law on you, I swear I will!"

"For God's sake, Agnes, you know this is not true," Charles exclaimed passionately, as he took out the daguerrotype of his son and held it up so that both women could see it. "Besides, Howard knows me. Take your hand away from his mouth, Agnes Strion! Do you hear me?"

Once again, they turned to go back into the house, and

Charles, desperate in the face of such a mendacious denial, was at the point of reaching for the concealed six-shooter in his inner coat pocket.

"Help, Joe!" the older woman called, as she beckoned with her free hand. "This here's my friend Agnes, it's her boy, and this crazy fool claims it's his kid!"

"You just get away from there, mister!" Charles heard a hoarse, angry voice call to him from across the street. Quickly turning, he saw a tall, cadaverous-faced man in dingy blue shirt, torn overalls, and heavy work shoes stride across the street toward him, followed by the surly bartender, who gripped a piece of steel pipe in his pudgy right hand.

"Now you men wait just a minute!" Charles drew out the six-shooter and leveled it at them both. "I'm from Chicago, and this is my little boy Howard. This woman"—quickly turning, he pointed to Agnes Strion—"was hired by my wife as a governess. She ran away Saturday with my son, and I can prove he's my son. Howard will recognize his father—tell her to take her hand away from his mouth and let him speak for himself!"

"So you say, mister," the bartender growled, as he came forward warily, drawing back the piece of pipe to use as a club. "Now if you'll take my advice, you'll get the hell out of here and don't ever come back. Me 'n Joe, we'd jist as soon cut yer tripes out as talk to you, git me?"

"I don't want to hurt either of you, but my God, if you try to interfere with me in this, I'll shoot you both, I mean it!" Charles cried out.

Then, seeing that they came slowly and steadily toward him, Charles swiftly turned and, with his free hand, pulled Agnes Strion's palm away from little Howard's mouth. "Now, do you know me, Howie boy?"

"You're my dada," Howard tearfully articulated. "I wanna go home, Dada. Agnes said I had to come with her, she said I was her boy now."

"There, did you hear that, you men?" Charles turned to confront his two assailants. The bartender scowled, turned to the tall man and muttered, "Could be there's something fishy about all this. The kid sure called him Daddy, plain as day—you heard it yourself." Then, aloud, he demanded, "You got any more proof you're his father, mister?"

"This birth certificate!" Charles drew it from his pocket,

keeping his six-shooter leveled at both men. "Now, all I'm asking you to do, fair and square, is go get a policeman. We'll find out what's right and what's a lie soon enough once you've done that. I told you, I don't want to hurt you, you're not involved in this. But that's my son, I swear before God!"

"Well, sounds like you're on the square, mister. Whaddya think, Joe?" the bartender glanced at the tall man.

"Yeah. All right, I'll go for a policeman. But you better not tell him we had anythin' to do with this, get me?"

"I promise that," Charles breathlessly agreed. He watched as the cadaverous-looking man, with a last hesitant glance at the bartender, began to run down the street. Then he turned back to the two women. "Now look, Miss Harley—" he began.

"It's Mrs. Harley to you, my man died three years ago," the fat woman snapped.

"All right, I'm sorry. Mrs. Harley, then. You know yourself that boy doesn't belong to your friend Agnes."

The older woman shrugged, and turned to Agnes Strion. "Honey, I done the best I could. I feel for ya. That bastid of a Mulvaney left you high 'n dry—you wanted a kid by him, and I know just how you felt about it. But, honey, you know what's right—this man, I sure guess, is the tyke's daddy. You better give him to him, or you'll get into real trouble, Agnes."

Agnes suddenly began to weep, sank down on her knees, letting go of Howard's hand, and covered her face with her hands as great, tearing sobs shook her shuddering body.

Charles, very pale, himself trembling in aftermath, pocketed his six-shooter, then scooped Howard up into his arms. His eyes were filled with tears. "Mrs. Harley, I won't bring any charges against your friend here. Poor woman. Don't you see, her mind's given way. When the policeman comes, you ought to tell him that she should see a doctor."

"Yeah, mister, I guess you're right about that. She was a good friend to me at Fritz's. Now, I won't get into no trouble, will I?"

"No, Mrs. Harley. All I want is my son back. I've got him now. I'm going to take him back to Chicago right away. You do what I tell you to about your friend."

"Sure." The fat woman turned to the kneeling, weeping

306

younger woman. With her knuckles, she rubbed her misted eyes and, in a matter-of-fact voice, declared, "All right, Agnes. Cry it out. He was a bastid, all right. But you oughtn't to have gone and done what you did. I tried to cover for you, but it's no use. I'll see that they take good care of you, though. I won't leave you in the lurch, Agnes."

Little Howard had begun to cry, linking his arms around Charles's neck. Charles walked back down onto the sidewalk and looked up at the weeping governess. He murmured a silent prayer and then quickly walked down the street and out of the slum.

"Oh, Charles, it's like a miracle!" Laurette tearfully exclaimed as she lifted Howard up and hugged him to her, covering him with kisses. "I was just beside myself, darling—then your telegraph wire came yesterday, just when I thought I'd go mad if I didn't hear something—oh Charles, Charles, thank God you found our little boy!"

"Thank God indeed, dearest." Charles stood close to her, an arm around her shoulders, his eyes moist. "Thank God for giving me the idea of looking in that valise of hers and that she'd left Ella Harley's letter in it. Otherwise . . ." He shrugged philosophically. "The poor woman's obviously deranged."

"But why did she keep saying he was her child, that his name was Frederick Mulvaney?" Laurette anxiously pursued.

"Frederick Mulvaney, as you know, happens to be a very prominent caterer and greengrocer here. I suspect there is a tragic story behind all this, but at this point, I'm not going to investigate it. My guess is that, somehow, this Agnes Strion got involved with Mulvaney, perhaps even had a love affair with him. Maybe he threw her over—after all, he's married to one of our society belles, which would be enough to prevent any happy outcome for that poor woman. So perhaps her mind just gave way and she believed Howard was the child she had or wanted to have by him."

"What will become of her, darling? I feel so sorry for her—"

"So do I. Before I left Indianapolis, I stopped over to see David Porter, the man who supplies my store with that fine furniture of his, you know."

Laurette nodded, looking earnestly at her husband, then again began to kiss and soothe little Howard in her arms.

"I left a bank draft for five hundred dollars with him. He's going to have his attorney call on Ella Harley and arrange to have Agnes examined by a mind doctor. And if there isn't any cure for her, I'll arrange to see that she's placed in an institution that will take care of her. In a way, I feel it's my moral duty, Laurette."

"You're such a kind, good man, Charles Douglas. Besides—well, I don't have any vindictiveness toward her at all. It's very strange—she was so loving and devoted, poor woman. And I'm so lucky to have you. And—and, Charles?"

"Yes, my darling?" he tightened his hold around her shoulders and kissed her on the cheek.

"Have you noticed anything different about me? I hope so—I'm going to have another baby."

"That's wonderful news, my dearest! This time, I want it to be a daughter, with your red hair and that combination of fiery temper and loving kindness that makes you the best wife a man could ever have."

Laurette blushed becomingly and turned to kiss him, smiling through her tears.

CHAPTER TWENTY-FOUR

The summer of 1872 was full of pleasant nostalgia for Luke Bouchard. The weather was unusually warm, with surprisingly little rain, just enough to aid the fruit and vegetable crops Marius Thornton was so ably supervising. Luke wryly thought to himself that if he had decided to plant cotton he could not have asked for a better season. But knowing the low price to which it had fallen, he remained doggedly convinced that his decision to bypass cotton this year had been a wise one. He was doing well enough with his other crops: chickens, hogs, even cattle. All these enterprises afforded him a decent profit for his labors, and at the same time created the very diversity that he felt was essential to the progress of Windhaven Plantation.

There were times during the summer when Luke ascended the steep bluff fronting the Alabama River and communed with his beloved grandfather. He prized these moments of spiritual union with the man who, more than anyone else, had shaped his own adventurous life. Always, on the high bluff, he felt as if the almost century-long period between Lucien's coming to Econchate and his own renascence on Windhaven Plantation had fallen away, leaving him face to face with the past. Perhaps the scenery had changed: no longer did the Creeks paddle their pirogues up and down the gently flowing river, or play their games of *tokonhay* in the vast clearings well beyond the rich land that the *mico* Tunkamara had given to his grandfather. But the spirit of those long-gone days was still alive, and Luke felt close to the soul of his noble ancestor who, motivated by a belief in the equality of men of all races, had come to seek a new life across the seas.

Best of all, Luke did not look upon himself as an old

man, even though he had just begun his fifty-seventh year. His grandfather had lived to be nearly seventy-three, and yet, as he looked back, he had never been conscious of Lucien as an old man: certainly not old in mind and spirit and heart. And like his grandfather before him, Luke was kept young and vital through his way of life, and through the strong ties he felt with all members of his family. Though separated by hundreds of miles, the members of such a family would remain true to their intrinsic beliefs, an inseparable clan. Just as kinship ties had been of paramount importance among the Creeks, just as they were today among Sangrodo's people, the Comanches, so were they also among the Bouchards, and would remain so, even after Luke's own demise.

Nor had he forgotten the gentle influence of Lucy Williamson, his first wife, that sweet and devoted companion to whom he had been unfaithful a single, thoughtless time—when he and Laure Prindeville had met in John Brunton's Union House on that fateful day in New Orleans seven years before. He knew that Lucy would not have rebuked him for that lapse; but, although he was not puritanical by nature, he was grateful that she had never known of his blind hour of infatuation with Laure. As he considered the past—and these days he found himself doing that more and more—he was convinced that morally he had righted whatever wrong there had been, in this union with Laure, for it had turned into a new life which was harmonious with what he had known before, with Lucy.

At thirty-one, Laure had reached the full flower of her maturity: she was his companion, wife, and lover, more devoted to him than ever. This was why he did not feel the weight of his years on this pleasant mid-July afternoon, as he mounted his stallion to ride to the land that once James Cavendish had owned and now belonged to Andy Haskins and his wife, Jessica.

Forty years earlier, James Cavendish, ostracized by his stern father, had come to Lowndesboro and bought fifty acres of land. He had produced forty bales of cotton that autumn, and yet, because of his womanizing and lack of business acumen, he had become heavily indebted to Luke's father, the dissolute Henry Bouchard. Henry had shrewdly maneuvered to take over ownership of the Cavendish acreage. Now, after all this time, it belonged to a

310

young Southerner whom Luke himself had found, along with Joe Duvray, looking for any kind of job on the New Orleans levee shortly after the Civil War had ended. Now Joe Duvray was a partner of his own oldest son, Lucien Edmond, on Windhaven Range. And by the stroke of chance, Andy Haskins had come back to join forces with Luke and, if the fates were kind, to take his place as an honorable and idealistic legislator for the state of Alabama. Surely there was a purpose behind the existence of these acquaintances who had grown into friends true enough to ally themselves with the Bouchard family. This, too, was part of old Lucien's legacy.

When he dismounted and tied his horse to the rail in front of the old but still durable Bambach house, Luke heard a lusty "Hello!" from the fields and strode toward them, recognizing Andy Haskins's voice. The genial, one-armed Tennesseean had dropped his hoe and come running, a grin on his pleasant, sun-browned face. "Good to see you, Mr. Luke!" he exclaimed as he tendered his hand, which Luke warmly shook.

"Likewise, Andy. Say now, I picked up this morning's *Advertiser* and I had the pleasure of reading one of the first of your campaign statements. It reads very well. Better than mine, indeed."

"Oh, shucks, Mr. Luke, now you know you're just being nice to me. Happens I went down to the *Advertiser* office myself just after I told Mr. Blount and his two friends that I'd run on their ticket, and I got copies of the paper from two years ago, when you were running yourself for the same office." Andy shook his head. "No, sir, Mr. Luke, well, I sure couldn't come anywheres up to that piece you wrote—let's see if I remember—sure I do, it was on April 10, 1870, that's when it was."

Luke Bouchard had to grin despite himself. "Now that's really flattering, Andy. Well, yes, I remember that. But you see, I had to go into a lot of detail about explaining that I wasn't a real scalawag, even if I'd been born a Southerner. Also, I had to go on record that I didn't endorse all of President Grant's doings, nor the people around him, either."

"Well, I'd go along with you there, Mr. Luke."

"Yes," Luke's face sobered. "I'm very much afraid that if he's reelected and doesn't look for abler men around

311

him, we're going to have a very serious economic crisis next year. You could say I feel it in my bones—except that to say a thing like that would make me sound like an old man, and I certainly don't feel it on this beautiful July day. Well now," he changed to a casual, almost bantering tone, "shouldn't a would-be legislator be out stumping the countryside instead of working in the fields with a hoe?"

"I don't hold with that, Mr. Luke. Mind you, I've already made a few trips to some of the nearby little towns and spoken at meetings, but I'm going to let Mr. Blount handle a lot of the details. I figure that if folks know me now as a settler here in Alabama, with land and workers and a wife who's going to give me my first child just about the time the election comes due, they'll know all of me there is to know. They're going to vote on issues, mainly, Mr. Blount tells me."

"Yes, they are, Andy. But I think they've had their stomachs full of men like Cletus Adams and the carpetbagging they stand for. Well now, how are your crops coming along?"

"First rate, Mr. Luke!" Andy grinned from ear to ear. "I tell you, I was mighty lucky I picked fellows like Matt Rensler and Burt Coleman. They're orphans, just like myself, and they lost a lot more in that war than I ever did, because their wives died. And what kinfolk they had left Alabama to go to Texas and California. Matter of fact, I was talking with them just this morning, and both Matt and Burt tell me that they haven't heard a word from any of their kin in over a year now."

"That's a shame. One of my projects is keeping in touch with all the members of our clan, Andy. That way, we can depend on one another when the going's tough, and we're all ready to pitch in once some member of the family gets into trouble. You know, if it hadn't been for my son Lucien Edmond, it might have taken a great deal longer to find my poor little kidnapped boy, Lucien."

"That's true enough, Mr. Luke." Andy nodded solemnly. "Anyhow, I can tell you that I'm sure looking forward to the first family I've really ever had, when my Jessica has our child."

"I suppose you're hoping for a boy, Andy. Most men do."

"No, sir, Mr. Luke, I'm not." Andy Haskins energetically shook his head. "The way I figure it, I'm so lucky to have my girl Jessica, I'd be just as content with a daughter if it's half as pretty as she is and has her sweet nature."

"Bless you, Andy. Maybe it'll be twins, a boy for her and a girl for you." Luke chuckled and patted Andy on the shoulder. "So you're doing all right with your crops. Melon, yams, tomatoes, corn, and beans. And you've got about ten acres of cotton going. Now that's not a bad idea, because I remember this piece of land, Andy. It used to belong to a fellow named James Cavendish, and my own father, Henry Bouchard, wangled it away from him when he couldn't meet his bills. So far as I can remember, there hasn't been too much cotton planted on these fifty acres, so I'm pretty sure that you'll do nicely with your ten. But I warn you, don't expect too much money on the crop."

"I don't, Mr. Bouchard. But you know, the Ardmore brothers, Cassius and Daniel, they were really the ones who talked me into trying those ten acres with cotton. You remember, I told you that they'd worked together on the same plantation near Talladega before the war. They know how to run a gin, and they tell me that they'll get good production out of the acreage come this fall."

"I'm glad to hear it. Grandfather's old gin is still in good working order, because he and then I kept it in tiptop condition all the years up to the war. And you're welcome to use it, Andy, that goes without saying."

"Thanks, Mr. Luke. I don't know how to begin to thank you for all you've done for me."

"You've already thanked me by being a good neighbor, Andy. And a good friend. Well, I'm going to ride on down to Lowndesboro and see Dalbert Sattersfield. Can I bring back any supplies for you from his store?"

"No, thanks, Mr. Luke. Happens I went down there myself yesterday morning. Say, Dalbert's got himself a new clerk."

"Oh?" Luke expressed mild interest at this news.

"For sure he has. Met him myself, matter of fact. Nice-looking fellow, hardworking, doesn't talk much, does his job. Dalbert says he walked in about two weeks ago and asked if there was any work he could do, and Dalbert took him on."

"It's gratifying to learn that Dalbert's doing so well in his store that he needs more help."

313

"He's doing just fine, Mr. Luke. You know, I've been selling him some of my melons and tomatoes and yams, and the fellows working for me are real happy with the money we're making. I'm putting aside a little nest egg for when Jessica has our kid, naturally."

"I'm proud of the way you're managing, Andy." Luke clapped him on the shoulder. "Well, I guess I'll be off. You just keep working on your campaign. It'll be a very nice present for your newborn child to have his daddy elected legislator for the county of Montgomery. I'll be seeing you again, Andy. Take good care of yourself."

"So long as I can still use a hoe and a spade and work with my boys here, I'll be fine, Mr. Luke. Good to see you. You keep well, too."

An hour later, Luke rode into the town of Lowndesboro, tied up his horse to the hitching post in front of Dalbert Satterfield's store, and walked inside. The one-armed former Confederate officer was behind the counter waiting on a portly, gray-haired woman, who had a long list of wants, so Luke seated himself on a barrel of molasses and looked around the store. Since the last time he had been here, it was evident that Dalbert had not only tidied up the store but added many attractive displays of merchandise to it, another sign that he was doing well.

Luke turned to look at a tall, wiry, black-haired man at the other end of the counter. He appeared to be in his late thirties, and he was listening attentively to a pretty blond young woman who was chattering aimlessly before coming to the point of what she needed. This, Luke told himself, must be the new clerk. He was certainly amiable enough, and when the young woman had finally stopped chattering, Luke heard him speak to her in a soft, drawling voice.

When at last Dalbert Sattersfield had finished with his customer and promised to have her supplies delivered that evening, he came from behind the counter to greet Luke, a warm smile on his distinguished face. "It's very good to see you, Mr. Bouchard."

"I really wish you'd call me Luke, Dalbert. We've been friends long enough, and you're practically one of the family," Luke Bouchard quipped, as he straightened and shook Dalbert's hand. "You know, you and Mitzi and the twins owe us a visit. Laure was mentioning that just the

314

other day. Can you come for dinner, all of you, this next Sunday evening?"

"I'd be delighted to, Mr. Bouchard—I mean, Luke. Forgive me, I guess I'm from the old school," Dalbert chuckled. Noticing that Luke's eyes were fixed on the tall, black-haired clerk, he murmured, "I see you've noticed Hugh. He's been quite a help to me, and I don't mind telling you. Walked in here a few weeks ago out of the clear sky, and as it happened, I really needed someone. It's partly your fault, Luke," Dalbert gave an apologetic chuckle. "You and Andy Haskins have been sending me such good fruit and vegetables, my business has increased and I've had to hire help. And he's working out very nicely."

"Where does he come from?"

"He didn't say too much about himself, Luke. Except that he was born in New Orleans, worked for a time as a roustabout on the docks there, and as a waiter in a restaurant."

"I see. I'll tell you what, Dalbert. Why don't you invite him to come to dinner with us on Sunday, when you and Mitzi and the twins visit us?"

"That's very kind of you. I'm sure he'd be delighted. He doesn't seem to know anybody around here, or have any friends. Keeps to himself, mostly. I found him a room with old Mrs. Stellman down the street. She's been a customer of mine, you see, ever since I opened the store. She tells me he's a wonderful tenant, makes no noise, very clean and personable in his habits, no trouble at all."

Luke nodded. He took another look at the wiry black-haired clerk who, having finished with the young blond housewife, was tidying up behind the counter and not looking at him. "I'm just curious about a man like that. He seems to be reasonably sophisticated, and I'm wondering what he's doing in a little town like Lowndesboro. It can't have much excitement for him after New Orleans. Well, you tell him what I said. Laure and I will be very pleased to have him as our guest. And as for you, Dalbert, don't you dare forget my invitation. Laure is just dying to see both you and Mitzi."

315

CHAPTER TWENTY-FIVE

On Saturday, Luke Bouchard rode into Montgomery to see Jedidiah Danforth, for the latter had sent him a message that he had urgent news which would be of great interest. The ailing old lawyer seemed to have obtained a new lease on life: he looked more vital, and his eyes twinkled with amusement as Luke entered his office and greeted him.

"Jedidiah, I swear I don't know how you do it. You know, earlier this spring, I was really worried about you, from what I'd heard from your housekeeper, Mrs. Cantwell.

"She's a dear woman, even if she meddles too much," was Jedidiah Danforth's reply, with a dry chuckle to preface it. "I'll tell you what decided me to forget all the nonsense my doctor's been telling me about slowing down—it was that excitement over your adopted son, Lopasuta. You remember how Mrs. Cantwell drove a buggy—and I didn't think she had it in her, I'll tell you that straight out—to warn me that the Ku Klux Klan was going after Lopasuta. Well, sir, that got my dander up in a hurry. And I've been riding high ever since. No, I'm not ready to cash in my chips yet. But enough about me. I've some news that will really make you happy."

"That's why I came in, Jedidiah. What's happened?"

"Sit there a spell and let me tell the story in my own way. You know, now that the North seems to be relenting a little bit about us poor old Southern rebels, what with the Amnesty Act and the discontinuation of the Freedmen's Bureau, I've been looking at some of the old deeds from before the war pertaining to the land you and your father used to own, and your grandfather before you both."

"And what have you found, Jedidiah?"

"Just this. I don't want to bring up anything distasteful, but I'm afraid I'm going to have to remind you about Barnabas McMillan."

"That's certainly a distasteful name. I'll never forget what he did to Laure."

"Yes, I know." Jedidiah closed his eyes and shook his head. "But he paid for it, since that slut of his, Stacey Hollbrook, shot him. She's never been heard of since, as you well know."

"Yes. Just the same, I'm still remembering those terrible hours when I thought poor Laure was going to die after Stacey kicked her so that she lost our child. Thank God Laure survived that viciousness, and was able to have our lovely, perfectly healthy little daughter, Celestine."

"Amen to that, Luke. But listen, what you ought to remember even more is that Barnabas McMillian finagled those four hundred acres of land which used to belong to old Williamson, your father-in-law."

"I shan't ever forget that. That's where I met my Lucy, and that's where I met Williamson's thieving, sadistic overseer, Amos Greer."

"My God, we're going back in time, aren't we?" Jedidiah cackled as he leaned back in his chair and shook his head. "One of the bright spots in my mind about you, Luke, is when you went after that son of a bitch and beat the hell out of him and fired him off the Williamson land. That surprised everybody in the county, believe you me."

"I'm not a fighting man as a rule, you know that, Jedidiah. But he really riled me, treating those helpless slaves the way he did. And all the time he was cheating poor old Williamson, backed, of course, by my father, Henry Bouchard." Luke turned away, strode to the window, and stood looking out for a long moment, wrestling with the emotions this nostalgic reminder of the past had evoked. "My father thought I was a milksop. He had the same contempt for me as he had for his own father, old Lucien. He looked down on idealists, because all he could see was profit and greed and taking land away from people who didn't know how to hold it. But he didn't know how to use it, to make it work for him. And he didn't know human nature. And that's all I'll ever say again about my father, Jedidiah."

"I understand that perfectly well. I'm sorry I had to

bring up these things. But what I'm getting at, Luke, is that I've managed to buy back that Williamson land, all four hundred acres of it."

"You mean it?"

"I certainly do. Now, I don't think it would be the smartest idea in the world for you to take title, but I'm thinking that maybe you'd like Andy Haskins to take it for the time being."

"I think that's a marvelous idea!" Luke said exultantly, as he came back to stand beside the old lawyer and put his hand on Jedidiah's shoulder. "McMillan did nothing with the land, just used it for his imposing house and his parties and his campaigning. It's rich land, and although it produced more than its share of cotton a generation ago, it should be as fertile by now as Windhaven Plantation. And Andy Haskins is just the man who can redeem it and make it productive again. He'll need more workers, but that's easy for him. He's likable, honest, and generous. I'm sure he'll find worthy tenant farmers in this area who have been down on their luck and would welcome the chance to work for a man like him."

"And maybe one day, when the time is right, Luke," Jedidiah said softly, "you yourself can make it part of Windhaven Plantation."

"I'm not sure I'd want to, to be honest with you, Jedidiah," Luke reflected. "Grandfather was never greedy for the acquisition of land just for its own sake. He was content to do the right thing with what land he had, rotating his crops so that the land would continue to be bountiful. Neither he nor I cared very much about accumulating property, or hoarding in a miserly way the resources of a country that gave us so much opportunity. I know it sounds sanctimonious—"

"No, it doesn't, Luke. Now you listen to me." Jedidiah leaned forward across the table and shook his bony forefinger at the tall, gray-haired grandson of old Lucien Bouchard. "If you'd been born in the North instead of down here in Alabama, Luke Bouchard, you might just find yourself running against U.S. Grant. No, don't shake your head that way and smile, I mean it. Now listen to me. We've come almost a hundred years since the Declaration of Independence, since a band of enterprising colonists broke away from the oppression and the taxes of George

319

III and declared themselves a republic. Well, we had Washington, and then we had Jefferson, and a few good men after that, but those folks who loved the British and didn't really want to see us break away from the English throne scampered on down to Florida and Georgia and set themselves up against all the freedom we were trying to earn."

"I follow you so far, but it's outlandish for you to imply that I could ever have any great political aspirations," Luke chuckled.

"I'm just thinking out loud. It's an old man's prerogative, Luke. One of these days, you'll come to it yourself. Just give me some leeway, because I'm in a very mellow mood right now. And that's the only fee I'm going to charge you for acquiring this Williamson property, by the by."

"I can't argue with that," Luke laughed.

"Well, to continue: when your father was growing up, we had Aaron Burr and that General Wilkinson, who was in cahoots with him. The pair of them really wanted to set up an empire, with a token acknowledgment to imperial Spain. And Burr killed Alexander Hamilton in a duel, taking from us one of the soundest, wisest men we've ever had."

"I'll agree with you on that score."

"Yes, and in the years that followed, all of us—particularly we Southerners—drifted away from the ideals of the founding fathers. The English-lovers got their licks into the deep South, in Florida and Georgia, and they started the landgrabbing. That led to Andy Jackson's shutting the Indians out of the South and putting them on reservations where they'd die and be forgotten."

"I know that only too well. I know how my grandfather sorrowed over what was done to the Creeks," Luke said softly.

"And then we muddled along until that angry old man John Brown went down to Harper's Ferry and got himself hanged and made himself a martyr for the cause of slavery versus freedom. By then, all the South was committed to cotton and to the indolence of having black slaves do the work, and the big plantation owners enjoyed an easy life without any burdens or responsibility."

320

"But as you know also, Jedidiah," Luke softly interposed, "my grandfather and I never countenanced slavery."

"That's precisely my point, Luke. Right now, what you're doing on Windhaven Plantation—arranging it into a sort of commune where whites and blacks work together and share the profits with you, even though you're technically the owner—is something the North would admire. But we hidebound traditionalists in the South can't quite comprehend it. And that's why I say, if you'd been born in the North, with your record for honesty and decency, you might have been nominated to run against the man who won his fame by saying, 'I propose to fight it out on these lines if it takes all summer.' And you see what we're into now, a real debacle if he's reelected."

"Yes, Jedidiah. I feel that in my bones. And from the letters I've had from my son Lucien Edmond, he's preparing for bad times ahead if Grant is reelected, as I'm afraid he will be. But that's enough of reminiscing and saying 'if' and 'but' and 'and'—let's come down to cases. I know that ought to please you, as a lawyer. What do you want me to do with regard to the Williamson acreage?"

"Have Andy Haskins come in here and make an application to the recorder of deeds, because by now we've got an honest one, and he happens to be a friend of mine. And I'll see that he can buy the land for cost. There are a few back taxes due on it, but they aren't excessive."

"Whatever they are, I'll pay them. It's the least I owe Andy, for what he's done for Lucien Edmond and for me," Luke interposed.

"That I don't want to hear about. It's collusion, and we lawyers shy away from things like that," Jedidiah cackled. Then, rising from his desk, his eyes still twinkling, he held out his hand. "You and I, Luke Bouchard, we've survived the worst and we've going to live long enough to see the best come back here. You mark my words."

Luke Bouchard, his beard neatly trimmed to a crisp Van Dyke and wearing a fawn-colored frock coat and trousers, with ruffled shirt and neat blue cravat, glanced admiringly at his wife, Laure, as they waited in the foyer of the red-brick chateau to welcome their visitors this Sunday evening. Laure wore an elegant taffeta gown to match her

321

golden hair, which was pulled back from the temples and sides into a thick chignon at the nape. Never had she seemed more beautiful, more desirable.

They had engaged a new governess for Lucien and Paul and baby Celestine, Clarabelle Hendry, a widow in her early forties whose little boy had died from river fever. Mitzi Sattersfield had recommended her, and she had moved into the red-brick chateau, replacing Clara Mathies, who had left to marry a Montgomery man. The children adored Clarabelle, and because of her own bereavement she lavished them with devotion and affection.

"I can hear Dalbert's horse and buggy coming, Laure," Luke smilingly remarked to his beautiful wife. "They're right on time."

"Hannah will like that. She's taken special pains to give us a very wonderful dinner, and you know how she fusses when it's ready and we aren't," Laure laughingly told him. "By the way, darling, I hope you won't mind if after dinner I take Mitzi off and have a nice long chat with her."

"Of course. Besides, I want to talk with Dalbert and, most of all, with his new clerk, that Hugh."

"Don't you know the rest of his name, Luke dear?"

Luke shook his head. "No. Dalbert just introduced him as Hugh, told me how he'd walked in there a few weeks ago looking for a job, and praised him to the skies."

"Well, it was very gracious of you to invite him to dinner."

"It's strange, Laure, but when I saw him, I had a feeling that I'd known him—I don't know why, it's completely irrational, and yet there it was. To be honest with you, that's why I invited him for dinner tonight. I want to know more about him. He seems like a personable young man. Well, here they are now." Luke opened the door at the sound of the knocker.

"M'sieu Luke, Madame Laure—oh, *mon Dieu*, how wonderful it is to see you again!" irrepressible, petite Mitzi exclaimed as she hurried up to Laure and flung her arms around her. Laure sent her husband an amused glance and then returned Mitzi's embrace with great affection. Dalbert Sattersfield stood by, indulgently smiling, while behind him stood the tall, black-haired clerk, who had been delegated to hold Courtney and Brandon while Mitzi enjoyed her reunion with her former employer. That relationship had be-

322

gun during the Civil War, when John Brunton, whose fiancée Laure Prindeville had been, had transferred the old Rigalle Bank to the Union House. To prevent its being taken over by General Benjamin Butler, the "Beast of New Orleans," he had turned the house into an elegant bordello to entertain high-ranking Union officers and thus camouflaged his real activities. And Mitzi Vourlay had been engaged by Laure as a hostess who greeted the clients—though she had never been one of the girls who went upstairs with them to the private rooms.

"Do come in," Luke urged. Then, to the tall clerk, he said pleasantly, "I must say, for an unmarried man, you're holding those children quite ably."

"Thank you, Mr. Bouchard. You're right about my being a bachelor, but I've always liked children," the clerk replied with a faint smile and a soft, pleasant voice that held the unmistakable inflection of a Creole.

"Mrs. Hendry has the high chairs ready for Courtney and Brandon, as well as for my own adorable little Celestine, Mitzi dear. Do please come in, don't stand on ceremony. Here, do let me take the twins—may I, Mitzi?" Laure gaily urged.

"Mais bien entendu, chérie!" Mitzi happily exclaimed. "M'sieu Entrevois, it was sweet of you to take them for me."

"Entrevois?" Luke echoed, his eyes widening as he turned to look intently at the tall, black-haired clerk.

"Yes, Mr. Bouchard, my name is Hugh Entrevois." As he carefully handed the twins over to Mitzi, the tall man unflinchingly met Luke's probing gaze.

There was a moment of almost intolerable silence which Laure, quickly sensing that something was amiss, broke by exclaiming, "Good gracious, you must all think I'm a perfectly dreadful hostess! Do come on into the dining room. Hannah will be furious with us if we're so much as a minute late."

CHAPTER TWENTY-SIX

Luke Bouchard was grateful for the presence of the children at the table. Six-year-old Lucien sat at his right and three-year-old Paul at his left, while across the table was Laure with Celestine in a high chair solicitously attended by the governess. Mitzi's twins sat on either side of her in high chairs, while her handsome husband, Dalbert, seated next to Courtney, added his own paternal attention from time to time.

As for Hugh Entrevois, he showed flawless table manners, though he did not often enter the conversation. At the beginning of the dinner, Laure politely asked him for news of New Orleans, mentioning that she herself had been born there. From Hugh's replies Luke had the impression that the tall, neatly dressed clerk purposely sought to be evasive, for he limited himself to a few chatty remarks about the special attractions of the Queen City that in no way gave any clue as to his own identity.

As for himself, Luke was guarded in his conversation throughout the dinner. He sought to give no sign that the name Entrevois had raised a sudden, appalling ghost out of the past. At times, when Hannah came into the dining room to refill the goblets with wine and to accept the guests' profuse compliments on the dinner, he glanced sharply at the soft-spoken man across the table from him, but took pains not to prolong that glance.

At last, at a nod from Laure, little Paul and Lucien asked to be excused, and Lucien led his younger brother off to their room, while Mrs. Hendry took Celestine to bed. Laure and Mitzi rose, each of them taking one of the twins, intent on their long-deferred reunion. As Dalbert Sattersfield rose, Luke caught his eye and covertly shook his head, then said aloud, "Dalbert, stay and have some brandy and more coffee. I'd like very much to have a private chat with your new clerk, if you've no objection."

"By all means, Luke. Hugh, you're in safe hands with Mr. Bouchard here. I'd trust him with my life—he not only helped me in my business venture but, thanks to him and his beautiful wife, I have Mitzi and the twins." And then, with a wry smile at Luke, he added, "To be frank with you, Luke, I'm not accustomed to feasting like this. I'd just as soon sit here and relax with the coffee and the brandy you offered."

"I'll send in Hannah at once, Dalbert. Let's go to my study, Mr. Entrevois," Luke proposed. As the clerk rose, Luke went to the kitchen to ask Hannah to bring fresh hot coffee for his guest and serve their best brandy, then returned to the dining room to beckon the clerk to follow him.

They walked into the study. Luke closed the door and then turned to Hugh Entrevois. "I must confess," he began somewhat uneasily, "that when I heard your surname for the first time tonight, I was taken aback. I'll come to the point and tell you why. My grandfather, Lucien Bouchard, was in love with a girl in France named Edmée de Courent. She preferred to marry his older brother, Jean, and they went to Haiti. There, Jean was killed in the uprising of slaves, and Edmée fled to Mobile, entering into an agreement of indenture with a ship's captain in order to save her life. In Mobile, my grandfather paid to free her from her indenture, and she went to New Orleans and married a Philippe Entrevois, whose grandmother had been a *griffe*."

He waited a moment, studying the blandly handsome face of the clerk, which reflected hardly a flicker of emotion. "Help yourself to some brandy over there at the sideboard, Mr. Entrevois. I'll have one with you," he proposed.

"Thank you, Mr. Bouchard. I believe I will." Luke watched him walk over to the sideboard, catlike, fluid of movement, and his eyes narrowed. He was remembering how his own half brother, Mark, had been very nearly entrapped by Edmée's daughter, Louisette, who had called herself Louisa Voisin and who had become the tool of the corrupt gambler and slave-trader, Pierre Lourat. Louisette Entrevois had purposely changed her name, he remembered, so that if her plan to force young Mark into marrying her was successful, she could enter the Bouchard family and strike back at old Lucien, who had disavowed her mother because of his idealistic honor. He found himself trembling as he watched Hugh deftly pour about an inch of the golden liquid into an exquisitely wrought snifter, then fill another, and turn back to him with one in each hand. *At least,* he thought to himself, *even if there's only coincidence in the similarity of names, this man has breeding, has good blood in him from somewhere.*

"Thank you, Mr. Entrevois," he said aloud as he accepted one of the snifters and raised it to his lips. Hugh Entrevois imitated him, and the two men stood measuring each other with their eyes.

"Forgive my being so blunt, Mr. Entrevois," he said after a moment, carefully choosing his words. "Are you by any chance the son of Louisette Entrevois and my half brother, Mark Bouchard?"

With surprise, the man facing him nodded, and again there was that suave, soft smile.

"Not of Louisette, Mr. Bouchard. But of Rosa, her half sister and, yes, your half brother Mark. It's true, I've Bouchard blood in my veins."

"Then, in God's name, man, why in all this time haven't you come forward to declare yourself a Bouchard?" Luke saw that the snifter in his hand was shaking from the sudden wave of emotion that surged through him.

Hugh deliberately took a sip of his brandy, then walked toward the window. He took a deep breath and then turned back to face Luke Bouchard. "For several reasons, Mr. Bouchard. For one thing, I've black blood in me. Oh yes, it's true. But you see, I can pass for white, and I'm not ashamed to say that I've done so all my life."

"Go on." Luke's voice was hoarse and unsteady.

"You see, Mr. Bouchard, Philippe Entrevois went to one of the quadroon balls in New Orleans after the death of his wife, Edmée. There, he arranged with the mother of a very attractive quadroon named Diana to provide for them both and to install Diana in a cottage on Rampart Street. Well, Rosa was born from that union. Philippe Entrevois took Rosa into his own house along with Diana. The plan was that everyone would believe that Diana was his slave housekeeper and Rosa her illegitimate child by an unknown father."

"Go on." Luke was very pale and terse.

"That child, as I said, Mr. Bouchard, was my mother, Rosa. And after the death of Philippe Entrevois, when both Rosa and her half-sister, Louisette, were on their uppers, they went to work for Pierre Lourat, the gambler."

"I know a great deal about him. Go on with your story, man!" Luke demanded.

"As you will, sir." Hugh inclined his head in a kind of mock obeisance. "Young Mark Bouchard came to New Orleans with his father and fell in love with Louisette. But Louisette let him go to bed with my mother, Rosa, and that's how I was conceived—in the year of 1836, to be exact, Mr. Bouchard."

"And Mark Bouchard never knew this?"

Hugh shook his head. "Pierre Lourat was stabbed to death and Louisette threw herself into the river. My mother, Rosa, told me when I was a little boy that she was very sure that Louisette had avenged her shame on the gambler and then committed suicide. Well then, as for my mother, she became manager of the pleasure house which Pierre Lourat had owned. Soon after my birth, a wealthy man from Ohio visited New Orleans and decided to settle there. He bought the house of pleasure and kept my mother on as his mistress."

"My God!" Luke softly ejaculated, shaking his head. He took a swallow of brandy and grimaced. His eyes did not leave the tall, black-haired man opposite him.

"Then," Hugh continued, "when I was five, she told me who my real father was. She told me that, because I had the taint of black blood in my veins, I would have to learn how to make my own way and not seek any alliance with the family of Mark Bouchard. My mother died in 1845, when I was nine. And she seldom spoke of Mark Bouchard after the time she first told me about him, except to say that she was ashamed of the way in which she had been used by my Aunt Louisette, and that she did not ever wish to remember Mark Bouchard again."

"I see." Luke took another sip of brandy, then set the snifter down on the escritoire. "And what happened to you after your mother's death?"

"The man from Ohio didn't want to have a 'black child' around the house of pleasure. He said it would drive away customers." Hugh uttered a cynical chuckle. "So he placed me as a foster child with a couple whom he knew could not have children, and they brought me up as their son. They were poor and, at times, they resented me because I was a drain on them. So when I was fifteen I ran away and went to work for another house of pleasure on Rampart Street. I would tell wealthy gentlemen of the joys they could obtain in this house, you understand."

"Yes, I'm quite familiar with the ways in which New Orleans houses of pleasure are touted to patrons," Luke tartly told him. "And then?"

Hugh shrugged diffidently. "Well, after that, I lived by my wits as best I could. I worked on the docks, and when the war came, I even helped smuggle contraband to Baritaria. As a matter of fact, I was once caught by Union troops, who could have hanged me. I managed to talk them out of it, and they put me in a guardhouse tent and said they'd wait for the captain to pass judgment on me in the morning. I was lucky enough to escape. Well, after the war, I learned to play faro, and I did reasonably well until one night a drunken gentleman was ill-advised enough to accuse me of cheating. I had to kill him to defend myself, and I went to Natchez, where I worked for a time as a clerk in a store very much like Mr. Sattersfield's."

"And now you've come here to Lowndesboro and you're working for Sattersfield. What prompted you to do that?"

Again, the black-haired man shrugged. "I suppose I was tired of all these changes, and perhaps, too, I wanted to find out for myself about the Bouchards. I'd been told in Natchez that Windhaven Plantation had been restored and was thriving. So I came here, you might say, out of curiosity. As it happened, Mr. Sattersfield needed a clerk, and here I am."

Luke began to pace the study, his face taut with concern. Suddenly, he turned to Hugh and demanded, "Have you a birth certificate to prove you're the child of Rosa and of Mark Bouchard?"

Hugh shook his head, his smile deepening. "I'm afraid not. You'll have to take my word for it, Mr. Bouchard. After all, it *was* an illegitimate birth, and because my mother was ashamed at being used as my aunt's slave girl—that was how the little farce was played with Mark

329

Bouchard, she told me that time she revealed who my father really was—I daresay she would hardly have wished to acknowledge the legality of my existence."

"Nevertheless, you are a Bouchard," Luke dully retorted. "What you don't know is that when Mark Bouchard deserted his wife, Maybelle, the younger sister of my dead first wife, I saw to it that he was given a third of Grandfather's legacy so that he could never claim we had cheated him out of his inheritance. And yet, because you are a Bouchard and Mark's issue, I can't ignore you. Tell me, does clerking appeal to you?"

"Well, it's as good as anything else, and it's an honest living, I'll say that for it."

Luke curtly nodded, paced the floor of the study for a moment, then abruptly turned back to Hugh. "It so happens that there are four hundred acres of land downriver which once belonged to a man named Edward Williamson, who was the father of my dead first wife, Lucy. They were purchased by a carpetbagger by the name of Barnabas McMillian, who died two years ago. My attorney has just arranged for the purchase of that land in the name of Andy Haskins, who worked for my son in Texas before settling here two years ago. He's married and doing very well."

Hugh Entrevois nodded, his eyebrows mildly arching as if to ask what all this had to do with him, but he did not speak. Holding the brandy snifter in his right hand, he studied Luke Bouchard with dispassionate calm.

"I'm told that you worked as a roustabout on the New Orleans docks," Luke resumed.

"Yes, I did for a time."

"Well, you look strong enough. Andy can use some good workers on the old Williamson land. I think you'd be paid more than what Sattersfield can give you, and you could be your own man there."

"But Mr. Sattersfield seems to need me at the store," Hugh began.

"That's a problem easily solved, I can assure you. On my acreage, there's a black man named Buford Phelps, who used to work for the Freedmen's Bureau and came here thinking that perhaps I was one of those oppressive plantation owners. He liked the idea of my commune so much that he left his job and came to work for me. Well, he's strained his back working in the fields, and since he did a good deal of clerical work before he came here, he'd welcome a chance to work in a store. I'm sure that Dalbert Sattersfield would agree to him as a substitute."

"It's funny that you should take such an interest in me, Mr. Bouchard." Hugh took a sip of his brandy and set the snifter down on the escritoire.

"I'm trying to be fair and just. My half brother, Mark, went away swearing vengeance on me even though I'd arranged to give him a full third of my grandfather's legacy. Well, you're his issue, there's no gainsaying it. In a sense, you've a right to some advantage here, now that you've come back as a Bouchard. Legally, it's quite true that it would be difficult for you to claim any monies due you. But, ethically and morally, I feel I must honor the family connection. What I propose to do is this: I'll put you in charge of recruiting men to work those four hundred acres—though it's really too late in the season to expect any crops except perhaps some vegetables, especially yams—and if you prove yourself capable and trustworthy, I'll have Andy Haskins deed over a hundred of those acres to you next year. After that, you can make up your mind if you want to stay here and settle down, build a house, be a farmer, perhaps even marry and have a family. Moreover, if you decide to do that and you need capital to get started, I'll lend it to you without any interest. Does that seem fair enough?"

"A great deal more than that, Mr. Bouchard." Hugh uttered a soft little laugh. "I'd like to try my skill on the land for once."

"If you're successful, you'll show that you're far more gifted than your unfortunate father was. Mark never cared for land, except for the money it would provide for his extravagances. But I shan't speak ill of the dead. And, from this moment on, you and I will have the relationship of partners, in one sense."

"You know, that's really damned decent of you, Mr. Bouchard. Here's my hand on it. I'll give it a good try, I can promise you that." He came forward and extended his hand, which Luke shook.

"Then it's agreed. Tomorrow, we'll ride over to see Andy Haskins and I'll tell him what's been arranged. Then I'll take you to my lawyer's office and sign a contract with you in which I, acting as factor, appoint you foreman of the old Williamson land at a stipulated salary. But it's up to you to recruit workers and get them started clearing out the weeds, building huts for their own living quarters, and seeing what can be done about that big house McMillan left standing there. I promise you, you'll work hard, and because you're only a short ride from me, I intend to visit regularly to see how you're coming along."

"I expect that. And thanks again."

"Good. Now let's go back to tell Dalbert of our new arrangement," Luke Bouchard urged.

Before the Sattersfields drove back to Lowndesboro that night, Luke Bouchard had brought Buford Phelps to meet Dalbert. The latter expressed himself quite willing to accept Buford as his new clerk, and Buford gratefully accompanied the Satterfields home. He would begin work in the store the very next morning, and he would make his quarters where Hugh Entrevois had roomed. Hugh Entrevois spent the night at the red-brick chateau in one of the guest rooms, breakfasted with Luke and Laure the next morning, and then rode with Luke to Montgomery. There the two men had Jedidiah Danforth draw up a contract stipulating that Hugh should be foreman of the Williamson land, whose title was to be registered in the name of Andy Haskins that very morning.

This done, Luke instructed Hugh to meet him that evening at Andy Haskins's house an hour before sundown, urging him to spend the day recruiting workers for the four hundred acres of old Williamson land. There were to be as many blacks as whites, if possible, particularly men who had worked on farms in the past and were familiar with the raising of crops and their harvesting. Luke suggested that there was still a chance of devoting perhaps twenty acres to cotton with a late fall yield, sufficient to prove that the Williamson land was still fertile and capable of excellent productivity, after being allowed to lie fallow for the past several years.

That evening, when Luke Bouchard knocked at the door of Andy's house, he found that Hugh Entrevois had already arrived and had introduced himself to the one-armed Tennesseean and his wife, Jessica. Andy, with his good nature and utter lack of cynicism, told Luke that he felt that Hugh could do a good job for him. Already the former store clerk had been able to enlist the services of a dozen quite capable men who would report the next morning to the Williamson property. Three of these had formerly been carpenters and could at once start building the quarters for the field workers. Two others had been employed in cotton gins or in the planting and harvesting of this staple crop which so epitomized the agrarian resourcefulness of the old South.

It was indeed an excellent beginning, perhaps even more successful than Luke himself might have believed. Yet when he rode back home in the gathering darkness to Windhaven Plantation, he turned his horse into the fields and rode toward the gentle slope which permitted the easiest access to the top of the towering bluff where his grandfather and Dimarte lay in their eternal sleep. Securing the reins of his horse to the branch of a live oak tree, he ascended the bluff.

Turning the day's events over in his mind as he walked, Luke had the strange presentiment that all of this had been preordained years before. It was as if, after he had eliminated the dreadful threat of the Cournier brothers, whose plotting had put Windhaven Plantation to its severest trials, he was destined to meet a new and sinister menace, lurking beyond the bourne of even his own awareness. Perhaps perversely, he told himself, he had countenanced and even encouraged this menace, in offering such generous terms to the illegitimate son of his amoral half brother, Mark. He thought again, as old Lucien must have done, of how divergent the various members of a family could be: Lucien, the true patriarch of the Bouchards, had been diametrically opposed to his hedonistic and ruthless brother, Jean. And Luke's own father, Henry, had been very much like Jean, and so had Mark Bouchard. Yet he himself, born of his father's rape of an innocent teenage Georgia girl, had retained the idealism of his grandfather. Against this family history, what would it mean to have Mark's bastard son working nearby? Had Luke himself gone out of his way to create danger to the Bouchards? Was it truly wise to have admitted Hugh Entrevois into his life, offering him a post of trust so close to Windhaven Plantation?

As he climbed to the top of the bluff in the warm evening and in the silence broken only by the twittering of the night birds, he told himself that, even if Hugh Entrevois proved to be an enemy, there could be no one left to challenge the integrity of the Bouchards. The Courniers had had no issue, and Hugh was a bachelor.

Thus he wrestled with his conscience, telling himself again and again that he could not have acted otherwise, once he had learned the identity of Dalbert Sattersfield's itinerant clerk. When Mark Bouchard had ridden away, defying Luke and vowing vengeance—even after Luke's generosity in granting his half brother a third of old Lucien's savings in gold—Luke had been constantly tortured by the lingering doubts that out of his own selfish inclinations he had driven Mark away and salved his own conscience by giving Mark that gold. Perhaps he had given it to him in order to be rid of him once and for all, so that he might be free to lead an untroubled existence with his young bride, Lucy, free to carry on his grandfather's precepts in the management of Windhaven Plantation.

Yes, he said to himself as he came at last to the summit of the bluff, in the farthermost recesses of his mind, there had dwelt all these years a vague concern that he had not acted out of unselfish generosity, but rather out of suppressed hatred for his half brother. Perhaps he had wished to push Mark out of his life forever. Well, if that were really true and if he had the courage after all these years to admit it, then it was best that he should face squarely the legacy of that old hatred: the presence of Mark's son in his life. He remembered from his reading of Shakespeare, how young Hamlet had failed to solve his dreadful problems because of his own indecision. Yes, it was better by far to face up to Hugh Entrevois, to repay with kindness whatever wrong might have been done to him and to his father, Mark, so long ago. The justice of this course of action was clear, and overrode any possible danger.

He knelt upon old Lucien's grave, bowed his head, and, as if his grandfather were there to hear him, spoke in a low, trembling voice to relate how this incredible meeting with Hugh had taken place, and how he had decided to do what he had just done.

"Grandfather, this Hugh Entrevois was conceived illegitimately in a cruel jest whereby the daughter of your faithless sweetheart, Edmée, forced her half sister to accommodate Mark as if Rosa were her slave. I could not blame him, in all justice, if he had come back to hate all the

334

Bouchards because of the wrongs done to him. But, Grand-father, you whose spirit has inspired all of us since the earliest times of the Bouchards, I ask you to search my heart and tell me whether I did not drive Mark away out of my own selfish self-interest. For if I did, then surely I owe a debt to his son. All I can do is pray God that, in seeking to pay it as I have now done, I do not bring peril upon Windhaven Plantation."

He knelt there in silence a long moment, eyes closed and head bowed, and when he rose, the moon had ascended to its full zenith in the heavens. He touched the grave of Di-marte and said a prayer for her. Then he started back down the slope, thinking that perhaps Laure would be worried about him. When he reached the tree where his patient horse stood waiting for his return, he heard in the distance the sound of an owl, a single, forlorn hooting call, and he shivered with that presentiment which still lingered within him.

CHAPTER TWENTY-SEVEN

By mid-August in this election year of 1872, Luke Bouchard's misgivings about Hugh Entrevois had been considerably eased. He and Andy Haskins had visited the old Williamson plantation at least twice a week, and both were satisfied that the tall, soft-spoken Creole had made an excellent start in preparing the land for cultivation and furnishing quarters for his workers, who now numbered twenty-six. He had also begun to refurbish the house, which the carpetbagger Barnabas McMillan had used only for his orgies and the fomenting of trouble against any bona fide Republican candidate for office.

Of the twenty-six workers, fifteen were black and eleven white, and their experience as carpenters, blacksmiths, stablemen, and field hands augured well for a diversification of enterprise on the four hundred acres. Some fifty acres had been immediately cultivated for the growing of yams, beans, okra, and cabbage, as well as melons and some field corn. Another twenty, the richest of the entire plot, were devoted to cotton. Four of Hugh's workers had constructed pens for hogs and cattle, and Luke lent the Creole two thousand dollars for the purchase of five sows and a boar, eight heifers and a bull, and a dozen horses. Two of the horses were dray animals, hitched to plows to turn up the sod in some of the acreage, which would prepare it for planting next spring. The other horses would be used by the Creole's workers to go on errands, bring back supplies, and confer, when necessary, with Luke and Andy Haskins. Luke instructed his own foreman, Marius Thornton, to work with Hugh and his men and acquaint them with the going market price for their crops, as well as give them such planting information as had proved so profitable at Windhaven Plantation.

The one-armed Tennesseean had begun to devote a greater portion of time to campaigning for the state legislature and had delegated to Matthew Rensler the post of foreman of his fifty acres, on which old Horatio Bambach and Jessica had settled over two years earlier. Twice during the first week of August, for example, Andy appeared at town meetings in Lowndesboro and Montgomery to declare his political stand and to outline his plans for fair and honest dealing with his constituents. He drew considerable applause, and the *Advertiser* printed an editorial recommending him over Oliver Perkins, the choice of the Democrats to replace their own incumbent, Cletus Adams, whose corrupt and dissolute way of life had thoroughly discredited him.

Luke was optimistic about Andy's chances for election, and he found fresh cause for this optimism in the exceptional unity that prevailed in the Republican Convention in Montgomery this month. The Alabama Republicans declared that the state ticket would be composed entirely of native Unionists, and that the major offices of governor, secretary of state, and treasurer would go to men from northern Alabama, a region that the Democratic state convention had ignored in selecting its candidates.

The leading Republican candidate for the office of governor was Unionist David P. Lewis of Huntsville, an ex-Democrat who had joined the Republicans after the 1868 presidential election. Since that time, he had not been actively embroiled in Republican party quarrels. He had few enemies in either major party and therefore appeared to be the most desirable candidate among the scalawags in the Republican party. All of Lewis's colleagues on this year's ticket were native white Southerners. In all, it was a ticket that united Alabama Republicans for the first time in at least three years, and it appeared to offend no influential group.

William Blount and his two associates called on Luke during the third week of August to ask his aid in speaking on behalf of Lewis, and he readily agreed. The dissatisfaction of Alabama Democrats with the record of the incumbent governor, Robert B. Lindsay, was a further indication that the Republicans had more than an even chance of capturing this year's highest state office. The Democratic gubernatorial candidate, Thomas Hord Herndon of Mobile, was

338

bound to appeal to former supporters of the Confederacy who remembered Herndon's record as a secessionist and Confederate soldier during the war. But some Democrats feared that Herndon's ticket would alienate the black voters. Clearly, this was a heaven-sent opportunity for the Republicans.

On Friday night of this third week of August, accordingly, Luke Bouchard mounted his roan stallion and rode to Lowndesboro to speak at a political meeting. His route took him along the gently flowing Alabama River, and his mind was filled with thoughts of the past, of how his beloved grandfather had followed this same trail all the way from Mobile almost a century ago. He thought of Emataba and his villagers, taken by soldiers from this beautiful country with its forests and glades, and set down in the midst of a desolate plain. He thought, as well, of Sangrodo and his tribe of Comanches who called themselves the Wanderers—for this they truly were now, having fled across the border into Mexico to pursue a new agrarian life in place of the old ways of hunting the buffalo and settling where they would. They, too, had been an impediment to the greedy ambition of those who lusted for their lands. Luke asked himself what this nation might have become if all white men had been like his grandfather, bringing about an alliance between white men and red so that all could work and prosper on the rich land.

As he neared his destination, Luke began to think of the speech he would make. His primary purpose, of course—aside from supporting Andy's and Lewis's candidacies—was to speak out against corruption in government, wherever and however it occurred. On the local level that meant support of the Republicans. On the national level, Luke continued to be intrigued and impressed by the Liberal Republicans' efforts to speak out against the evils of the Grant administration, and to promote their candidate, Horace Greeley.

Luke had always admired the founder of the *New York Tribune*, now sixty-one years of age, ever since he had attempted to provide for the laboring classes an inexpensive newspaper that would be both honorable and intelligent. Greeley had supported protective tariffs and many social reforms. His humanitarian hatred of war had often embarrassed Lincoln's administration; yet at the end of the Civil

War, he had generously advocated amnesty for all Southerners. Although he had been among the first to support Grant, like Luke himself, he had been appalled by the corruption of the Grant administration and thus encouraged the growth of the Liberal Republicans. His candidacy for the presidency had been recently strengthened immeasurably by the fact that the national Democratic Party had also endorsed him in July, during its convention in Baltimore.

But in the state of Alabama, Luke ruefully reflected, it would be well nigh impossible for men like himself to support Greeley. Because Greeley was the Democratic choice, and because the state and national candidates were on the same ballot, a vote for Greeley would mean a vote for the very Democrats whom Andy and Luke both were opposing, on the state level. Luke realized that, in the end, he would probably be compelled to vote for Grant, simply to make certain that good Republicans would be elected in the state along with the incumbent president; to vote Democratic would mean that he would endorse the clandestine, murderous activities of the Ku Klux Klan, which the Democrats had so unscrupulously used to further their political party. And he could only pray that if Grant were reelected, this bluff soldier who had been acclaimed by the North as an intrepid hero would have wisdom enough to pluck away at the rank weeds of corruption that grew about him and to restore the Republican party to its rightful principles, those laid down by the martyred Lincoln.

Andy Haskins, Dalbert Sattersfield, and Buford Phelps warmly greeted Luke as he dismounted from the roan stallion, tied the reins to the hitching post, and followed them both toward the town hall. There was a good attendance, at least two hundred citizens, Dalbert enthusiastically informed him. And David P. Lewis himself had promised to put in an appearance and speak to the crowd.

The meeting was an exceptional success. Luke's speech was short and to the point, and greeted by great applause. Then he introduced Andy Haskins, speaking warmly of the one-armed Tennesseean's war record and steadfast loyalty on the Texas ranch, and underlined the facts that Andy now owned land, was married and expecting a child, and that he was truly a man of the people who would work for the people in the state legislature.

Dalbert Sattersfield also introduced Andy, and then the

340

young Tennesseean made his own speech. His directness and candor, together with his friendly, almost self-effacing demeanor, won him enthusiastic applause. Next David P. Lewis ascended the rostrum and spoke for about ten minutes on the need for all loyal Unionists to support the Republican ticket so that the party might withstand Democratic attempts to steal votes, particularly from the freed blacks.

"We must show the nation," he firmly declared, "that the Republican Party in Alabama is one guided by Southern whites and sustained by black voters. Remember, the Democrats will have difficulties this fall because they themselves want to shelve Governor Lindsay." And he concluded with a flattering remark directed at Andy Haskins's campaign, stating that the resurgence of a young Southern-born campaigner on the Republican ticket was indeed a fortunate omen and indicated that, perhaps at last, the North was ending its vindictive tyranny over the South and allowing the South to choose its best men to express the will of its people.

After the meeting, Luke, Andy, Dalbert, and Buford Phelps returned to the back of the store, and the one-armed former Confederate officer brought out a bottle of old French cognac to toast Andy Haskins's campaign.

"Well, Dalbert," Luke genially asked with a smile at Buford, "are you satisfied with Buford here behind the counter?"

"Absolutely! He's already made many friends among my customers and brought in a few freed blacks who never used to patronize me. In fact, I'm seriously thinking of increasing his salary," Dalbert cheerfully avowed. Then, in a more serious vein, he pursued, "And now it's my turn to ask you if my former clerk is working up to *your* satisfaction, Luke."

"Very much so. He's got himself a good, hard-working crew, and you wouldn't recognize that weed-ridden acreage. Strong new huts for the workers, the house even has a new coat of paint, and the crops are already showing good promise for a fall harvest. Naturally, he's going to give you the first pick of fruits and vegetables, and maybe you can use a side or two of salted pork."

"I can always use that if the price is right," Dalbert smilingly agreed. "Here, let me refill your glasses. And now, a

341

toast to my wife, Mitzi, who told me just this morning that we're going to have another Sattersfield.".

"Well, now, that's wonderful news! I'm happy for you, Dalbert," Luke lifted his glass. "And Andy's going to be a father too, just about the time he's swept into office by a landslide of sensible voters!"

"I hope you're right, Mr. Luke—I mean, about Jessica's being all right and such—you know, I—well, this is her first baby and I've never—"

They began to chuckle at Andy's obvious embarrassment, and all of them reassured him that it would be a fine, strong boy who would one day take his father's place in the legislature, or perhaps even the governor's mansion. On that happy note, Luke and Andy left the store and rode back to their homes.

The heat had been oppressive all this August Sunday, intensified by the humidity from the Alabama River. Luke and Laure had kept Lucien and Paul inside most of the day, greatly to their displeasure, and he had made up for it by playing games with both little boys most of this afternoon till supper. Tomorrow, he decided, he would ride into Montgomery and give the *Advertiser* an account of the successful Friday meeting at Lowndesboro. During Andy Haskins's speech, he had jotted down some of the young Tennesseean's remarks, and found them particularly quotable. They would help to get votes from Montgomery's influential citizens, he was certain.

It seemed hard to believe that two years had gone by, two years in which he himself had run for the legislature and been defeated. The birth of his daughter, Celestine, and the success of his adopted son, Lopasuta, had more than made up for what he and Laure had suffered at Barnabas McMillan's hands. He had peace now, and serene contentment with his life. By next year, the transfers of the separate parcels of land that had once been Windhaven Plantation would have been effected by Jedidiah Danforth so that all of the acreage that had once belonged to venerable old Lucien would be restored to a strong, unified, and thriving Windhaven Plantation.

For himself, he could be thankful that even the stifling heat did not seem to sap his physical energy too much; at fifty-six, his health remained excellent—a blessing no

342

money in the world could buy. And in his union with Laure there was that indescribably priceless combination of spiritual and physical love to bind them. Yes, in all bounties in this new life of his, God had been generous.

He was happiest of all for Andy Haskins. He felt that in a sense he had given new purpose to Andy's life. And now, from what Lucien Edmond wrote him, Andy's friend, Joe Duvray, had become a full-fledged partner in expanding Windhaven Range. Joe, like Andy, was happily married, and he already had his first son. Both of these loyal men had added courage and strength to Windhaven; allies and defenders like these would make Windhaven continue to grow and prosper. No, it was not wealth and power that brought contentment, but discipline and work and prayer and a reliance upon good friends to give a relish and purpose to life.

Then he caught his breath, suddenly remembering, Toward the end of May, Laure had told him that she thought it wouldn't be very long before they had an addition to their family. In all the furor of getting Andy Haskins to accept his political debut, then the Klan's murderous attack on his son Lopasuta, and finally the unforeseen encounter with Diana's daughter's son, he'd given very little thought to that exciting prediction. Well, that certainly didn't speak well for his role as Laure's devoted husband and lover! He felt his pulses tingle at the thought of how he would make it up to her, and reassure her that he hadn't fallen back into what she had teasingly used to call his "old sobersides" nature.

The chateau was silent now, and in the cloudless August sky the half-moon sent down its pale silvery tracery on the twin towers. Making his way to Laure's bedroom door, Luke knocked gently and entered, silently closing the door behind him. In the darkness of the room, he could see his beautiful wife standing at the window, her body silhouetted by the faint light which filtered in through the partly drawn shutters. Her hair, to his delight, was unbound and fell in a soft cascade nearly to her waist. She wore a blue cotton wrapper, and her feet were bare. He felt himself trembling with the sudden urgency of protective love and fierce desire that she never failed to rouse in him.

He came to her noiselessly and bent to kiss the nape of her neck, his hands lightly caressing her rounded shoulders. With a little sob of joy, Laure turned, locking her arms around his neck and straining to him as her lips met his. "My dearest, how wonderful that you should come to my summons!" she whispered when the kiss was done.

In the darkness, he stared into her exquisite face, meeting her eyes and seeing the whimsical little smile curving her red lips.

"Oh yes, Luke my darling," she murmured, pressing herself against him till he could feel the swelling of her bosom. "I was waiting for you. I sent thoughts to make you come to me. Do you remember reading that story in Lord Bulwer-Lytton's anthology, that Greek myth about the Thessalian sorceress who summoned her lover from afar by incantation? I was pretending I was she just now, my dear one."

"And the proof is that I am here. You are still the sorceress who draws me to you in unending desire and adoration, my beloved Laure," he told her as he lifted her and carried her to the wide bed.

It was well after midnight when, fitfully emerging from a dreamless sleep, he heard a hoarse voice shouting anxiously, "Mr. Luke—Mr. Luke, please, please wake up!"

The urgency in that voice made him spring out of bed; then, remembering, he looked anxiously down to make certain that Laure had not been awakened by the clamor. He bent to kiss her cheek and earlobe. Then, drawing on his britches, he tiptoed to the door and opened it, a finger to his lips to caution the intruder.

It was Hughie Mendicott, a worried look on his face. "Mr. Luke, there's a black man that come from Andy Haskins's place, saying there's terrible goin's-on over there! The Klan's out and that's where they went tonight, Mr. Luke! I couldn't find out any more—that black man was so scared, he just ran off!"

"My God! And Jessica with child—Hughie, do me a favor and saddle my roan, I'll be down in a minute. Can you and Dan Munroe go with me?"

"Sure we can, Mr. Luke. I already told Dan what was happenin'. He's got hisself a pistol all primed and loaded, and he's just waitin' the word!"

"Then get three horses, and we'll ride there. I'm glad you brought me the news. My God, and it's all because

Andy's running as a Republican!" Luke said to himself, for already Hughie had hurried back out to the stable.

Luke dressed quickly, then closed the door gently so as not to disturb his sleeping wife, and hurried to join them. From the closet in the study, he took the Spencer carbine and its cousin, the Spencer rifle, which he had brought from Windhaven Range six years earlier.

Hughie Mendicott had armed himself with an old six-shooter, but Luke shook his head and handed him the carbine. "This'll do you a lot more good, Hughie. That old pepperpot is obsolete by now—it's a lot older than the ones my son Lucien Edmond's vaqueros used on the range back in Texas. And it'll likely go off in your hand the first time you pull the trigger. Use this. You can pump seven shots with good effect. Now let's ride!"

Twenty minutes later, they rode into the winding narrow driveway which led to Andy Haskins's little house, and the three men dismounted, their weapons readied. Luke swore under his breath as he saw the flickering flames leap from a half-consumed wooden cross planted about a hundred yards south of the house.

Then, as he strode to the door and called out, "Andy, it's Luke!" he saw three men clad in the infamous white hooded robes of the Klan lying sprawled on the ground, one almost at the door of the house, the other two near the burning cross.

Andy Haskins slowly opened the door, warily peering out, the barrel of his Spencer carbine poked out ahead of him. As he recognized Luke Bouchard, he opened the door and came out, calling back, "You just stay in bed, Jessica honey, now don't you fret, everything's fine, we drove the scum off, thank God!

"I certainly wasn't expecting anything like this, Mr. Luke." Andy shook his head and uttered a long, heavy sigh. "About a dozen of them came up the road from downriver a spell, can't rightly say where they were coming from, and the next thing I knew, they'd planted that damned wooden cross of theirs and set fire to it. Then the leader, he was in a black robe, called out that I was a dirty, black-hearted Republican and that I should come out to judgment. I took a shot at him but missed, dagnabit!"

"So it's politics all over again, just the way it was two years ago for me when Barnabas McMillan and his Demo-

345

cratic backers called out the Klan," Luke said, half to himself. "But you only have five men here."

"Four now, I'm afraid," Andy's face fell. "Matt Rensler
took a bullet in the side, and it's real bad. His friend Burt's
doing the best he can for him right now, but I don't think
even a doctor's going to help. Anyway, those two and the
Ardmore brothers and Jasper Cooper—now there was a
brave man, Luke. All he had was a pitchfork, but he came
running at one of them just after he'd shot poor Matt, and
he stuck that dirty, white-robed skunk right in the throat
and stretched him out, over there by the cross. I know I
picked one off after I missed the leader, and Burt got one
himself with his old Whitworth. I don't think they expected
my folks here to have any weapons. Trouble was, they
were circling the house and I was scared sick that maybe
Jessica would catch a stray bullet if I opened up on them. I
tried to play 'possum most of the time."

"Who was the man who came to give Hughie the warning about them?" Luke anxiously asked.

"There's an old darkie, some folks say he's touched in
the head, he sells watermelon and pickled preserves and
such. Happens he was just walking down the road when all
of a sudden he saw those skunks ride up. His name's Ezekiel Tompkins, and he knows you, Mr. Luke. First thing he
thought of was running as fast as he could to tell you what
was going on. Poor old man, it must have taken him nigh
unto an hour to reach Windhaven Plantation from here on
foot, but he did it."

"I didn't see anyone around when Hughie and Dan and
I saddled up and rode out here, Andy. I'll try tomorrow to
locate this Ezekiel Tompkins and see that he gets something for his trouble."

Even as he spoke, Jasper Cooper hurried up, still clutching his bloodied pitchfork, his sweaty face twisted in grief.
"Mistah Andy, suh, poah ol' Matt's daid, suh. Mistah Burt
tole me to tell you—ain't no use gittin' no doctuh now,
nossuh! He sho' was a fine man, Mistah Matt was—dem
dirty, yeller-livered Ku Kluxers murdered him for fair,
Mistah Andy!"

"I know they did, Jasper," Andy softly said with another
agonized sigh. "We'll bury him, Jasper, and we'll all hold a
service for him. I'll miss him a lot."

"Wut you wants us to do 'bout dem daid Ku Kluxers,

346

Mistah Andy?" Jasper Cooper was very close to tears, his stubby fingers twisting and clenching around the handle of the pitchfork as he spoke.

"I'll bury them myself, Jasper. But first I'm going to pull their hoods off and see if I know any of them."

"And I," Luke Bouchard fiercely declared, "am going to ride into town first thing tomorrow morning and write a piece for the *Advertiser* demanding that Governor Lindsay call out the militia to quell the murderous attacks of these cowards who come skulking like jackals at night and are too ashamed of what they do to show their faces!"

CHAPTER TWENTY-EIGHT

Shaken by the tragedy that had struck so close to Windhaven Plantation and that brought back abhorrent memories of other depredations of the Ku Klux Klan, Luke Bouchard rode early the next morning to the office of the Montgomery *Advertiser* and demanded an interview with the editor. He detailed what had taken place the previous night and asked permission to write a story that would be not so much a political harangue against the Klan as an appeal to the sanity of the decent citizens of Alabama. The editor, who shared his views, gave him a free hand, reserving only the right to correct such language as might be too intemperate—understandable though it would be because of Luke's righteous indignation over what had taken place.

The next day, there appeared on the editorial page a statement signed by Luke Bouchard that was both an appeal to reason and a defiance of the forces of evil. It ended:

. . . It is now seven years since Appomattox. There are still those in the North who contemptuously view the South as a conquered nation that seeks to strike back by fair means or foul. The continued existence of the outlawed Ku Klux Klan gives weight to their accusations against us all; it maligns the majority of decent, law-abiding citizens who want only to lead their own lives, make their own decisions, and choose their own representatives in our legislature without coercion from their rivals.

I believe that the people of Montgomery County are intelligent enough to see this issue as I do; to unite with those who desire sane, judicious government, and to repudiate once and for all any party or any candidate for public office who espouses the infamous and cowardly tactics of the Ku Klux Klan.

I have this day sent a letter in my own hand to Governor Lindsay, urging him to call out our state militia to quell any further attacks by this malignant society whose members are not honest enough to show their faces. I trust that our governor will for once show courage and thus prove that, whatever else might be thought of his administration by his friends and foes alike, he, as the highest-ranking executive of our beloved state of Alabama, cannot countenance any more than you or I can this scourge of lawless evil which has been inflicted upon us.

Luke Bouchard

After he left the *Advertiser* office, Luke stopped in to visit old Jedidiah Danforth, to tell him what had happened and to show him a copy of the letter. The crotchety attorney sighed and shook his head. "Luke, you never cease to remind me of Don Quixote—I'm sure you're familiar with Cervantes' hero?"

"Are you implying that I am somewhat mad?" Luke humorously countered.

"Of course I'm not. What I'm getting at, Luke, is that you're always championing the causes of idealism in a world that, alas, has grown much too practical and greedy to care about ideals. I know—you think that if you tilt at windmills, you'll be catapulted into the stars. But the sad fact is that, all too often, those of us who try to do that find ourselves flung down into the mud and jeered at by our fellows—fellows who wouldn't have the all-fired guts to try what we did. You know that Governor Lindsay is going to ignore that letter, just as he's ignored a great many other basic issues during his administration."

"But I've learned to be a *practical* idealist, Jedidiah," Luke firmly retorted. "So much so that I'm going to arm Andy Haskins's workers as well as the men on my own land. And I may even bring a few weapons over to Hugh Entrevois so that his men will be prepared in case the Klan decides to strike there."

"You've told me about this Entrevois. It's really curious that you should befriend him, knowing what you do about his background."

"Well, Jedidiah, for a good long while—perhaps without consciously knowing it but certainly inwardly—I've been asking myself if I wasn't really leaning too much to my own interests by sending Mark away from Windhaven Plantation. Yes, I paid him off with a third of Grandfather's gold, but I never really tried to patch up things between us."

"From what I've known about that unfortunate young man, Luke, I don't think any gambit you could have tried with him would have been successful. And I wish you'd stop reproaching yourself for something you've no real reason to feel guilty about. Here you are in the prime of your life, you don't even look your age, and you're looking back into the dead past, trying to rectify it. How can you be sure that Hugh Entrevois doesn't mean you some harm?"

"I really can't. It's troubled me greatly ever since I first was introduced to him and learned his last name. But I think also that since I'm being a practical idealist these days, as I said, I'd much rather face an enemy and know him for what he is than have him come up behind my back without any warning and deal me a low blow. At least, I've given him an honorable chance to build a future for himself. So far, he hasn't betrayed that trust. But if he should—well, at least I'll be prepared for it."

"You're a remarkable man, Luke Bouchard. I think your grandfather would be very proud of you if he were alive today."

"That's the finest compliment you could ever pay me, Jedidiah. And you know, I think he'd take a great liking to you too. Well, I'll be getting back to Laure and the children now. And by the way, there'll be another Bouchard early next year, Laure tells me."

"That's wonderful! I envy you, Luke. Here I am, a cranky old bachelor, tolerated only by my much put-upon housekeeper, and look how many hostages to fortune you've given life. You can take pride in knowing that they'll go on after you and continue in your footsteps. You've given them a wonderful beginning."

"I couldn't do less than my grandfather, who gave me such a wonderful heritage. If I can set such an example for my children, then I shan't be ashamed of what I've done in this life. Good day to you, Jedidiah."

* * *

Throughout all the next week, Luke redoubled his vigilance over his own fields and urged Andy Haskins to have his workers keep their weapons nearby in the event of an attack by the Ku Klux Klan. On Wednesday morning, he rode down to the old Williamson plantation to meet with Hugh Entrevois and admonish the latter to be equally cautious. The tall Creole took him on a tour of the fields, and Luke complimented him on the diligence he had shown in supervising his workers to restore the rich land.

"You've done very well," Luke commended him. "If the weather continues good, you should be able to turn quite a tidy profit by fall harvesting time. That's why I'd hate to see any interruption by the Klan's cowardly vandals. Make sure your men keep their weapons handy, Hugh. From what I've learned about them in the past, I'd say they don't relish having a counterattack made on them when they come calling to do their dirty work. And the law's on your side: if they invade your property, you're legally justified in repelling them, even if it means having to kill a few of them. God knows I'm not a bloodthirsty man, but I will not tolerate this brand of treacherous cowardice which preys mainly on the helpless and seeks to take the upper hand by sheer terror."

"I understand your feelings, Mr. Bouchard," Hugh replied suavely as he reached for a hoe, which had been left on the ground nearby by one of the workers, and zealously chopped away at a small patch of weeds near a row of yams. "But I wouldn't go so far as to say that all of them are cowards. Do you think it was right for the North to treat us Southerners like criminals and traitors just because we fought to keep our way of life? They flooded the South with their carpetbaggers and their swaggering black Freedmen's Bureau delegates who acted like thieving policemen—that's all they really were, Mr. Bouchard. Was it wrong for us to try to strike back before they robbed us of everything we had left?"

"I'll agree that the North had more than its share of greedy profiteers, Hugh. But that still didn't give us the right to take the law into our own hands. The proper way would have been to have stopped our internal squabbling and elected a strong, unified people's government to cope with our own problems. Yes, and to form our own militia,

352

which could have acted as a legal restraining force against outright thievery."

"I'm afraid, Mr. Bouchard, you're more of an idealist than I am. On the contrary, I'm a realist. Now what about the vigilantes in San Francisco—you've heard about them, I imagine?"

"Indeed I have. But the difference there is that those vigilantes were public-spirited citizens who didn't try to disguise themselves, who punished crimes like murder by giving the perpetrators a public trial and presenting evidence, the way you might do in a courtroom."

"Oh to be sure." There was a trace of a sneer in Hugh's softly accented voice. "But just the same, they hanged them out of hand. What would you do if a freed black slave came into your house and raped your wife, for example, just because he knew that his Northern masters would justify anything he did as a part of keeping the conquered South in bondage?"

A shadow passed over Luke's face, for the Creole's chance remark had brought back to mind Henri Cournier's despicable conspiracy to degrade Laure and to kidnap little Lucien. Swiftly controlling his reactions, he coldly replied, "If I were on the scene, it wouldn't happen. The man would be taken prisoner, charged with a crime, and suitably punished—unless I had to defend both my wife and myself against his violence, and then, alas, I'd be forced to kill him."

"That's all very high-sounding, Mr. Bouchard. But you see, I was born in New Orleans and I lived there a good while. I can remember how Ben Butler's soldiers treated decent Southern women like whores—yes, and raped quite a few of them." He uttered a short, bitter laugh, picked up the hoe again, and viciously slashed at another patch of weeds, then dropped the hoe and turned to add: "It so happens, Mr. Bouchard, I knew one of those women. Her name was Désirée Lagrande. She was just nineteen and had been married to a man nearly three times her age who owned a sugar-cane plantation upriver from New Orleans. She happened to be in the city visiting her cousin, whose husband was wearing the Confederate gray and fighting for the South up near Vicksburg. Unfortunately, both of them had left the house early in the evening to visit a sick neighbor and to take her some comforts, when a platoon of Butler's brutes stopped them and asked them for their passes. Naturally, they didn't have any." Again he uttered a bitter little laugh. "Then the corporal decided that both of these gentle, well-bred young women hadn't shown enough respect for their blue uniforms—you may recall, Mr. Bouchard, Butler's General Order Number Twenty-eight?"

"Only too well."

"Well, Mr. Bouchard, that platoon herded both those unfortunate young women into an abandoned house, abused them repeatedly all night long, and then, in their drunken brutality, obliged them to go home stark naked, as best they could. When Désirée's husband learned what had happened to his wife, the scoundrel abandoned her—she had to become a prostitute in one of the houses on Rampart Street. Now, sir, I tell you this because, perhaps, you will better understand that I don't entirely condemn the Klan for retaliatory measures against such crimes as the North has perpetrated upon us!"

"I understand your feelings, Hugh." Luke sought a conciliatory tone. "But I would remind you of an old cliché that still has a good deal of truth in it: two wrongs do not make a right."

"As I said before, Mr. Bouchard, you're an idealist, a dreamer. I've had to be just the opposite, practical and shrewd enough to survive disaster. Well, I'd best get back to my work."

"Of course. I only came to caution you to have your men ready in the event of any attack by the Klan. I assume you've allocated the weapons I brought you?"

"It's been done, of course. Good day to you, Mr. Bouchard." Hugh bent down to retrieve the hoe, curtly nodded, and went down the rows, scanning them to detect any more patches of weeds.

It was nearly midnight on the first Sunday of September. The weather had been scorching, and to its discomfort had been added a slight rain that made the humidity intolerable. The Alabama River moved sluggishly along its winding course beyond the towering bluffs, and there was hardly any breeze to stir the leaves of two massive hickory trees that vigilantly guarded the graves.

Luke had left Laure's bedroom after a tender conjugal reunion. The child she was bearing had begun to stir in her womb, and the heat and the sudden qualms of this pregnancy had made her restless, almost feverish. He had been content to hold her, to soothe her and kiss her, to reassure her. She had clung to him as a child might to its father, and this union had been chaste and gentle. Out of consideration for her, he had waited until she had at last fallen asleep, and then gone back to his room. He would have Dr. Medbury call on her tomorrow, for this time her symptoms caused him some anxiety, and he made a mental note to tell the new governess to look after Laure as conscientiously as she did her three little charges.

He wore only his britches and an unbuttoned shirt, and he sat on the edge of his bed, wanting sleep and yet unable to relax. From deep within him came a sudden swarm of memories, disjointed, confusing. He rose, walked abruptly to the window, opened the shutters, and let the night air in. It was moist and warm, and he grimaced with distaste. The silence was almost oppressive. In this brooding night, he found himself thinking of his father, Henry, and of the mother he had never known, poor little teenaged Dora Trask who had drowned herself after his birth. He shuddered, and he found himself saying a prayer for the innocent girl who had given him birth. How little happiness she must have known, the daughter of an unscrupulous Georgia land speculator who had killed his grandfather's faithful Ashanti, Ben, and who had been cudgeled to death by Ben's young son, Thomas, in agonized retaliation.

His beloved grandfather, old Lucien, had told him Dora's story only once, and even then, young though he had been, Luke had sensed how abhorrent it had been for Lucien to discover that his only son had been capable of such ruthless treatment of his family. He thought, too, with a kind of awed wonder, how fortunate he had been to have his grandfather's influence, rather than his father's, in shaping his own life. But for the grace of God, he might well have taken the same road his half brother, Mark, had taken—yet here he was, at the very zenith of his life, content, with a family he could be proud of.

He was luckier by far than Mark, yes, and luckier even than his grandfather, who had had to struggle so hard for survival, and for even one heir to carry on his name. Old

Lucien's first two children had died, as had their mothers: Dimarte and her baby were bitten by a water moccasin; Amelia Duggins's child perished of river fever, after Amelia herself had given her life to save old Lucien from a murderer's bullet. Only Priscilla Wellman's child, Henry, had survived, and Priscilla had died in giving birth to him. As Luke stood at the open window and stared off into the sticky black night, he pondered the capriciousness of fate.

He turned with a start, for there was someone knocking on the door of his bedroom, and there was a woman's voice choked with sobs. "Mr. Bouchard, sir, it's Hughie! He's gone—I'm real scared, sir! Please, Mr. Bouchard, wake up!"

Puzzled, he strode to the door and opened it. It was Hannah, her face stained with tears, wearing an old cotton robe over her nightshift, her feet bare, twisting her hands in anguished grief. "Hughie's gone, Mr. Bouchard! He said he was going out in the fields, to check on his melons. He told me to go to bed, 'n he'd be right back. But that was nigh unto an hour ago! Now Moses is here, Mr. Bouchard, and he says he heard some strange noises!"

"Hannah—please, Hannah, don't cry like that! We'll find him—now, think carefully—you said Moses heard a noise out in the fields?"

"Yessir, that's what he said! You know what I'm scared of, Mr. Bouchard, sir? You 'members poor ol' Phineas—"

Luke uttered a cry of consternation. "The Klan!" he hoarsely ejaculated. "All right, Hannah. It'll take a minute to dress." Then, muttering to himself, he added, "I think I can guess who's behind this. I played right into his hands from the very start. I thought that even if he were an enemy, if I had him where I could see what he was doing, he'd reconcile himself and forget the past and accept what I was trying to offer."

"What's that you say, Mr. Luke? I don't understand. What man you talking about?"

"Never mind, Hannah, it's not important now. Go back and wake Dan and Marius. Tell them to get their guns and saddle up their horses. I'll meet them at the stable."

"Thank God, Mr. Luke, you always help us poor folks when we need you the most—God bless you! I'll go right now and tell them what you said, Mr. Luke."

Ten minutes later, carrying his Spencer rifle and car-

356

bine, Luke listened intently to arthritic Moses Turner, as Dan Monroe and Marius Thornton, armed with Spencer rifles, prepared to mount their horses. "Hannah says you heard something suspicious out in the fields, Moses. Tell me, did you know Hughie was going out there?" Luke asked.

"Yessir, Mr. Luke, I knew. Hughie stopped by 'bout an hour 'n half ago, seems like, said he was gonna take a last look at those rows of melons we put in last month way back in that corner of the fields."

"Yes, go on, Moses," Luke impatiently urged.

"Well, I didn't think no mind much about it, Mr. Luke, 'cause ever since Hughie's done jumped over the broom with Hannah, he's been workin' harder than anybody else round here. So I went on back to sleep, real quiet-like 'cause I didn't want to wake Mary up, she been feelin' poorly again, you know—anyhow, Mr. Luke, 'bout twenty minutes after I went back, I heard some funny noises way off by that bluff you goes up to all the time. I got up 'n looked out, but it was so awful dark I couldn't see nuttin'. Jist then I heard horses, and they was goin' off east, and then that was all. Then when Hannah come round real upset and sayin' Hughie hadn't come back yet, I told her."

"It's the Klan," Luke said to himself. "And now I've got an idea where they've taken Hughie. All right, Dan, Marius, we'll ride downriver to Andy's place."

"You think that's where they took poor Hughie?" Marius anxiously asked.

"No. They've already been to Andy's. But we'll need Andy and his men, especially Burt Coleman; he was Matt Rensler's best friend and he'll want to get back at the Klan for killing Matt. Let's go, and pray God we'll be in time!"

A quarter of an hour later, the three riders drew up in front of the little Bambach frame house and found Andy Haskins, the Ardmore brothers, and Burt Coleman about to mount their own horses and ride off downriver. Jasper Cooper had been left behind to guard Andy's pregnant wife, Jessica, and stood defiantly in front of the door, holding a loaded Spencer carbine.

"Mr. Luke!" Andy cried out as, just in the act of leading out his three workers, he saw Luke and Marius and Dan ride up. "You've heard about what's happening too? One of my men heard riders going by, and caught a glimpse of them. It's big trouble."

"They took Hughie Mendicott from the fields when he went out late tonight to check the melons," Luke tersely retorted. "And Moses Turner told me that he heard the noise of horses. They'd have to go downriver—and I was pretty sure they wouldn't stop here, they've already had an overly warm welcome."

"Look there, Mr. Luke!" Cassius Ardmore cried out as he pointed downriver. A faint red glow could be seen, at a distance which Luke judged to be about a dozen miles away.

"It's the old Williamson place, I thought it would be," he said, half to himself. "That's where they've got Hughie! Come on, let's ride! By God, if they've harmed him, they'll pay for it—and it's all my fault, I'm the only one to blame!"

"I don't understand you, Mr. Luke," Andy curiously peered at him as he mounted up. "Why do you say a thing like that? We all know how you beat off the Klan yourself when that Parmenter fellow ran the store that Mr. Sattersfield's got now."

"No time for talk, Andy, just ride!" Luke spurred his stallion into a gallop, racing ahead of the others, who quickly joined him. His face grim, he followed the winding trail downriver to what had been the old Williamson plantation.

As they neared the Williamson acreage, the faint glow grew more intense, and when they reined up at Luke's sign a quarter of a mile before the driveway that led to the two-story house, Luke had guessed the worst. "They've set fire to the house," he called back to the others. "Now, there are seven of us, and we've all got repeating rifles and carbines. We'll circle from the north and Marius and Dan will cut in toward the end of the fields at their easternmost boundary. You two"—he gestured toward the Ardmore brothers—"cut in just behind that burning house. Andy, Burt, you come with me; we'll go up the driveway and around the house to the beginning of the fields. Don't fire till you have to, but if any of the Klan show weapons, don't wait for them to fire at you. Now, let's go!"

So saying, he spurred his whinnying stallion forward.

Andy Haskins and Burt Coleman, whose face was twisted with anger and in whose eyes tears glinted at the thought of the cold-blooded murder of his best friend, rode abreast of him till they neared the driveway of the house. The second floor was already catching fire, the first was nearly all consumed, and sparks danced on the rooftop. But beyond, and to the south, at the very edge of the fields, there stood a burning cross. And ten yards east of it was another cross to which the naked body of Hughie Mendicott was bound. His arms were around the cross and his wrists bound together; his neck was tied so that his face was mashed against the vertical upright. Another cord tethered his ankles. Behind him and at his left stood a white-robed figure holding a carriage whip that trailed on the ground, its long lash streaked with blood. Hughie had fainted, his body crisscrossed by bloody marks from shoulders to calves.

In a wide circle around the burning cross stood ten Klansmen, and directly behind the man with the carriage whip, his arms folded, stood a tall, robed figure, whose peaked hood was colored red. He raised his hand now, as the man with the whip turned back to look to him for orders. "Cut him down, bind his hands and feet, and throw him into the burning house!" he intoned in a sepulchral voice.

"Cut him down, yes, but if any of you try to throw him into the fire, you'll be shot down like the cowardly dogs you are!" Luke Bouchard cried as he spurred his stallion toward the Klansmen.

One of the ten hooded men in the circle round the burning cross suddenly plunged his hand beneath his robe and drew out a pistol. Instantly, Burt Coleman leveled his Spencer carbine from the hip and pulled the trigger twice. The Klansman coughed, slumped down on his knees, then rolled onto his side and lay sprawled dead. "That's for Matt, you dirty, murdering skunks!" he shouted. "And there's more where that came from! Anybody else want to try marksmanship with me? Matt and I won sharpshooter medals, and I was just a mite better than he was—draw, you lily-livered skunks, draw on me, I'm begging you to do it!"

"You'd best cut Hughie Mendicott down," Luke called

to the red-hooded leader. "I've other men flanking you from the east, and they're all armed with repeating weapons. But what I'm wondering is why the men who work on this land aren't here now to defend against scum like you—and I think I know the answer already." He dismounted, flung down the carbine, and started toward the red-hooded leader. The man with the carriage whip drew back the lash as if to strike at Luke, but Marius Thornton, riding in from the east, leveled his carbine and triggered a shot that smashed the Klansman's wrist. With a scream of agony, the Klansman dropped his whip, clapped his other hand to the bleeding wound, then sank to his knees and began to whimper like a child in his pain.

"Take your horses and ride out of here while you're still alive to do it," Dan Munroe bawled, firing his carbine into the air. The nine men around the circle broke ranks and, to a man, ran blindly into the night and into the fields, where they had tethered their horses. As they ran, Andy, Burt, and the Ardmore brothers rode after them, firing their weapons into the air.

Luke Bouchard strode purposefully toward the red-hooded leader, his eyes blazing with anger. As he neared him, the leader suddenly thrust his hand under his robe and sought to pull out a weapon. Luke uttered a cry of rage and threw himself upon the man, his right hand gripping his adversary's wrist. They stood locked in mortal combat, and Luke could hear the Klansman's hoarse gasps as he struggled and see his dark eyes blazing through the slits of the hood. Exerting all his strength, the leader of the klavern managed to draw out a six-shooter, and Luke ground his teeth as he twisted his opponent's wrist with all his strength. Suddenly, there was a sharp report, and Luke could feel his opponent's body sagging against him. With a final wrench, he pulled the weapon away from the Klansman and flung it into the night, then stepped back.

"Jesus—you've done me in—" the red-hooded Klansman groaned as he sank down on one knee, bowing his head before Luke as if to signal his capitulation.

With an imprecation, Luke ripped off the hood. "Yes—I knew it would be you—but why, in God's dear name?" he groaned.

Hugh Entrevois slowly raised his tortured, sweating face. He fought for breath, and gasped: "I guess—I guess be-

cause what my mother told me—I—I hated the Bouchards—she told me how they'd kicked Mark, my f-father,
out—and—"

"But that's not true!" Luke interposed passionately. He
sank down on his knees, gripping Hugh's shoulders, forcing
the man to stay alive until he could reason it out, trying to
understand this treachery. "Mark Bouchard left of his own
will. I gave him his fair share of his inheritance, and he
said that he hated us all."

"Maybe—maybe so—" Hugh bowed his head and was
silent a moment. Then, with a ghastly cough, blood oozing
from the corners of his mouth, he gasped, "All I know—
my mother was ruined by Mark Bouchard—all these
years—yes—I've wondered if there wasn't something due
me—I wanted to get back at you—you're so mighty and
rich and proud—you're so sanctimonious—I think you
knew what I was going to do—and you thought you could
outsmart me—oh Jesus—Jesus, forgive me—aaaah!"
There was a long-drawn sigh, and Hugh Entrevois's eyes
closed, his head bowed, and he fell against Luke Bouchard.

"Amen," Luke said softly. He gently eased the Creole's
body to the ground. Then, still kneeling, he touched the
dead man's forehead. "God forgive me, too. Yes, Hugh,
perhaps I knew all along that you would try to strike at
me. And perhaps you were right—I *was* smug and sanctimonious in thinking I had given you this chance because of
what I thought I had done to Mark. And my folly has cost
the life of a good, fine man, Matt Rensler. My God, I
have been guilty of the sin of vanity, and that is the worst
sin of all. I have sinned grievously in my own selfishness,
and I have paid for it tonight in the turmoil of my conscience, in the knowledge of my own secret flaws. Tonight,
as I near the end of my life, I have learned a long-delayed
lesson in humility, and at what a price—"

The men around him were silent, glancing among one
another and waiting. Wearily Luke got to his feet. He
turned to Andy Haskins and said in a low voice, "Will you
and your men help me get Hughie home? I only pray he's
still alive. If he dies, my guilt will be all the harder to bear
after tonight."

Andy nodded and whispered orders to the Ardmore
brothers, who advanced toward the cross and cut the
thongs binding Hughie's unconscious body. Gently they

lifted him and tied him onto one of their own horses, then both mounted astride the other.

"We'll take him to my place, it'll be easier that way, and Jessica'll help nurse him, Mr. Luke," Andy murmured.

Luke Bouchard nodded, scarcely hearing. He had turned to look upriver, and he stared as if his eyes sought the towering bluff. His lips framed the words, although he did not speak them aloud, "Grandfather, forgive me. I have learned tonight I am not the man you were, nor ever shall be. But I shall learn from you, Grandfather, this I vow."

CHAPTER TWENTY-NINE

Hughie Mendicott was not able to resume his work in the fields until the end of September but, thanks to his devoted wife, Hannah, and the frequent visits of Dr. Medbury, he regained his strength with no seeming ill effects. He remained a week at Andy Haskins's house, nursed there first by Jessica and then by Hannah who came the very next day to tend him. A week later, carefully bandaged and supported by pillows on a thick quilt, he was brought back to the red-brick chateau in a buggy.

When Luke Bouchard rode back to Windhaven Plantation after his tragic confrontation with Hugh Entrevois, he went directly to the chapel. There, for more than an hour, he prayed, abject in his discovery of his own almost incredible naiveté, in believing that Hugh would not think of vengeance once he had been offered what Luke believed was more than generous restitution for any possible claim made upon the Bouchards. He had been so confident that Mark's son would meet him at least halfway that he had ignored the potential danger that had cost the life of one of Andy's loyal workers and almost had cost that of Hughie Mendicott. By way of reparation, he visited Hughie ten days after the flogging and handed him a deed to fifty acres of the old Williamson land.

"You've earned this, Hughie. It's yours from now on to do with as you wish. The rest of the acreage goes to my good and loyal friend Andy, and if you prefer, you may work with him and his friends. There's room enough there to build your own little house for you and Hannah and your children, and the land's just as rich as on Windhaven. It's the least I can do after getting you involved through my own folly, Hughie, and I hope you'll forgive me for it."

Hughie's sons, Davie and Louis, stood near his bedside

363

and eyed Luke wonderingly. Wanly, their father shook his head and murmured, " 'Twarn't your fault, Mr. Luke, not hardly. I ought to have had better sense than to go out there by myself alone at night without having Dan and Marius and maybe Moses come along with me."

"No, that's not really true, Hughie. I knew that Klan leader's background, I should have anticipated what he'd do. And what we both forgot, although I'm sure it was in the back of his mind all along, was that although his father was white, his mother was an octoroon. So you see, Hughie, he could exist in neither world with security and self-esteem in himself, because he had black blood as well as white. I think now that element turned him from what he really could have made of himself if he'd gone along and worked honestly with me. Yet it was my fault for not foreseeing it. No, Hughie, the land's yours. And you have my deepest apologies and regrets that through my own lack of insight, I subjected you to such a terrible beating. Now you just rest and get well in your own time."

The very next day, after a late breakfast with Laure, Luke went out into the fields with a hoe and worked as assiduously as he had used to do beside his grandfather. When sunset found him exhausted and dripping with sweat, he sank down on his knees and murmured a silent prayer as he looked up at the bluff and again asked old Lucien to understand and to condone his lapse in judgment.

On the next day, he rode into Montgomery with another letter for the *Advertiser* in which he described the Klan's attack against the Williamson land and its workers, urging the county's clear-thinking citizens to repudiate once and for all those who employed the Klan as a weapon of terror and coercion. Meanwhile, Andy Haskins, at the urging of William Blount, spent one day of each succeeding week until the November election visiting neighboring farms and going into towns to advance his own candidacy and to speak on behalf of the Republican ticket.

As the election neared, it was evident that this year's campaign would be quiet by comparison with that of 1870. The Republicans emphasized the necessity of party unity and appealed to the northern Alabama whites. Their only problem was a shortage of campaign funds. They received a much-needed assist from the national party three weeks

364

before the election. Partly as a result of this, the Republicans swept into office easily. Fortunately, those Republicans who, like Luke, had been tempted to cross over and support Greeley, realized that to do so would be to ensure victory for the Democrats and their candidates sympathetic to the Ku Klux Klan. Accordingly, these Republicans stuck with their party. The Democrats were undermined by their own dissatisfaction with Governor Lindsay's administration, and this further helped the Republicans. David P. Lewis was elected governor with 89,020 votes, as against 78,524 votes for Herndon, his Democratic opponent. Andy Haskins defeated Oliver Perkins by over a thousand votes, and Luke held a celebration party for him on the morning after the election.

Exactly eight days after her husband had been elected to the state legislature, Jessica Bambach Haskins gave birth to a son, and Andy urged her to name the child after her beloved father, Horatio. Luke sent off a letter to his son Lucien Edmond, for he had already received the news that Maxine was again pregnant. If it was a son, Lucien Edmond had written, they were thinking of naming it Charles, by way of tribute to the intrepid young Chicago merchant who had visited with them and who was now back in Galveston supervising the final stages of work before the opening of his new department store.

In his letters to Luke during the fall, Lucien Edmond had continued to talk of what he feared would be hard economic times ahead, saying how glad he was that he had held back part of his herd from market this year. Luke applauded his son's wisdom in emulating the industrious ant of Aesop's classical fable: laying away resources against a foreseeable hard winter of economic recession showed far sounder judgment than pursuing the grasshopper-like tactics of those who took immediate profits and spent them without concern for the future. He hoped that Charles Douglas's new business venture would be backed not only by the Chicagoan's good business sense, but also by sufficient merchandise and reserve capital to weather what Luke also believed would be the coming economic storm.

Already the clouds of this storm were gathering for those who could perceive their meaning. In Alabama, the state government was hovering near bankruptcy, because of the tremendous expenditures since 1868 and the resulting strain put upon the state's economy. The state treasurer's report revealed an abysmally low reserve for the administration of Governor Lewis. The problem of trying to sell the ill-fated Alabama and Chattanooga Railroad, which was virtually bankrupt, was certain to plague the new administration.

Nationally, the signs were even more ominous. Two months before the national and state elections, the *New York Sun* had begun the exposure of the infamous Credit Mobilier. And Luke's own misgivings about President Grant's cabinet and his greedy and corrupt coterie of advisers were strengthened by Grant's sweeping victory. Lincoln's favorite general had been reelected President, with Henry Wilson as vice-president. As if to underscore the somber note of trouble ahead, a great fire swept the downtown area of Boston four days after the election, causing many deaths and over seventy-three million dollars, worth of property damage.

Despite all these gloomy portents, however, Luke had cause to be optimistic about the future of Windhaven Plantation and the welfare of his family and his loyal workers—though he was still unable to expunge entirely from his conscience the results of the ingenuous pact he had made with Hugh Entrevois. When he had told Laure what had happened on that terrible September night, he had said in a self-recriminating tone, "Looking back, Laure, I see that I tried to play the role of a master puppeteer, pulling the strings, fatuously confident that because I acted in good faith, he would completely forget his enmity against the Bouchards and live by my own code. What a fool he must have thought me, tossing him a sop when he wanted the whole bowl to avenge the wrong he felt poor Mark had done his mother and him! It has taught me a bitter lesson, Laure. Matt Rensler's death and Hughie Mendicott's suffering will forever weigh upon my conscience. I've tried to make some small restitution, by giving Hughie fifty acres of land, and I've decided also to give Matt's best friend, Burt Coleman, another fifty—but even these are at most inadequate gestures."

Laure had put her arm around his shoulders and tenderly replied, "My darling, you mustn't try to shoulder all the burdens of the world. When I first met you in New

Orleans, and I learned of your grandfather's courage and wisdom, I thought to myself that you were trying to shape your life out of a book, that you were a colorless perfectionist. But since then I have learned how very warm and human you are, my darling. And when you tell me what troubles you now, I see only that you're very human, still very trusting and good and decent. Reproach yourself if you must, my dear, beloved husband, for this shows your integrity as a sensitive man concerned with others. But please don't flagellate yourself constantly with a guilt that is really based on the evil-doing of others. Would you blame yourself for Pierre Lourat, or for the Courniers, or Hurley Parmenter? No, my darling, no more than I can blame myself for that Union corporal who took my virtue as a part of the spoils of war." Then she kissed him and whispered, "Think rather of the good you've done and of the happiness you've given me, and think most of all of the child I'm going to give you early next year."

Thus, in the autumn of his adventurous life, Luke Bouchard found comfort and consolation. By mid-November, when he and Marius Thornton drew up the accounting of the profits made from the produce, crops, chickens, cattle, hogs, and dairy products, which formed the highly diversified harvest from Windhaven Plantation—a far cry from those early days when cotton was the primary crop—he had reason to rejoice in his stewardship of the land. There were ample profits to be returned to all the workers, a tidy sum to be put aside for his own family's expenses in the year ahead, and even money to invest in such repairs and remodeling as would be needed, as well as for the purchase of tools and machinery to facilitate next year's work upon the fertile land.

During November of 1872 there were two letters, which cheered him as well. One was a chatty, lengthy missive from Arabella Hunter, telling him how her husband, James, was taking to his new career with zest; he had even gone so far as to tender his outright resignation as Cousin Jeremy's cotton factor, in order to devote all his time to Charles Douglas's new department store.

As for herself, Arabella wrote, she had never been happier. Melinda's marriage was serenely happy, and little Gary was thriving. Andrew, now nearly nineteen and quite the young man, not unexpectedly had decided to work for

Cousin Jeremy and was already displaying signs of his father's business acumen. James's new work gave the two of them more time to go out socially, to the theater and to the symphony, to visit friends, to have dinners at their home and ripen old friendships as well as develop rewarding new ones. Little Joy would be three in December, and Luke could not help chuckling when he read Arabella's doting comment, "I swear, Luke dear, when she grows up, she's going to be lovelier even than Melinda—maybe even lovelier than I was back in those Alabama days!"

The second letter was from Dr. Ben Wilson in Wichita. He wrote to wish Luke and Laure well, and to say that he was busy and happy in his medical practice. His post as Quaker deacon gave him great spiritual joy as well, and as a further blessing, he reported that his sweet young wife, Elone, was with child. His letter concluded, "I pray God that He will give all the Bouchards, to whom I feel myself so inseparably linked, as much joy in the year ahead as He has seen fit to grant me. Pastor Hartmann and I are trying to raise funds to build a small hospital here in Wichita. If this is successful, there will be a ward for the poor, and I mean to name it after Fleurette. If it had not been for her, I should never have known all of you and found inspiration in the courage and family love you display. The children she gave me will be brought up to know their heritage. And our little daughter, Sybella, will remind me constantly of that valiant, wonderful matriarch who lived nearly seventy years and was as indomitable a pioneer in your home in Texas as she was in your own birthplace."

Thus it was that Luke Bouchard's trial of torment was greatly eased.

CHAPTER THIRTY

Eddie Gentry's wound from Jim Bradshaw's derringer had been a clean one, without complications. Lucas, Simata, and Nacio Lorcas had taken him at once to the hotel where Lucien Edmond Bouchard was quartered. The young Mexican girl whom Eddie had rescued from her life of prostitution had insisted on accompanying them. Hysterically, she kept repeating that Eddie had saved her, that he was a good man, and that they must not let him die.

When Nacio knocked at Lucien Edmond's door and was admitted, he quickly told the tall young trail boss of the events in Bradshaw's dance-hall. Lucien Edmond went at once to Joseph McCoy's room and begged him to find a doctor. Happily, there was an elderly doctor staying in the hotel at that very moment. And as it happened, he had left Abilene at Joseph McCoy's own suggestion to accompany McCoy to Newton. He was frail but still capable, and once the three men had gently laid Eddie down on the bed in his room, he tore away Eddie's shirt and examined the wound. Then, straightening, he said, "I can take the bullet out in a jiffy, if you fellows will hold him down. It's going to hurt a mite, but it's a small pellet, the Lord be praised. He'll be just fine in a couple of days."

"We'll stay in Newton just as long as it takes till you're back on your feet, Eddie," Lucien Edmond assured him, bending over the lanky young cowboy. Then, remembering his own leg wound sustained during the attack by Jack Martin's bushwhackers, he wryly added, "You'd better swill down as much whiskey as you can hold, Eddie, and chew on something." Turning to the old doctor, he asked, "Do you have any whiskey handy, Doctor—Doctor—"

"Doc Silas, mister. Amos Silas, that's my monicker. Sure as you're born, I've got whiskey. Sometimes, when I don't

369

have any practice in this one-horse town, I take a nip now and again for the miseries. Whiskey's not a bad idea, 'cause laudanum's hard to git out in these parts, and when Joe McCoy had me move out of Abilene, he didn't leave me much time to stock up on medical supplies. Well now, here it is." The old doctor turned to the closet, opened the door, and brought out a half-filled bottle of cheap whiskey. Nacio Lorcas took it with a grateful nod, drew the cork out with his teeth, then tilted the bottle to Eddie's lips. "*Amigo*, I know you don't like it, but it will make you feel less pain."

"Sure, I'll have the pain in my belly instead of my shoulder," Eddie wanly joked. He grimaced, closed his eyes, and opened his mouth, then swallowed till at last he shook his head and turned it away with a violent cough. "Seems like the cure's worse than the disease," he gasped. "That's foul stuff."

"Sorry, son," Dr. Silas commiserated as he opened his bag, took out a scalpel, then took the bottle of whiskey back from Nacio and poured some of its contents onto the scalpel to sterilize it. "Newton's still a young cowtown, you can't expect civilization to be here in a jiffy. Now git the young man something to chaw on and, mind you, hold him real steady. 'Pears to me at first glance that that derringer pellet didn't smash the collarbone—that's a good thing, too. That'd put him out of action a lot longer."

Simata drew his hunting knife out of its sheath and proffered it, handle foremost, to the young Texan. "Hold this, Eddie. You can bite down hard, it's made of bone."

"Thanks, Simata. Mr. Lucien Edmond, I'm sure sorry as hell I'm holding up your getting back home. And with that girl now—" Eddie began faintly, as he turned his head toward the tall, blond trail boss.

"Stop feeling so sorry about everything, Eddie," Lucien Edmond grinned. "There isn't a vaquero in the outfit who isn't proud of you for what you did to save that Mexican girl. And don't worry about her, I got her a room in this hotel, and Pablo Casares is standing guard there just in case any of that fellow Bradshaw's friends think of coming after her. You just grip hold of that knife handle and let Doc Silas do his work."

"Thanks, Mr. Lucien Edmond. All right, Doc, do your worst." With this, Eddie doggedly gripped the bone handle of Simata's hunting knife between his teeth and closed his eyes, while Nacio, Simata, and Lucas bent over the bed and held his arms and legs as firmly as they could to prevent his thrashing about when the doctor began to probe.

As the latter had predicted, the derringer bullet had missed the collarbone. However, since Eddie had turned at an angle when Maria Elena Romero had pushed him out of Jim Bradshaw's line of fire, the bullet had entered at an angle and penetrated deeply. It took fully a quarter of an hour before the sweating old doctor straightened and held up the pellet in his forceps for all to see. Eddie · had groaned and arched, but toward the end of the operation a merciful unconsciousness had claimed him, and he now lay still, breathing normally.

"Nasty little bugger! Good thing it didn't go the other way, or it might have got plumb near his heart. He's got guts, this cowboy of yours, mister." He respectfully eyed Lucien Edmond.

"That he has, Doc Silas. We're all indebted to you. Now, how soon do you think it'll be before he can ride again? We're going back to Texas, now that the herd's been sold."

"He'd better rest two, three days, I'd say. And I'll fix up a sling for him. You better put him on a nice gentle horse he can rein in with his other hand."

"We'll do better than that," Lucien Edmond promised. "He'll ride in one of the supply wagons with the girl he saved. Now then, here's your fee. And thanks for helping out in an emergency like this." He handed the astonished old doctor a twenty-dollar gold piece.

"Hey, you don't owe me that much!" the doctor protested.

"You've earned it. Eddie Gentry's life is worth a lot more to us, believe me. Now then, would it be safe to carry him back to my room?" Lucien Edmond demanded.

"Sure it would. He's passed out, as you can see. There isn't any arterial bleeding or anything like that. Just let him rest. And he can eat himself a good steak as soon as he feels like it. It'll get back the blood he lost and his strength with it."

"Thanks again. Let's lift him, men."

* * *

Three days later, Lucien Edmond Bouchard's outfit began the return journey to Windhaven Range. Eddie Gentry, his left arm in a sling and his shoulder thickly bandaged, protested when Ramón smilingly urged him to get into the wagon, where an improvised bed had been made. "Gosh, Ramón," he blurted, his face reddening almost to his ears, "I'm no baby. I don't have to be coddled any. I can't even feel where the bullet was now. Go ahead and let me ride a horse."

Ramón stared at him, then put his hands on his hips and shook his head. "Absolutely not. And if you stand here arguing, we won't leave. Then the vaqueros will blame you for delaying them in getting back home. If you get on a horse, you're certain to use that wounded arm, even if you try not to. And it might start the bleeding again. Get into that wagon, and that's an order." Then he winked. "Besides, I don't think you'll mind the companion you'll have on the trip back."

"Companion?" Eddie wonderingly echoed.

"Of course. Maria Elena especially asked to be your nurse. You should like that—you seemed to enjoy seeing her when she visited you at the hotel," Ramón teasingly replied.

The young Texan's face was almost scarlet with embarrassment as, clambering up into the driver's seat and peering into the back of the wagon, he saw Maria Elena Romero sitting there beside the improvised bed. At the sight of him, she sprang to her feet and let out a cry of joy. "Señor Gentry, how happy I am to see you well!" Then, solicitously, "Do you still feel pain? I worried so—you were so very brave."

"I—I'm just fine, ma'am," he stammered, more and more ill at ease as he heard a muffled snickering outside the wagon. Nacio Lorcas, Lucas, and Simata had come up to watch, alongside Ramón, who was listening to them. He half turned, wanting to tell them to mind their own business, but the young woman put her hand on his good elbow and murmured, "Please, Señor Gentry, do not disturb yourself. It is good for you to rest. You've lost much blood, they say. I will look after you, I promise. I want to—did you not save me from that terrible man?"

"Well, I suppose—I guess it wouldn't hurt to rest a little.

But I'm not going to stay here all through the trip, I can tell you that. I belong on a horse, ma'am."

"Why are we so formal, Señor Gentry? For three days now, Señor Lucien Edmond has permitted me to visit you in your room, and you still don't call me Maria Elena. For shame, señor!" She winked shyly and flashed him a dazzling smile.

"I'm sorry, Maria Elena, I'll remember next time."

"*Gracias*, señor. Now come, I will help you be comfortable. The bed is the best we could make. And I told the driver he must be very careful so the wheels do not go over rough places that will bump and hurt you."

The young Texan groaned softly. He tried to turn his head, then winced with pain from the sudden jerk to his bound left arm, as he saw the black-haired girl—he could think of her in no other way, for she had seemed so forlornly young in that dance-hall—make her way to the driver's seat of the wagon and begin to talk to the vaqueros who had gathered around it, secretly amused as well as delighted that their *gringo compañero* had found so outspoken and lovely a champion.

"*Linda*," Nacio Lorcas swept off his sombrero with a low bow, "have no fear. I myself will drive the wagon, and I will avoid all the gopher holes and the wagon ruts so that Señor Gentry will ride as if he were on the clouds going into paradise."

"*Por Dios*, señor," Marie Elena cried, aghast, "do not speak of *paraíso* in such a way—he will not die, you know he will not die! I will not let him, señor vaquero!"

"Be assured, señorita *linda*," Nacio again made a low bow and then climbed into the wagon and took up the reins. "Of course he will live. With such an angel as you to care for him, who would not defy death? *¡Adelante, caballos!*"

Nonetheless, Eddie Gentry proved to be a restless patient, and several times Lucien Edmond himself had to drop back and ride to the supply wagon to remonstrate with the lanky, towheaded Texan.

"Get it into your mind, Eddie, once and for all, you're not going to be allowed on a horse until we reach the Colorado River—maybe not even then, if you keep annoying everybody. Remember, there aren't any more cattle to round up, you've done your job, and a great deal more than that. Just rest and get your strength back, that's all I ask of you." Then, doffing his sombrero to the attractive, black-haired young Mexican woman, he wryly added, "If you have to hogtie him, señorita, and you can't do it yourself, just tell Ramón or Nacio or myself; we'll see to it. Now you behave yourself, Eddie Gentry!"

Then the young Texan would mumble to himself, his face turning a fiery red as he saw Maria Elena quickly eye him, with an enchanting little smile playing around her soft, red lips. "The idea! I'm no invalid, and I don't much take to being treated like one," he grumbled after the last time Lucien Edmond told him to remain in the wagon. "By the time I get back to Windhaven Range, they'll all be laughing at me."

"Now you stop such talk, Señor Gentry!" Maria Elena scolded, shaking her forefinger at him. "When I go each night to the *cocinero*—how do you say that—oh yes, cook—when I go to bring your supper, everyone says that you are *muy hombre*."

"Shucks, Maria Elena," he groaned again, turning his face to the canvas flap of the wagon so that she wouldn't see his embarrassment. "I'm not used to this, and I won't ever be. Besides, my arm feels just dandy. I don't know why they won't let me ride a horse. It's just downright ornery of Mr. Lucien Edmond to keep me in this wagon."

"Oh, so perhaps I am not good enough company for you, is that it, Señor Gentry?" she ingenuously inquired, widening her dark eyes and feigning a hurt look on her lovely face.

He sat up with a start, his own eyes widening with alarm. "Oh no, I didn't say that at all—I don't mean that—you—you're so good to me—but you know what it is, I'm used to riding by myself and doing my work as a cowhand—and here I am lollygagging around and you taking care of me—it's just not right, Maria Elena!"

"But I would like to take care of you, Señor Eddie," she softly confessed, and then it was her own turn to blush and look away. "I owe you my life. I have no one left. I can never go back to my father now—and I would not, after he sold me. Where would I go—to that terrible old *hacendado* who wanted to marry me? *Dios*, when I think of how brave you were against that awful man, how you stood up

374

to him even when he was behind you—I owe you my life, I owe you everything, Señor Eddie!"

"Maria Elena, I—I've been meaning to talk to you about that," he said uncomfortably, easing himself into a more restful position and propping himself up against the bolster that served as a pillow. "I know we can use a cook at the ranch. I've already spoken to Mr. Lucien Edmond, and he's certainly willing to give you a chance and to pay you good wages. But that's just for starters. I mean, you don't want to stay on a Texas ranch the rest of your life—you're too young and pretty—"

"Do you think me so?" she archly whispered, leaning toward him, her eyes tender and misty, her lips quivering and tempting.

Eddie Gentry squirmed uneasily. "Yes, you sure are awful pretty—I mean—aw shucks, Maria Elena, that's not fair! And you don't owe me anything—any fellow would have done what I did, once he saw Bradshaw take a quirt to you. I'm not sorry for what I did at all, you hear me?"

"*Sí, conozco,*" she softly murmured, leaning closer to him, as she put a hand on his shoulder. "But you were the only one who thought of doing it. It is true—I owe my life to you, I am yours. I would be your *criatura,* because you'll need someone to wash your clothes and to bring you your food—"

"Oh no—Maria Elena, now you stop talking like that!" he stammered, his face flaming with confusion. "I'm a man, and we're in the bunkhouse, and we do our own washing and such, and we get our own meals—I mean, there's a cook—maybe you can help her—and we bring our food into the bunkhouse and we eat it. Nobody waits on anybody. That's not Mr. Lucien Edmond's way, not likely."

"Then if you do not like me, Señor Eddie, I will not stay very long at this *rancho* where you work. Because I told you already, I belong to you, I owe you my life, you see. But if you do not want me, then I shall not stay. Perhaps I will find another place somewhere, perhaps back in Mexico—though I will never go back to my father, that I promise."

"But I don't want you to go—I mean—darn it all, Maria Elena, you got me all upset now—" he blurted, flustered by her nearness and the sweet tenderness she showed him.

"I do not mean to. I do not want to cause you any trouble, truly I do not, Señor Eddie." She drew back, her eyes clouding with tears. "But I have no family now. You took me from that dreadful place and you brought me back to life. Why do you not wish to be responsible for me? I can work very hard, I am young and strong—"

"But then you'd be a servant or a slave, like they'd want you to be back in Mexico—no, Maria Elena, please don't talk like that. Doggone it, I just have to get out of here and ride my horse again!" Eddie despairingly exclaimed as he tried to struggle to his feet.

The very next day, when they came in sight of Emataba's village, Eddie clambered onto the driver's seat and, to Nacio's great amusement, pulled the reins away from him and declared, "Dagnabit, Nacio, my shoulder's as fit as it ever was! Now you just let me hold these reins and keep your mouth shut to Mr. Lucien Edmond, or you and I are going to have words, savvy?"

"*Sí, comprendo,*" Nacio grinned broadly.

Lucien Edmond and his men spent a day and a night with Emataba and the Creeks, and these two men, blood brothers and linked beyond their own immediacy to the ancient days of old Lucien Bouchard and Tunkamara, smoked the calumet in the *mico*'s tepee and talked of many things. Lucien Edmond related how well he had found Dr. Ben Wilson and his family, and Emataba, in turn, related how satisfied his people were with the new shaman who had replaced the kindly Quaker.

"Thanks to you, my brother, our people will have milk and meat for the winter. The cattle you brought last year and also last month will keep us well fed, and the new Indian agent is an honest, good man. Ibofanaga will bless you for what you have done to help us all. And I will be impatient until the moons have come and gone to bring your here again. Thinking of you and what you have done for all of us will keep our brotherhood strong, and will keep us all remembering our good white-eyes friends."

"And if ever the need arises, Emataba, you have only to send one of your braves to Windhaven Range to fetch my men and me. I pledge you that I will stand by you if ever there is trouble for you and your people," Lucien Edmond solemnly replied.

Eddie Gentry at last had his way about not being treated

like a convalescent wagon passenger, for the wound was now completely healed. He had the full use of his arm and shoulder, as he ably demonstrated by carrying in some of the supplies Lucien Edmond had purchased in Wichita for the Creek village. While in Wichita, the trail boss had also stopped to visit with Ben Wilson again, and he had brought with him a note in the latter's hand for Emataba. The *mico* was able to read English quite well, thanks to the language classes Ben had initiated when he was living in the village. Some of the braves had also become proficient, so that they now acted as teachers for the young children and the elders.

Maria Elena visited the Creek village and made friends at once with some of the children. Eddie Gentry observed this, and he began to see for the first time how extremely attractive she was, soft-spoken, gracious, honest, and open. Yet he told himself that it wasn't right for him to look at another woman when he was still remembering sweet Polly and how much she had meant to him. Nonetheless, he found himself worrying about what was going to happen to her. Sure, Mr. Lucien Edmond would find work for her at the ranch, but she wouldn't have any kinfolk or any real friends except, of course, himself. And with all the vaqueros around, she might feel out of place. And then maybe one of them (although nobody better try it, or they'd have to reckon with him, Eddie Gentry!) might say something out of line to her, because she was so pretty, and then there'd be trouble. He shook his head and went about his work, more and more troubled.

It didn't help matters when, just before they were ready to resume their journey back home, Nacio Lorcas came up to Eddie and jovially accosted him. "*Hombre,* you are a very lucky man, I think. That *muchachita linda* has eyes only for you. *Sí, es verdad.* Do you know, the first nights that we spent on the trail back home, she would not sleep? I know. Once, late at night, I found myself awake and I climbed back into the driver's seat to look in and see how you were. And there she was, *hombre,* sitting there looking down at you, with the smile of an angel. I tell you, señor Eddie, that one *te quiere mucho!*"

Eddie turned a furious red, and growled, "You're crazy, Nacio, plain loco! Anyway, you won't have to be looking into the wagon any more. I'll be on a horse from now on.

But you better take good care of her and don't bump her when you're driving those horses, or you'll have me to deal with, *comprende*?"

Nacio grinned from ear to ear and nodded. "*Pero sí*, Señor Eddie. Everyone understands very well. It is only you who does not, I think."

So once again Eddie Gentry mounted his gelding and rode back with the others. It was noticed that from time to time during the long days he would slacken his horse's gait and wait for the supply wagon to catch up, then ride abreast of it and call out to Maria Elena a greeting or a question as to whether she was comfortable. The vaqueros chuckled and winked at each other, for they felt that their *gringo compañero* had truly been cured in more ways than one, and that very soon he would be a happy man. All of them found Maria Elena Romero exactly as Nacio Lorcas had described her, a *muchachita linda con mucho corazón*.

Thirty-five miles south of the Colorado River, Simata raced ahead of the outfit on his gelding and then galloped back to Lucien Edmond with the news that smoke was rising from a farmhouse and barn. They had altered their return trail somewhat, a precaution Lucien Edmond always took on the return from the cattle market to avoid possible ambush by rustlers, bushwhackers, or thieves, and this was an area through which they had not previously passed.

"There were settlers there, Mr. Lucien Edmond," Simata breathlessly reported. "And the signs are of a raiding party of Kiowa Apaches. I saw the marks of horses—the Indians took those from the barn after they had killed the people who lived in the house. There are the bodies of an older man, a young man and his wife, and on the doorstep of the house I found the dress of a little girl. It is possible the Indians took her with them as a captive, perhaps to keep or to sell as a slave to some other tribe. And there was a little dog there, crying and barking."

"I hadn't thought there were any more Indian raids so far south, Simata. We'll bury those people and say prayers over them," Lucien Edmond gravely declared.

He turned to Ramón and explained what had to be done, and his young Mexican brother-in-law chose two vaqueros and himself for the burial detail. Eddie Gentry had

378

heard the news, and volunteered, but Ramón replied, "No, Eddie, you've had enough sorrow. Stay behind and keep Maria Elena company."

The young Texan looked at Ramón, bit his lips, then nodded. Suddenly tears came to his eyes. All through the cattle drive and now on the way home, he had held himself back, kept away from these good friends, while all the time they were doing their best to console him, to make him forget the loss of Polly Behting. Almost wonderingly he said to himself, "My God, Polly will always know how much I loved her. But it's over now, and I have to go on living. I've shut myself away from all these *compañeros,* even from Mr. Lucien Edmond who's been so good to me. No, I can't go on like this. She'll understand. I'll never forget her, God. And now I've got to do something for Maria Elena to show her I haven't forgotten what she did to try to save my life."

He wheeled his gelding and rode down with the two vaqueros and Ramón, although Ramón shook his head and frowned at him. Reaching the still-burning farmhouse ahead of the others, he dismounted. A shaggy little dog stood barking over the body of the young woman, who had died from the thrust of a feathered lance which rose like a grisly semaphore from her lifeless body.

"Come here, little fella, don't be scared. I know someone who will take real good care of you," he said, and his voice broke with a sudden well of long-pent-up emotions. He gathered the dog up in his arms, carefully mounted his gelding, and rode back to the supply wagon. Maria Elena had clambered onto the driver's seat alongside Nacio Lorcas. Her eyes widened as she saw Eddie galloping toward her.

"Señor Eddie, *qué pasa?*" she gasped. "I see the fire—what is it?"

"Indians, Maria Elena. There were settlers there, and I guess they killed them."

"How horrible! May God rest their souls!" she fervently murmured as she crossed herself.

"Amen to that, but here—there's a little dog left behind, and he hasn't got any family. I thought, well, I thought you might like to keep him. He'd make a fine pet back at the ranch."

She stared at him, and then her dark eyes filled with tears, and a tremulous smile curved her soft lips as she reached for the whimpering little dog.

"How sweet it was of you to think this, to make me less lonely, Señor Eddie! *Gracias*, for my life, for everything you have done—do you not see how much I care for you? You have made me shameless, but I cannot help it. I swear to you before the good Señor Dios that no man has ever touched me—though I know how it would have been if you had not taken me away from the Señor Bradshaw. Señor Eddie, please do not make me say it again—*te quiero mucho*. There—do you know what that means?"

His glacial reserve broke. In a voice that was hoarse and shook with suppressed sobs, he ordered Nacio Lorcas, "Go take my horse and ride away some, Nacio. I'm going to drive this wagon from now on, do you hear me?"

"*Pero sí*, Señor Eddie, with the greatest of happiness! Here, the reins await you!" Nacio chuckled affectionately as he climbed down from the wagon and mounted Eddie's gelding. Then, with a flourish of his sombrero, he shouted, "Give her a kiss for me too, *mi compañero!*"

Eddie Gentry, the reins in his hands, tears streaking his weatherbeaten face, turned back to stare at Maria Elena Romero. She cradled the dog in her arms as, on her knees, she moved forward to give him her lips. And at last Eddie understood that in the cycle of life, there is an eternal balance, and that when love has been taken away, it can be restored also.

CHAPTER THIRTY-ONE

After gathering herself together and walking about the streets to calm herself down, Alice Fernmark had at length gone back to the frame house on Dorado Street, where she lived with her older sister, Jeanette, and the latter's husband, David Perring. She was dazed by the swift turn of events on this February day, on which she had thwarted Calvin Jemmers and Arnold Shottlander's scheme to defraud Charles Douglas, and then had been beaten by Shottlander. Even more amazing had been Mr. Douglas's sudden entry into her employer's office, accosting him and ordering him to leave town. Then—Alice still could not believe her good fortune—Mr. Douglas had given her two hundred dollars so that she could move to Galveston and work in his store. It was like a miracle, she thought to herself.

When Alice entered the Perrings' house Jeanette hurried out of the kitchen where she was cooking her husband's supper. He was still at the stable, for his business was constantly increasing and he was a diligent worker who never looked at the clock.

"My goodness, your face is all red, Alice dear—whatever happened to you?" Jeanette Perring, a tall, willowy, chestnut-haired woman of thirty-two, exclaimed.

"Mr. Shottlander slapped me," Alice stammered. "Jeanette, would you mind awfully if I moved to Galveston?"

"Why, whatever made you think of a thing like that? You know that David and I like having you here—after all, you're my own sister, and just about my only living relative," Jeanette expostulated. "Come into the kitchen and let's talk. I only hope Davey'll be home soon, but you know how he is about horses, especially when someone comes in and just wants to talk about them. Now, what were you saying about Galveston?"

Quickly, Alice explained what had happened. Jeanette wonderingly shook her head. "I just don't know, honey. It all happened so fast. But are you sure you can trust this man, this Mr. Douglas?"

"I know I can. Besides, why would he give me two hundred dollars unless he really meant it? And he said that half of it would be my first month's salary when his new store opened—that would be in about half a year's time."

Jeanette frowned and shook her head. "You're such a trusting soul, honey. You and John had a wonderful marriage, and he was your first and only sweetheart, so you really don't know too much about men."

"I know enough to know I'll never work for men like Calvin Jemmers and Arnold Shottlander again, not ever! And I know what you're thinking, Jeanette, and you're all wrong. Mr. Douglas is happily married—he told me so— and he's got three lovely little boys. Anyone could see right off he's very devoted to his family. I just wish—" Alice bit her lips and turned away to hide her tears from her older sister.

"I know, I know, honey," Jeanette soothingly placated her. "You've been eating your heart out for poor John ever since that dreadful raid on your farm. But you mark my words, you'll find a nice man one of these days. Lord knows you're attractive enough." She gave a self-conscious little laugh. "I only wish I had your skin and your figure."

"Thank you, but the trouble is that the only men I knew in Houston were those two, and you know how that awful banker wanted me to—to be with him," Alice could not bring herself to use a more explicit term.

"Yes, I agree with you there. But what are you going to do in the meantime?"

"Well, my job with Mr. Shottlander is over—in fact, Mr. Douglas told him to leave town or he'd have Mayor Scanlan run him out. So I'll have to find something else—I'm going to go on paying room and board as I always do, until Mr. Douglas sends for me. He took my address down, and he said he'd get in touch with me when his new store was ready."

"Well, that's fair enough," Jeanette grudgingly admitted. "Now I know one thing for sure, they need a waitress down at Loring's—you know, that little restaurant near the theater. The tips ought to be pretty good. The work shouldn't be too hard. I mean, if you really have to get a job right away until you're ready to go to Galveston."

"I do need a job right away, because I'm going to keep this money for exactly what Mr. Douglas said I should use if for. So I'll go there tomorrow and I'll apply. You and David have been terribly good to me, Jeanette, I won't ever forget it. But I know it'll do me a lot of good to move to Galveston eventually and to find some other kind of work. I never did like working for that nasty Mr. Shottlander anyway, to tell you the truth."

"Well, maybe it'll all work out for the best. I do wish Davey would remember that I'm not running a restaurant myself," this last with an exasperated frown. "I tell you what, it's stew, and it'll keep hot for him. You look as if you could stand a really good supper after all you've been through, you poor darling. We'll just sit down and eat ahead of Davey. He can have his when he gets home."

Charles Douglas had not forgotten Alice Fernmark. In early May, some two weeks after his return from Indianapolis with little Howard, he sent off a letter to her at the Dorado Street address, enclosing a bank draft for three hundred dollars and suggesting that she move to Galveston even before the new store was ready—in fact, as soon as it would be convenient for her. He urged her to visit his new partner, James Hunter, to introduce herself, and then to spend a few weeks visiting the rival general stores in Galveston and making notes about what she observed there. These she would turn over to James Hunter, who would in turn forward them to him. In this way, he pointed out, she could be very helpful to him in revealing what his future competitors were currently doing so that he could make his plans for strong merchandising that would win more sales volume for his new store.

When the letter arrived, Alice excitedly discussed it with her sister. "Now you see, Jeanette? He wouldn't be sending me this draft if he didn't really want to hire me, now would he?"

"No, I guess not, honey. Besides, I know you've made your mind up. The restaurant job hasn't really turned out too well, has it?"

"It certainly hasn't," Alice snapped. Only last night, one of her customers had pinched her bottom and obscenely detailed a relationship for which he would be willing to set her up in a hotel room at more money than she could earn waiting on tables. She had slapped his face and burst into tears, and the restaurant owner had taken her into the kitchen and angrily censured her. "Mr. Zimmerman happens to be one of my best customers, Alice, and if he doesn't show up here again because of what you just did to him, you might as well hang up your apron and call it quits. You're going to be strictly on trial from now on till the next time he shows up, understand me? I know what you said he did, but you just don't go around slapping an important man like Mr. Zimmerman, not in my place you don't!"

Remembering all this, Alice defiantly said, "Jeanette, I'm going to take a chance. Maybe a change of scenery will help get me out of the doldrums. I'm sure I'll never be able to forget what happened to John, but at least I'll have something new to occupy my mind."

Jeanette gave her sister a searching look. "If you ask me, honey, I think you've sort of fallen for this Chicago fella."

"You know, Jeanette, you're right." Alice gave her sister a tiny smile. "Only I know he's married. He couldn't see me for dirt, and I wouldn't even try. The first time I met him and he started talking about his wife and kids, I knew he was a fine, decent man. He's a doer, Jeanette, just the way poor John was. Maybe, if God's good to me, I'll find someone like him in Galveston. There's certainly no one here—at least so far I haven't met anybody. I'm going to do just what he wants me to, and maybe I can start a new life there. We'll still be in touch, because after all it's only fifty miles away. Maybe I can come up and visit you on my first vacation—that is, if you still want to have me."

"Now don't you dare talk nonsense like that, Alice Fernmark!" her sister righteously exclaimed, and then they began to cry and hug each other.

After Ramón Hernandez had driven the remuda back into the corral at Windhaven Range in August, he turned his horse and galloped toward the little house he had built for his wife, Lucien Edmond Bouchard's sister, Mara. Maybelle Belcher was on the porch and beamed at him as

384

he hurried up the steps. "It's good to have you back, and she'll be very glad to see you, Ramón," she exclaimed as she put her arms around him and kissed him on the cheek. "You're a father again!"

"*¡Gracias a Dios!*" the handsome young Mexican joyously exclaimed, as he took his sombrero and whacked it against his thigh in sheer delight. "Tell me, is it a boy or a girl?"

"Why don't you go see for yourself? It was born just three days ago. I've been helping Mara a little, but you've got a strong, good girl there."

"Maybelle, thank you for saying that. But the truth is that I've said it to myself every day that I've been away from her. I thank the good *Señor Dios* that she once took her quirt to me."

"I don't understand you, Ramón." Maybelle questioningly peered at him.

"It's a long story, and one day I'll tell you. But I'm very glad she did. And now, if you'll excuse me, I'm going in to see my *querida*, my *novia*, my *esposa!*" he jubilantly exclaimed as he opened the door of the house and hurried into the bedroom.

Mara lay propped up in bed on two pillows, a tender smile on her lovely face, as she cradled her baby son to her breast. He stood, awe-struck, and then sank down on his knees and crossed himself. He had thought, not irreverently, of the Holy Madonna at the sight of his beautiful young wife nursing their newly born son.

"Mara—my dearest one—I have been praying all the time I was away on the drive," he hoarsely murmured.

She looked up, her eyes soft and tender. "My husband, my lover, here is our new son. What shall we call him, my dear one?"

"I once said I wished to call him Edward after your grandfather Williamson, Mara, my *muy linda*," he said, as he rose to his feet and came toward the bed. He bent to kiss her on the mouth, and she circled his neck with one arm.

"Kiss our son, my beloved. Yes, I would like that too."

"My sweetheart, you have given me such joy as few men are ever blessed to know. I thank the dear God for you— and I am grateful to you, and humble in your love," he murmured, and tears streaked his face as he kissed her again and then their little son.

Pablo Casares and Lucas knew the same proud, paternal joy when they were reunited with their wives. Kate Casares, who had been Kate Strallis, had given birth to a son, in July and she told the good-hearted, middle-aged vaquero that she wished to name him after himself, Paul. Pablo Casares brushed his eyes with the back of his hand and told her that it would be better if she named the child after her first husband, Brett.

But black-haired Kate shook her head, her eyes sparkling with a feigned anger. She made tears come to his eyes with her fierce declaration, "*Hombre,* will you keep on wasting so much time all the rest of our lives together by humbling yourself to me? I'm yours now. I'll remember Brett through my sons. But with you, I have come alive again—it will be Paul, or I will be very angry with you."

Pablo Casares snorted and pretended to be indignant, as he fought to hide his own tears at this avowal of his young wife's love for him. "*Querida,* of course I would not have you angry with me. Yes, I know I am old and stupid, but I know that you are the wisest of all. Very well, it shall be Paul, as you say." And then, with a fierce glare, "But I will have something to say about how he is brought up, *comprende*? And if he does not obey you, I will have a long and serious talk with him, you may believe this!"

Felicidad had given Lucas a girl this time, a delicate-featured baby scarcely two days old, who had her mother's dark eyes and sweet mouth. Lucas knelt down before his wife's bed, his eyes rapt with wonder at the sight of the child. He looked at Felicidad and murmured, "What name shall we call her by, dear Felicidad, my sweetheart?"

"I would like you to decide, my husband," Felicidad tenderly whispered.

"Then I would like to call her after my mother, Celia. I'm an orphan now too, the way you were, Felicidad. We have a son we've called James, after my father. So let's name our daughter after my mother. And after that—" He hugged her and whispered into her ear, and she blushed. "And I promise you will have the right to name all the rest of the babies we're going to have, dear, wonderful Felicidad!"

* * *

386

Two days after she had decided to move to Galveston, Alice Fernmark made the journey to that city and then had a driver with a horse and buggy take her to the Hunters' home. Arabella received her, and after Alice introduced herself and explained her mission, Arabella urged her to wait and take some refreshment until James returned, which would be in about two hours.

The auburn-haired young widow took an immediate liking to vivacious Arabella Hunter. Indeed, the two hours passed quickly while they exchanged anecdotes about their lives, their hopes and aspirations, and when James entered, he found them both absorbed in conversation. Alice quickly sprang up, her cheeks reddening, and stammered out the reason for her visit, handing him the letter Charles Douglas had written to her.

"I already know who you are, Mrs. Fernmark. Charles wrote to me from Chicago, you see. Well now, we'll try to find you a decent place to live, which won't cost you too much—and I have some good ideas on the subject already," he genially informed her. "Rest a couple of days, and then you and I will go out to see the site of Mr. Douglas's new store. The contractor, Max Steinfeldt, has really done wonders so far. He's got an experienced crew of men, they've already laid the foundation, and there's already been some mention in the Galveston newspapers about the enterprise. Meanwhile, I'd like you to be our guest at supper and then stay the night. Tomorrow morning, you and I will go out and find you a good place to live, not too far from the store."

The next morning, he installed the attractive young widow in a boarding house half a mile away from the new department store, and Alice Fernmark found an immediately sympathetic bond between herself and her new landlady. The latter, Hattie Denver, was a spinster in her early fifties, whose brother and cousin had run a small ranch near San Antonio and like Alice's own husband had fallen victims to Indian attack.

Two mornings later, James Hunter called for Alice in a carriage and drove her to the site of her employer's store. Max Steinfeldt, who was directing his men, came out to welcome James and his attractive companion. "Mrs. Fernmark, this is Max Steinfeldt," James made the formal introductions. "He's the man responsible for all these hardworking men who are putting up the store where you're going to work by Christmas—maybe even sooner, if I know Max."

"Now, now, Mr. Hunter," the genial contractor chuckled, shaking his forefinger at James, "I'm only human, and all I promised Mr. Douglas and you was that we'd be open in time for Christmas shopping. That we will, sir, have no fear of that." Then, turning to Alice Fernmark and respectfully inclining his head, "It's a pleasure to meet you, Mrs. Fernmark. Well, you can see for yourself how far we've gone. We'll start with the second floor by the end of the summer, and with any sort of luck and not too bad weather, we should be ready for a December opening. I had a letter from Mr. Douglas, and he tells me that he's preparing to have goods shipped that will reach us by the middle of November. By then we'll have storerooms ready, and we'll be able to get everything set up by the very first week of December; at least, that's what I'm aiming at."

"It's just wonderful how much you've done already. You see, Mr. Steinfeldt, I met Mr. Douglas in Houston back in February," Alice smilingly explained. The candor and geniality of the German contractor had proved infectious, and she already felt confident in his presence. "Mr. Douglas wants me to visit the other stores in town and report my impressions to Mr. Hunter so that they'll be able to have an edge on the competition."

"That's a very smart idea, and it's typical of Mr. Douglas. I can tell you he's a very smart man, and I like him a great deal," Max Steinfeldt unhesitatingly declared.

"Well now," James grinned, "I appreciate that. But on to practical matters. I'm hungry. Max, do you think you could take time off for lunch? I think the three of us might have something to talk about. And then I'll write Charles a letter and tell him how we've progressed. I'm sure he'll be pleased."

James intuitively sensed Alice Fernmark's needing to come to terms with her new situation. Charles had already written to him some of the details of the young widow's background, and he was extremely sympathetic toward her. He understood her feeling of being a stranger about to begin a new life in a new city where she had neither friends nor relatives.

James could also see that Max Steinfeldt was greatly attracted by the auburn-haired young woman, mainly because of Alice's forthright and innate honesty. He made up his mind to get to know her better. Accordingly, for the next several weeks he saw to it that she was included when he and Arabella and his daughter Melinda and her husband went to the theater or to symphony concerts or simply out to dine. In his conversations with her on these occasions, he observed that she had good common sense, an admirable sense of humor, and the ability to hide any certainly pardonable traces of self-pity because of her widowhood and her consequent loneliness.

Because of this, he was able to write perceptive letters back to Chicago to assure Charles that his hiring of Alice had been extremely judicious. She had already begun to pose as a potential customer in two of the general stores that currently provided Houston citizens with furniture, clothing, dress materials, and sundries. The notes she brought him on her shopping experiences were, so far as he was concerned, well thought out and quite astute.

Knowing Charles as he did, the tall Southerner was extremely optimistic about his own impulsive decision to resign his post as his cousin's factor. He had initially been impressed by Charles's concern for attentive service and his wish to offer a variety of stock of primary interest to women shoppers. From Alice Fernmark's comments on what she had observed in the two rival stores, it was apparent to him that the Chicagoan's concept of long-range merchandising and personalized service would quickly appeal to the citizens of Galveston. And this would certainly reflect in profits on his own investment.

Thus in his fiftieth year James Hunter felt very much like Luke Bouchard, who had begun a new life and was savoring it to the fullest. This new venture whetted his mind, and his behavior toward Arabella constantly continued to delight and surprise her. What pleased him most was that he and Arabella had become steadfast friends as well as increasingly devoted lovers, and because of this cordial turn of events, he took an almost paternal interest in Alice Fernmark, recognizing as he did her estimable virtues. By the middle of July, he smilingly hinted to Arabella over supper one evening, "Do you know, Bella dear, I think Alice and Max have a great deal in common and I, for one, would like to see them married."

Arabella giggled, as she often did these days, so happy was she in her new relationship with James. It was one of the few girlish traits that she still retained. She was more mature, and yet paradoxically felt younger than ever. She no longer feared the advent of her fiftieth year: she had achieved an inner peace and contentment, and the idea that her husband was continuing to court her as romantically as he had when they had first been married had at last freed her from insecurity, immaturity, and most of her girlish foibles.

"Do you know, James darling, I feel exactly the same way. Of course, it would be much too obvious if we tried to bring them together. But I think it'll happen by itself, and that is the best way of all."

He chuckled as he poured more coffee into her cup. "In a way, Bella, I rather envy them. You know, the second time around is sometimes the best. Both of them were married, both of them lost their spouses, and they both are in need. Now here are you and I, gracefully advancing toward our autumnal years, if I may say so, but I find you even more enticing than when I first married you. When I first met you, I said to myself that I'd have real problems in disciplining you—"

"And you certainly did, James," she teased with a sly wink at him.

"I know. But you know, down deep inside, Bella, you're not really angry with me for having spanked you."

"Gracious no. Where would our darling Joy be today if you hadn't? You're a very devious young man, my husband. I'm glad I've grown up enough to appreciate you for all you are." Arabella winked at him and raised her cup in tribute.

He broke out into a hearty laugh. "I am, too, to put it selfishly, my dearest Bella. Well then, I've a hunch that, by the time Charles's store is ready to open and dazzle all our Galveston elite, Alice and Max will have found each other to be very compatible. As Shakespeare might say, 'tis a consummation devoutly to be wished.'"

"I do hope so, James. She's such a sweet woman, and Max is such a dear, thoughtful, hard-working man. They're really meant for each other, aren't they?"

"As you and I were long ago, Bella, and still are," he murmured. Then, with a boyish grin that made her giggle again, he left the table and came to her side to take her in his arms and kiss her passionately on the mouth.

"James, my goodness! You're the most amazing man!" she gasped.

"And you the most amazing woman. Since nobody's home, and I don't think we'll have to worry about any consequences, can I seduce you from the table long enough to spend a little private time with your loving husband?"

Arabella didn't answer, but as she kissed him back, a blush flooded her lovely, unwrinkled face.

During the first week in September, Alice Fernmark walked down the street from her boarding house to the new store. The first floor had been completed, and the second floor was in the process of being constructed. That very morning she had received a laudatory letter from Charles Douglas commending her for her accurate and extensive notes on his competition, forwarded to him by James. He had enclosed another bank draft for a hundred dollars as a bonus for her labors and told her that he planned to come down to Galveston some time in mid-November. Charles had added that his wife, Laurette, was expecting a baby about a week or two before his intended visit, and Alice sighed deeply when she read that personal note, remembering her own barrenness. Fortunately, the new job absorbed most of her energies, and she did not waste much time feeling sorry for herself.

Alice had written many glowing letters back to her sister in Houston, saying how graciously the Hunters had treated her and also mentioning the name of Max Steinfeldt several times. He was of course older than Charles Douglas, and quite a bit older than Alice; nevertheless, his personality and his straightforwardness had made a great impression on her. Having resigned herself to widowhood, Alice tried to ignore her feelings. She thrust all thought of a relationship into the farthermost recess of her mind. After all, Mr. Steinfeldt had taken her to lunch and dinner several times and had never shown her more than a general amiability, which she knew to be a part of his nature. He had talked mainly of his work on the store, often describing to her the lives of some of the workers he had hired, their personal troubles and aspirations. Alice was aware—though she didn't want to admit it to herself—that this very selflessness was attracting her to him. But until he gave some sign—and perhaps not even then—she would not permit herself to acknowledge anything beyond admiration and respect for the man.

She stood for a long moment, watching the masons lay bricks in a neat row above the foundation of the second floor. It would be a wonderful store, she knew. Mr. Douglas had written that he planned to start shipping the merchandise for the store by the end of October. By that time, a great deal of it could be put on display on the already-completed first floor, and Max Steinfeldt would hire an additional crew of a dozen men to set up and decorate the various departments, according to the instructions he had already received. The balance of the merchandise would be kept in a nearby warehouse and installed by the first week of December. Thus far, everything was on schedule, even ahead of it, and the cordial German widower was exuberantly optimistic about fulfilling his obligations to his Chicago boss.

She smiled as she saw the passersby stop to look up at the structure, and she played a little game with herself, wondering how many of the spectators who watched would come into the store in December and up to her counter. She knew there was already considerable interest in the venture: the Galveston daily newspaper had printed several stories about Charles Douglas and his store, and that would certainly draw many shoppers. She wanted everything to succeed for the man who had given her such a wonderful opportunity, as well as for James Hunter who was his partner. They were both the finest men she had ever met—since she had lost John. There was no higher praise she could give them.

She saw Max Steinfeldt emerge from the entrance of the store, talking to one of his workmen, a young, moustachioed Mexican who was one of the masons. Glancing around to make sure that there were no horseback riders or buggies coming down the street, she crossed to meet him.

There was a scaffolding on the left side of the store, just above the floor of the second story, and three of the workmen were waiting for a plank to be drawn up by a hoist, on which a container of newly made bricks was set. Max turned, nodding to the young Mexican, who went back into the store, and then waved his hand at Alice. With a little cry of pleasure, she hurried toward him.

"It's good to see you, Mrs. Fernmark," he exclaimed. He turned to point at the second floor. "You see how well we're coming along. I've got good men here, they work hard and they take pride in what they're doing. That's the sort of men I like."

"Oh yes!" Alice breathed. "I just know it's going to be a great success. We're going to take all the business away from those other stores, aren't we, Mr. Steinfeldt?"

"Of course. Matter of fact, Mrs. Fernmark, I'm going to send off a wire to Mr. Douglas this very day and tell him that we're doing very well indeed. By the end of the week, my men will be ready to uncrate whatever merchandise he ships and put it where it belongs. You see, I've had detailed plans from him. I really have to hand it to him, he knows exactly what he wants, and I'm glad I can help him get it."

"So am I, Mr. Steinfeldt. Yes, he's really a wonderful man!" Alice smilingly agreed.

Max Steinfeldt glanced upwards, then suddenly uttered a cry and, grasping Alice around the shoulders, pulled her far to one side. The ropes holding the scaffolding had broken, and the bricks crashed down upon the sidewalk only a few feet away from both of them.

"My God, that was much too close for comfort! I'm sorry, Mrs. Fernmark—I didn't mean to startle you, but I just saw that scaffolding give way!" he panted.

Alice turned to look at the bricks strewn along the sidewalk. Then, feeling his arms around her, she began to tremble and suddenly buried her face in his chest. "Oh, Mr. Steinfeldt, you saved my life—you did, you know—oh, you—you might have been hurt—I couldn't bear to think of that—"

In her nervous reaction, she burst into sudden tears. The German widower, holding her tightly, hastened to reassure her. "Oh no, Mrs. Fernmark—Alice—there wasn't really any danger—it's fine now, everything's all right. Please, *meine* Alice, *Liebchen*, everything will be fine now."

Slowly she lifted her head, her face crimson with emotion, and they saw in each other's eyes what neither so far had had the courage to evince.

He tightened his embrace of her, and whispered, "Do

393

not be afraid, *Liebchen*. I will take care of you always. I am not sorry this happened, if you want to know something. I think—I know—I want to protect you like this for always, Alice."

She was trembling as she sheltered herself in his embrace. "I would be so happy, dear Max. I want you too. But there's so much you don't know about me—maybe you wouldn't want me. I was married, and my husband was killed by Indians—and I couldn't have a child——"

"Hush, my *Liebchen*," he softly whispered. "I am a lonely man, no longer young, and you are a beautiful young woman. That you should care for me at all is so much more than I could hope for—I do not care what else may be. But all I know is that I want you very much. You will have dinner with me tonight, and we will talk about all this, and then when Herr Douglas comes to see what I have built for him, you will be my wife—that is, of course, only if you wish it, my *Liebchen*."

CHAPTER THIRTY-TWO

When Lucien Edmond Bouchard's outfit returned to Windhaven Range, Maria Elena Romero was graciously welcomed by Maxine Bouchard and invited to live in the ranch house as a respected guest. Lucien Edmond's beautiful wife quickly divined the relationship that was beginning to exist between the black-haired, gentle Mexican girl and Eddie Gentry, and rejoiced in it. She had further news for her own husband when he came to her room that night.

"You'll be a father again by the end of the year, my dearest," she happily informed him. "And this time, I'm hoping it will be a son. After all, I've given you three girls to only one boy, so I want to be sure that your great-grandfather's name is carried on."

Lucien Edmond took Maxine in his arms and gently kissed her. "I'm sure it will, my sweet Maxine. Besides, you're forgetting my father's other sons, little Lucien and Paul. I have a feeling the name of Bouchard is going to persevere for a good long while. Besides, there's another side of the coin too, Maxine. One day these three girls of ours, with all the virtues they'll have acquired because of their upbringing by you, will marry good, fine men and give them strong, lasting families. And those same fine Bouchard qualities will be carried on wherever they settle down."

"I know that, darling," she smilingly nodded as she clung to him and put her head against his chest.

"Why, of course. And I've always felt that the wife deserves a lot more credit than she gets for the success of a family. Take you, for instance. When you came to visit from Baltimore that summer, I fell in love with you at once, and I knew even then not only what happiness you'd give me, but also how you'd help shape my character as a man.

No, Maxine darling, it would be fine to have another son, but if it's a daughter, I'll still say that I'm the most fortunate of men to be given such a loyal, beautiful, and devoted wife."

"You weren't so sure at first," she playfully teased him, reaching up to tug at a lock of his blond hair. "You thought I was one of those intellectual bluestockings—at least, I know that's what your father said about me."

Lucien Edmond tilted back his head and laughed heartily. Then he kissed her soundly and said, his eyes twinkling with humor, "If you really want to know what he said, he told me that he and Mother had been invited by your Uncle Ernest and his new young wife, Lucille, to come for a housewarming. You may recall that your uncle had bought fifty acres of land from my Uncle Mark's overseer and built a house on it. Father said that you'd be visiting and if I didn't have any other social plans, he thought I'd like to come along."

"And what did you say to that?" Maxine gaily inquired.

"Well, I told him that the only social plans I had at the time were to study Dubow's *Planter's Manual*. And he said it would be much more enlightening for me to meet you, because, like Mara, you believed that a woman should have the right to cast a vote and even to hold public office. And I said that by all means I'd like to meet so imaginative a girl and that I could learn a great deal more from you than even from an authority like Dubow. So you see, darling, the news that you were a bluestocking didn't deter me in the least—if anything, it increased my interest in you."

"And do you still have the same interest?" Again she tugged at a lock of his hair.

He kissed her so lingeringly that there was no time for an immediate reply. When he straightened, her face was flushed and her eyes warm with happiness. Then he said, "I don't think there are many ranchers' wives out here in this huge state of Texas who combine being a wonderful hostess, an incomparable mother, a devoted wife, an indescribably tender sweetheart, along with the ability to cook a meal and to play the spinet and to divert me with stimulating conversation when I need it most. Yes, Maxine, I'd say my interest has increased over the years and it always will."

"That, sir, is an answer I'm willing to wager few wives

ever get from their husbands. And I love you more than the first day we met, that's for certain." She kissed him ardently on the mouth and then slipped out of his embrace, arranging her tumbled hair and smoothing her dress with a most becoming blush. "I'm so happy that Eddie Gentry found someone to care for. I was praying that he would."

"I'm sure before very much longer they'll be married. And that reminds me, there's no one on the ranch who can perform the ceremony. I only wish Friar Bartoloméo were here." Lucien Edmond thoughtfully frowned. "But then, they can always ride to San Antonio, be married there in one of the missions, and spend their honeymoon there. It's a lovely old town, and quiet enough for a honeymoon too."

"That's a splendid idea!" Maxine excitedly agreed.

"And I plan to give Eddie that fifty acres I reserved for him, and have the vaqueros help build a house for him and Maria Elena when the time comes, just as I would have done if he'd been able to marry Polly Behting."

"Never you mind, Lucien Edmond, I'll keep after them both until he gets over any shyness he may still have and actually proposes."

"I'm afraid, darling, you really won't be needed as a matchmaker, though I'm certain your talents are as outstanding as in everything else. When Eddie brought that puppy back to Maria Elena, she just about made him propose to her, from what Ramón tells me. So I don't imagine it's going to be very long before he comes in to see me, sombrero in hand, shifting from one foot to the other and trying hard to tell me what's on his mind." Lucien Edmond chuckled again.

True to Lucien Edmond's prediction, Eddie Gentry hesitantly approached him a week later as Lucien Edmond and Ramón were standing beside the corral selecting horses to be trained for the next spring roundup. Despite the intensive cross-breeding which Lucien Edmond and his new partner, Joe Duvray, were doing, they would still have to do a certain amount of "brush-popping" to round up the strays, the mavericks, and some of the wild Mexican cattle that had crossed over the border to graze on the perimeter of Windhaven Range.

"Yes, Eddie, what can I do for you?" Lucien Edmond turned to smile at the Texan.

"Mr. Lucien Edmond—I mean, if it wouldn't be inconvenient—I'd like to take about a week or so off. 'Course I know I haven't earned any furlough yet, but I was thinking of getting married—if you've no objection," the young cowboy stammered, flushing hotly as Ramón amusedly eyed him and nodded encouragement.

"Of course, I've no objection. And I don't suppose Maria Elena has either, or you wouldn't be telling me this. Now here's what I want you and her to do, Eddie. You'll hitch two of the strongest horses we have to one of our extra wagons, and the two of you will drive off to San Antonio. You'll find a priest there who'll marry you, and then you just stay and have yourself at least a week's honeymoon. It's on me. Before you go, come see me and I'll give you the bonus you have coming—it'll come in handy for expenses with a new wife and all." Then, glancing at Ramón, he added, "And don't you worry about that fine new mustang you broke—I'm sure Ramón will take special care of it for you while you're gone."

"My gosh, Mr. Lucien Edmond, this is too much. You don't owe me anything—I'm the one who owes you—"

"Now I'm giving you an order, Eddie." The twinkle in Lucien Edmond's eyes belied the words. "I say that you've a bonus coming, and when you get back from your honeymoon, there's a section of fifty acres to the northwest of Joe Duvray's land that I've earmarked for you and your wife. I know the vaqueros will be happy to help you build a nice little house there."

"Gosh, I—I don't know what to say—you—oh gosh, thanks—I'll work my tail off—I'll—"

"You already have, Eddie. You deserve everything I'm giving you and a lot more. Now you go see your girl—she's in the kitchen with Maxine right now—and you tell her to get ready and you can leave whenever you want."

Eddie Gentry could hardly speak, but as he turned to go back to the ranch house, he sent Lucien Edmond a look of gratitude, and his face was like that of a man who had just been told to enter paradise.

Laurette Douglas fulfilled her husband's wish on the Saturday of the first week in November by giving birth to a red-haired baby girl. It was an easy delivery, and the helpful cooperation of the new governess who had replaced unfortunate Agnes Strion had considerably eased Charles's preoccupied mind. He had recently completed arrangements with his suppliers to begin shipping the goods to go on display, hopefully by the very first week of December.

His Indianapolis friend and furniture supplier, David Porter, had undertaken the project of placing Agnes Strion in a private mental institution where she would receive decent care and treatment. Charles had forwarded a draft to him to cover the expenses for the first six months. He also threw business in Porter's direction, signing a binding contract to purchase furniture only from Porter for the next five years for all of his outlets—and he had already been in touch with the Houston bank president, Dennis Claverton, who had confirmed the availability of a likely piece of property on which a subsidiary store could be built in Houston whenever Charles Douglas desired.

Charles was reluctant to leave Laurette so soon after the birth of their child, but the attachment his wife had formed with the new governess enabled him to feel less guilty about not being with her. The governess had already proven herself. A month before the birth of the baby girl, whom Laurette and Charles had agreed to name Fleur, in memory of Fleurette Wilson, the twins, Kenneth and Arthur, fell ill after lunch. The governess, suspecting that some meat obtained from the butcher was responsible, and having had some practical nurse's training herself, alertly recognized the signs and took preliminary measures. When the doctor arrived nearly two hours later, he commended her on her quick thinking and remarked to the distraught Laurette that, thanks to the governess's quick action, the twins were quite out of danger.

When he arrived in Galveston in November, Charles Douglas quickly discovered that James Hunter had ably discharged all his duties. He had spent a great deal of time with the contractor, the architect, and the workers, as well as with port officials to inquire about shipping goods to Galveston.

James had seen to it also that the Galveston newspaper carried occasional reports of the progress of the store, as well as little human interest notes to arouse public interest in the new enterprise.

One of these notes had a romantic bent: Alice Fernmark and Max Steinfeldt, the first sales clerk hired and the contractor for the store, would be married the day after the opening. And already, James enthusiastically informed the delighted Chicago merchant, he had taken many applications for positions in the new store from local residents whose character and background he had himself personally investigated. When the store opened, it would be staffed with the kind of employees Charles would himself have selected, had he been on hand to do so.

And so the Douglas Department Store opened its doors for the first time on December 2, 1872. Two weeks earlier, Charles's original Chicago store had reopened, thanks to the efforts of Lawrence Harding, Charles's Chicago partner. Harding had taken over much of the responsibility of rebuilding that store while Charles was preoccupied with his new store in Galveston.

By the end of the first day of business at the Galveston store, the number of sales as well as the constant throngs of interested shoppers made Charles turn to his affable partner and joyously declare, "James, some people say we're going to have a panic next year, a recession. Well, judging by what I see here—and a great deal of it is due entirely to you—I think we're going to weather the storm. And now, I'm bone-tired. Let's you and I go have ourselves a bite of late supper and a good stiff drink, and toast the wedding of two of the nicest people I've ever met!"

CHAPTER THIRTY-THREE

It was December 18, 1872, and if Lucien Bouchard had been alive, he would have celebrated his hundred and tenth birthday. On Windhaven Range, one would have believed it still to be late autumn. The sun was warm, and only a faint wind stirred the clumps of mesquite and the tall reeds that grew along the banks of the Nueces River. At dawn, Lucien Edmond Bouchard went to the chapel, and there, alone, he prayed for the souls of his great-grandfather and Dimarte. He thanked his Maker for the many bounties of happiness and prosperity that had been vouchsafed him during the year now ending. Also, he offered prayers of gratitude for his wife's safe delivery of the child they had both wanted . . . a girl whom they had named Gloria, after Maxine's grandmother.

He prayed also for blessings upon Joe Duvray and his Margaret, and their little son, Robert; upon Eddie Gentry and Maria Elena; Dr. Ben Wilson and Elone and their reunited family; Charles and Laurette Douglas and their children; James and Arabella Hunter and their children in Galveston. Finally, he prayed for his father, Luke, and stepmother, Laure, and their children. Then, crossing himself, he gave thanks for the loyalty of the men who had worked with him to make Windhaven Range strong and defensible; for the souls of Sybella Bouchard Forsden and the stouthearted Mandingo, Djamba; then finally for his blood brother, Emataba, *mico* of the abandoned Creeks in Indian Territory.

The new year loomed upon the horizon of both Windhaven Range and Windhaven Plantation. The soothsayers, the harbingers of disaster, and the pessimistic Cassandras of the young nation that was four years away from its centennial all prophesied ill tidings and economic unrest in the year ahead. Yet with his father's legacy of courage and straightforward thinking, Lucien Edmond looked to the future as a challenge, not a threat. He had only to think back to those grim days after Appomattox to realize what an advance the Bouchards had made upon the pages of history: burned out of their ancestral home near Lowndesboro, they had come here to begin a new life. They had fought the elements, hostile Indians, bandits, and bushwhackers, and they were stronger because of it.

There were many portents for good to outweigh any fears about the future. Lucien Edmond had only to think of courageous Charles Douglas, caught up in his new venture, with James Hunter to help him. Both men, through their marriages into the Bouchard family, had added immeasurably to its strength. Yes, the unity of the Bouchards had never been stronger. And Lucien Edmond was sure that his father, far to the east of him—perhaps at this very moment—was praying in his own chapel, as was his yearly custom, to pay tribute to the gallant young idealist who had left Yves-sur-lac to found a veritable dynasty built on loyalty and hard work.

He left the chapel, his face as serene as his spirit, and walked slowly back to the ranch house. There he stood looking toward the west, savoring the sweep of verdant land that was now joined with Windhaven Range: Robert Caldemare's land, now under the stewardship of loyal Joe Duvray, married to Caldemare's daughter.

He experienced a momentary pang of sadness as he recalled how much sorrow Caldemare had brought upon his daughter. There was some good in every man, it was true, but it was up to each man to make the most of his virtues and to discipline himself so as to minimize what was weak and harmful in his nature. At least, Lucien Edmond thought, Caldemare's grandson and namesake, little Robert, had a good chance of traveling the right path in life, given the guidance and love of two such parents as Joe and Margaret.

It was a week away from Christmas, and Lucien Edmond's thoughts now turned to practical matters. A week earlier, he had sent Simata and two new vaqueros, Antonio Morales and Esteban Verdugo, to San Antonio to bring back supplies. They would also bring the Christmas gifts which he had ordered for the members of his household and for all of his workers as well. On Christmas Eve, they would have a joyous fiesta, to which all would be welcome. It would be a time for thanking even the humblest vaquero for his loyalty and diligence through this prosperous year. Perhaps financially it might not compare so favorably with previous years, but for Lucien Edmond Bouchard, it was rich in the satisfaction of seeing his family thriving and Windhaven Range doubled in size with Joe Duvray a loyal partner to work beside him. And now Eddie Gentry would become one of the true defenders of this greater Windhaven.

The men should be back by tomorrow, he estimated. He smiled to himself as he thought of the gifts he had ordered for Maxine: a red velvet gown and a pair of exquisite slippers to go with it, an edition of all the Beethoven piano sonatas, and a ruby ring. The ruby ring was a symbol: it was just such a ring that the Countess Laurette de Bouchard had given to her younger son, Lucien, when he had determined to leave France forever and seek a new life across the seas. And Lucien had given that ring to his beloved Dimarte as his pledge of eternal love.

He was about to go back into the ranch house when he saw a lone rider galloping from the north. Puzzled, he hurried to the gate and went out to meet him. He recognized the gray mustang as Simata's, and raised his hand in salutation. The half-breed scout reined up and dismounted, his face troubled.

"Has something happened to Antonio and Esteban?" Lucien Edmond anxiously asked.

"No, they are coming with the wagon. But I rode on ahead to tell you what has happened in San Antonio. A very terrible thing, Mr. Lucien Edmond. The night we arrived there, Esteban and Antonio went to a saloon for tequila. They overheard two men talking near them, men who had already drunk more than was good for them. There was music and there was dancing and there were girls around them, so they thought what they said would not be heard by our vaqueros. And they spoke the name of Sangrodo."

"That's strange indeed, Simata. Go on!" Lucien Edmond urged.

"One of them said that after they had done what they had come to do in San Antonio, they meant to ride across the border. They would attack Sangrodo's stronghold and kill the Comanches and take their horses and their treasures."

"What treasures could they mean? Sangrodo's people have been living like simple farmers for the past several years," Lucien Edmond indignantly averred.

"That is so, Mr. Lucien Edmond. I don't know how these men knew of Sangrodo. Antonio said to me that one of the two drunken men who spoke was a half-breed. And he boasted that when they robbed the Comanche stronghold, they would find jewels, even gold and silver."

"The only jewel I know of was the great turquoise of the tribe, which Sangrodo gave to my father," Lucien Edmond gravely replied. "Do you think they know where Sangrodo's stronghold is, then, Simata?"

The half-breed nodded. "This man who had Indian blood in his veins said that he knew. And he said that it was not far from the village of Miero, to the west of it."

"Wait—" Lucien Edmond closed his eyes and thought back. "Yes, four years ago, Simata, when Carlos Macaras and his band attacked our ranch and were routed—thanks to the intervention of Sangrodo and his men—there were two bandits who escaped: Macaras himself and a henchman. Those two then rode across the border and attacked Sangrodo's stronghold, before Sangrodo and his men had returned there. They tried to kidnap Menigasay's wife, Dolores, and Macaras tried to kill Sangrodo's son, Kitante. Catayuna saved the boy by knifing the bandit leader, and paid for it by losing her unborn child." Lucien Edmond paused and frowned. "Simata," he continued, "we thought that, after that, there was nothing left of Macaras's band. But someone must still be alive who knows where the stronghold is—perhaps one who wasn't killed in the raid on Windhaven Range."

"Yes, that could well be, Mr. Lucien Edmond. But wait, I haven't told you all of this. The next morning, just as we were going into town to buy the gifts and the supplies you ordered, we heard gunfire from a distance. And when we came to the Citizens' Bank, where I was to cash the draft you had given me, the sheriff and his deputies were there and many people were crowding around and we could not get in. When I asked what had happened, one of the depu-

404

ties told me that outlaws had robbed the bank and killed the president, two of his clerks, and two of the customers who were in the way when the shooting started."

"My God, poor old Pericles Lysander! I remember him when Father and I opened our account there and one for Djamba. He was very hostile, but he later became a good friend to Father and me. Murdered by outlaws, how horrible!"

"The deputy told me that the outlaws were riding south. That is why I hurried back ahead of Antonio and Esteban to tell you this, Mr. Lucien Edmond. You will want to warn Sangrodo if those evil men are heading for his stronghold."

"Yes, I will, for they have few weapons to withstand any such attack. Have you any idea of how many men are in this outlaw band, Simata?"

"This deputy told me that one of the women customers who had been in the bank, and whose friend had been killed, said that there were about fourteen or fifteen men who came into the bank, all with guns."

"They would slaughter Sangrodo's people with such a force of arms, Simata."

"That is what I think too, Mr. Lucien Edmond. And they have taken a trail west of here to cross the border. This I know because yesterday, riding to the west, I found the marks of their horses. There was also a little camp where they had stopped for the night. They would be coming through Eagle Pass, and then, across the border, head southeast to the stronghold. Unless they manage to steal fresh horses, theirs must be exhausted by now. I think that if we send our men now to the stronghold we might arrive ahead of them—and that is why I drove my mustang without mercy to reach you."

"Thank God you found out what you did. Get Lucas—his sister Prissy is in that village, and he'll want to protect her. I'll go to the bunkhouse and ask for a dozen of our best riders to come with me. Have Lucas pass out the Spencer rifles and carbines and plenty of ammunition for each man!"

Half an hour later, Lucien Edmond came out of the ranchhouse, armed with a Spencer carbine and a holstered Starr .44, to mount his gelding and lead his men to the aid of the valiant Comanche chief. Maxine had tearfully pleaded with him not to undertake so dangerous a mission. But he had withstood that poignant appeal.

"I must, Maxine," he had gently told her. "It's a debt I owe. Yes, the men would obey my orders and go without me, but they'd never respect me again. I'll be careful, you know I will. I mean to come back to you and to our children, my darling Maxine. Now don't cry, we'll enjoy ourselves at the fiesta on Christmas Eve, I promise you."

There were fifteen of them, all outlaws whose individual exploits had terrorized the Panhandle as well as southern Texas and many a helpless Mexican village. Their leader was a gaunt, black-bearded, forty-five-year-old Kansan, Fred Morley, who had been a Union deserter during the Civil War, ridden with the infamous William Clarke Quantrill in the brutal raid against Lawrence in 1863, and gone on to form his own band of five bank and train robbers. Five months earlier, having recruited another ten men across the border, *pistoleros* and outlaws with a price on their heads offered by the Mexican government, he had robbed a bank in Austin, shot down two of the officers in cold blood, and ruthlessly gunned down a horrified woman customer who had screamed when she had seen the two men fall dead near her.

One of his Mexican recruits was Luis Ademar, whom Morley had made his lieutenant, because Ademar had both a savage lust for killing—it was he who had shot down old Pericles Lysander as well as the two officers of the Austin Bank—and a fertile imagination for planning new and daring acts of plunder and bloody violence. Luis Ademar had been one of the members of Carlos Macaras's band four years earlier. He had been wounded in the attack on Windhaven Range and had crawled away undetected by friend or foe. He had hidden in the underbrush until all was quiet, and then had dragged himself to the hut of a peon whom he had killed and whose wife he forced to nurse him and satisfy his carnal lusts. When he recovered, he killed her too, and then rode off to Nuevo Laredo where he soon joined several of his renegade compatriots to raid helpless little villages. He was one of the two men whom Antonio Morales had heard boasting in the San Antonio saloon.

Before the attack on Windhaven Range, Luis Ademar had been a friend of Juan Cortigo, also a member of Carlos Macaras's band, and the one who perished with him in the attack on Sangrodo's stronghold. Cortigo had had an Indian mother, and although Ademar's mother had been of a different tribe, he had become one of Cortigo's few trustworthy friends, because of their common Indian background. Like Cortigo, Ademar was ferociously sadistic and lecherous.

In the months following that raid, Ademar had heard rumors of how both Luis Cortigo and Carlos Macaras had perished in an attack on a Comanche stronghold. Ademar concluded that this must be the same stronghold from which Comanches had marched forth to thwart the attack on Windhaven. He had heard Cortigo and Marcaras discussing this *Comancheria,* saying that there were certain to be attractive squaws and treasure there. In the four years since that time, Ademar had burned with the obsession both to find that treasure and to avenge himself on the Indians who had killed Cortigo, his friend. Thus it was that he now proposed an attack on the *Comancheria* to the ruthless Kansan, Fred Morley.

The four other white men whom Fred Morley had originally recruited, and who had ridden with him into many a daring robbery before he had decided to enlarge his forces, were a scabrous lot. Dan Weinhold, like Morley, was a Kansan, and a rapist, murderer, and rustler. Hans Durst was a twenty-two-year-old German-born runaway from his uncle's home in Sedalia; his vanity was flattered by seeing himself described on "wanted" posters for the crimes of strangling a dance-hall girl in Abilene and knifing a Sedalia stable owner whose best horse he still rode. John Hazelhurst, thirty, was a Confederate deserter who had robbed and killed two wealthy Creoles in New Orleans. Subsequently he fled to northern Texas, where he murdered an isolated settler and compelled the latter's wife to be his harlot until he tired of her and drowned her in the little creek nearby. Lee Shaw, from Emporia, Kansas, was a tall, wiry, gray-bearded man in his late forties who had murdered his own father and older brother when he learned that his father planned to leave the farm and its livestock to his brother. He had robbed three banks on his own and killed five bank clerks before he met Fred Morley.

Nine of the Mexicans of Morley's enlarged band were armed with knives and Belgian and French pistols, while Luis Ademar, wearing a knife sheath at his left hip and a holster for a Starr .44 at his right, was proudest of all with a new Sharps rifle. Morley's four white cronies each wore a pair of holstered six-shooters, and Lee Shaw and Dan Weinhold had, in addition, Henry rifles sheathed in leather scabbards bound to their saddles. Morley himself wore a Bowie knife in a sheath at his left hip, a holstered six-shooter at his right, and flamboyantly brandished an old but still murderously effective Whitworth rifle in his right hand as he rode at the head of this ominous procession.

They had galloped out of San Antonio and taken a little-used trail which veered to the southwest, then veered to the southeast once they had crossed the Colorado River. Twenty miles farther south, they stopped at an isolated farm, shot down an ex-Confederate captain and his two teenaged sons, raped and then killed his wife, and stole the four horses they found in his barn. They had indeed, as Simata predicted, headed for Eagle Pass, and Luis Ademar, who knew the terrain well, directed them to the southeast and toward the stronghold of Sangrodo. There, he had promised them, they would find *dinero* and *muchachas* in abundance. And beyond that stronghold, once they had slaughtered the Indians and taken their women and treasure, there were many little villages he knew which they could profitably raid or even take over and use as their headquarters while they planned their next exploits.

Late in the afternoon of December 20, Ademar reined in his horse, turned to Morley, and excitedly gestured southward. "There it is, Señor Morley!"

"I see it, Luis. Now, off to the left, southeast of the camp, where you see all that tall, thick grass, there's a passel o' trees—we'll get in there and wait till it's dark. They won't see us so well once we're inside those trees."

"*Es verdad*, Señor Morley," the half-breed smirkingly agreed. "It is about two hundred yards from the *Comancheria*, which is on higher ground, and all those little hills which circle it. I can just make out the light of their campfires. They will be preparing the *comida de noche*."

"Sure. Now you, Luis, and you, Diego," Morley turned to a thickly moustachioed, stocky Mexican in his mid-thirties, "the two of you, once it gets real dark, will get up

408

as close as you can to the stronghold. They're bound to send some of their squaws out for water—d'you see that little creek just this side of the stronghold? Well, you'll grab them and bring them back into the woods with us. That'll draw the murderin' redskins out for certain, and we'll pick them off like ducks in a pond. All right, the rest of you, into the woods with me!"

Lucien Edmond Bouchard, Lucas, Simata, and the vaqueros who had eagerly accompanied the blond trail boss of Windhaven Range had ridden hard for two days, taking only a few hours' sleep the first night. Now, at nightfall of the second day, they came within sight of Sangrodo's stronghold from the west. They could see the campfires from a distance, and a few yards ahead of them was a wide, deep ravine. Lucien Edmond held up his hand to halt his men, then quickly whispered to Simata, "There's no sight of the outlaws yet. But it's possible they're hiding in those woods over to the east, southeast of the stronghold. Let's all dismount, and there, to our right, are heavy mesquite bushes to which we can tie the reins of our horses. We'll wait here in the ravine. If they intend a surprise attack and are really here ahead of us, we'll be able to halt them with our long-range Spencer fire before they can enter the stronghold!"

Swiftly Simata transmitted Lucien Edmond's orders, and the men tied their horses' reins to the branches of the mesquite bushes, drew out their rifles and carbines from the saddle sheaths, and crouched down in the ravine, which was as deep as a man's full height. It was a warm evening, but there was a silent wind from the northwest which blew gently above them and rustled the mesquite. Their well-trained horses stood docilely, occasionally tossing their heads and flicking their tails. All that could be heard was the sound of an occasional night bird and the cheerful drone of the cicadas.

Ademar and Diego had crawled on their bellies toward the entrance of the stronghold and lay waiting, their senses keen. Now night fell swiftly, and the moon was obscured by thick clouds which heralded an oncoming storm. Indeed, far to the northwest, there were already the faint, ominous rumbles of thunder. Over Eagle Pass, through which the outlaws had ridden, lightning flashed in the dark sky.

Just then, a buxom young Mexican woman, Conchita Regales, wife to Migrante, Sangrodo's war lieutenant, came out of the entrance of the stronghold with a bucket and headed for the creek. Swiftly, Ademar sprang from his hiding place, and with one hand clamped over her mouth and the other menacing her with his sharp knife, bade her accompany him back into the woods if she valued her life. The terrified young woman obeyed without a sound, her eyes rolling in fright as much from the ferocious look on the half-breed's face as from the gleam of the weapon he lifted above her head.

Once inside the woods, two of the Mexican outlaws seized her, bound and gagged her, and forced her to lie on her belly between them while they squatted, amusing themselves by pinching and stroking her shuddering body and gloatingly promising her all manner of lubricious ordeals.

Half an hour later, beautiful Catayuna, who three weeks ago had borne Sangrodo a daughter she had named Consuela after her long-dead mother, came hurrying out of the stronghold in search of her missing friend. Diego sprang at her, and when she turned to struggle he dazed her with a blow of his fist to her jaw. The stocky Mexican outlaw trundled her inert body over his shoulder and hurried back to the woods.

Lucien Edmond had seen this second abduction follow the first, but he had held back the order to fire because he feared that in the darkness a stray bullet might kill the women captives. He did not recognize Catayuna, but what he saw told him that the outlaw band was hiding in the woods. Simata murmured to him, "It is too dangerous to go in there after them, Mr. Lucien Edmond."

"I know. But if I'd fired each time those scouts captured the women and took them back into the woods, I might have hit one of the women, and I certainly would have given our position away. We don't yet know how well they're armed. And those trees are large and thick and grow close together; it's almost impossible to see where anyone is."

"The wind is rising, Mr. Lucien Edmond." Simata moistened a finger and held it above his head. "It is very strong, a warm wind that speaks of rain and storm, and it comes from the northwest."

"A northwest wind," Lucien Edmond repeated and then stifled a gasp as he remembered what Charles Douglas had told him of the great Chicago fire. That fatal wind had come from another direction, the southwest. "Yes, that's the answer! You see that grass ahead of us that grows all the way toward the woods? Light a fire, Simata, and the wind will drive it toward the outlaws to the southeast of us. It will not touch the stronghold, which is to the north. They'll have to come out in the open where we can see them, and they won't be able to think about their captives."

Diego had carried the unconscious Catayuna to where Fred Morley crouched beside Lee Shaw. "Señor Morley," he gloatingly whispered, "here's a *señorita muy linda*. And she is not Indian, but *Mejicana*."

"I can see that," Morley muttered, licking his lips as he stared down at Catayuna's lithe body, clad in buckskin jacket and skirt. "Well, it's as Luis said, there'll be heifers enough for all of us—but this one's mine. Don't look at me like that, Diego—I'll blow your brains out. When we take the stronghold, you'll find someone else to take your fancy, and I'll see that you have an extra share of the treasure when we find it. Now get back to the lookout post. When they start missing this one, perhaps some of those redskins'll come out and start looking for her. Then we open fire!"

"*Sí, mi jefe*," Diego grumblingly agreed. With a last covetous glance at Catayuna's sprawled body, he crept out of the woods and toward the entrance of the stronghold to lie in wait, drawing his six-shooter and leveling it at the gateway.

Simata had started a fire with his tinderbox. The wind caught it, and the dry grass crackled and bowed before the surge of bright flame. Waves of smoke began to drift toward the woods, while Lucien Edmond's men crouched down in the ravine to keep out of sight.

Fred Morley uttered a blasphemous oath. "Now where did that fire come from? The wind's catching it, it's coming this way. Hey, see over there, Lee? Those horses tied to the mesquite branches—it must be the posse from San Antone! But how the goddamned hell could they get here without our seeing them, the way we rode?"

"But I don't see any men anywhere, Fred," Lee Shaw growled, as he peered down the sight of his rifle, aiming at the entrance of the stronghold.

"We're going in," Morley angrily decided. "Pass the word to the men, you, John! Crouch down low and on the double, the way the soldier boys do it! And keep crouching. Once we get inside that stronghold, if there is a posse, they'll have a helluva time weeding us out from the redskins, and by then we'll be ready for them. They'll have to attack us. Let's go when I give the word."

With this, drawing his holstered pistol and transferring the Whitworth to his left hand, he straightened and carefully began to move out of the woods. John Hazelhurst had whispered back to the other men what the outlaw leader proposed, and now Morley barked, "Go!" and ran forward. Four of the Mexicans of his band followed him, as did Hazelhurst and Shaw, guns ready. Lucien Edmond gripped the top of the ravine and hoisted himself enough to see this frontal attack. "Open fire, *amigos!*" he called to his men.

As the outlaws began to fire into the village, aiming at the first tepees they saw, Lucas, Simata, and two of the vaqueros crawled up out of the ravine and, lying on their bellies, fired at the onrushing outlaws. Two of the Mexicans fell dead at once, and Shaw swore with pain and anger as a bullet ripped through the muscle of his right arm, but Morley whirled and, flattening himself on the ground, emptied his Starr .44 at Lucien Edmond's vaqueros, killing both of them. Then, flinging away the empty pistol, he aimed his Whitworth and snapped off a shot. Lucas uttered a strangled cry and rolled over onto one side, Morley's bullet embedded in his left hip. A sudden swirl of wind seemed to lift the fire and obscured the vision of Lucien Edmond and Simata. Morley, cursing under his breath, ran back at full speed into the shelter of the woods.

By now, the fire and the sounds of gunfire had roused the *Comancheria*. Sangrodo and his young war lieutenant, armed with the Spencer repeating rifles Luke Bouchard had given them to retaliate against the treacherous attack by Captain George Munson five years earlier, hurried out of the entrance of the stronghold, followed by a dozen of the younger braves who were armed with bows and arrows, lances, and old muskets.

"Sangrodo, they are in the woods, the rest of them!" Lucien Edmond cried, cupping his hands to his mouth. "We set the fire to drive them out of there. Be careful, don't give them a target. They have two of your women."

"Yes, and one is Catayuna!" Sangrodo cried, his voice hoarse with anguish and fury.

"All the rest of you, out of the ravine, on your bellies and aim your weapons at the woods—but fire only when you see men. They've got two of Sangrodo's women with them!" Lucien Edmond commanded.

Simata had quickly bandaged Lucas's wound to stop the bleeding. Gritting his teeth against the waves of pain, Lucas crawled forward, nosing the butt of the Spencer carbine against his shoulder, covering the eastern side of the little forest. The flames had by now reached the edges of the trees, and there were frightened cries from the men who hid there. Suddenly the moon emerged from behind the clouds, and as three of Fred Morley's Mexicans broke their cover and headed toward the horses, a withering fire from Lucien Edmond's men dropped them in their tracks.

Dan Weinhold and Hans Durst fired their pistols simultaneously, wounding one of Lucien Edmond's vaqueros, but Simata whirled and triggered his carbine till it was empty. The young German outlaw staggered back, his eyes huge with pain and terror as he saw the blood welling from a hole in his belly, then toppled to the ground, his fingernails scrabbling the earth in his final agony. Dan Weinhold swore as he pulled the trigger on the now-empty pistol, flung it away, and ran toward the horses, only to be killed by a shot from one of the vaqueros' repeating rifles.

Sangrodo and his war lieutenant had circled to the southernmost end of the woods and, both of them seeing John Hazelhurst crawl out toward the edge and lift his rifle to fire at them, fired at the same time. The outlaw's body jerked, then slumped in death.

Fred Morley, cursing violently, reloaded his Whitworth and fired toward the ravine, killing another of Lucien Edmond's vaqueros. Catayuna, who had been neither bound nor gagged, dazedly wakened from her unconsciousness. Lifting her head, she saw the gaunt, black-bearded outlaw leader standing with his back to her, reloading the Whitworth. Putting her right palm down on the ground to steady herself, she straightened. Then, as Morley turned

413

around to see what was happening, she made her fingers like claws, stepped forward, and thrust her fingernails at his eyes. With a hideous shriek, the outlaw leader dropped the rifle and fell onto all fours. "You bitch—you've fair blinded me—oh, you dirty bitch—wait till I get my hands on you—Gawd, it hurts fierce—oh, you dirty greaser bitch you!"

Luis Ademar heard his leader's cries and crawled forward out of his hiding place, his knife between his teeth. As he rose to his feet at the very edge of the woods and saw Catayuna standing there, panting with the exertion of her effort and emotion, he snarled and seized the deadly sharp point of the knife between right thumb and finger, about to throw it into her back. But Sangrodo, too, had seen this, and he ran forward now, sank down on one knee, quickly leveled the carbine, and pulled the trigger. Ademar spun around, his eyes blank and staring, the knife dropping from his lifeless fingers.

The few survivors of Fred Morley's band managed to get to their horses and ride off. Before Lucien Edmond could stop them, the Comanche war lieutenant and two other braves strode round the sprawled bodies of the outlaws and, finding that some still stirred, killed them with savage thrusts of their feathered lances. Conchita was found, her gag and bonds removed, and her Comanche husband soothed her as he led her back to their tepee.

Catayuna, forgetting for once the tradition that a squaw does not show affection to her husband before others, flung herself into Sangrodo's arms, bursting into hysterical sobs. And his taciturn face was radiant as he murmured, "Once again, beloved woman, you have shown how truly you are Comanche. Come, we must honor the son of the great *Taiboo Nimaihkana*. The father is my blood brother; the son shall be that also, for I respect and honor him for what he has done to save us from these evil men."

Great campfires were lit, and the villagers assembled. Before Sangrodo's tepee, Lucien Edmond and the tall chief stood facing each other. The young war lieutenant took the ritual knife and cut the wrist of each man, then pressed them together and bound them with a thong and repeated the mystic words of Comanche avowal of lasting brotherhood by blood and spirit, which would last as long as mor-

414

tal lives lasted upon the earth where once the Comanche had been proud and free.

When it was done, Sangrodo turned to his people and said, "It is beyond this, even the lives of my white-eyes blood brother and myself, who am yet your chief. I pledge all of you and your children and your children's children to keep this pact of lasting brotherhood and friendship with all those of the Bouchards and their descendants. Thus it will be proved that white man and red may endure in peace and friendship against those enemies who would not believe such a peace could ever be made. I, Sangrodo, chief of the Wanderers, of the people, so swear before the Great Spirit who hears us all."

CHAPTER THIRTY-FOUR

On December 18, 1872, the same day that Lucien Edmond learned of the planned outlaw attack on Sangrodo's village, Luke, Laure, and Lopasuta Bouchard came to the towering bluff surmounting the Alabama River to commemorate the birthday of Lucien Bouchard. The headboard on which he had carved the names of his beloved Dimarte and of his tiny son Edmond had long since crumbled away, and only its jagged edge remained just above the ground. A soft wind from the southwest stirred the branches of the massive hickory trees that framed this hallowed burial ground.

Each of these three Bouchards, the grandson and his wife and the adopted son in whose veins there ran the proud blood of the Comanches, knelt and touched each grave and murmured prayers. Lopasuta had waited till the last, that he might add his own special prayer for the patriarch who had been blood brother to the mighty Creeks, that he might express his mystical awareness of the immortal bond that had been made between old Lucien and those who had given him sanctuary, sustenance, and a new way of life, just as he himself now had been linked through adoption with the grandson of that far-seeing, compassionate pioneer.

When at last it was done, and Lopasuta began to help Laure along the easier pathway down from the summit, Luke stood a few moments alone at the grave of his grandfather. He said softly, "How well I remember, Grandfather, that you told me you were troubled by the thought that the evil blood of your brother Jean had been passed to your own son Henry and then to my half brother, Mark. Can this blood be truly extinct now? I pray today also for the spirit of that misguided Hugh Entrevois, the son of my half

417

brother. I pray you too, Grandfather, to pardon my conceit and arrogance in believing that he would not seek to do harm to the Bouchards simply because I placed him near me and trusted him. But now at last the evil that pursued you throughout your long, honorable life and came to its deadliest fruition when the Couriers struck against all that I hold dear, has—I humbly pray—come to an end with the passing of that descendant of the last flawed Bouchard."

He knelt down again beside his grandfather's grave, clasped his hands, and prayed silently. Then he rose and said aloud, "I am here, Grandfather, as a staunch defender of Windhaven. And in what years remain to me, I promise you that my vigilance will increase, not slacken as it did this time because of my own mortal failings. And in the children that my beloved Laure has given me, we will constantly seek to plant the seeds of truth and honesty and righteousness, that they too shall be the defenders of Windhaven so long as men exist upon this rich and wondrous earth."

Preview

WINDHAVEN'S CRISIS
by Marie de Jourlet

This is the eighth novel in the phenomenal best-selling Windhaven Plantation saga by Marie de Jourlet. Once again, she weaves the compelling story of the Bouchard family, its towering hopes, its profound tragedies, its great loves and its legacy, passed from one generation to the next.

"It's a mighty cool evenin', Miss Judy ma'am, Dat sky look lak we might jist git a storm." Old Josiah respectfully touched his forehead to greet the tall blonde girl as she entered the rickety stable over which he presided and where he slept at night on the small Branshaw farm. After the death of the girl's parents two years earlier, he and three other free blacks who had once been Branshaw slaves had loyally stayed on to help her eke out a meager living from a few acres of cotton and produce. The stable quartered her spirited pony and two milk cows. A hundred yards away, toward the river, stood the dilapidated old frame house that Martin Branshaw and his young wife had built, working side by side with their slaves, nearly twenty-five years earlier. They had left their birthplace of New Orleans to live near Martin's cousin on the outskirts of the little Alabama town of Tensaw.

"I know, Josiah." Judith Branshaw gave him a quick smile, her large dark-blue eyes warm with affection. "I declare, you and Nate and Jerry and Tom watch over me as if I were a baby. I'm all of twenty-one and I've managed—thanks to all of you—"

"Yassum, dat you shonuff have, Miss Judy. 'T'ain't right, though, 't'ain't right at all that a nice sweet gal like you should go on runnin' this farm all by herself, no ma'am." He dolefully shook his head. " 'Scuse me

421

fer speakin' out of turn, Miss Judy, ma'am, but you know yourself wut folks in Tensaw keep sayin'."

Judith Branshaw was five feet, nine inches tall, her face oval, with a pert nose and determined chin. Her mouth was full and sweet, but it tightened now and her eyes narrowed coldly as she angrily retorted, "I've heard till I'm sick of it, Josiah. Yes, I know. These pious God-fearing townsfolk think I'm a fallen woman because I keep running Daddy's farm and staying here without any white kin to look after me. But I'll tell you this, Josiah, I feel safer here with just you four hard-working, loyal helpers than I'd ever feel with anybody in town, and that's a fact."

"Jist the same, Miss Judy, ma'am—" Josiah began to protest.

"Please saddle my pony for me, Josiah," she broke in, softening the brusk tone with a warm smile. As he reluctantly nodded and headed for the stall, she added in a confidential tone, "Besides, maybe Mr. Fales'll make an honest woman out of me, and then my disapproving neighbors won't have any more chance to gossip about me."

"Ah hears you, Miss Judy," Josiah led the black pony out of its stall and expertly applied the sidesaddle, with a sidelong look at his young mistress. "Dat be the fella from Stockton who been sparkin' you?"

"The very same, Josiah. When we met last Friday, he told me to meet him near old Fort Mims by the river after sundown tonight. Said he had something important to ask me." Her eyes sparkled with a sudden happiness. "So you see, Josiah, if it's what I think it's going to be, I'll be marrying him and selling this farm to you and Nate, Jerry, and Tom. And I promise I won't ask much for it. You almost deserve it for nothing, for the hard work you've put into it ever since you started working for my poor daddy."

Josiah helped her up into the saddle, holding the pony's reins tightly in one hand, frowning as he digested this news. "Ah dunno, Miss Judy. Sho, we'd mighty lak to have disyere li'l piece of land foah ouahselves, only not if you jist up'n married any man jist to get away from Tensaw. 'Pears lak to me—'n Nate thinks lak ah do—disyere Mistuh Fales, he doan nebbah come round heah so we kin size him up'n see wut he looks lak. It's always you ridin' over to Stockton oah down by de rivah to meet him when he wants." He shook his head dubiously, his frown deepening. "Mebbe ah's got no right to say disyeah, Miss Judy, but effen ah was young'n white lak dat Mistuh Fales and cared foah a purty, sweet gal lak you, ah'd come callin' on you, not make you traipse off ebry time to see me, 'n dat's a fact!"

As she adjusted her shawl around her shoulders, she smiled down at him. "You're mighty nice to pay me such a compliment, Josiah. But in a way it's just as well Mr. Fales doesn't come calling on me here, the way folks are so quick to jump to conclusions. Why, they'd be saying, like as not, I was just carrying on with him— and I'm not."

The white-haired black indignantly clucked his tongue and shook his head. "No need for you to tell me dat, Miss Judy. Why, Nate'n me, we know'd your mammy 'n pappy before you wuz born, 'n Tom and Jerry, they done come to wuk when you wuz a li'l baby. No, ma'am, all us niggers know you'se the nicest, sweetest gal in the county. Dat's jist why we doan wanna see you come to git mixed up with any flighty fella that mightn't do the right thing by you."

Judith Branshaw's eyes misted. Deeply touched, she leaned to pat his shoulder reassuringly. "I said before, Josiah, you mustn't worry so about me. And I'm sure he's not flighty. And now, you look after things till I get back, and then maybe I'll have wonderful news. I surely hope so!" With this, wheeling the pony toward the west, she rode off toward her rendezvous.

It was the evening of January 13, 1873. Lincoln's most successful Union general, Ulysses Simpson Grant, was about to start his second term as President of the United States, eight years after he had received Confederate General Robert E. Lee's surrender at Appomattox. Now at the helm of a reunited nation, he would preside over the punitive carpetbagger government, which was doing great harm in the South, yet which— despite the anguished protests of reputable citizens from those once Confederate states—he fully supported.

Yet the new year augured well for the prosperity of this vigorous young country, which was three years away from its centennial. The Great Bonanza silver mine had been discovered in Nevada. The Remington Fire Arms Company had begun the manufacture of the typewriter, after having bought the rights from its inventor, Sholes, for a paltry $12,000. The Bethlehem Steel Works, destined to be one of the nation's largest, had established its huge plant in Pennsylvania. Transportation by rail was increasing, would connect cities and towns and bring staples as well as luxuries to thousands. By leasing the Lake Shore and Michigan Southern Railroad, Cornelius Vanderbilt had completed his railroad control from New York to Chicago. Yet, despite all this, 1873 would be a year of crisis. . . .

Nate, a stocky, bearded man in his late fifties, came out of the little cottage that he shared with the two other blacks, and headed for the stable. "Dat Miss Judy jist ridin' off, Josiah?" he inquired.

"Sho was, Nate." Josiah scratched his chin reflectively, shook his head. "She say she goin' fer to meet disyeah Mistah Fales. She say she think he gonna pop de question foah shoah tanite."

"Ah doan lak dat none at all, ah doan, Josiah," Nate gloomily confided. "It ain't none of ouah business, but jist de same, ah done heard things 'bout dat man in Stockton."

"Wut things, Nate?"

The bearded freed black scowled and spat. "You 'members ah went to help ma fren' Amos kill a passel ob coons just aftah Christmas?"

"Sho do," Josiah emitted a delighted cackle. "You brought us back two ob dem tasty critters foah supper. Even Miss Judy liked coonmeat de way ah fixed it foah her—de sweet chile!"

"That ain't all ah meant, Josiah. Amos hires hisself out to some ob desyeah rich white folks in Stockton, 'n when ah tol' him Miss Judy was sorta sweet on dat Mistah Fales, Amos said he didn't think nuttin' was gonna come ob it."

"Why he say dat, Nate, why, man?" Josiah anxiously inquired.

" 'Cause disyeah Mistah Fales, his ol' pappy left him a big plantation 'n not much cash. He been scrapin' a long time to pay the niggers he got wohkin' fer him, Josiah. Amos say, he doan think Mistah Fales gonna up'n marry wid no gal dat ain't got herself rich folks to put up de cash Mistah Fales needs to run his place," Nate patiently explained.

Josiah emitted a low whistle and shook his head, then turned to look westward in the direction in which his young mistress had ridden off. "Ah doan lak de soun' of wut you jist tol' me, Nate, not one mite ah doan. If disyeah Mistah Fales got Miss Judy's hopes so high to marry her 'n take her away from dese nasty folks wut am puttin' her down—'cause she lib alone out heah wid only us niggers—'n den he let her down, it gonna break her heart foah sho, Nate."

"Ah knows dat, Josiah. Ah sho does wish Miss

Judy'd take herself off to n'Awleans. She'd shonuff fin' herself a proper man dere. Ain't nobody in Tensaw ah knows of is good enuff fer Miss Judy."

"Dat's so," Josiah dispiritedly agreed. Then, with a sigh, he added, "Mebbe dat fren' Amos, he might be wrong 'bout dat Mistah Fales. Mebbe things gonna turn out all right. Ah sho does hope so, fer her sake, Nate."

"Ah does too. Ain't gonna be easy this year to make any money on cotton. Price keep goin' down, 'n cost ob wut we need keep goin' up. Even if Miss Judy gits herself married 'n sells us dis place lak she tol' us she'd do, there's gwine be hahd times ahead foah all ob us, Josiah."

It was a ride of about seven miles from the little farm to the abandoned site of old Fort Mims on the banks of the sluggishly flowing Alabama River. Sixty years ago, on a stiflingly hot August day, a thousand Creek warriors had massacred more than five hundred whites, soldiers, Indians, and blacks congregated in the inadequate fort. And eighty-four years ago, Lucien Bouchard had made camp near its site on the second night of his lonely journey from Mobile to the fertile lands of Econchate, where he would live with the Creeks and begin the dynasty of the Bouchards in America.

Judith Branshaw slackened her pony's gait as she came within sight of the ruined fort. All that was left was a jagged rectangle of rotted timbers nearly hidden from view by the luxuriant moss and weeds and grass. It was outlined by clumps of pignut hickories and butternut, and just north of it stood an old, gaunt, lightning-scarred pine.

The soft, thick darkness of early nightfall made this rendezvous an eerie one, but the tall blonde girl was exhilarated by it. She had met David Fales in the general store at Stockton not quite a year ago, and she had been attracted to him at once because of his good looks and courtly manner. In the ensuing months, having learned that she rode her pony, Beauty, nearly every day, he had ridden out on his own sturdy dappled gelding, Aaron, to ride with her.

Because she had lived a sheltered, isolated life with her parents, Judith knew nothing of men save to be wary of their glib promises—her mother had taught her that. But David Fales had conducted himself like a perfect gentleman; never once had he tried to kiss or embrace her. Then, early last month, he had hinted that he was in love with her and that he would count himself proud to be her sweetheart. Judith had naively replied that her sweetheart would be her husband, to whom alone she could give all her love. As they walked hand in hand through the verdant forest, having tethered their mounts to a live oak tree, he had suddenly turned to her, taken her into his arms for the first time, and kissed her on the mouth, saying, "I'll make you happy, Judy, honey, I promise that. Trust me. Soon I'll share my plans with you."

She had felt herself respond eagerly to his embrace and kiss, and told herself that this indeed was love. And in the intervening weeks, when they had met between the towns of Stockton and Tensaw, she had impatiently waited for him to divulge these plans, which she believed would make her his wife and free her from the lonely life of this impoverished little farm where gossiping neighbors condemned her for her courageous quest for independence. *Tonight,* she happily thought to herself, *it will all come true, it will have been well worth the waiting!*

She dismounted from her pony, patting its sleek head with one hand while she held the reins loosely in the other. "Good girl, Beauty," she murmured. "Now there's nothing to be afraid of. We'll stay away from the edge of the bank, just in case there are any snakes. He'll be here soon, I know he will."

Behind her, there was the sound of brush being trampled, and she turned, with an expectant little cry of "David!" only to drop the pony's reins and clap her hand to her open mouth. Before her stood four men in white hooded robes, and the eyes of the burly leader, dark and cruel, glowered at her through the slits of the hood.

"Wh-who are you?" she quavered.

"Are you Judith Branshaw, girl?" the leader's voice was hoarse and vibrant with cruel anger.

"Yes, I am. What business is it of yours? Why are you dressed like that?"

"To dispense justice and to punish wickedness, as you'll find out, Judith Branshaw. Turn loose that pony and come along with us!"

"No, I won't! You've no right to—stop it—Beauty—no—oh, you brutes—how dare you treat me this way—" For one of the quartet had advanced, pulled the reins out of her hand, and cut the pony across its withers with a hickory switch. With a loud whinny of pain, the terrified animal had bounded off along the riverbank and disappeared.

Judith Branshaw turned to run, but her assailants had anticipated that. The two others, stocky and short of stature, seized her by the wrists and dragged her, struggling, kicking, and indignantly crying out, back into the forest till they reached a clearing.

The leader followed, folding his arms across his chest, while the third accomplice hurried to a gray stallion tethered nearby and came back with a coil of rope. The other two men drew out her wrists to be tightly secured with one end of the rope; the third man then slung the other over a thick, high-perched branch on the towering pine tree and squatted down, holding it with both hands. Judith Branshaw was forced to stand on tiptoe to ease the chafing tension of the coarse rope, and she turned her fear-congested face back over her shoulder to entreat the leader: "Why are you doing this to me? What have I done? For God's sake, tell me why!"

"You low bitch, you can't guess?" the leader sneered as he approached her and cuffed her with the back of his hand across the mouth, drawing blood and a strangled cry of pain from the helpless young captive. "The whole town knows all about you, *Miss* Judith girl. Living way out of town with those four niggers, keeping away from decent, God-fearing white folks so's you can have yourself a high ol' time with them in your bed." His voice grew viciously ingratiating. "Tell me, Miss Judith, which one of those four niggers gave you the best poke, hm?"

"That's a filthy lie! I've never been with any man, and I won't till I marry!" Judith Branshaw hysterically cried out, arching and swaying to ease the torturing bite of the rope against her slim wrists.

"We know better, girl. Right now, we're going to show you how we punish dirty nigger-loving sluts like you. Peel her down, boys," the leader ordered.

The two men approached the distraught blonde girl and, despite her frenzied twisting and kicking and shrill, tearful protests, ripped off her dress and camisole, leaving her in pantaleetes, gartered stockings, and shoes. They sniggered coarsely at the revelation of this last intimate garment: "Wal, I'll be hornswoggled—she's wearin' trousers, jist like a man!—Sho nuff, she is at that—so why don't you see if she is a man?"

Naked to the waist, her face scarlet with shame and wet with tears, Judith tried desperately to kick as one of the two hooded men now thrust his hand down under the waistband of the batiste pantalettes, but his companion, stepping behind her, hugged her above the waist with both arms, effectively hampering her attempts to evade this supreme indignity.

"She's a gal, all right," the first man lewdly announced, as he rubbed his hand up and down. "Got my hand right on her cute li'l hairy snatch, I have!"

"Oh my God! Cowards, brutes, you filthy cowards to treat an innocent girl this way—take your hand away—oh, David, my God in heaven, David, where are you?" Judith shrieked as she writhed and shuddered, twisting her contorted face this way and that in the poignant hope of seeing her lover there to save her.

"Innocent, hell! All right, I said peel her down!" the leader commanded, lusting and impatient.

A strident shriek burst from Judith's mouth as the man in front of her ruthlessly ripped the pantalettes down to her calves and then stepped back. A faint ray of moonlight, filtering through the forest, tinged the carnation sheen of her slim, full-breasted nudity with a nacreous glow, and the eyes of her four assailants glistened with ferocious lubricity.

"First, Judith Branshaw, we shall punish you in the name of the God-fearing people of Tenshaw," the leader intoned as he gestured to the second hooded man, who handed him a slim hickory switch. He made it whistle in the air, then muttered, "Best put that shawl round her eyes 'n mouth, it'll quiet her a mite, as she's purty likely to start screeching like a hoot owl 'fore much longer."

This done, he stepped back, planting himself at the naked captive's left and, savoring the sadistic joy of what was to follow, slowly lifted the switch in the air, poised it a long torturing moment, and then cut it viciously across the tops of her lovely hips.

A wild cry of pain was torn from the victim, who lunged forward, while a bright crimson welt leaped across the shuddering flesh. Slowly, with obvious relish, the hooded leader flogged the naked girl, prolonging the interval between strokes so as to delectate over her convulsive, uncontrollable gyrations and to gloat over her screams and babbled entreaties for mercy. When he flung aside the switch, her hips, buttocks, and upper thighs were cruelly welted, and blood oozed from a cut at the base of her buttocks. Judith Branshaw sagged, head bowed, her bosom wildly heaving, feeble moans escaping her lips which, in her suffering, she had bitten to the blood.

"And now, girl, so's you'll learn that a white man can service you better'n any low nigger, we're goin' to give you a little fun. But remember, when we're done, you'd best move out of Tenshaw for good. Or the next time we might not be so easy with you. All right, you boys, grab her legs'n spread them for me. I'll do as much for you when it's your turn," the leader ordered in a thick, unsteady voice.

Her eyes blindfolded by the shawl tied over her face and knotted tightly at the back of her head, Judith Branshaw was hardly conscious, in the burning pain that swirled through her, that the two hooded men had squatted in front of her, each well to one side of her and gripped her ankles to spread them hugely apart. But, moments later, when she felt the leader's virile organ pierce her hymen, she uttered clamorous shriek upon shriek till the forest resounded with her cries of agony.

In turn, all four of them had their way with her. And then, when they had finished, they let go of the rope and let her slump to the ground as they mounted their horses and rode away into the quiet night.

She lay sprawled on her belly, arms flung beyond her head, the trailing rope still remorselessly biting into her cruelly bruised wrists. She moaned wanly, half-

431

conscious. In the forest, the night birds had resumed their soft twittering. Presently, there was the sound of a horse's hooves, which stopped nearby, and then the sound of a man's voice: "Judith! Oh my poor Judith, what have they done to you?"

He came toward her, a tall, wiry blond man in his early thirties, with well-groomed spade beard and a supercilious mustache, in riding breeches, shining new black boots, and red riding jacket. For a moment, he stood staring down at her naked body, pursing his fleshy mouth and caressingly stroking his beard, then repeated, "Judith—Judith, my dearest—can you hear me? I was late for our appointment—I never dreamed they'd be so cruel to you!"

Slowly, dazed with her suffering, Judith Branshaw raised her swollen face, still covered by the knotted shawl. "David—David—I prayed you'd come—to save me from them—oh those dreadful men—they—they wh-whipped me, D-David—and—and then—oh my God, oh I want to die!"

He knelt down and carefully unknotted the shawl, casting it to one side. His mild brown eyes fixed avidly on the smooth estuary of her deeply hollowed back and the contrast between its unmarked sheen and the savage pattern of livid welts that marred her upper thighs and buttocks. Very lightly, he put out his right palm to glide it over one of her ripely rounded hips, and shuddered, licking his lips as, affecting a deeply solicitous tone, he inquired, "But surely they—they left you after—after they had whipped you?"

Judith Branshaw had dragged her bound wrists toward her and now laid her face against her arms, slowly shaking her head while choked sobs wrenched her. "Oh God—if only they had—no—they—they—f-forced me—oh, David—why were you so late?"

Gentle now, he slowly turned her over and laid the shawl over her loins, yet his eyes feasted on her heaving bosom. With his left arm under her shoulders, he again passed his right palm over her bare flesh as he murmured, "I couldn't help it, Judy dearest. I wasn't armed, so when I heard you scream and heard those men, I didn't dare try to rescue you—all I could pray was that they'd whip you and have done—"

Slowly she turned to stare at him, her face stricken with mingled pain and lack of comprehension. "You—you were there—you saw?" she at last quavered.

"Yes—forgive me—"

She made an effort to sit up, and groaned at the pain the movement cost her. Her dark-blue eyes scanned his effetely handsome face as if for the first time. Then, fighting for breath and control of her voice, she demanded, "You said—you said—all you could do was pray th-they'd wh-whip me and have done—then you-you must have known that they were here waiting for me—David—David—don't let me think what I'm thinking—"

"It'll be fine, you'll see," he glibly sought to reassure her. "I told you you'd be my sweetheart. Well, you will be. We can't get married, but I'll take good care of you—"

"W-what are you saying?" she gasped as she tugged at her bound wrists. "Please—g-get this rope off—it's cutting my wrists in two, please, David."

"Yes, of course, dear." He drew a penknife out of his breeches pocket and cut the rope as she watched him intently, her face suddenly congealed, aloof, harsh with the twisting of her pain and degradation. "There. I'll get you some water from the river—"

"No! Don't leave me now—I—I want you to tell me what you mean, David. You just said we can't get married. Why?"

He shrugged noncommittally, tightening his grip round her slim, bare shoulders. Again his right palm strayed down her shivering naked body, smoothing the deeply dimpled belly. Judith Branshaw uttered a hoarse, indignant cry, and with all the strength she could muster, struck his hand away. "Stop it! Do you understand me? Now I'm beginning to understand, myself, for the first time, David Fales! You—you never wanted to marry me from the start, did you?"

"But I couldn't, Judy dear. I mean—well, you've no money, only that little farm, and everybody knows it won't ever be profitable. And then your reputation—I mean, what are people to think, your living out there all alone with four niggers—"

"I see! That's what you think, too, isn't it? But you'd like me to be your sweetheart—naked like this in your bed, I suppose?"

"Yes, of course, and I'll take very good care of you—"

With a cry of agonized desperation, she struck him across the mouth with all her might. "It was you who sent those men to whip and force me, wasn't it? I can see it now—oh, what a stupid little trusting fool I've been all this past year! All you really wanted was for me to be your trollop, wasn't it?"

"But I couldn't marry you now, my dear," he smugly answered, as he drew out a cambric handkerchief and patted his mouth, eyed it to see if her blow had drawn blood, then replaced it. "For one thing, my own plantation is in debt, and I'm marrying Henrietta Aylmers, who'll bring me a very handsome dowry. And for another, since we may as well face up to it now, Judy dear, you're damaged goods."

"You—you—you horrible, conniving bastard—and

434

you're a Southern gentleman, are you?" She spat at him.

He rose to his feet, his face cold and contemptuous. "How could you expect a decent man to marry you after you've been living alone with those niggers since your parents died? Do you think I could face the smirks, the gossip, the innuendos of the townspeople if I married you, I myself always wondering if perhaps you hadn't been to bed with your hired black help? No, my dear, no respectable Southern gentleman will ever want to marry one of your kind."

"Get away from me. I don't ever want to see your lying, treacherous face again. And the townspeople will have their wish—so will your henchmen, whom you must surely have hired to do all this to me, David Fales! I'll sell my farm to my loyal blacks and I'll leave Tenshaw forever!"

He shrugged again. "As you please, my dear. Though I was prepared to make you a suitable offer—it would give you financial security so you wouldn't have to sell yourself to any man who came along with the price—"

"Damn you to hell forever, you—you stinking bastard—you're worse than those men ever would be!"

"I'm sorry you choose to look at things that way. But I've a last piece of advice for you. You might think of moving to Montgomery. There are plenty of rich Northern carpetbaggers there who'll take a fancy to your charms."

She dragged herself to her feet, panting and groaning, dragging up the ripped pantalettes over her loins, tying the shawl with shaking fingers over her heaving bosom. "I just might do that, David Fales," she gasped. "Maybe they'll help me find a way to pay *decent*

435

Southern gentleman back! And now, be kind enough to get out of my sight before I try to kill you."

He uttered a mocking laugh, untethered his gelding, and rode off into the night, leaving her standing weeping in the dark forest. . . .